FAMILY LIES

TITLES BY KAREN ROSE

Dirty Secrets (enovella)

BALTIMORE NOVELS

You Belong to Me
No One Left to Tell
Did You Miss Me?
Broken Silence (enovella)
Watch Your Back
Monster in the Closet
Death Is Not Enough

CINCINNATI NOVELS

Closer Than You Think
Alone in the Dark
Every Dark Corner
Edge of Darkness
Into the Dark

SACRAMENTO NOVELS

Say You're Sorry
Say No More
Say Goodbye

NEW ORLEANS NOVELS

Quarter to Midnight
Beneath Dark Waters
Buried Too Deep
Knife in the Back

SAN DIEGO CASE FILES

Cold-Blooded Liar
Cheater
Dead Man's List
Family Lies

KAREN ROSE

FAMILY LIES

BERKLEY | NEW YORK

BERKLEY
An imprint of Penguin Random House LLC
1745 Broadway, New York, NY 10019
penguinrandomhouse.com

Copyright © 2026 by Karen Rose Books, Inc.
Penguin Random House values and supports copyright. Copyright fuels creativity, encourages diverse voices, promotes free speech, and creates a vibrant culture. Thank you for buying an authorized edition of this book and for complying with copyright laws by not reproducing, scanning, or distributing any part of it in any form without permission. You are supporting writers and allowing Penguin Random House to continue to publish books for every reader. Please note that no part of this book may be used or reproduced in any manner for the purpose of training artificial intelligence technologies or systems.

BERKLEY and the BERKLEY & B colophon
are registered trademarks of Penguin Random House LLC.

Book design by Elke Sigal

Library of Congress Cataloging-in-Publication Data
Names: Rose, Karen, 1964- author.
Title: Family lies / Karen Rose.
Description: New York: Berkley, 2026. | Series: The san diego case files; 4
Identifiers: LCCN 2025032494 (print) | LCCN 2025032495 (ebook) |
ISBN 9780593817209 (hardcover) | ISBN 9780593817216 (ebook)
Subjects: LCSH: Mystery | Suspense fiction | LCGFT: Novels | Fiction.
Classification: LCC PS3618.O7844 F36 2026 (print) | LCC PS3618.O7844 (ebook)
LC record available at https://lccn.loc.gov/2025032494
LC ebook record available at https://lccn.loc.gov/2025032495

Printed in the United States of America
2nd Printing

The authorized representative in the EU for product safety and compliance is
Penguin Random House Ireland, Morrison Chambers, 32 Nassau Street,
Dublin D02 YH68, Ireland, https://eu-contact.penguin.ie.

To Terri and Kay. You've both always been there for me.
I wish everyone could have friends like you.
Love you so much, sisters of my heart.

And, as always, to Martin. How can forty years have passed?
I'm so grateful that I've gotten to spend them with you.
I love you.

FAMILY LIES

PROLOGUE

Carmel Valley, San Diego, California
Saturday, December 27, 2:45 p.m.
Sixteen years ago

Katherine Matthews clutched the gift in one hand and the barn door in the other. She hated giving gifts nearly as much as she hated apologizing. Both of which she was going to have to do.

She didn't hate apologizing because she hated admitting that she was wrong. She was wrong all the time. But this time she'd hurt someone. Someone who didn't deserve her unpleasantness. Someone who'd tried to be a good friend.

Trouble was, Katherine didn't want friends. She'd had a friend once—her sister. She'd loved Wren, but Wren was gone. Taken from them.

Murdered.

It was coming up on a year, and the cops still had no idea who'd done it.

This had been the first Christmas without her and . . .

Katherine swallowed hard. She would not cry. She needed to get this apology out of the way so she could go back to being angry at everyone and everything.

She drew a deep breath and pulled the door open enough to slip through. She stood quietly, letting her eyes get used to the darkness. There was an overhead light, but it hadn't been turned on. The only illumination came from a lamp in the stall where Katherine's foster father carved his little figurines.

She appreciated the darkness. Things like apologies tended to be easier to say in the dark. And . . . there was the person she owed the apology to.

Akiko was gliding silently through the martial arts moves she did so gracefully.

In some ways, she envied Akiko Jones. Her current roommate was tidy and kind, smart and graceful.

Katherine bumbled through life, usually annoying people who got too close until they backed away. She was too much. She knew it. Everyone knew it.

Somehow she still had a place here, though. McKittrick House was a safe place—for her and for any child who walked through the front door.

Or, as in Katherine's case, any child who snuck into the barn to get away from the cold. She and Wren had been twelve-year-old runaways when they'd stumbled into this barn. Into the path of Harlan and Betsy McKittrick.

The McKittricks were the reason Katherine stood here,

watching her roommate do her karate dance. Kata, Akiko called it.

Be respectful, Katherine told herself. *Use the right words. It's important.*

Akiko abruptly halted, spinning to stare open-mouthed at Katherine, who still stood next to the barn door.

"You scared me," Akiko said quietly.

"I didn't mean to."

"I'll leave. I know this is your place."

Katherine winced. "It's just as much your place."

Akiko tilted her head, her long black ponytail swinging slightly. "Why are you here, Kit?"

Katherine started to correct the name but stopped herself. For a while, only Harlan had called her Kit. But after Wren had died, others had picked up the habit. Katherine thought she should mind, but she really didn't.

She might even like it.

"I'm sorry," she blurted out.

Akiko's brows shot up. "For?"

Katherine sighed. This was the part she hated most. "For being a jerk. I've been awful to you."

"You have," Akiko agreed. "For months. Why apologize now?"

Katherine's cheeks heated uncomfortably. "I made you cry."

Akiko crossed her arms over her chest. "You did not."

But she had. Katherine knew it. She'd snapped at Akiko and told her that she wasn't welcome, that she wasn't wanted. And she must have been convincing, because Akiko *had* cried.

Katherine swallowed. "Then I made you feel unwelcome at least."

"That you did do."

"You should have called me a jerk. I *was* a jerk."

One side of Akiko's mouth lifted sadly. "I understand. Well, I don't understand because I've never had a sister murdered. I've never even had a sister. I can't imagine losing one. So I got why you were angry. I moved into your room. Took her bed."

"It's not your fault, though."

"No. And I could say that I'm sorry I came here, but I'd be lying. My last home was . . . well, not good."

Katherine wasn't sure if she should ask questions about that or not. She didn't like talking about her past placements, but some of the kids who came through McKittrick House found it therapeutic. She was saved from her dilemma when Akiko spoke again.

"Why now, Kit?"

Katherine stared at her own feet. She was wearing new boots, a Christmas gift from her foster siblings who'd aged out of the system and were living good lives in town. She'd never had nice things before coming to McKittrick House.

She'd never been able to sleep before coming here, either. She'd always been waiting for the next assault.

She owed a lot to Harlan and Betsy McKittrick. More than she'd ever be able to repay. Importantly, their approval had come to mean a lot. She'd deserved their anger and disappointment many times in the past four years, but they'd never been anything but proud.

Until she'd made Akiko cry.

Which had totally happened, even if Akiko denied it.

"I didn't realize what I was doing to you and the others."

Meaning the two other fosters currently residing in the best foster home in the world. "Mr. McK . . ." She sighed, remembering the sad look in his eyes. "He let me know that I messed up."

Akiko seemed to understand. "Sucks when he does that. I feel like I've kicked a puppy or something." She blinked. "Not that I've ever done that."

Katherine's lips tipped up in a reluctant smile. "Me either, but yeah, that's how it felt." That Akiko had disappointed Harlan and Betsy was a surprise. "But you never fuck up." She winced. "Mess up."

Akiko huffed. "I'm not gonna snitch on you, Kit. That's not who I am."

Katherine bit her lip. "I'm not sure I know who you are."

Akiko's chin lifted. "You never gave me a chance to show you."

Katherine stepped forward until she stood a foot from Akiko. "I know. And that was wrong of me. I wanted to fix this—fix me—for a while now. I got you this." She held her hand out, palm up. The little figurine was more beautiful than she'd expected. She'd known Harlan would do a good job. He was a wizard with wood and a carving knife. "Merry Christmas."

Akiko stared at the figurine, her crossed arms falling to her sides before she clasped her hands behind her back. Like she was afraid to touch it.

"It's a crane," Katherine supplied when Akiko said nothing. "Because when you do your karate dance, you look like a crane."

Akiko looked up abruptly, and Katherine was stunned to see tears in the girl's dark eyes. "Pop made it?"

Katherine was the only resident of McKittrick House who didn't call Harlan "Pop." He'd offered several times, even straight-out asked her to call him that, but she didn't want to.

No. It's that I'm afraid to. Because once they really knew her, they wouldn't like her anymore. They'd make her leave.

He's always been nice. He wouldn't make you leave.

And she'd think about that later. For now, it was taking all her energy to do this apology. "He did. I asked him to. I bought it from him. Like a . . . commission." That was what Harlan had called it when Katherine had approached him.

Akiko shuddered out a breath. "You paid him for it? In money?"

She knew what Akiko was asking. Harlan McKittrick had never done anything sexually inappropriate. Not even once. That it had occurred to Akiko made Katherine's heart squeeze painfully in her chest.

"Half money. Half chores."

"That's why you've been mucking out stalls all week?"

"For the last three weeks," Katherine grumbled. "And I've been washing dishes every night. But I still think he gave me a good deal. His carvings bring in hundreds of dollars. I didn't pay that much," she added ruefully.

Akiko slowly brought her hands to her eyes to brush the tears away before they spilled. "For me?"

"For you. I . . . I wanted to make nice a while back, but . . ." She sighed. "Mr. McK finished it about a week ago and I wanted to give it to you then."

Akiko still hadn't touched the offering. She just stared at it longingly.

Katherine understood that. Foster kids rarely got things of

their own. When they were offered, it was hard to believe there wasn't a catch.

"Why didn't you?" Akiko asked.

Katherine's eyes suddenly stung. "I . . ." She pursed her lips and willed the tears to recede but they didn't listen. Keeping the hand with the carved crane where it was, she angrily dashed them away with her other hand. "The detective who's been working Wren's case thought he had a lead."

"Detective Constantine?"

Katherine nodded. Baz Constantine came to McKittrick House at least once a month to give Harlan, Betsy, and Katherine an update on Wren's case. He'd been doing so for the past nine months. Ever since Wren's body had been found in a dumpster.

She tried to speak but the words were stuck in her throat.

"The lead wasn't a lead after all?" Akiko asked gently.

Katherine shook her head, frustrated when the tears kept falling. "That bastard's still out there. He killed her and he's walking around free."

Akiko wiped a few tears of her own. "Could have been us," she whispered.

"I wish it had been me."

Akiko shook her head. "You can't say that, Kit. Promise me that you won't say it again."

"I can't. I don't lie."

Akiko hiccupped on a small laugh. "You are exactly who you seem to be, aren't you?"

Katherine shrugged one shoulder. "I don't know who else to be. Sorry."

"Don't be. I like you. I'd like to, anyway."

Katherine rolled her eyes. "Then take the damn bird."

Akiko giggled and took the crane, taking care not to touch Katherine's skin.

Katherine appreciated that. She didn't like to be touched. Even Harlan and Betsy didn't hug her like they hugged the others. They understood.

"Thank you," Akiko whispered. "But I didn't get you anything."

"You didn't have to. You weren't a jerk to me like I was to you."

"Wanted to be," she admitted. "But you're Mom and Pop's favorite and I didn't want them to get mad at me."

Katherine's eyes widened. "I am not their favorite."

"Well, maybe not their favorite," Akiko allowed. "But they love you. You get that, right?"

Katherine nodded slowly. "I think so."

Akiko sighed. "I hope I can stay long enough for them to adopt me."

"They won't throw you out. You don't do drugs or try to run. You're safe here."

Akiko smiled. "I'm starting to believe that."

Katherine found herself smiling back, because she might be starting to believe it, too. Finally. "Good."

"Can I ask you a question?"

Katherine stiffened. "You can ask."

"Why won't you let them adopt you? The other kids said that Mom and Pop have offered. But they say you refuse. Why?"

Wasn't *that* a good question?

"I don't think . . . I'm not a nice person. Not like you. Not like Wren was. They just don't know it yet."

Akiko looked like she wanted to argue, but she finally just shook her head. "I thought something had happened last week. You almost warmed up to me and then it was like Alaska again. I'm sorry that the detective failed."

Katherine was, too. "He says he'll keep trying. I guess we'll see if he does. Mr. McK and I have been out looking for months, talking to runaway kids on the street in town. We show Wren's photo and ask if they saw her and if they saw anyone with her, but it's like her killer is a ghost."

"Next time you go to town to search, I'll go with you."

Katherine's throat tightened once again. "Why?"

"Because I'd want someone to fight for me like you fight for Wren," Akiko said simply. "Because I want to help."

"Thank you." The words came out as a whisper.

Akiko sighed heavily. "Now I feel like I should get you something, but Christmas has passed. You've made me look bad."

Katherine hesitated, then decided to just ask. "That karate thing you do. Can you show me?"

Akiko smiled brightly. "Yeah?"

"Yeah. I need to know how to protect myself."

"Everyone should. I've been studying with Shihan Ito since I was in kindergarten. I can give you lessons." She carefully set the carved crane aside. "Let's start from the beginning." She offered her hand. "Hello. I'm Akiko Jones."

Katherine stared at the girl's hand for a long moment before giving it a brusque shake. "Hi, Akiko. I'm Katherine Matthews, but everyone calls me Kit."

"It's nice to meet you, Kit. Let's get started. I'll need to touch you sometimes, to show you how to hold your arms or legs. Is that okay?"

Katherine nodded, impressed that Akiko had asked. "Yes, but warn me first."

"Understood. Okay. Lesson one."

An hour later, Katherine and Akiko wandered back to the big house only to find Harlan McKittrick sitting on a bench outside. He was wearing a heavy jacket and his cheeks were a little pink from the chill in the air.

He gave them a nod. "Mom's putting dinner on, Akiko. She said to send you in to help when I saw you." He winked. "It's fish and chips night."

Akiko grinned. "She promised she'd show me how to fry them." She glanced at Katherine. "See you later?"

"Sure. Thank you for the lesson."

"Thank you for the crane." Akiko skipped into the house.

"I noticed that Mrs. McK didn't ask me to help," Katherine said wryly.

Harlan's lips twitched. "You've got many talents, Kit. Cooking doesn't have to be one of them." He patted the bench beside him and Katherine sat down. "Akiko likes the crane?"

"Loves it."

"Worth the cash and the chores?"

"Yeah." Katherine thought she should have paid more. Done more. "Thank you for making it."

"You're very welcome. How did the apology go?"

"She forgave me. She's a lot nicer than I am."

Harlan frowned. "Don't say that. You, Kit Matthews, have the biggest heart of anyone here. You just hide it well. One of these days you're going to realize you don't have to hide it."

"Maybe." She sighed. "I can't even call you Pop."

"You will. In time. Or you won't. Either way, it doesn't

change the way Mom and I feel about you. You're ours, Kit. Ours to protect. Ours to love."

Katherine sucked in a breath that burned. "You said that to me before."

"The day we buried Wren. I remember. I remember everything I've ever said to you and everything you've ever said to me. I also said that I was sure of you and that's still true. I know apologies aren't easy for you. I know they make you feel things you don't want to admit to. But you did it because you couldn't let Akiko go on being hurt. You have a good heart, Kit. And if you don't believe it yourself, believe me. I will never lie to you."

"Okay," she whispered. "It's . . . a lot."

"I know. But I'm here. Always. So is Mom."

Katherine believed him and that scared her to death. She couldn't speak and wasn't sure she'd know what to say if she could. So she sat in silence as Harlan carved and the shadows of evening began to fall.

She was safe here. In this house. With this man and his wife.

A window opened, and Betsy stuck her head out. "Dinner!"

Harlan blew her a kiss, then stood, holding out his hand for Katherine. "Ready to eat?"

She stared at his hand. She somehow knew that if she didn't accept his hand, he'd still like her. He'd still be nice to her. He wouldn't throw her out.

That made it easier to accept his gesture. Easier to give him something back.

So she took his hand and let him pull her to her feet. "Thank you. Pop," she added before she chickened out.

He smiled down at her and she felt . . . loved. "You're

welcome, Kitty-Cat. Let's go eat before it's all gone. That Akiko is a little thing, but she can put away food like crazy."

Katherine followed Harlan McKittrick into the big house that always smelled like apple pie, fresh laundry, and lemon furniture polish.

It smelled like home.

CHAPTER ONE

La Jolla, San Diego, California
Saturday, January 28, 4:30 p.m.
Present day

Police psychologist Sam Reeves wasn't certain about what they were about to do, but he believed in homicide detective Kit McKittrick and she *was* certain.

So . . . here they were, knocking at the front door of a woman who'd claimed to know about Akiko McKittrick's mother. It was an intriguing mystery, to be sure.

Sam glanced at Akiko, who was biting her lip. "You okay?"

They were supposed to have met Mary Sherman at a diner about two blocks away, but the woman hadn't shown up. Kit had, however, traced Mrs. Sherman's initial phone call to Akiko and now knew nearly everything about her, including the woman's home address.

Kit insisted she hadn't broken any rules to get the information, that the woman's phone number had been easily traced on the internet. Sam had checked that out for himself and it was true. Whoever Mary Sherman was, either she was not adept at covering her tracks or she had nothing to hide.

She was forty-six years old and of Japanese descent, as was Akiko, so that part worked. Mary had been married to Leo Sherman for twenty-four years and was the mother of twenty-two-year-old fraternal twins—two daughters. Both were seniors at San Diego State—one was majoring in accounting as their mother had, and the other was a pre-med student, following in their father's footsteps. Leo Sherman was a cardiologist, and Mary had her own accounting firm.

Sam had acquired all this information in about fifteen minutes of online searching. They seemed to be an ordinary family.

Akiko probably would have been fine meeting Mary Sherman on her own, but Kit's spider-senses were telling her to accompany her sister. Kit almost always listened to her gut, for which Sam was grateful. Her intuition had saved her life several times.

Sam was along to pay attention to what Mary shared, as Kit wasn't sure if she could do that and support Akiko at the same time.

Sam was just happy to assist. He loved helping Kit, largely because she rarely asked for anyone's help. That she trusted him gave him hope that they did, indeed, have a future together.

He wanted a future with Kit more than he'd ever wanted anything. But he knew her well enough by now to know not to rush her. She'd get there in her own time. He could wait. She was worth it.

"I don't know if I'm okay or not," Akiko murmured as the three of them gathered on the woman's front porch. "If she got cold feet, maybe I need to respect that."

Normally confident, Akiko had been uncertain about meeting this woman ever since Mary Sherman had first made contact. But, above all else, she wanted to learn more about the mother who'd left her at a firehouse thirty-two years before.

Kit arched a blond brow. "We can turn around right now."

Akiko winced. "But you took today off just for this. Just for me."

Kit smiled at her sister and the sight warmed Sam's heart. Kit wasn't overly demonstrative, but she loved her family fiercely. It was one of the many things Sam found so appealing about the homicide detective who'd stolen his heart nearly a year ago.

"I'd take off a million days just for you," Kit said, stroking her hand down Akiko's long black hair. "If you want to set up another meet for a later date, I'll be there for you."

"Thank you, but I've come this far. I might as well see it through while I have you two. I really need to settle this so that I can get back to work." Akiko ran a charter fishing boat business. She took anglers out to do deep-sea fishing off San Diego's coast, but her nerves over Mary Sherman's call—amplified by Kit's gut telling them that something wasn't quite right—had kept her from taking her boat out. She'd canceled a few charters in the weeks since receiving that call. She met Sam's gaze. "I'm okay."

He didn't really believe her, but he nodded anyway. "Then let's knock."

Kit did so and the three of them stood for a moment, waiting. But no one came to the door. Kit leaned in to put her ear to the door.

"Noth—"

Her words were cut off by the crack of gunfire.

Sam stared for a moment at the bullet hole in the door, just inches from where Kit's head had been only moments before. Then his brain kicked in and he yanked both Kit and Akiko down, but there was no cover. There was no porch railing and only a small overhang.

They were sitting ducks.

Another shot was fired and Kit made a muted noise of pain.

"Kit!" Akiko screamed.

"It's not bad," Kit said with a grimace. "Just a graze. We need to get out of here."

Sam moved to cover Kit's body with his own, looking around for a better place to hide. It would take them too long to get to their car.

Inside, he thought. *We go inside.*

He lurched to his feet, prepared to use his shoulder to bust through the door. *Which is gonna hurt.* But that didn't matter.

Someone was shooting at Kit.

From the corner of his eye, he saw Akiko cover Kit with her body, her hand fumbling at the left sleeve of Kit's blazer, which was already dark with blood.

No more shots were fired, but that didn't mean they were safe.

Sam put one hand on the doorknob and braced himself for

the pain of shoving open the door. But the doorknob turned and he fell into the house.

It was dark. Too dark for this time of day. And too quiet.

And none of that mattered right now.

"Move," he barked, taking care not to touch Kit's left arm as he scooped her up and entered Mary Sherman's home. Akiko followed and closed the door behind them, visibly trembling.

"Kit?" she asked.

"I'm fine," Kit bit out. "Just a graze."

"Liar," Sam said mildly, even though his heart was pounding with fear and adrenaline. "Let me look. Akiko, call 911."

That Kit didn't argue about calling 911 told him that it was far more painful—and potentially far more serious—than she was admitting.

Carefully he removed her blazer, leaning up to hit the light switch so that he could better see. But no lights came on.

The power was off, which explained why it was so dark and quiet. No appliances hummed and the living room drapes shut out the waning afternoon sun.

Akiko put her phone on speaker so that she could shine her cell's flashlight on Kit's arm.

"Thanks," Sam said, listening to the 911 operator assure Akiko that help was on the way as he examined Kit's arm as gently as he was able. "It appears to be a through-and-through. Entry and exit wounds."

"Listen to you," Kit said with forced lightness. "Sounding like a cop."

Sam pushed a lock of hair off her cheek. "I've been hanging

out with the best. The bleeding has already slowed down. I'm going to try to find Mary Sherman and see if she's got any bandages. You two stay here."

Kit gripped his jacket sleeve. "Stay here with us. Someone has been in this house. Power's off and it's on in the other houses on the street. I could see lights."

So had Sam. "I need to find bandages to dress this wound."

"You said the bleeding had slowed. Stay here. Please. I don't know where the shooter is. I can defend us here." Kit drew her service weapon from the hip holster he'd rarely seen her without.

"Kit," Sam protested. "Let me have that."

She shook her head. "Right-handed, so I'm okay to shoot if necessary. Just . . . stay down. Please, Sam."

Sam sighed. It was pointless to argue with her when she got that stubborn look on her face. "Fine." But he twisted on his heels to take in the rest of the room, the flashlight from his phone illuminating a very normal-looking living room.

Someone was planning a trip to Germany, based on the two travel books and one German-English dictionary on the coffee table. Someone wore size thirteen shoes. And someone—

He sucked in a breath. "Oh shit."

"What?" Kit demanded.

"What?" Akiko echoed.

"What's happening?" the 911 operator asked.

"Mary Sherman," Sam said, recognizing her from her Facebook photos. He shined his light on the woman who lay in a crumpled heap on the floor. The wall behind her was streaked with blood, the source of which appeared to be the bullet hole in the middle of the woman's forehead.

"Oh shit," Kit muttered.

"Now we know why she didn't show up at the diner," Akiko said, her voice hitching up in fear.

Even though the windows were covered with drapes, Sam kept his head down as he crawled across the floor and touched Mary's throat. "No pulse. She's dead." Which he'd surmised from the bullet hole, but miracles sometimes happened.

Kit reached for her blazer. "I need my phone. I have to call Navarro."

Sam crawled back to her. "I'll call him. You stay quiet until the medics arrive." He took Akiko's phone, keeping his touch gentle since Kit's sister appeared to be holding herself together by a thread. "Ma'am?" he said to the operator. "This is Dr. Sam Reeves. I'm with Detective Kit McKittrick, who was shot. We took shelter in the home of Mary Sherman, who I just discovered dead. The body is still warm and the blood on the wall behind her is still dripping, so I think her death was quite recent."

"It was probably her shooter who shot at me," Kit said loudly.

"I'm sending help," the operator said. "Please stay on the line."

"We will," Sam promised. But he needed to call Navarro, so he muted Akiko's cell and used his own to call Kit's lieutenant.

"Dr. Reeves?" Navarro said when he answered. "What's wrong?"

Sam sighed. "Found a body."

Navarro groaned. "You two. It's always you two."

"Three today. Akiko's with us."

"All right. Tell me what you know."

Sam filled him in, hearing sirens approach as he came to the end of his explanation. "Medics are here. What should I tell the cops who show up?"

"To touch nothing. I'll call the ME and CSU. I'm coming to the scene. I'll make sure they don't take you away in cuffs."

"Thank you," Sam said dryly, because that had happened to him in the past. Just once, but that was enough. "See you soon."

He ended the call and unmuted Akiko's phone. "The medics are here," he told the operator. "Thank you for your assistance." Then he ended the call and returned Akiko's phone. "You okay?"

"No," Akiko said honestly. "What just happened?"

"That's what I'm going to find out," Kit said.

"Will they let you?" Akiko asked. "Conflict of interest and all?"

"What they don't know won't hurt them," Kit said. She glanced at Sam. "You okay with me conflicting the interest?"

He cupped her cheek, gratified when she leaned into his touch. "As long as you know that I'm not letting you do this alone."

Hell, he wasn't going to leave her side. Someone had shot her. *Shot. Her.* It was starting to sink in and Sam thought he might be sick.

Until she smiled at him. "I know I'm not alone. Not anymore."

His spinning mind began to settle and he pressed a kiss to her forehead. "Good."

"Okay." She turned her head to one side, just in case her eyes opened accidentally. "Did you talk to Navarro, Sam?"

He squeezed her hand lightly. "I did. He arrived shortly after you left with the medics."

He hadn't wanted to leave her side, but Akiko had been borderline hysterical, so he'd let her sister ride in the ambulance with her. He'd stayed to answer all the lieutenant's questions.

"What did he say?"

"He sighed a lot."

Kit let out a sigh of her own because she and Sam were gaining a reputation for finding bodies when they least expected it. "I bet he did."

"Luckily at least three of Mrs. Sherman's neighbors rushed up to say that they'd seen the 'whole thing' and that they had security camera footage to back up our story. So we're in the clear."

"I should hope so," Kit said grumpily. "Not like it's our fault we keep stumbling over bodies."

The doctor made a strangled sound. It sounded like he'd choked on a laugh.

Good thing someone is happy today.

"Did Alicia come or did she send one of her techs?" The ME was supposed to have had the day off. She and her wife were taking their kids to the zoo.

"Alicia came, right about the time I was released from the scene. I stuck around until she'd had a chance to look at the body. She said that she'd know more when she got her on the table."

"She always says that. What did she say off the record?"

"That Mrs. Sherman had been shot not too long before we arrived."

Kit winced, and it had nothing to do with the sutures the doctor was apparently still doing. She barely felt a thing. But she knew Akiko would feel guilty about Mrs. Sherman. "If we hadn't waited at the diner so long, we might have been in time to stop her killer."

"I said as much, but Alicia said she was probably dead by the time we arrived at the diner. That our waiting for her to show up hadn't changed a thing. Off the record, of course."

"Of course. Has the victim's husband been notified?"

"Navarro said he'd take care of it."

"Who is he assigning?"

"Your best pals. Marshall and Ashton."

Kit had to steady her heart. She liked Kevin Marshall and Alf Ashton. They were amazing cops. But they were supposed to be working another case.

"I texted Kevin," Sam said. "He says they won't stop working on Wren's case. Said to tell you that they won't let you down."

Because they'd finally gotten a lead on Wren's killer, after years of nothing. It had been nearly seventeen years since Wren's death, and it physically hurt that she'd been unable to solve her sister's murder. She knew that Navarro had been right to give the case to Marshall and Ashton. There was no way she could be objective.

She also knew they'd do their best, but cold cases were a lot of hurry up and wait. Marshall and Ashton had to work Wren's case in between the fresh cases, like Mary Sherman's.

"I know they won't let me down," she murmured. "Is Akiko okay?"

"She's calmer now. I saw her in front of the hospital when I came in. She's waiting for your folks. Said she needed to move and that there wasn't enough space for that in the waiting room."

"She must have really long legs," the doctor deadpanned. "The waiting room isn't that small."

"She's only about five-two," Sam said with a smile in his voice, "but she's a powerhouse."

"By needing to move, she means she has to do her kata," Kit explained. "She's a black belt and doing the kata makes her less stressed. I used to call it her karate dancing."

Sam chuckled. "Seems accurate. When was that? When you were fifteen?"

"And last week." Kit's ears perked up at a trio of familiar voices. "We're about to be invaded."

The privacy curtain swooshed open.

"Kit." Betsy McKittrick sounded like she'd been crying. "My baby."

"I'm okay, Mom. I promise. Sam took good care of me."

"Of course he did," Harlan said gruffly. "He and Akiko both contacted us right away. We weren't at home so it took us a while to get here." His scent filled her head. Wood chips, hay, and lemon. He always smelled the same. It was a comfort. "You really okay, Kitty-Cat?"

"I am. Just a little hole in my arm. Didn't hit anything important."

"She's not lying," the doctor said cheerfully. "I'm all done. I'll send someone in with the aftercare instructions. She shouldn't be alone for the next few hours."

Kit opened one eye in time to see Harlan, Betsy, Akiko, and Sam all nodding.

"She won't be," they all said in unison.

Kit groaned. "My life."

Harlan's big hand trembled as he stroked her hair, then cupped her cheek. "You've got a good life, Kitty-Cat."

She let go of Sam's hand to cover Harlan's. "Because of you and Mom. You promised me I'd have a good life and you never lie."

"I don't. Now, how about you and Akiko stop lying and tell me what's going on. Why were you at that woman's house to begin with?"

She glanced at Akiko, who was staring at the floor. "You didn't tell him?"

"No," Akiko whispered. "And don't ask me why not, because I'm not sure."

Kit exhaled quietly, then brought her parents up to speed, telling them about Mrs. Sherman's call to Akiko more than two weeks before. How, out of the blue, this woman had come forward, claiming to have known Akiko's mother. And how Kit hadn't wanted her to meet the woman alone, that she'd had a bad feeling about the whole thing. *And I was right.*

All the while Akiko kept staring at the floor and her parents kept shooting concerned looks in Akiko's direction.

"We just figured we'd have a sit-down with Mrs. Sherman and get Akiko's questions answered," Kit finished, "but . . . well. It didn't turn out that way."

Betsy turned to Akiko with wet eyes, because she'd started to cry again in the middle of Kit's tale. "You didn't trust us?"

Akiko's head flew up, her expression horrified. "No! I . . . I didn't want to hurt you. I didn't want you to think I cared more about finding my mother than you. Because you are my mother, Mom. You and Pop are my parents."

"I know that, you silly girl. It's okay that you want to know about your biological mother. It's all okay." Betsy engulfed Akiko in a hug and Harlan embraced them both. There were a lot of tears.

Even Harlan was crying and that always tore Kit's heart.

Kit reached for Sam's hand, knowing he'd still be there. Still close by.

Sam brought their joined hands to his lips. "It's going to be okay, Kit," he murmured. "However this turns out, it'll be okay. I won't let anyone shoot you again."

She stared up at him. "I know." Because she did. Sam appeared to be everyone's idea of a nice guy—and he was. But he was no pushover. He was strength and safety. He kept his promises.

And he was extremely easy on the eyes with his messy dark hair and nerdy glasses. She brought their joined hands to her lips and echoed his kiss.

I'm lucky. In so many ways.

She was lucky to have Harlan and Betsy. And Akiko.

She was lucky to have Sam.

I'm lucky to be alive.

If she hadn't ducked to listen at the Shermans' door, that first bullet would have struck her in the head, too.

Now the biggest question was why.

"Why me?" she said. "Why did he shoot at *me*?"

Because the shooter hadn't fired at Sam or Akiko, even when they'd put their bodies in harm's way, defending her.

"I don't know," Sam said, his voice going grim and cold, and she realized that he'd been wondering the same thing. "But you can be damn sure we'll find out."

Kit nodded once. "Together."

CHAPTER TWO

Carmel Valley, San Diego, California
Saturday, January 28, 8:30 p.m.

Sam liked Detectives Kevin Marshall and Alf Ashton. He really did. Kevin often joined Sam and Connor Robinson at the lanes for bowling night, and the Ashtons had sent a fruit basket to Sam's parents in Scottsdale when Sam's father had had a mild stroke six weeks before.

Sam had been very grateful for that basket because the fruit was the only nutrition he'd gotten while his father was in the hospital. A man could only eat fast food for so long.

He not only liked Marshall and Ashton, he respected them, too. They were good cops. Smart and loyal. They had Kit's back.

But at the moment, they were getting on Sam's last nerve. He'd sat in relative silence in the McKittricks' living room watching Kit answer the same questions a third time. She looked pale, sitting on the sofa with her legs propped up and one of Betsy's homemade quilts pulled around her shoulders. She was shivering, too, and her jaw was tight.

"But *why* did you ask your sister to wait to contact the woman?" Marshall asked.

"I told you," she said, far too quietly. Sam's Kit was passion and exuberance. Not this muted shell. "I had a bad feeling. This woman calls out of the blue from a local area code saying she has info on Akiko's mother. Why now? She's lived here for decades. Why call Akiko now? It felt wrong, so I asked my sister to wait."

She was in pain and she was pushing through it so that Marshall and Ashton as the primary detectives on Mary Sherman's case could get the answers they needed.

But enough was enough.

How many different ways could they ask Kit why she'd insisted Akiko wait?

"But why—" Ashton began.

Nope. No more.

Sam cleared his throat, interrupting the detective. "Guys, we know you're trying to cover all your bases, but Kit needs to rest. She's held off taking a pain pill so that she could talk to you. You've interviewed Akiko, me, and Kit. It's time for you two to go."

Harlan appeared in the doorway from the kitchen and gave Sam an appreciative nod. "You can always come back, boys," the older man said mildly, but Sam could see the tension Harlan carried in his shoulders.

The man's daughter had been shot today. He was worried

and trying not to show it. He was always strong for everyone at McKittrick House.

Marshall looked aghast, as if he was seeing Kit's pain for the first time. Maybe he was. Maybe Sam just knew her well enough that he could see it clearly.

"I'm so sorry, Kit," Marshall said. "We didn't realize."

"And we should have," Ashton said. "We'll be going now."

Kit smiled weakly. "Thanks, guys. You'll pass on anything you find, right?"

Marshall hesitated. "As much as we can."

Kit sighed. "I figured you'd say that."

"At least none of you are suspects this time," Ashton said brightly.

Kit glanced at Sam, then returned her attention to the two detectives. "Too soon, guys."

Because Sam had been a suspect in a murder the year before. Several murders, actually. He'd been cleared quickly, but the memory was still a disturbing one.

Ashton nearly pouted. "Still too soon? God, Sam."

Marshall smacked his partner in the arm. "Still too soon, asshole." Then he winced when Betsy came through the doorway from the kitchen holding two plastic grocery sacks.

"Sorry, Betsy," Marshall muttered.

"I've heard far worse," Betsy said. "I made you boys some dinner to take with you. You *will* keep us updated."

Marshall took the bags with a vigorous nod. "Absolutely, ma'am."

"We will happily trade need-to-know-only information for your food," Ashton added with a grin. "Nobody wants to be on your bad side, Betsy."

Betsy's lips twitched. "Drive safely." She ushered them to the front door. "See you soon." She sagged against the door when she'd closed it. "I thought they'd never leave. Thank you, Sam."

"Looks like you had a plan, too," Sam said. "To bribe them to leave—and to share info."

"It's what I do best." Betsy pressed the back of her hand to Kit's forehead. "No fever." She sat in the chair closest to her daughter and dug a bottle of pills from her pocket. "They're not the opioids the doctor prescribed. They're just over-the-counter ibuprofen," she said before Kit could protest. "You will take two. Do not argue with me, Kit McKittrick."

Kit snapped her mouth closed and held out her hand, scowling. But she took the ibuprofen.

"Where's Akiko?" she asked.

"In the kitchen," Betsy said with a worried frown. "Punching bread dough."

"Like mother, like daughter," Kit said wryly. "You always bake when you're upset, too. Akiko was rattled, seeing Mrs. Sherman's body. Most people would be."

"She's more rattled that you got hurt," Sam said. He sat at the end of the sofa, settling Kit's feet in his lap.

"You're right," Harlan said. "She's feeling guilty."

"That's just stupid." Then Kit sighed. "And I'd be feeling the same way in her shoes. We need to figure out our next steps. I have faith in Marshall and Ashton, but Akiko's scared. I can't just sit here while she's scared."

"Yes, Kit," Akiko said from the doorway. She leaned on the frame, wiping her hands with a towel. "You *can* just sit there, and you *will*. You got shot."

"I know," Kit said. "I was there. What are you baking?"

"Cinnamon bread. The girls are getting it ready to go into the oven." The "girls" were the six foster children currently living in McKittrick House. Soon to be five, since Rita's adoption would be finalized within a few weeks, and she'd no longer be a foster. "And don't change the subject."

"Busted." Harlan took some wood and his carving knife from his pocket. "She's right, Kitty-Cat. You need to rest. Let Marshall and Ashton do their jobs."

Kit scowled and Akiko looked smug.

But Harlan jolted before either of the sisters could say another word. "Someone's coming." He frowned at his phone. "Cameras are showing a black Audi coming up the driveway."

Kit opened her mouth, then snapped it closed.

Sam knew that expression. She'd done something that she didn't want anyone to know about. "What is it, Kit?"

"Leo Sherman owns a black Audi," she said.

Akiko crossed her arms over her chest. "How do you know? You can't find that out in a normal internet search."

Kit winced. "I might have checked them both out a little more thoroughly than I originally let on."

Sam pushed himself to his feet. "At least forewarned is forearmed. Betsy, can you take Akiko back to the kitchen? Harlan, let's see what this guy wants."

Harlan nodded, stopping at his gun safe to retrieve a rifle before following Sam out the door.

"Hey!" Kit called. "You can't just go out there by yourselves." She flung the quilt off her shoulders and rose to her feet, her stance shaky.

Sam shook his head. "You're not wearing any shoes."

"Fine. Where are my shoes?"

"Where you can't find them," Harlan said. "Sit yourself back down. You can watch with the cameras."

Kit looked outraged. "You hid my shoes?" She followed them anyway. "It's not that cold."

Harlan shook his head. "We don't know what this guy wants. He could blame you, Kitty-Cat. You're not as nimble as you usually are."

"Sam is. And you have a rifle." She pushed past them to the front porch. "Don't let all the heat out. Close that door."

Harlan sighed. "Stay in front of her, Sam."

"Already planned to."

Sam walked down the porch steps and put his body in front of Kit's, unsurprised when he heard her rack the chamber of her gun. Together, he, Kit, and Harlan waited until the Audi emerged from the trees and pulled into the driveway, stopping behind all the McKittrick Subarus and Sam's RAV4.

The driver sat in the Audi for a full minute before shutting off the engine and getting out of his car. He was five-eight at the most. He looked older than his wife, maybe mid-sixties. And, in the light of Harlan's security spotlights, he appeared to be utterly exhausted.

"Hello," he said quietly, then pointed at Harlan's rifle. "I mean you no harm."

Sam drew a breath. "You're Dr. Sherman? Leo Sherman?"

Sherman nodded. "I am. And you'd be Dr. Sam Reeves."

"I am." Sam kept his tone gentle. Assuming this man hadn't been involved in the murder of his wife, he'd sustained a terrible shock today. "How can we help you, sir?"

"I . . ." Sherman's shoulders sagged. "I don't know. But

those detectives said my wife's body was discovered by three people, one of whom was shot. That was you, Detective McKittrick."

Sam felt Kit move from behind him to his side. He wasn't going to look at her, though. He wasn't taking his eyes off Leo Sherman.

"How do you know that?" Kit asked. "The news doesn't have my name. Do they?"

Sherman shrugged. "I have no idea. I was in surgery when my Mary..." He closed his eyes. "When I came out of surgery, a lieutenant was waiting to talk to me. Navarro."

"He's my boss," Kit said.

"I figured. He told me the bare facts but wouldn't disclose the names of the three people who'd entered my home. He said they'd been cleared of any wrongdoing, that one of the three had been shot, and that he was sorry for my loss. I... I say that to every family whose loved one dies on the operating table. No one's ever said it to me. Not like this."

"I'm so sorry," Kit said softly. "But if Lieutenant Navarro didn't tell you our names, how did you know to come here?"

"Because hospitals are like beehives," he said bitterly. "Everyone buzzing with gossip. In less than ten minutes I'd heard from three different people that Detective Kit McKittrick was in the ER after having been shot at the scene of a murder. I don't think anyone knew it was my wife."

"I see." Kit started to take a step closer to the man, but Sam held her back. She didn't fight him, and for that Sam was grateful. "What do you need from us, Dr. Sherman?" she asked.

"Answers. Why were you there? Why did you knock on my door?"

Harlan leaned into Sam. "What do you think? Is he safe? Can we ask him to come inside? Because Kit is shivering again."

Sam put his arm around Kit, still not taking his eyes off Leo Sherman. She *was* shivering, this time because she'd come outside in *January* with no shoes. It wasn't a particularly cold night, but . . . *no shoes.* "I think he's sincere in his grief," he replied, but didn't drop his voice. He wanted Sherman to hear him. "But I'd ask him to let us check him for weapons before asking him into the house."

Sherman immediately stretched out his arms. "Check me."

Harlan glared at Kit. "You go inside. Now."

Kit made a face but complied. "Check his boots."

"I'm not wearing boots," Sherman said softly. "I don't own a gun."

"I know," Kit said, and then she went back into the house but stood in the open doorway, two dogs having come to flank her sides. One was her standard poodle, Snickerdoodle. The other was Petunia, a mix of some very large breeds, including mastiff. Petunia was still a young dog but already stood as tall as Kit's hip. The dog growled loudly enough to be heard, and it was an impressive growl, Sam had to admit.

Sherman would have to be a fool to try anything with Petunia on the scene.

Together, Sam and Harlan checked the cardiologist for weapons, then escorted him into the McKittricks' living room.

Kit returned to her place on the sofa, the quilt now tucked around her bare feet. Sam put his jacket around her shoulders and she smiled up at him.

"Thank you."

"You're welcome. And if you get sick, I'm telling your mother that you went outside without shoes."

"I already know," Betsy said, coming in from the kitchen. "I was watching the camera feed. Dr. Sherman, can I get you some coffee?"

Sam turned to the doctor when the man remained silent. He was staring, open-mouthed, at Akiko, who stood at Betsy's side. All the color had drained from his face.

Suddenly he swayed, and Sam rushed to his side. "Are you all right, Dr. Sherman?" he asked, lowering the man into a chair.

Sherman waved him away. "I'm . . ."

He didn't finish the sentence because he clearly wasn't "fine." He was staring at Akiko as though he'd seen a ghost.

"Who are you?" he whispered.

"This is my daughter," Harlan said. "Akiko McKittrick."

"Dr. Sherman?" Sam asked. "What is this?"

Sherman clutched his hands together so tightly that his knuckles were white. "My Mary," he whispered. "She's . . . I'm sorry, Miss McKittrick," he said to Akiko. "You look just like her when we were first married. You could be my Mary's twin."

Carmel Valley, San Diego, California
Saturday, January 28, 8:55 p.m.

Kit's gaze went from Leo Sherman to Akiko and back again. If the man was faking it, he was a master actor. She didn't think he was faking it.

Who was Mary Sherman to Akiko?

Was she Akiko's mother?

That had, of course, occurred to Kit when Akiko had first told her about Mary Sherman's phone call. It had occurred to her when she'd seen Mary's driver's license photo and the woman's Facebook feed.

There had been a resemblance, to be sure.

But to see Leo Sherman's face right now . . .

"Was Mary my sister's mother?" Kit asked softly, because no one else was saying a word.

Akiko stood with Betsy's arm tight around her shoulders. Both she and Betsy still stared at Sherman, who was dangerously pale.

"Rita!" Sam called. "I know you're there listening."

A teenage girl with blond hair streaked with pink and blue entered the room, her expression sheepish. "Sorry, Dr. Sam."

Sam waved the apology away. "Can you get our guest a glass of water? And maybe something to eat? Cheese and crackers or something? But the water first."

"On it." Rita disappeared and Kit heard the activity of six teenagers snapping to attention in the kitchen.

They'd likely been listening to every word all evening. Kit couldn't blame them. She'd have done the same at their age.

"Dr. Sherman," Kit said softly, "can you tell us about your wife? All we know is that she called Akiko a little more than two weeks ago and said she'd known her mother. They arranged to meet at a diner today, after what your wife said would be a trip out of town, but your wife didn't show up. So we went to your house."

Sherman quietly thanked Rita when she brought him a glass of water. "How did you know where I lived?"

"I reverse searched your wife's phone number and found your address. All available online, sir."

That she'd searched the police databases for photos, past arrest records, and gun ownership was something she'd keep to herself. She shouldn't have done it, but she'd felt a visceral *wrongness* in her gut. And she'd been right.

The shots fired at them and the bullet hole in Mary Sherman's forehead were proof positive.

"And when you got to my house?" Sherman asked.

"We knocked," Kit said. "No one answered. I leaned in to listen at the door, which was a good thing. The first shot hit the door where my head had been." She glanced at her father. "Sit down, Pop. You're scaring me right now."

Because Harlan had grown pale, just as he had the other times she'd shared this part of the story in his presence. But all the other times he'd been sitting down. Now he was swaying.

Sam was at his side before the words were out of her mouth, helping her father to a chair. But he returned to where Leo Sherman sat.

Just in case the man was a good actor. Sam would never let her be threatened if he could help it.

Many people thought that Sam Reeves was just a really nice guy. A golden retriever in a world filled with Dobermans. And he *was* a really nice guy. But he was so much more.

He'd saved her life in the not-too-distant past.

The man had her back. He was unfailingly loyal.

And for some reason, he wants me.

That still floored her.

Rita reappeared with a glass of water for Harlan and a

plate of cheese and crackers for Dr. Sherman. Then she left the room, but Kit was certain that all the girls continued to listen.

Kit refocused on Dr. Sherman, who had politely moved the plate of food away from him. "I can't eat," he said apologetically. "But thank you. What happened next, Detective?"

"The next shot hit my arm," Kit went on. "Dr. Reeves and my sister, Akiko, both tried to shield me with their bodies and the shooting stopped. I don't know if the shooter just ran or he was waiting to get another shot at me, but there were no more shots. We didn't know that at the time, though. There was no cover. No place for us to hide."

"So you went into my house," Sherman said, regaining some of his composure.

"The door was unlocked, sir," Sam said. "We wouldn't have trespassed had the situation not been so dire."

"I understand," Sherman said. "And then? You . . . found her?"

"Yes, sir," Kit said. "I'm so sorry, but she was already gone. There wasn't anything we could do. So we called 911 and waited for help."

"You had a gun," Sherman said.

Kit's brows went up. "How did you know that?"

"I didn't. I guessed. I know many off-duty detectives who carry their service weapons. Did the police confiscate yours?"

"They did." She couldn't assume that this man was too distraught to clearly think. He was more on the ball than she'd expected. "I hadn't fired it in several days. Not since I went to the range for target practice. Ballistics will show that my gun was not the one that killed your wife."

Sherman nodded once. "I believe you." He turned to Akiko, who stood huddled against Betsy's side. "What exactly did my wife say to you?"

"Only that she knew my mother," Akiko murmured. "When I asked how she knew her, she said she'd tell me everything when we met in person. Was she . . ." She swallowed hard. "Was she my mother?"

"I don't know," Sherman admitted. "But you look just like she did when she was thirty, which is about how old you look now."

"Thirty-two," Akiko said numbly. "She would have been fourteen when I was born. I guess the box at the firehouse makes sense now."

Sherman shook his head. "I don't understand."

"My sister was left on the steps of a firehouse when she was just a baby," Kit explained. "She and I both grew up in the foster system. We were adopted by our parents, Harlan and Betsy."

"I was told that there was a piece of paper pinned to my blanket," Akiko said, "with my first name written on it. I was also told that there had been a photo of my mother in the box with me, but that was lost long ago. I never even saw it."

Kit had often wondered about the photo. Had it really existed? She'd always thought the photo seemed like the kind of thing a foster parent might tell a kid, intending to soften the rejection. If it had existed, was it really a photo of Akiko's mother or someone else? If there had been any name written on the back, it hadn't been recorded anywhere. Might it have been a photo of Mary?

They'd probably never know, but the existence of a photo had always been a comfort to Akiko, so Kit had never questioned it out loud.

Sherman nodded silently, studying their faces one at a time. Finally, he exhaled. "Something terrible happened to my wife when she was young. Before I met her. She would never tell me what that was. Sometimes she'd have nightmares, but she never shared with me what they were about. Once, when she was coming out of sedation after dental surgery, she said she was sorry, so sorry. That she did the only thing she knew to do. But when she was fully lucid again, she said that she didn't know what I was talking about. My wife loved me. Of that I am certain. She loved our daughters. Might she have had a child in her teenage years? Perhaps. But I don't know that much about her background." He rubbed his hands over his face. "I don't think her name was actually Mary, though."

Kit looked at Akiko. "Do you want me to ask the questions?"

Akiko's nod was shaky. "Please. I can't breathe. Can't think."

Harlan was on his feet immediately, helping both Akiko and Betsy to chairs.

I should have thought of that. But Kit would cut herself a little slack. It had been a difficult day.

"What do you think her real name was, Dr. Sherman?"

"Mari," he said, pronouncing it like the last part of *calamari*. "I heard her talking to a man a long time ago, before we were married. I was jealous at first. He was Japanese and they seemed to know each other. He called her 'Mari,' and she hissed at him, like an angry cat. She spoke to him in Japanese. Something about him knowing better and that wasn't who she was anymore. There was more, but that's all I caught. I studied for a year in Japan as an undergrad, so I was only conversationally fluent."

"What happened then?" Sam asked.

Sherman shrugged. "He begged her pardon and called her Mary after that."

"When and where was this?" Kit asked.

"A few months before our wedding, so twenty-four years ago. We'd just finished dinner and were coming out of a restaurant when this man called her name. Mari. I don't think I'll ever forget her expression when she saw him. Angry, but also afraid. So afraid. I thought he was going to hurt her. I was ready to hit him, but then she talked to him, like I said, and then they calmed down and spoke like old friends. Well, maybe not friends. Acquaintances."

"Do you remember what he looked like?" Akiko asked.

"I do. As I said, he was Japanese, like my Mary. He was older than she was, by at least twenty-five or thirty years. Once he'd walked away, I asked if he was a relative, and she said 'no' in a way that told me not to ask again. I drove her home and, when we got there, she apologized. She said the man had been her mother's friend, but not hers. I trusted her, but I watched for him for years. I never saw him again. I don't know his name. She never introduced us."

"Did you tell this to the police?" Kit asked.

She wanted to believe him. She really did. But his story was just a little too . . . good. His memory a little too clear. On the other hand, surgeons typically had a good memory.

But until she knew differently, she wasn't going to trust Leo Sherman.

"No," Sherman said. "I didn't tell them because I didn't even think of that night. Not until I saw your sister." He turned to Akiko. "I apologize. You've brought back a lot of memories."

"No need," Akiko said. "I'm so sorry that your wife is gone. I wish I knew more to tell you."

"I wish you did, too. I have to go. I left my daughters with my sister at her house. They're distraught, as you can imagine. And our home is a crime scene."

Kit started to ask Sam to drive the man home because Sherman didn't look like he was capable of driving, but Sam, as usual, was a step ahead.

"I'll drive you back, sir," he said. "I don't think you should be behind the wheel."

Sherman closed his eyes. "I hate to admit it, but you're right. Thank you, Dr. Reeves. You're very kind."

"He is," Kit said, letting the man hear the sharp edge of her voice. "He's very kind. I would hate to have something happen to him."

Sherman met Kit's gaze squarely. "He's safe with me. Even if I wanted to hurt anyone—which I do not—I'm too tired right now."

"I'll follow you, Sam," Harlan said. "So I can drive you back here. I assume you're staying here tonight."

Sam nodded. "I planned to, yes. I have to go home and get my dog, but I can sleep on the sofa. I know you have a full house. Every bed is taken. Dr. Sherman? Are you ready?"

"I am."

"Wait," Kit said. "Can you sit with a sketch artist? Since you remember what this man looked like, I mean."

"Of course." He pulled a card from his wallet and wrote on

the back. "My cell. Call me when you're ready for me to sit with the sketch artist. I'll make the time."

"Thank you," Kit said. "And we really are sorry. All of us have lost someone to violence. We know the pain."

Sherman swallowed hard. "Thank you for speaking with me."

Akiko rose to her feet. "Sir? I . . . hate to ask you this, but it could be important. Can we have a DNA test done? To see who I am to your wife?"

Kit could have told her that it didn't matter what Leo Sherman wanted. Until he was formally cleared, he was still a suspect in his wife's murder, and Detectives Marshall and Ashton would be doing that DNA test as part of their investigation. But she held her tongue, wondering what Sherman would answer.

"I think that would be wise," he said quietly. "But I want to talk to my daughters first. Finding that they might have a sibling is going to be a shock, on top of this tragedy. They may not want to know."

Too bad, Kit thought, *because we're going to find out.*

"I understand." Akiko inclined her head. "Please give them my condolences."

Sherman nodded, then stood and gave his car keys to Sam. They left, with Harlan following behind them.

The room was quiet for several long minutes after the front door closed. Then Rita and the other girls came into the room and surrounded Akiko in a group hug. Of the six teenagers, Rita had been with them the longest—nearly a year now. Emma and Tiffany had joined McKittrick House in November after Sam had found them homeless on the streets of downtown

San Diego, and the newest three—Dawn, Amy, and Stephie—they'd discovered just last month through New Horizons, a local shelter for homeless teens. They were good kids, all of them.

Watching them made Kit remember her own early days with Harlan and Betsy. She remembered finally feeling safe, like she could finally breathe. It was a debt she could never repay, but Harlan and Betsy would never expect her to even try. She knew Akiko felt the same. So the two of them spent a lot of their spare time here, paying it forward to these six girls and to any others who entered this wonderful place.

The group hug must have shaken something loose in Akiko, because she began to cry, sucking in great gasping breaths. "She's gone. I came so close to meeting her, but she's gone."

Rita met Kit's eyes. *What do I do?* she mouthed.

Love her, Kit mouthed back.

Rita laid her cheek on Akiko's head. "We're here. We love you."

"But she's dead," Akiko cried.

"I know," Rita whispered. "And you found her body. I know how that feels, too."

Because Rita had been the one to find her own mother's body after her murder. She'd been only eleven years old at the time.

"But I at least got to know my mom," Rita said sadly. "You didn't get that and I'm so sorry. But we're here. It's not the same, I know. But we're your sisters, and we're here."

"We're here," the others echoed. "We're here."

"Oh my goodness," Betsy whispered, pressing her hand to her heart. Tears slipped down her cheeks.

"We're raising them right, Mom," Kit whispered back, pride for Rita and the other girls mixing with her grief on Akiko's behalf.

And with the nagging feeling that Leo Sherman hadn't told them everything.

CHAPTER THREE

Carmel Valley, San Diego, California
Sunday, January 29, 7:15 a.m.

Sam rubbed at his eyes, grimacing when Siggy licked his face. "Dammit, Siggy."

Siggy sat on his haunches, grinning a doggy grin.

Sam pushed himself up to sit on the McKittricks' sofa. It was comfortable and he'd fallen asleep as soon as his head had hit the pillow.

Kit had slept in the room she shared with Akiko when one or both of them stayed over. Which was far more often than Kit stayed in her own place. Sam couldn't blame her. There was something about this house. He felt more at ease here than anywhere else.

Knowing Kit was just upstairs... he was content. Someday he'd wake up beside her, holding her in his arms. But until that day came, this was enough.

Plus, someone had made coffee. Probably Betsy.

Sam shoved his feet into his shoes and clipped Siggy's leash to his collar. It was going to be a gorgeous day. He loved it out here on the McKittrick farm. It was peaceful.

He'd taken Leo Sherman to his sister's house the night before, then driven back with Harlan, stopping to get Siggy on the way. Of course, Harlan had had questions.

How long had Sam known about the woman claiming to know Akiko's mother? *Two weeks.*

Why hadn't Sam told them? *It wasn't my story to tell.*

Did Sam think the woman could be Akiko's mother? *Of course it entered my mind, but I was waiting to see.*

Why had Kit asked Sam to join them?

That was a harder question to answer, because the real question was: why hadn't she asked Harlan?

Harlan had quickly retracted that question with an apology.

His daughter, his Kitty-Cat, had allowed someone new into her heart.

Sam was ecstatic. He'd been waiting on Kit to come around for nearly a year. Harlan was happy for them, Sam knew, but it was still an adjustment. He was no longer her only go-to person.

Harlan would get there. Sam had faith in the burly farmer who'd created this amazing place for kids in need.

Sam stiffened when he heard the roar of a car engine. He took out his cell phone, ready to dial 911.

A few seconds later, Harlan joined him in the front yard. "Morning, Sam. Hope you slept well."

"Like a rock. Who's coming?" Kit's father knew, or he would have been armed.

"It's Baz."

A moment later, a familiar SUV emerged from the trees.

Basil "Baz" Constantine had been Kit's partner when Sam met them the spring before. He and Baz hadn't started out well, as Baz had been convinced that Sam was a killer.

And he'd threatened to shoot Siggy.

But he'd apologized and he and Sam were now . . . mostly friends. They'd never bowl or play squash together like Sam did with Kit's new partner, but Sam didn't want to sock the man in the nose anymore.

Harlan huffed when Baz got out of his vehicle. "She's *fine*, Baz. I told you that when you called me yesterday afternoon and yesterday evening and first thing this morning."

Baz looked slightly abashed. "I know, but . . . dammit, Harlan. Someone shot our girl."

Baz wasn't only Kit's first partner in the Homicide division. He was the detective who'd investigated Wren's murder. He'd known Kit since she was a grieving fifteen-year-old and considered her his second daughter.

"I know," Harlan said grimly.

Baz nodded to Sam. "Sammy. How's it going?"

It was hard not to like Baz. He was a jovial guy who loved Kit. "Better than yesterday."

"I have a treat for Siggy." Baz smirked. "Can I give it to him or do you need to sniff it first?"

Baz was ridiculous. "Just give it to him." Snickering, Baz held out the treat for Siggy. It looked like one of those fancy dog biscuits that were sold at the bakery on Sam's street. "Did you go by my place first?"

"I did. You weren't home so I figured you'd be here." Baz winked salaciously. "You go, Sammy."

Harlan frowned. "Leave the boy alone. Also, that's my daughter you're talking about. Stop it."

"Fine, fine. What do we know?"

"No more than we knew last night when you called," Harlan said, sounding perturbed. "I don't want to let either of them out of my sight. Kit or Akiko."

Sam agreed. "He wasn't shooting at Akiko, but she's clearly at the center of all of this. As for not letting Kit out of your sight, you know that isn't gonna happen, right? She's gonna do what she's gonna do."

Harlan sighed. "I know. What do *you* know, Baz? You're grafted onto the SDPD grapevine. I know you've got news."

"Just a little."

"Don't say anything until I come down!" As one, they turned to the house, where Kit waved from a second-story window. "Be there in a minute."

Eager to be sure that Kit was feeling better this morning, Sam put his curiosity on pause. "Let's go get breakfast. Come on, Siggy." He followed his dog into the house, where the aroma of coffee had been joined by that of sausage.

He expected to see Betsy at the stove but found Akiko there instead. He fed Siggy, making enough noise that Akiko wouldn't be startled by his presence.

"You okay, Akiko?" he asked quietly.

She turned to face him, her eyes red and swollen. "Not really. But you two will figure this out. You and Kit."

"And Baz," Sam added, hoping he didn't sound too rueful.

Akiko chuckled. "He said he was sorry for threatening Siggy, Sam. You need to let it go."

He was happy to see her smile. "Siggy loves him, but Siggy is easily bribed with a dog biscuit. I, on the other hand, am easily bribed with people biscuits."

"I know my mom's recipe. I'll make you some."

Sam washed his hands and began to set the table. "Should I set places for the girls?"

"Nah," Kit said, coming down the stairs. "It's Sunday. They'll be in bed till at least ten. That's as late as Mom lets us sleep."

He studied Kit carefully, his heart tripping in his chest like it did every time he saw her. She was so pretty with her blue eyes and her golden hair. "You look like you rested."

She smiled up at him shyly. "I did."

She didn't kiss him. Not in her parents' home. They were too new for that, and that was okay with Sam. She'd called him her boyfriend yesterday and that was progress enough.

"She slept all night," Akiko said. "Which I know because she snores like a bear."

Kit's mouth dropped open in outrage. "I do not."

Akiko laughed. "She really doesn't, Sam, but it's always fun to tell her she does. Good morning, Pop," she said when Harlan and Baz came in from outside. "And Baz. So good to see you."

And that quick, the kitchen was filled with chatter. Betsy joined Akiko at the stove and soon breakfast was on the table. It wasn't until everyone sat down that Kit pointed a fork at Baz. "Spill. What have you heard?"

"Trouble in paradise," Baz said. "Mary Sherman's neighbors

said that the good doctor hadn't been home in three weeks. Turns out he's got a hotel room right next door to the hospital. One of those suites with a kitchen."

"Who told you that?" Kit asked.

Sam nudged her plate closer. "Eat. You can listen and eat at the same time. I've seen you do it."

"Aw," Baz said when Kit took a big bite, "she's doing it for you. When *I* used to tell her to eat, she just flipped me the bird. I heard it from Connor, who heard it from Marshall and Ashton."

Kit sipped at her coffee. "I *thought* Leo Sherman was hiding something."

"So did I," Sam said. "His memory of that night twenty-four years ago was a little too on the nose."

"I need to tell Ashton and Marshall about his visit," Kit said. "I meant to do it last night, but I fell asleep."

"I already did," Sam said and winced internally, waiting for her to be annoyed.

But she only smiled at him. "Thank you."

Baz's eyes widened. "Thank you? He scoops your news and you thank him?"

Kit regarded Baz seriously. "This isn't about scoops. This is about keeping Akiko safe."

"And you," Akiko said. "You were the one who got shot."

"I know," Kit said dryly. "And before anyone asks, yes, I took some ibuprofen this morning. It hurts but not as bad as it could be. I checked the wound in the mirror and it looks fine. Sam, did you ask Marshall and Ashton to run a DNA on Mrs. Sherman?"

"I did. I told them that Dr. Sherman had indicated he might

not want to know, but they assured me that it didn't matter. Especially now that he and his wife were sleeping apart."

"He must feel so guilty," Akiko murmured. "If he'd been home, she might still be alive."

"Unless he did it," Kit said. "I'm glad he came by last night. We got a lot more information than we gave. Unless he was lying, but that would be helpful information as well." She filled Baz in on the incident with Mary's old friend, the Japanese man who'd called her Mari. "I assume Marshall and Ashton have searched the house."

"They have," Sam confirmed. "I told them about the Japanese man and they're going to search Mary's photo albums to see if they can find a picture of him. They also said that the security cameras in the Sherman household had been deactivated before the power was cut. Which happened an hour and ten minutes before we arrived."

"But he was still there," said Kit. "Her shooter, I mean. Why shoot her, then stick around for an hour? He couldn't have known we'd come by. Or could he?"

Sam shrugged. "If this is about Akiko, and it almost certainly is, maybe he knew Mary was going to meet us. But he still couldn't have known we'd stop by. Marshall thinks he was searching the house when we knocked. The shooter appears on the neighbor's security system less than a minute after we parked in the driveway."

"What does he look like?" Kit asked.

"A guy in a hoodie," Sam said.

"Dammit." She scowled. "Always with the hoodies. Cause of death, Baz?"

"Cause of death was the bullet in her brain," Baz said, "but she did have finger-sized bruises on her wrists, like she'd been restrained. Also had defensive wounds. She scratched her attacker. ME got skin cells from under her nails. Full autopsy should be done by end of day." Then he grimaced. "I'm sorry, Akiko. I forgot that this woman might have been a relation."

"It's okay," Akiko said quietly. "I never knew her, so . . . I guess I haven't lost anything."

Betsy took Akiko's hand. "You lost a potential connection with someone who cared about you. That's not nothing. You're entitled to your grief and your anger."

"Why do you think Mary cared about Akiko?" Baz asked.

Betsy bit at her lip. "Like Kit said yesterday, Mary lived here for decades. Why choose now to contact Akiko? And what if whatever it is she had to share got her killed? Did she know Akiko was in danger?"

"Good questions, Mom," Kit said. "I'll add another. Do we know where Mary went for the past two weeks? If Sherman didn't come home for the last three weeks, why stay away? If Mary was out of town like she said she was, why wouldn't he just come home to his own house? Where did she go? Who did she see? What did she do?"

More good questions, Sam thought. "Akiko, when Mary told you that she couldn't see you for two weeks, how did she sound? Relaxed or upset?"

"Disappointed, I think. And maybe a little upset, but not mad. More . . . frustrated."

"How long has it been since that first phone call?" Harlan asked. "Exactly?"

"Almost three weeks," Akiko said. "I sat on it for a few days before I told Kit."

Kit glanced at her father. "And she didn't volunteer the information, she only told me because I asked, Pop. She didn't seem like herself."

"It's fine, honey. You told me that you knew what was bothering Akiko, but she hadn't given you permission to tell me. And I told you that I was glad one of us knew. I meant that."

"You do remember everything, don't you?" Kit asked with a smile.

"I try." Harlan pushed his empty plate aside. "So something happens that triggers Mary Sherman's call to Akiko. Right about the same time that her husband picks up and leaves their house, getting a hotel. Sounds like a connection to me. You need to find out what happened three weeks ago."

Baz cleared his throat. "I think you mean 'we' need to find out."

Kit met Baz's eyes. "Are you in?"

Baz's eyes gleamed. "With both feet."

Kit lifted her brows. "And Marian? Won't she be angry?"

"She's gone on a cruise with her sister through the Panama Canal. I'm home all alone." He tried to look pitiful and failed. "Just don't tell her when she comes back."

"Maybe you should talk to your cardiologist first?" Sam asked gently.

"Did it," Baz crowed. "My EKG was totally normal. I'm not coming back to SDPD, because I like retirement, but this is personal. This asshole messed with my kids. Kit and Akiko are mine, too."

Akiko's smile was tremulous. "Don't go having another heart attack on my account."

"Mine either," Kit said. "But if you promise not to do anything physical, I'll keep your secret. Unless she finds out from someone else, then I'm totally throwing you under the bus, old man."

"I've missed you, Kit." Baz winked at Sam. "You too, Sam. Of course."

"Of course," Sam said dryly. "What about Connor? Should we include him in our little caper?"

"No," Kit said, serious again. "He's still healing. Maybe a phone consultation or two, but he stays home."

"Because he was *shot*," Betsy said. "Just like you were."

"Not the same, Betsy," Harlan said. "You know that, just like you know that we can't hold Kit back."

"I know. I just worry."

Kit leaned forward to take her mother's hand. "I'll be okay. Now that I know someone's gunning for me, I'll take precautions."

"Don't get hurt anymore. I thought *I'd* have a heart attack yesterday when Sam called us."

"I promise I'll be careful." Kit took another biscuit and slathered it with butter. "Let's make a list. We have to figure out who in SDPD we can get information from. I don't want to put Marshall and Ashton in a bad spot."

"Leave that to me," Baz said. "I have resources. Are we going to feed what we learn to Marshall and Ashton?"

"Of course," Kit said. "I'm not in competition with them and I trust them. But I also can't sit still when Akiko might be in danger. I've got vacation coming, plus I can milk this injury for a few days of sick leave. We need to come up with a plan."

"Wait." Akiko appeared to be stunned. "You're going to take vacation? For me?"

"I'd do *anything* for you," Kit said fiercely.

Akiko swallowed. "Thank you."

Kit nodded once, then looked at Sam. "Can you spare some time?"

"I'd already cleared my calendar for this week." That Kit would take time off for Akiko didn't surprise Sam at all. His next words, however, were going to surprise her. "My, um, parents are coming."

Kit's eyes grew wide as saucers. "Here?" she squeaked. "They're coming *here*?"

"On Tuesday. They want to meet you and your family."

Kit stared at him, horrified.

"You broke her, Sam," Baz said, barely holding back a laugh.

Harlan patted her hand. "It'll be fine, Kitty-Cat. Let Mom and me plan the family dinner for Sam's folks. You make the plan for solving Mary Sherman's murder."

Sam gently squeezed her thigh under the table, because Kit still looked like she'd bolt. "My parents are going to love you. And you already have something in common with my mom."

"What?" Kit asked.

"Neither of you can cook worth a darn."

Kit surprised him by laughing. "I suppose that's as good a place as any to start. Let me change my shoes and feed Snickerdoodle and we can be off. I want to find out where Mary Sherman went for two weeks."

La Jolla, San Diego, California
Sunday, January 29, 10:05 a.m.

"It's this house, Sam," Kit said, pointing to a bungalow. "The one with all the rocks."

It was the home of Glenda Baker, who was at the top of Kit's list of interviewees. Glenda and Mary had, apparently, been close friends.

Sam parked his RAV4 at the curb. "Those rocks are a zen rock garden, based on a famous one in Japan."

Kit's focus quickly diverted from the perfectly groomed rocks to the woman trudging around the corner, a bucket in one hand and a rake in the other.

She was crying.

"I think that's Glenda," Kit murmured.

"And I think she knows that Mary's dead," Sam murmured back.

"How did you find this woman?" Baz asked from the back seat.

Kit held up her phone so that he could see. "Mary's Facebook page. Glenda posts a lot and Mary always comments. There are dozens of photos of the two of them together. They belong to the same garden club. She seemed like a good place to start."

"I agree," Baz said. "You just got a new text, by the way. The notification flashed on your screen."

Kit scowled at her phone. "The story hit the news and I've been getting nonstop texts and emails and calls from the media, asking about the shooting and why I was at Mary Sherman's house with my sister and Sam. I've silenced my phone, but I'm still getting the notifications. I need to start blocking numbers."

"Has the media identified us as the people who found her body?" Sam asked.

He loved his job, but the publicity was something he could do without. Every time they closed a high-profile case, the media descended, robbing them of privacy until the next big story came around.

"Not yet," Kit said, "but it's only a matter of time."

"Then we deal with it then," Sam said. "I'm wondering if she knows whether or not Mary had a child thirty-two years ago."

"I'm wondering if Marshall and Ashton have already been here," Baz said.

"I hope they have," Kit confessed. "I'm not looking to step on their toes by poaching their witnesses."

"Who are you and what have you done with my Kit?" Baz demanded.

Sam chuckled. "She's softening."

"I am not. But I like those guys and I don't want them thinking that I'm butting in."

"Then let's do this." Sam turned off the engine and got out of the vehicle, Kit and Baz following behind him.

Glenda Baker, fifty-four, was a civil engineer and the mother of a twenty-two-year-old son, Brian, who was majoring in art at San Diego State. And who was also watching them suspiciously from the front door. Quickly he joined his mother, standing slightly in front of her.

"We're not interested," the young man said.

"We're not selling anything. My name is Kit McKittrick.

These are my colleagues, Sam Reeves and Basil Constantine. We'd like to talk to you about Mary Sherman."

"You and everyone else in town," Brian said. "My mom just wants to be left alone, so please leave."

"We found her body," Sam said quietly. "We just have a few questions."

Glenda gently pushed her son aside. "If you're the ones who found her, then I have questions for you, too. Please follow me."

"Mom," Brian started.

"You can stay," his mother said. "You can even dial the first two digits of 911. But I need answers and those detectives didn't give me any."

So Marshall and Ashton had been here. That was good.

Did your friend have a secret baby? was on the tip of Kit's tongue, but she held it back. They were here to discover where Mary had gone for the past two weeks, but if Kit could, she'd find a way to ask about secret babies. And the status of the Shermans' marriage.

She, Sam, and Baz followed Glenda to the back of her house. She led them to a patio table and chairs, gesturing for them to take a seat.

"Full disclosure," Sam said, "we work with the San Diego PD, but we're not here in an official capacity. I'm a police psychologist, Detective McKittrick is Homicide, and Mr. Constantine is a retired homicide detective."

Glenda eyed Kit's arm. The outline of the bandages was slightly visible through the sleeve of her sweater. "I heard one of you got shot. I assume it was you, Detective?"

"It was. Dr. Reeves and I accompanied my sister to meet Mrs. Sherman. I was shot while we stood on her front porch. Mrs. Sherman was already dead when we entered her house."

"To get away from the shooter," Sam added. "Otherwise, we never would have trespassed."

"I believe you," Glenda said. "Why are you here if not in an official capacity?"

You need to answer our questions first, Kit thought. But she wasn't here as a cop. She was here as Akiko's sister. She decided to be as transparent as possible.

"I'm adopted. So is my sister, Akiko. Both of us grew up in foster care. Akiko was abandoned as an infant. Nearly three weeks ago Akiko got a call from Mrs. Sherman." She explained the call and what followed, hiding nothing. "I'm protective. I didn't want Akiko going alone."

"I can understand that," Glenda murmured.

"Why was *he* with you?" Brian demanded, pointing at Sam.

"Because he's my boyfriend," Kit said, the word easier to say every time she uttered it. "And he's a good listener. I wanted to be there for Akiko. Sam wanted to be there for me."

Sam nodded his agreement. "The meeting was scheduled for yesterday because Mrs. Sherman had been out of town for two weeks. We were wondering if you knew where she went."

Glenda's lips pursed. "I don't know."

Lie. Glenda knew, but she didn't want to tell them. Not yet, anyway. Kit considered arguing but then silently took her phone from her pocket and found a recent photo of her and Akiko. They were standing on Akiko's fishing boat, a monster tuna hanging between them.

She needed to earn this woman's trust.

"This is my sister."

Glenda's eyes widened. "Oh," she whispered brokenly. "Oh my."

"We understand that there's a strong resemblance," Kit said, "between Akiko and Mrs. Sherman when she was that age."

Glenda closed her eyes. "Yes."

"Do you know why?" Kit asked, holding her breath.

"I'd only be guessing. But my guess would be what you're thinking. That Mary was her mother."

"But you don't know for sure," Baz pressed.

Glenda opened her eyes, her grief nearly tangible. "No. Mary was my best friend. We met years ago, when Brian and her twins were in the same preschool class. We told each other many secrets, but that was never something she shared."

"I'm so sorry you lost your best friend," Kit said. "My sister is my best friend. I need to know if she's in danger."

"I'd say so," Brian said. "Someone shot you."

Kit gave him a rueful nod. "True. But they shot me, not her. And they could have shot her. They had ample opportunity."

"Mrs. Baker, do you know where Mary went for two weeks?" Sam asked gently.

Glenda's shoulders sagged. "I told the two detectives that I didn't know. But they didn't show me a photo of your sister. She went to LA. I don't know exactly where she went or why, and that's the truth. But she was upset, I do know that. She was upset and worried and had been for the past three months." She hesitated. "This was her third trip to LA. I took care of her dog, so I know the dates." She took out her phone and scrolled through her calendar. "She was only gone for a week the first two times. October sixteenth to the twentieth and November thirteenth to the seventeenth."

Sam tilted his head. "We didn't hear or see a dog yesterday when we were at her house."

"Because Pochi is still here. Mary was supposed to pick him up last night, but she never showed up. I called her cell and it went to voicemail each time. I was worried sick, so I finally drove over there and saw the police cars. One of the neighbors told me that she was dead. I was . . . stunned. I called Leo but he didn't answer." She hesitated again. "Leo and I aren't on good terms."

"Because?" Sam asked.

"Because he's an asshole. He accused her of having an affair. He assumed that's why she went out of town. But Mary would never cheat. That's not who she was."

"Is that why he's been staying at a hotel?" Baz asked.

"Yes. He left about three weeks ago. I say good riddance. He wasn't much of a husband anyway."

Kit's brows went up. Now they were getting somewhere. "Was he abusive?"

"Emotionally. He never hit her."

"Would have damaged his precious million-dollar hands," Brian said with contempt.

Clearly Leo Sherman was not a fan fave.

Glenda sighed. "Leo is a surgeon. He's got a very healthy ego and he expected Mary to bolster it every day. She never really minded because she believed he was the best, but lately she was . . ." She drifted off, frowning at her son as if he could better describe her friend.

"Frazzled," Brian said. "Mary was always so together. She

had lists and plans and spreadsheets. But lately she'd forget things. Like Pochi. She'd drop him off for a few days and forget to pick him up. She never forgot things like that before."

"When did this start?" Sam asked.

"Three months ago," Brian said, "around the time the trips to LA started."

"And Leo lost his mind," Glenda added. "If dinner wasn't ready when he got home from work, he'd yell at her. If she forgot to pick up his dry cleaning, he'd blow up. I ended up doing some of that stuff for her. We kept the marital problems from the girls—Raisa and Dahlia. At least, I think we did. It was important to Mary that the girls believe everything was perfect at home."

"So they probably wouldn't know where she went in LA, either," Kit said.

"I don't think so," Glenda answered. "Mary called me on Friday night to let me know she was back and asked if I'd keep Pochi till Saturday night as she had meetings on Saturday. I guess one of those was with you."

"Did she often have meetings on Saturday?" Baz asked.

"No. She kept a strict Monday through Friday schedule with her accounting business. Tax season was always crazy, of course. She'd hire a housekeeper from January through April to make sure Leo was fed and the house was clean. She didn't often travel for her job. A few training seminars, but rarely overnight."

"How do you know she was in LA if she was so secretive?" Kit asked.

"I wasn't supposed to know. She came here to pick up Pochi

after the trip in October and I saw a receipt from a restaurant in LA." Glenda smiled sadly. "The accountant in her could never throw away a receipt. I asked her about it. She snatched that receipt right out of my hand. Begged me not to tell. She ripped it into tiny pieces. She was scared, but she wouldn't tell me why."

"Where did she tell Leo that she was going?" Baz asked.

"To a training class. She was a terrible liar. He checked on her, found there was no class. I suppose I might have been suspicious, too, but I knew Mary Sherman. She was no cheater. Leo should have known her better, too."

"Do you think Leo would have had her killed?" Kit asked. Glenda gasped. "No. Never."

Sam's brow had creased into a thoughtful frown. "Was Mary planning a trip to Germany?"

Germany? Oh. The books on Mary's coffee table. Kit had seen them, too.

"Raisa and Dahlia were. It's their graduation present. They wanted Mary to go with them. Leo was always too busy, but Mary was considering it." Glenda swallowed hard. "I guess she'll never get to go now."

"I'm sorry," Kit said softly.

"Do either of her daughters have boyfriends?" Sam asked.

Glenda's eyes narrowed. "Why?"

"I saw some shoes in her house yesterday. They were big, maybe thirteens. They weren't Leo's shoes. He's a size ten at the most."

Kit warmed with pride. *My Sam's no slouch.*

My Sam. She liked the sound of that. *Look at me, having feelings.*

Brian shook his head. "I'm friends with both the twins. They're not seeing anyone right now."

"Thank you," Sam said. "That's helpful to rule them out." He glanced at Kit. "Do you have what you need? Mrs. Baker is looking tired."

So was Kit. It had to be the bullet wound. She didn't like being tired in the middle of the day.

"Thank you for your time, Mrs. Baker," Kit said, taking a notepad from her pocket. She wrote down her cell as well as Sam's and Baz's. "If you think of anything, can you call us?"

"I will, of course." Glenda hesitated. "Will your sister do a DNA test?"

"We're hoping to," Kit said. "When we know for sure, and if Akiko is okay with it, we'll let you know."

"Thank you. Tell your sister that Mary was the best friend anyone could ever have. If they are related, your sister should consider herself blessed."

Kit didn't think Akiko felt blessed at the moment, but hopefully things would turn out so that she could be satisfied, at least. "Thank you. And thank you, Brian. You've both been a big help."

Brian walked them to the street. "You're gonna talk to Raisa and Dahlia, right?"

"We will," Baz confirmed. "Why?"

"Because Dahlia just got a gun."

Kit had to fight the urge to blink. "How do you know this?"

He winced. "Because I helped her find it. Some guy at school was selling it. She said that someone was following her."

Kit wanted to lecture the kid but bit it back. *Not the right time.* Plus, he knew he'd done wrong.

"Did her mom know?" Sam asked.

"I don't think so. Dahlia said she didn't want to worry her mom because Mary had stuff on her mind."

"What kind of stuff?" Kit asked.

"Just stuff. That's the word Dahlia used. I know that she was genuinely scared—and Dahlia's not afraid of much. She's a black belt. Both of the twins are. They can take care of themselves. But Dahlia said a bullet wouldn't care what color her belt was. Have I gotten her into trouble?"

Kit gave the kid a look that made him squirm. "She needs to register the gun, Brian. ASAP. And she can't carry it around without a concealed carry permit."

"I'll tell her."

Oh, so will I, Kit thought.

"What kind of gun?" Baz asked.

"Glock 43."

"Thanks, Brian." Kit waved as they got into the vehicle. "Take care of your mom."

They said no more until Sam had driven away from the Bakers' house.

"What next?" Baz asked.

"We figure out where Mary went in LA," Kit said. "We're going to be watching a lot of traffic cams."

"Assign that to Connor," Sam suggested. "He can do that from his bed and he'll feel left out otherwise. Then we can use our time to pay a visit to Raisa and Dahlia. Leo said last night that they were staying with his sister."

Kit nodded. "Maybe they know where their mother went."

"Maybe," Sam said, "but I'm more concerned that Dahlia felt like she was being followed. It might not be connected, but if it is, it could be a lead."

Kit smiled at him. "Excellent point, Dr. Reeves."

Sam looked pleased. "Thank you."

Baz made a gagging sound from the back seat. "You guys. Stop it."

"Shut up, Baz," Sam said mildly, but he was smiling.

"Okay. But if you're going to be all sappy and shit, can you at least get me some lunch?" Baz whined. "I forgot how hungry I get investigating."

Sam headed for the freeway. "That we can do."

CHAPTER FOUR

La Jolla, San Diego, California
Sunday, January 29, 1:15 p.m.

Leo Sherman, it turned out, had three sisters. And, as their luck would have it, his daughters were staying with the third sister on their list.

Sam parked on the curb a few houses down from the aunt's address, because the driveway—and the street—was filled with cars. "Three's a charm?"

Kit made a frustrated sound. "Seems like the whole neighborhood is here. Fat chance we'll get the twins alone to chat."

"Maybe we just give them our condolences and come back later," Sam said.

Kit shook her head. "All these cars and not a single black Audi. Leo isn't here and I'd like to take advantage of that." She turned around to talk to Baz in the back seat. "Have you heard from Marshall and Ashton?"

"Nope. I asked if we could meet them somewhere, but I haven't heard back."

Kit frowned. "Same. I texted them twice and haven't gotten a reply. That's not like them. I hope they're okay."

"Maybe they're upset that we're investigating," Sam suggested.

"Nah," Baz said. "They told me that they figured Kit would be poking her nose into things. They just asked that we give them whatever info we find."

That made Sam feel much better. He didn't want to be going behind the other detectives' backs. "Well, we know they interviewed Glenda Baker. They may have already been here, too."

"Let's find out." Kit got out of the car and rolled her shoulders, wincing.

"You're in pain," Sam said when he'd rounded the SUV.

"A little," Kit confessed.

Sam sighed. "Kit." He pulled a bottle of pain reliever from his pocket and shook two into his palm. "Baz? Can you get a bottle of water from the back seat? Betsy sent a cooler. Thank you," he said when Baz had done so. "Take these. Or I'll tell your mom."

Baz snickered. "He already knows you so well. That's the only threat that works."

"I know," Sam said dryly, gratified when Kit took the medicine with only a little bit of attitude. "Thank you."

"Hate pills," she grumbled.

"I know," Sam soothed.

She scowled. "Don't manage me, Sam Reeves."

"Wouldn't even dream of trying. Shall we? We've accumulated an audience." He gestured to the front of Ella Sherman's house, where he counted at least five people watching from the window and the now-opened door.

"Yep. But first, let me get the plant." She retrieved the succulent that Betsy had taken from her own indoor garden and had potted prettily. It would make a lovely bereavement gift for the victim's daughters.

Kit led the way, solemnly walking to the front door where an older woman stood. She bore a strong resemblance to Leo Sherman.

"Miss Ella Sherman?" Kit said when they'd reached the door. "I'm Detective McKittrick. My associates Dr. Reeves and retired detective Constantine."

"Why are you here?" Ella asked, an edge of impatience in her tone.

"To talk to Raisa and Dahlia." Kit held out the plant. "We'd like to express our condolences and maybe ask the girls a few questions, if we can."

Ella studied them for a long moment but finally nodded once. "You upset them and I'm throwing you out. I don't care who the hell you are. You may sit." Ella pointed to a sofa, a love seat, and some chairs in a comfortable-looking living room. "I can offer you a plate of any one of ten casseroles." One corner of her mouth lifted sadly. "My neighbors figured we'd be gathering here. People always bring food."

"Kind neighbors," Kit said.

"They are," Ella agreed. "They mean well."

Baz sat in one of the chairs and Sam and Kit took the sofa under the watchful gaze of Ella and four other women—two about the same age as Ella and two much younger.

Ella gestured to the other two older women. "My sisters, Liz and Hannah." The sisters nodded a greeting but said nothing. "My nieces," Ella continued.

The two younger women glanced at each other warily before sitting on the love seat.

"I'm Raisa," the smaller of the two said. "This is Dahlia."

Like Akiko, they were brunettes, but their facial features more closely resembled their father's. Raisa was petite like Akiko, but Dahlia was taller, closer to five-eight.

Raisa had streaks of bold purple in her long, curly hair, while Dahlia's was cut short with wispy bangs. Raisa wore four necklaces while Dahlia's throat was bare. Raisa's nails were painted the same color purple as the streaks in her hair. Dahlia's nails were ragged and short, her cuticles torn.

A nail biter, Sam thought. He wondered if she'd always been so or if the stress of her mother's murder had initiated the habit.

Both young women had red eyes, but their shoulders were squared, their postures battle-ready. Dahlia appeared defiant, like she'd punch anyone who came too close.

Kit introduced herself, then Sam and Baz. "First off, we're not here officially. Mostly to express our condolences, but we do have a few questions if that's okay with you. Your mother contacted my sister. She said she knew my sister's mother."

Again, the twins shared a look, then Raisa nodded. It appeared she was their spokesperson. "Our father mentioned that."

"We are so sorry about your mother," Sam said quietly. "We were too late to help her."

"I know," Raisa said, then took her sister's hand. "We both know. It's a shock, not gonna lie. Our mom is an accountant." Her eyes filled with tears. *"Was* an accountant. She was a mom. Normal and ordinary. A little boring but very sweet. We don't understand any of this."

Dahlia pursed her lips, her eyes filling as well.

"Murder isn't usually understandable," Kit said. "Is your father here?"

Raisa shook her head. "He had surgery. He's at the hospital."

"He's always at the hospital," Dahlia muttered. "Nothing new."

There's animosity here, Sam noted. Definitely anger.

Kit gave Dahlia an assessing look, then turned the conversation in a different direction. "Did your mother ever mention being afraid of anyone?"

"No," Raisa said. "But we haven't been home too much the past few weeks. The semester just started and we've been . . ." She sobbed once, then sucked in a breath. "We were too busy."

Ella laid a hand on Raisa's shoulder. "She understood. She wanted you to be busy. To have full lives. Don't feel guilty."

"She's right," Kit said, "although I know that it's hard not to feel that way right now. We just talked with Glenda Baker, who told us that your mom had been doing some traveling. Did you know your mother had gone out of town several times recently?"

Once again, the twins shared a look. "I didn't," Raisa said.

"But you did, Dahlia?" Kit prompted.

Dahlia nodded. "I knew about one of the times. I had to go

home to get a book I'd left in my bedroom and nobody was there. Not even Pochi. The house had an empty feel to it. So I called Mom. She said she was at a training seminar in LA."

"When was this?" Kit asked.

Dahlia glanced at her sister. "October."

"But you know now that it wasn't training?" Sam asked gently.

Dahlia looked miserable. "Yes. Dad checked up on her and decided that Mom was cheating on him, but . . . I can't believe that."

Raisa set her jaw. "Me either."

Sam glanced at Ella, who appeared torn. "I don't think so," the older woman said. "But she was unhappy."

"She was," Liz agreed. "But I don't think she was a cheater."

"I don't think she was unhappy with Leo," Hannah added. "Not until he started accusing her."

"Then you all knew about his accusations," Kit said.

"Oh yes," Ella replied wearily. "Leo isn't one to suffer in silence."

"He's the baby," Liz said. "We coddled him."

"Too much," Hannah muttered.

It appeared the sisters were Team Mary.

"Why don't you think it was Leo who was making her unhappy?" Baz asked.

Hannah hesitated, choosing her words carefully, it appeared. Which was interesting. "Mary was always . . . content. She was grateful. It was a little annoying, to be honest. She deserved so much more. Leo was . . . well, he loved her, in his own way."

"In his own way?" Sam repeated, because that phrase never boded well.

Hannah and her sisters nodded in unison. "He provided," Hannah clarified, then sighed. "I hate to say anything negative about him in front of the girls."

Raisa turned to fix her gaze on her aunt. "Say it. I don't think we'll be all that surprised."

Okay, Sam thought. So Leo Sherman was not the family man he'd portrayed himself to be.

"He kept other women from time to time," Hannah said with a sigh.

Raisa closed her eyes. Dahlia clenched her teeth. Neither seemed surprised.

"You knew?" Kit asked softly.

Both girls nodded. "Mom knew, too," Dahlia said bitterly. "I hated that for her. I hated him for doing it to her. But . . . I love him, too. I always felt like I was betraying my mother by loving my father."

Raisa opened her eyes and gripped her sister's hand. "Same. I didn't find out about the other women until this past year." She grimaced. "When *I* came home to get something for school, I wasn't lucky enough to find an empty house. Mom was at her garden club. It was their yearly sale of rosebushes, so she'd be gone all day. Dad had a . . . a guest."

Ella made a hurt sound. "Oh, honey. I'm sorry."

Raisa shrugged like it didn't matter when clearly it did. "Me too. I heard them. In Mom and Dad's bedroom."

Hannah's mouth twisted. "I'm going to murder him." Then her gaze shot to Kit in dismay. "I didn't mean that."

"I know," Kit said, although Sam thought it was possible Hannah had meant exactly that. "But," Kit continued, "we really need to find out where exactly Mary went and who she saw the three times she went to LA. Who might know?"

The twins looked at each other, as did the aunts. As one they shrugged.

"We're not trying to be unhelpful," Raisa said. "But Mom wasn't a traveler. She never went anywhere. Not that I knew about. She worked from home from the time that we were in kindergarten. She was always there when we got home from school, always went to our events. She was always . . . just there."

Dahlia choked on a sob. "And now she's gone."

Baz cleared his throat. "Did she ever call any of you during these training trips?"

Raisa and her three aunts all shook their heads, but Dahlia nodded. "I mean, she called me back when I left her a voicemail."

"Did you hear anything in the background?" Baz asked. "Other voices? Traffic? A train?"

Dahlia looked away, her expression one of concentration. "I don't think so. I'm sorry."

Kit smiled at her. "Don't be sorry. We'll keep working on it. I'm sure the other detectives—the ones in charge of her case—are requesting her phone records, so we can see who she called and who called her."

Raisa and Dahlia frowned in unison and, in that moment, they looked like the twins they were.

"*Other* detectives?" Raisa asked.

Kit met Sam's gaze, hers startled. "Didn't two other detectives come talk to you?"

All five women shook their heads. "You're the first," Ella said.

"Oh," Kit murmured. "That's . . ."

Concerning, Sam thought. Marshall and Ashton should have been here already.

Recovering, Kit nodded once. "Marshall and Ashton. I'm sure they'll be by to talk to you soon. They're good cops. I'm only here because my sister is involved. Dr. Reeves is here because he's our police psychologist and a very good listener. And retired detective Constantine is here because he's my mentor and he's known my sister nearly as long as he's known me. As I said, we're not here in an official capacity."

Sam looked up and found Kit watching him. "He's also here because he's my boyfriend," she added. "Just laying all my cards on the table here. We're not here as cops. We're here as my sister's family."

All five women gave Sam approving nods. "Good," Ella said. "Support is an important boyfriend job."

Sam had to smile, both at the women's approval and the fact that Kit was acknowledging him so freely. "Thank you, ma'am."

"Another question, please," Kit said. "Did your mother have any other family? Brothers and sisters? Parents we might talk to?"

They'd found no records of any family members, but Sam knew that Kit was looking for anyone who might know what Mary had been to Akiko, if the DNA showed that she wasn't Akiko's mother.

The twins dropped their gazes to their hands, studiously not meeting any of their eyes. "Our father said that your sister looks like Mom," Raisa said quietly. "That she might be our sister. But that seems really unlikely, considering how young she would have been."

"Only fourteen," Kit said, equally quietly. "It might be that they weren't related at all, but . . . Like I said, I'm here because Akiko's my sister. She and I grew up in foster care. She never knew her family and she's curious. I hope you understand. I'm sorry if my question makes you uncomfortable, but we need to know if there are other possibilities, other people who might be related to my sister."

"Mom was an only child," Dahlia said. "She said that she never knew her father, and her mother died when she was young. She went into the system, but she never wanted to talk about it. How will you . . ." She looked up, her eyes glassy. "Will you do a DNA test on your sister and our mother?"

More foster kids, Sam thought. They needed to find Mary's foster parents. They might know if she'd had a child at fourteen.

Kit smiled gently. "Yes. If there is a familial connection, would you like to know?"

Again, the twins shared a look. "Yes," Raisa said. "But . . . not right now."

Dahlia nodded. "Same. I'm sorry, and I know this isn't your sister's fault, but this is a lot."

"I do understand." Kit glanced at Baz. "We have a few more questions for Raisa and Dahlia, if we might."

Baz pushed himself from the chair and faced Ella. "May I speak with you and your sisters, Miss Sherman? Privately?"

Ella frowned. "Okay . . . I guess. Liz, Hannah?"

From Dahlia's expression, she knew what they wanted to ask, but Raisa looked confused.

When Baz and the three aunts had left the room, Raisa

turned to her sister, searching her face. "What's going on?" she asked quietly. "And don't you dare say nothing. I can tell when you're hiding something."

Dahlia exhaled. "You talked to Brian Baker?"

Kit nodded. "Should we tell you what he told us or do you want to do the talking?"

Dahlia's shoulders sagged. "It's probably nothing."

"But if it's not . . ." Kit prodded.

Dahlia met her sister's eyes. "I thought someone was following me. It kind of freaked me out."

Raisa's eyes widened. "When?"

"For the last month. It's probably nothing."

Raisa pursed her lips. "Mom's *dead*, Dahlia."

"I *know*," Dahlia hissed. "Dammit, I *know*."

"What if it's connected? Were you going to tell me?"

"Maybe," Dahlia muttered. "Someday."

Raisa abruptly straightened as if she'd been slapped. "*Someday* when I come home to find *you* dead on the floor because Mr. 'It's Probably Nothing' shot *you* in the head?"

"Shh." Dahlia looked toward the kitchen fretfully. "If they hear, they'll never let me leave the house."

"Maybe they shouldn't!" Raisa cried, raising her voice.

Dahlia lifted her hand, cupping it like she planned to cover her sister's mouth, but Raisa pointed a finger at her.

"If you even try it, I will kick you in the ribs."

Dahlia winced. "You broke one."

"I know. I didn't mean to do it the last time, but I'm seriously considering it now."

Whoa. Sam was mostly impressed. These two girls were legitimately hardcore.

"Ladies," Kit cautioned. "Take a breath, calm down. Raisa, I understand why you're upset, and Dahlia, I understand that you didn't want to worry anyone. But the situation has drastically changed, so tell us about it. Please."

Raisa crossed her arms over her chest and glared at her sister. "Yes. Please, do tell us about a stalker that you told Brian about and not me."

"I only told Brian because he could get me a gun," Dahlia snapped, then winced. "Shit. I didn't mean to say that part."

Raisa's mouth had dropped open. "You have a gun?" she whispered. "In our apartment?"

Dahlia winced again. "No?"

Kit sighed and put her hand out. "Give it to me. Now."

Swallowing hard, Dahlia rose to retrieve her purse from a side table. She took a small gun from her purse and handed it to Kit, who'd pulled on a pair of disposable gloves—an accessory Sam had never seen her without.

"It's loaded," Dahlia said guiltily.

"I figured it would be," Kit said dryly. She emptied the chamber, popped the magazine, and put everything in an evidence bag. "You don't have a license to carry this, Dahlia."

"I know."

"Then why did you?" Raisa demanded, her voice still a panicked whisper. "We always said no guns. We *agreed*."

"I know," Dahlia said again, then sank down onto the love seat next to her sister. "I didn't kill my mother."

"I didn't think you did," Kit said. "But I'm going to have Ballistics run a check. It'll protect you later."

Dahlia closed her eyes. "He scares me," she admitted.

"Who is it?" Raisa asked, her voice softening, but only a hair.

"I don't know. I never actually saw his face. He wears a hoodie. He's not too big. Maybe my height, five-eight. But he's . . ." She opened her eyes and met Kit's. "He's . . . menacing. He makes me feel like . . . spiders are crawling over my skin. He's never directly approached me. Never spoken to me. But he's always *there*. Every time I turn around. Waiting outside a lecture hall. Outside our apartment. At the student union. The coffee shop where I sometimes study. In the library."

"And you didn't tell me?" Raisa asked quietly.

"I thought at first I was imagining him. I did ask you if you'd seen a guy following me."

Raisa blinked. "One time, Dahl. I thought you meant he was trying to ask you out."

"I thought he might have been. But it kept going."

"Did you report him to the campus police?" Kit asked.

Dahlia nodded. "But they said they couldn't do anything until he actually approached me." She scowled. "Or hurt me."

Kit sighed. "I hate that you felt you had no options other than a gun. I want you to make a list of all the times and places you've seen him. We'll check with campus security for surveillance footage and see if we can ID him."

"Thank you," Dahlia whispered. "For pursuing this and for not arresting me." She winced. "You're *not* going to arrest me, are you?"

"No." Kit's tone became stern. "But only because I'm not here in an official capacity."

Sam had to bite back a smile. *Liar*, he thought affectionately.

Kit shot him a nasty look. "Shut up."

"I didn't say anything," he said mildly.

"You thought it."

"Maybe."

Dahlia had relaxed. "Whatever your reason, thank you. I was just so scared."

Raisa hugged her sister. "Sorry I got mad. Next time, tell me."

Dahlia nodded, hugging Raisa back. "I promise. I'm sorry I didn't tell you. I would have if you'd seen him, too." She looked at Kit. "Do you think that guy killed our mother?"

"Don't know. But we're going to find out. Can you make me that list right now? Even a few times and places would help, so I can get started. You can add to the list later as you remember."

Dahlia took out her phone and began typing.

Raisa continued to look upset. "Where should we go? Can we go back to our apartment? I don't want Dahlia in danger." She frowned. "And why follow Dahlia? If he meant harm, it would have been smarter to follow me. I'm smaller. Everyone thinks I'm a pushover."

"She's not," Dahlia muttered. "Broke my fucking ribs."

Raisa huffed, exasperated. "One time!"

Dahlia didn't take her attention from her phone, continuing to type her list. "Was enough."

"You make a good point, though, Raisa," Sam said thoughtfully. "Why you, Dahlia? Why not both of you?"

Dahlia shrugged. "I don't know. Maybe he has nothing to do with what happened to Mom."

"Maybe not," Kit said, "but I don't like coincidences. We

will be following up and bringing the detectives on the case up to speed."

They sat in silence for a few more minutes until Dahlia looked up. "I've written down what I can remember."

Kit gave her a business card. "Send it to my email, please."

Dahlia did so. "It's done."

Just in time for Baz to return with the aunts. Baz lifted a brow and Sam gave him a nod. They'd gotten what they'd come for.

"Don't go back to your apartment for now," Kit told the young women. "There will be a media presence, I'm sure. They'll bother you with questions. For now, stay here with your aunts." She looked at Ella. "Do you have a security system, Miss Sherman?"

"Yes," Ella said grimly. "I do."

"Then use it. Please." Kit rose, favoring her left arm. "Thank you for talking to us. Please don't hesitate to call if you remember anything or if you get any unwelcome attention."

Ella's eyes narrowed. "Such as?"

Raisa rolled her eyes. "We have something to tell you, don't we, Dahlia?"

Dahlia looked miserable. "Yeah."

Kit patted Dahlia's shoulder as they walked to the front door. "Stay safe. Also, close your drapes and stay away from the windows."

Dahlia nodded shakily. "Okay."

Sam opened the door for Kit, then paused behind her when he remembered something he'd forgotten to ask. "Are either of you dating anyone?" he asked the twins.

Both shook their heads. "Why?" Raisa asked.

"Because someone left a pair of men's size thirteen shoes in your parents' living room," Sam said. "We'd like to know who they belong to."

All five women shared puzzled looks. "That's a big shoe, right?" Ella asked. "I don't know anyone with feet that big."

The others agreed.

Raisa looked troubled. "A man came to visit Mom when Dad wasn't there. Check the security cameras. See who it was."

"Mom wasn't cheating," Dahlia insisted. "There has to be another explana—" A sharp, loud crack of a gun firing had Sam instinctively ducking. He looked to his right to find a large chunk of the doorframe . . . gone.

"Gun!" Kit shouted, grabbing Sam's shirt and hauling him down as she dropped to the ground. "Everyone down!"

Sam landed on his knees as more gunfire exploded outside the house, screams erupted inside, and tires squealed in the street. The missing chunk of the doorframe was where Kit had been standing.

They'd missed her by a fraction of an inch.

Sam sucked in a harsh breath and, from where he lay on the floor, stared wide-eyed at Kit. "Kit?"

Because she was breathing hard, grimacing in pain. "Motherfucking sonofabitch."

CHAPTER FIVE

La Jolla, San Diego, California
Sunday, January 29, 1:55 p.m.

"Kit? Are you hit?" Sam asked, reaching out to touch her.

Kit shook her head, disgusted to have been shot at two days in a row. "No. Just fell on my arm." Clutching her gun, she struggled to her knees, shaking Sam's hand off when he tried to pull her back down. "It sounded like the shooter drove away, but I need to check for sure. Baz?"

"I'm okay," Baz said, but his breathing was labored. "Ladies? Is everyone okay?"

Five pairs of eyes stared at them, all glazed over with shock and panic. But they were alive.

"Was anyone hit?" Sam asked them, calling 911 while Kit knee-walked her way to the door, which still stood wide open.

Sheltering behind the door, she studied the street before closing the door. Whoever had been out there seemed to have escaped. There had been several cars parked on the curb when they'd arrived. One—a white van—was now gone.

"No," Ella said. "We're not hit. We're . . . okay."

"No, we aren't!" Hannah's voice was high and thin. "Someone *shot* at us."

"Fine," Ella said sarcastically. "We're not wounded. Is that better, Hannah?"

"Yeah. Sure." Hannah closed her eyes. "We should call 911."

"I'm on the phone with 911 now," Sam said, his voice soothing, but his jaw was tight. "Kit, you should call Navarro."

Baz groaned. "Marian is going to kill me. I told her I was going to a hockey game."

"No," Kit said, punching her finger angrily at her phone screen, bringing up her contacts. "She's going to kill *me* for letting you come with me."

"We have a hockey team?" Liz asked numbly.

"Minor league," Ella told her.

"Oh. Okay."

It was a ridiculous conversation between the sisters, but that happened sometimes when people were in shock. Kit couldn't blame them. She was particularly concerned about the twins, who'd gone way too pale.

Their mother had been murdered only the day before and Dahlia had been stalked. Kit would check on them when she got her breath back, but right now the pain in her left arm was too great.

She'd probably pulled out her stitches from the day before. Which meant more needles. *Dammit.*

Sam was speaking with the 911 operator, and Kit had a rush of déjà vu.

They'd been shot at again. And now she had to tell her boss. Again.

"You guys have sucky dates," Baz grumbled.

"Fuck off, Baz," Kit muttered. "Sorry," she said to the ladies.

Raisa giggled, sounding hysterical. "It's okay. We've heard worse."

Kit closed her eyes when Navarro answered on the first ring.

"You better have a good explanation," he snapped before she could say a word.

"For?" she asked, feeling belligerent.

"Not calling me back. I've called you three times."

Kit checked her phone and, sure enough, he had. "I'm sorry. I had my phone silenced. I was getting constant calls from the media about yesterday's shooting."

"Where are you?" Navarro asked, his voice low and ominous. "And don't even think of saying you're at home, because I'm at your parents' house and you are not here."

She winced. "Why are you at my parents' house?"

"Because you didn't answer my calls. I've got two detectives in surgery right now and I didn't want there to be three!"

Kit blinked. "Hold up. Who's in surgery?"

"Marshall and Ashton. They were shot while they were on their way to interview the victim's daughters."

"That's why they didn't answer our texts." She pulled the phone away from her ear. "Marshall and Ashton were both shot."

"Fuckin' hell," Baz snarled.

"Yeah," Kit said, then put the phone back to her ear. "Well, sir, you're going to be unhappy."

"Kit," Navarro said quietly. "Where are you?"

"At the home of Leo Sherman's sister, talking to the daughters. And we just got shot at."

"Fuckin' hell," Navarro snarled.

"Yeah," Kit agreed. "That's what Baz said."

"Baz is with you?"

"He is."

"Throw me under the bus, why don't you?" Baz whined.

"He's gonna find out sooner or later," Kit told him. "Lieutenant, a white van was parked on the street but it's gone now. We need a BOLO for it. We've called 911 and we're all hunkered down. Five family members of the victim—her daughters and three sisters-in-law, plus Baz, Sam, and me. No one was hurt."

Sam had moved close enough to touch her arm, grimacing when his hand came away bloody. "Except you. You busted your stitches when you fell."

"I know." Kit looked over at Ella. "I'll have your carpet cleaned, ma'am."

Ella looked helpless. "Okay."

"We have information to share with whoever you call in to replace Marshall and Ashton," Kit said.

"You do." Navarro's voice had no inflection whatsoever.

"We do indeed," Kit said, injecting cheer into her tone. "It's a solid lead, sir."

"Fuckin' hell," Navarro said again. "Why the hell are you even there? You know you're not assigned to this case."

Kit tightened her jaw, suddenly angry. "Do you want to know what we learned or not? Sir?"

"You are on thin ice, Detective," Navarro warned. "Watch your fucking tone."

"Watch yours, Lieutenant," a tart voice said in the background.

Kit nearly laughed at the sound of her mother's voice. "Tell my folks I'm okay."

"Physically, perhaps," he said ominously. "Text me the address and I'll get there ASAP."

"I will. How badly are Marshall and Ashton hurt?"

"Bad enough," Navarro said, then sighed wearily. "Marshall got hit in the arm, but it was an artery. Ashton took a bullet to his back, but the vest stopped it. They shot him in the leg as he was trying to get Marshall to safety. He's probably the better off of the two, but the doctors said that neither was critical."

Kit exhaled the breath she'd been holding. "Oh good. And their wives?"

"I met them at the hospital. They're doing as well as can be expected."

Kit looked at Baz and Sam. "Marshall and Ashton aren't critical."

Sam heaved a heavy sigh of relief. "Thank God." Then he took the phone from her hand. "Kit needs medical assistance, Lieutenant. She's bleeding again. An ambulance is on its way."

"I don't need an ambulance," Kit protested.

Sam gave her an intense glare that had her shutting up, because mixed with his determination was fear. "You *will* be seen in the ER. I'll go with her, Lieutenant." Wincing, he handed her back her phone. "He said that he's on his way here first, then he'll 'deal' with us at the hospital. Then he hung up."

"Great," Kit muttered.

"Are you going to get fired?" Dahlia asked tremulously.

Kit tried to smile, because Navarro might have a case for termination if he got angry enough. "It's highly unlikely. But I knew there would be hell to pay before I decided to investigate. Sometimes you gotta pay the piper."

"Like me," Baz said mournfully. "Marian is going to kill me. She won't touch you because you're already shot."

"How long is her cruise?" Sam asked.

"Three weeks, but she's already been gone for two."

Sam patted Baz's arm. "That gives you a whole week. This will be old news by then."

Baz brightened. "I like the way you think, Sammy."

Sam met Kit's gaze. "Navarro won't fire you."

"I know. But it ain't gonna be fun."

"Are you going to stop investigating?" Sam asked.

"No way in hell. Someone wants the cops off this case. Navarro would do the same thing in my shoes. Are you going to continue investigating with me?"

"Like you even have to ask. Are you really okay?"

"Yeah. Just pissed as hell."

He squeezed her hand. "Me too, Kitty-Cat. Me too."

Baz coughed. "God. You two."

Kit glared at him. "You got a problem, Constantine?"

"Only that it took you so damn long to pull your head out of your ass."

Clamping one hand over her bleeding arm, Kit stood, embarrassed by Baz's words. Mostly because he was right. She had taken way too long to let Sam into her life. And after two shootings in as many days...

Life was too damn short to be as stubborn as she'd been.

"Let's get to work," she said. "Ella—may I call you Ella? It'll be less confusing than Miss Sherman, since there are so many of you."

Ella was looking a little more in control. "Of course. What do you need?"

"Bandages," Sam said.

"Access to your security system," Kit said at the same time.

Ella nodded, looking grateful to have something to do. "I can get you both."

San Diego, California
Sunday, January 29, 3:45 p.m.

"You need to stop," Akiko said, her arms tight around Kit's neck. Her parents and Akiko had, once again, descended on the local ER, where Kit was waiting to have her arm restitched, this time in an actual room with a door. "This isn't worth losing your job over."

"Or your life," Harlan added quietly. "Or Sam's."

Troubled at the thought of Sam being targeted, too, Kit glanced over Akiko's shoulder to the man in question, who stood leaning against the wall of the small exam room.

Sam shook his head. "Harlan, you know that isn't going to work with her."

"It might for *your* life," Kit admitted.

"I knew the risk when I signed on to be the SDPD psychologist," Sam said evenly. "Plus, they weren't aiming at me. Not today or yesterday. So leave me out of it."

Harlan glared at him. "You're not helping."

Sam shrugged. "I wasn't trying to. Sorry, Harlan. Whoever

is shooting, is shooting at cops. Not me. Telling Kit to stop investigating is like telling her to stop breathing. That's not who she is and you know it."

Kit froze for a moment, her heart tripping in her chest. She met Sam's gaze, finding him to be as sincere as he always was.

He gets me. He really gets me. It was a gift she hadn't been expecting when she'd met Sam Reeves the year before.

And, not only did he get her, he still wanted her, which was even more of a gift.

"It's like we aren't even here," Betsy murmured.

"Sam's definitely figured her out," Harlan added wryly. "That was the right thing to say, son."

Kit realized she'd been staring at Sam. Sam had been staring at her.

Sam's gaze shot to Harlan, his cheeks pinking up. "Thank you? I think."

Kit winced, hating that she probably looked as sappy as Baz had accused her of being. She tapped Akiko's back. "Let go. Can't breathe."

Akiko stepped back, wiping her tear-streaked face with hands that trembled. "You could get fired, Kit."

"She's right," Navarro said, entering the room and closing the door behind him. "You've put me in a bad position, McKittrick."

Kit started to apologize for her independent investigation, but she wasn't sorry. Still, she needed to say something. "I'm sorry you're in a bad position."

Navarro's laugh was sardonic. "You're something. You know that?"

"I'm aware," Kit replied. "He's targeting cops, sir."

Navarro slumped, looking more tired than she'd seen him in months. "I know. But Marshall and Ashton are both going to be okay. Just out of commission for a while. As are you. Both okay *and* out of commission, I mean."

"This is just a scratch." It was a lie. Her arm throbbed.

Navarro pressed his fingertips to his temples. "You might have been killed, Kit."

"But I wasn't."

"Dumb luck," Navarro muttered. "Both times."

Kit said no more, because that was true. She'd been incredibly lucky. Both times. No one else said anything, either, the moment growing heavy and somber.

"What about the Sherman women?" Sam asked, breaking the tense silence. "The aunts and the twins?"

"I've sent them to a safe house. They'll be guarded."

"And the campus security tapes?" Kit asked. She, Sam, and Baz had already updated him on everything they'd learned about Dahlia's stalker and Leo's infidelity.

"I've contacted the head of security for the university," Navarro said. "They filed a report when Dahlia first complained about a stalker, so they have more times and dates than she was able to remember for you. I should have the security footage within the hour."

"And the security footage from Ella Sherman's neighbors?" Sam pressed. "Did they catch the shooter's face?"

Because Ella Sherman's security system had not. The shooter had been lurking across the street, out of Ella's camera zone.

"No," Navarro said. "Guy wore a hoodie. He appeared to be the same guy as yesterday, but Dahlia Sherman said the shooter had the same build as the man who'd been following her. We'll see what the campus footage shows. And that, Detective, is the last update you'll be getting from me today. From here on out, you are on paid leave."

Kit sucked in a breath. She'd known it was a possibility, but she hadn't really thought Navarro would follow through. "Disciplinary leave?"

She'd never been on disciplinary leave before.

Navarro huffed. "No. Medical leave. But I will put you on paid administrative leave if you continue to investigate. I'm serious, Kit. You could fuck up the whole case. I don't think you have yet, but I don't want a killer to go free because you thought you were above the rules."

Harlan cleared his throat. "This conversation should probably happen privately. You should have asked us to leave, Lieutenant."

Navarro met Harlan's disapproval head-on. "No, I needed to do it this way. You all need to be aware of what's on the line here. Don't encourage her."

Betsy lifted her chin, eyes crackling with anger. "We didn't. She makes her own decisions."

Navarro sighed wearily. "Okay. But now you all know. If Detective McKittrick continues to investigate the murder of Mary Sherman, she will face a disciplinary board. I have to go. Marshall and Ashton are in recovery."

"Am I allowed to visit them?" Kit asked bitterly.

Navarro gave her a look that made her a little ashamed. But just a little. "Of course. I know you're friends." He rubbed the back of his neck. "I'm not trying to break you, Kit. I'm trying to save your job."

Kit understood his position, but he needed to understand hers. "Okay. But I won't stand by and do nothing. I can't."

Navarro's lips thinned. "What is that supposed to mean?"

"It means that I can and will ensure my sister's safety. And, with all due respect, sir, if the detectives you assign to this case aren't effective, I'll step in. This isn't just a case. This is my *sister*. And if whoever you assign isn't doing their job, I will. You can write me up now, if you want."

Navarro closed his eyes. "Kit. Please."

Kit slid off the bed and stood before him. "Please what, sir? Let my sister be harmed by whoever doesn't want Mary Sherman's murder solved? I won't do that."

"Kit," Akiko murmured. "Don't do this."

Kit reached for Akiko's hand. "You're worth it. I'm not letting another sister be hurt. Or killed. I'm just not." She returned her attention to Navarro. "Who have you assigned?"

"Lennox and West."

What? What the hell? No fucking way.

Kit had to bite her tongue to keep her words from escaping. Lennox was new and, in Kit's opinion, too untrained. West was old and, in Kit's opinion, too lazy to do a good job. Plus, the man did not like her. West was the worst detective Navarro could have assigned.

"Why?" she asked when she was sure she could speak without digging a deeper hole for herself.

"They're next up for a case. Don't say it," Navarro warned. "I know what you're thinking. Just . . . don't say it."

Kit drew in a deep breath, then startled when warm hands settled on her hips. Sam.

"Easy," he whispered.

She nodded, not breaking eye contact with Navarro. "I see."

Navarro looked like he wanted to say more, but he turned and left the room, closing the door behind him.

"You okay?" Sam asked quietly.

"Yes." She shuddered out a breath and let him have the truth. "No. I don't think that I am."

"You will be," he promised.

"Let's go home," Harlan said. "You're riding on adrenaline right now. A good meal and some rest might bring some clarity."

Kit turned to Akiko, noting her sister's guilty expression. "Don't even think it. This is not your fault. You didn't ask to be dragged into whatever this is." She slipped her hand from Akiko's and cupped her sister's cheek. "I meant it. You're worth it. You're worth everything." She pressed a kiss to Akiko's forehead. "You'd do the same for me."

Akiko's nod was shaky, but her eyes were clear. "I would. Because you're worth everything to me, too."

Betsy pulled them both into a hug. "Let's go home. We'll figure this out."

"Um . . ." They turned to see Sam looking hesitant. "We can't leave yet. Kit hasn't been seen by the doctor."

Betsy laughed. "I'm so glad you're here, Sam. I'd all but forgotten why we were here."

Kit made herself smile up at him because he looked so upset. *For me.* "I'm glad you're here, too."

It was the truth and it was time she let him know.

"We'll wait in the cafeteria," Harlan said. "Text us when you're ready to go home."

The door closed behind them, leaving Kit and Sam alone. "Thank you," she whispered.

He leaned his forehead against hers. "For?"

"Being you." She wrapped her arms around his waist and leaned into him. His arms came around her, warm and strong. Safe. "For giving me the time to . . . get my head out of my ass, as Baz so eloquently put it."

He chuckled. "You're welcome. Would this be a good time to remind you that my parents arrive day after tomorrow?"

She started to pull away, but he held her close and she melted back into him. "Not really. I've never met anyone's parents before. Not like this."

"It's going to be fine."

She wasn't so sure. "I honestly think I'd rather face a shooter."

He kissed the top of her head. "I'll be right there. Not going anywhere."

She drew a breath, taking him in. Hoping he was right. Hoping his parents didn't hate her. Hoping they'd think she was good enough for their son.

CHAPTER SIX

Carmel Valley, San Diego, California
Sunday, January 29, 6:20 p.m.

Baz was waiting for them at McKittrick House, Harlan having asked him to keep watch over the teenagers. Baz had called his daughter and granddaughter to meet him there and, when Kit walked through the front door, she was met with . . . glitter.

So much glitter.

There was a banner that read **Welcome Home, Kit!**, the letters outlined in silver glitter and filled in with gold. And beneath that, a smaller banner that read **Stop Getting Shot!** in so many different colors of glitter that Kit had to blink.

She laughed.

Rita stood beneath the banners, her arms held wide. "She's back!"

And then Kit was surrounded by six teenage girls, all

speaking at the same time. All glad she was home, all worried about her safety.

A few years ago—hell, a few months ago—she'd have been overwhelmed. She might have even turned tail and run. But she was getting better at being touched. Getting more comfortable with the worry and care of others.

She gave Sam a lot of the credit for that. In opening herself up to him, she'd opened herself up to a lot of other people.

"Give her room to breathe," Akiko commanded, and then she chuckled. "That's a lot of glitter, girls."

Baz's daughter leaned against the archway, smiling. "We cleaned out the craft store. You're going to be finding glitter in your . . . well, your everything for weeks."

"Years," Betsy murmured faintly, staring at the banners with wide eyes.

Rita's smile faltered. "Mom? I'm sorry."

Betsy gave herself a shake. "Don't be ridiculous. It's beautiful."

Rita bit her lip. "We did the glitter outside."

Betsy's relief was visible. "Then it's even more beautiful."

Rita laughed, such a sweet sound. "We also made dinner." She took Betsy's hands and danced her into the kitchen. "We warmed up meatloaf you had in the freezer. And then we cleaned. See?"

Akiko and Harlan followed them into the kitchen, but the other five girls remained, crowding Kit despite Akiko's command to give her space.

Emma and Tiffany were fairly well settled. Dawn, Amy, and Stephie were still finding their feet, and Kit remembered what that felt like. Remembered the uncertainty of not belonging, of wondering when she'd have to move to the next house. Especially when some crisis affected the "main" family.

She could see that uncertainty on all five faces to varying degrees.

As far as Kit and her parents were concerned, every one of these girls had become "main" family the moment they'd walked through the front door.

"I'm fine," she assured them. "And you're fine, too. Everyone's safe. Everyone has a place. I promise." All five girls smiled, but it was tentative. "Nobody is leaving. If you don't believe me, ask Sam. He'll tell you true." All five turned to Sam, and Kit had to laugh again. "I guess I see where I stand."

"What she said," Sam said simply.

"Are you hurt, Dr. Sam?" Emma asked.

"Nope. Not a scratch."

"Your shooter isn't a very good shot," Dawn said pragmatically.

She was the most outspoken of the group, sometimes speaking before thinking.

Stephie gasped, horrified.

Amy nudged her hard. "Dawn! That's awful to say."

Dawn grimaced. "Sorry, Kit. I'll shut up."

"Don't be sorry." Kit regarded Dawn thoughtfully. "And never shut up. You could have a point. He got me yesterday. Tried a headshot and when that didn't work, he got me in the arm. By that point, Akiko and Sam were shielding me. He only missed my head yesterday because I moved at the last minute. Today, he tried another headshot, but I was standing still, right in the doorway. I was a perfect target." She looked over her shoulder to Sam. "He legit missed, didn't he?"

"He had a bad angle," Sam said grimly. "He didn't come close enough to the house to get a good line of sight."

Kit frowned, going over the scene in her mind, because Sam was right. Ella's security footage hadn't captured him. After she, Sam, and Baz had dropped to the floor, he'd continued to fire, but there'd been no additional hits to the house. "I wonder why he stayed back."

"That white van was parked in front of Ella's house," Sam said, "and it kept the shooter from getting any closer."

"Did you shoot back at him?" Dawn asked. "Maybe he didn't come closer because you hit him, too."

"I didn't fire my weapon, yesterday or today." Kit looked at Baz, who had his feet up in her father's recliner. "Did Marshall and Ashton get any shots off before they were hit? If he's been injured, that could account for the missed shot. He was pretty accurate yesterday."

"They did," Baz confirmed. "According to the officers who were first on the scene, Ashton said he fired as he was running to assist Marshall. He wasn't sure if he'd hit the guy or not. Seems like he did." He gave Dawn a nod of approval. "Good thinking, honey."

Dawn beamed. "Thank you."

Kit bit back a smile. "So we could be dealing with an incapacitated shooter. That's good information."

"How are you going to find him?" Amy asked.

"Not sure yet." She glanced at Baz. "Navarro assigned Lennox and West."

Baz's eyes went wide. "No fucking way." Then he caught himself. "I mean, no freaking way."

Dawn rolled her eyes. "We know that word, Baz. We just try not to say it around Mom and Pop."

"You, me, and everyone else," Kit agreed. But her mind was still on the shooter—and those extra shots. "You girls go on and help Mom. I need to chat with Baz and Sam."

"Case stuff," Emma said. "We get it. But you'll come eat what we made?"

Kit gave Emma's hair a stroke. "You bet I will. It smells amazing."

"Just warm-ups," Tiffany said.

"Better than Kit can do," Baz said. "She can't even microwave leftovers."

Kit stared at him. "I can so."

"Well . . ." Sam said, his smile brittle. "I've had your microwaved food, Kit. It's not great."

He was forcing humor for the girls, Kit knew. Now that they were home, in a safe place, he was showing signs of strain. "Everyone's a critic. See you girls in a few." She took Sam's hand and led him to the sofa, close to where Baz was relaxing. "Sit down, Sam. Everything is okay."

"I know. I just . . ." Sam sighed as he sank onto the sofa. "It's not like Dawn's question made me remember the shots. Those few seconds have been playing on constant repeat in my mind all day."

"What did you want to chat about, Kit?" Baz asked.

"I'm thinking about those shots. He fired, hit the doorframe. We all dropped to the floor. And he kept shooting, but none of the bullets hit the house."

Baz lowered the recliner and leaned forward, a frown on

his face. "You're right. I kept expecting a bullet to come whizzing through a wall or the open door, but none of them did."

Sam went still. "He was shooting at someone else?"

"Maybe," Kit said, having come to the same conclusion. "But who? And why?"

"And," Baz added, "how can we find out without getting you into even more hot water? Your father told me what Navarro did."

Kit sighed. "Yeah, well. I get why he's pissed off. When it was Marshall and Ashton, I was merely gathering information to pass on to them. Mostly," she allowed. "I do want to solve this thing, I'm not gonna lie. But now? With Lennox and West on the case? I don't trust that they'll do a good job."

"West might be motivated to show you up," Baz said. "He really doesn't like you."

"Why doesn't he like you?" Sam asked.

"I worked a case with him when Baz was on vacation, years ago. I was new to the department and West thought he was going to be my mentor like Baz was. But every day I had to correct his work. Go back and reinterview witnesses, fix reports, that kind of thing. Navarro noticed and West got a reprimand. Just a verbal one. Nothing in his file, but he was mad. Called me a stuck-up bitch."

Sam frowned. "Do you think West will do a shitty job to get back at you?"

"It could go either way," Kit admitted. "He's not good at getting people to talk to him. He's like a bull in a china shop. Yells when he should listen."

"Why is he still around?" Sam demanded.

He was incensed on her behalf. It was sweet.

"I think Navarro's hoping he'll retire so he won't have to deal with him. He gives him the easy cases. Until today, anyway." She shook her head. "I've always trusted Navarro, but he's making it hard with this assignment."

"I'll do some digging," Baz said.

"Thanks." Kit closed her eyes, replaying the scene one more time. "Did either of you hear another kind of gunshot? Like maybe bigger?"

"No," both men said at the same time.

"It was all semiautomatic rifle fire," Baz added. "I wonder if CSU has recovered any shells. I'll dig into that, too. Navarro can't fire me."

Kit smiled at him gratefully. "Thank you. You've always had my back."

Baz patted her knee. "And I always will, kid. Now, let's eat. I'm starving."

Linda Vista, San Diego, California
Monday, January 30, 11:00 a.m.

Sam pulled his RAV4 to the curb in front of Alf Ashton's house. "What do you think Baz has up his sleeve?"

Baz had called them that morning and told them to be at Ashton's house by eleven. So here they were.

Kit counted all the vehicles. "I have no idea, but it looks like there's a party going on. Let's find out."

Sam opened her door and held out his hand. It was becoming easier to take it. He pulled her to her feet and kissed her cheek. "How's your arm?"

"It's okay." She lifted a brow. "You saw me take the pills Mom gave me."

He'd stayed over again, sleeping on the sofa. It seemed to settle him and . . . it had settled her, too, knowing he was close by.

"I know. I just worry."

She lightly bumped her head against his shoulder. "I'm okay. I promise."

"Have you heard back from Navarro?"

She'd texted him the evening before, telling him that they thought the shooter might have been shooting somewhere other than at them. He'd texted back that he'd check it out and that was all.

"Not since last night. I expected Lennox and West to come by to interview us, but . . ." She shrugged.

"Well, we won't think about it for a while," Sam said. "Let's enjoy whatever this is."

Baz met them at the door. "You're late," he snapped.

"One minute," Kit snapped back, then froze. "Oh my God. What is this?"

Because Alf Ashton's living room coffee table was covered in laptops and a whiteboard had been set up in front of a giant TV screen.

Sergeant Ryland from CSU and Alicia Batra, the medical examiner, sat on the sofa, reading on their phones. On a love seat was Kevin Marshall, whose arm was in a sling. Kevin's wife Leslie sat beside him. Alf Ashton sat in a recliner with his leg elevated.

Baz grinned. "Marshall and Ashton are having a party. We all came to see how they're doing. Come on in."

She and Sam stepped into the house, staring numbly at all the activity. A woman came up to greet them. "Kit! And you must be Sam. I've heard so much about you two. I'm Alf's wife, Stacey. Please, come in. Make yourselves comfortable. There's soda and water in the cooler. You'll find subs and chips on the table. Help yourselves."

Kit was still blinking. "What is this?" she asked again.

"I told you," Baz said patiently. "Some of the team is on their lunch break, so they don't have much time. Come, come. Check out what Ryland brought for show and tell."

He tugged Kit, who tugged Sam, not willing to release his hand. He looked as gobsmacked as she felt.

"Wow," Sam murmured. "They've been busy."

Everyone waved as Baz led them to the whiteboard, Kit's lips curving in a smile as she began to understand what they'd done. Everything—all the evidence—was listed on the whiteboard, including photos of the two crime scenes and a map of the spent shell casings found in Ella Sherman's neighborhood.

Kit leaned in to study the photo, taken in front of the house across the street and two doors down from Ella. She counted twenty markers in total. "Twenty shots fired," she murmured to Sam, and then her breath caught. There were markers of a different color in another photo. "Three more shots."

She let go of his hand to run her finger down the legend identifying the markers taped to the whiteboard next to the photos. "These are the casings from the gun that fired at us."

"At you," he corrected, his jaw tight.

"At me," she agreed. "The bullets came from an AR-15. He only fired once at me. The other bullets were aimed elsewhere.

But these"—she pointed at the second photo—"are from an M40."

"A sniper rifle?" Sam asked.

"Very good," she said with a smile. "Yes. Not a very commonly owned firearm in the civilian world. It'll make tracing it a little more viable than the AR-15."

"So there *were* two shooters," he said.

"So it would seem. I wonder where the second shooter was hiding?"

A throat clearing had her turning to Kevin Marshall, who was pointing to a laptop that was playing the surveillance footage provided by Ella's neighbors. Everyone seemed to be ignoring their presence while, at the same time, tracking her every move.

Kit was torn between gratitude and mirth. These people wanted to keep her updated without getting her into any more trouble with Navarro.

She stood watching the laptop for a few minutes while Ryland quietly chatted with Alf, and Stacey Ashton refreshed their drinks.

"Ah." Movement on the screen revealed a man in a hoodie emerging from a brown Ford sedan long enough to brace his rifle on the roof of the car and fire toward Ella's house.

"That was the shot that hit the doorframe," Sam said. "He can't hold the rifle in both hands."

She nodded. "You're right. And . . . look at that." A white panel van pulled up alongside the sedan. The van's windows were so heavily tinted that they couldn't see inside. The van stopped for about five seconds, after which the man in the hoodie opened fire, spraying the van's windshield, which cracked into a hundred spiderwebs.

"That was the van that was sitting in front of Ella's house," Sam said. "It moves up to the sedan right after the shooter shot at you."

"That was the other gunfire we heard." Kit watched as the van sped away. "The shooter wasn't shooting at us that second round. He was shooting at the van. And if the casings belong to the driver of the van, he must have had a suppressor. Ooh, look at that. The first guy was hit."

The man in the hoodie was clutching his left leg as he threw himself into the sedan and sped after the van.

Kit turned to Sam. "If he wasn't hurt before, he's hurt now."

"Nice shooting yesterday, Alf, hitting that asshole in the right arm," Marshall said conversationally.

"Thank you," Ashton replied, looking pleased with himself.

Kit pressed her palms together in a *thank you* to Ashton. "This also answers why the shooter didn't come closer to Ella's house. He needed to brace the rifle on the roof of his car to get his shot and the white van was in the way."

"Makes sense." Sam looked at the laptop, which had started to replay the surveillance footage. "Did they get any blood from the shooter's leg wound?"

Ryland walked by them on his way to the food, pausing to tap another page taped to the whiteboard. He never said a word.

Bless him, Kit thought. Ryland could honestly say he hadn't told her a thing.

"No blood," Kit said after reading the report. "Dammit."

Alicia Batra came to stand on her left side, holding a plate of food. "I just came for lunch," she said.

Kit chuckled. "That tracks. You okay?"

"Better than you, girl. How's it going, Sam?"

"Not bad. Worried."

"I guess you are," Alicia said sympathetically. "I don't have anything to tell you that you don't already know."

"Mary Sherman died by gunshot wound," Kit said. "Hmm. I wonder if there were any DNA hits from the skin scraped from under her nails?" She asked the question as if to the universe rather than to the woman standing beside her.

"This is a good sandwich," Alicia said, shaking her head. "Takes a long time to make a sandwich this good."

Kit sighed. "Got it." So . . . nothing. Yet, anyway. "But were someone to find that brown sedan he was driving, there might be blood traces on the seat or in the carpet. I'm betting the team has already thought of that, though, and has BOLOs out on the sedan."

Ryland walked past them again, giving her a smug look.

Of course he'd thought of that already.

Kit chuckled. "All right, then."

"I need to be getting back," Alicia said. "My lunch hour is over. I'll see you soon. You take care of yourself now, okay?"

"She will," Sam said. "I'll make her take care of herself."

"You've got the hardest job of all, Sammy." Alicia gathered her things, said goodbye to Stacey, and left for work.

Kit moved to the second of the two laptops. It was running more surveillance footage, this time from the university's campus security cameras.

She only had to watch for a minute when a man wearing a hoodie walked into the frame. He had the same body type as the man who'd shot at them.

"Dahlia's stalker," Kit said. "I wonder what he planned to do with her. He didn't shoot her and never came close enough to grab her."

"Psychological terror?" Sam guessed. "He's not trying to hide that he's there. He's hiding his face, but not his presence. He wanted her to be afraid."

"And why only Dahlia?" Kit wondered. "Why not Raisa, too?"

"You'll figure it out," Sam said with a confidence Kit wasn't certain she shared.

"Navarro can stop me from interviewing people," Kit said, "but he can't stop me from thinking."

"Exactly," Baz said, coming to stand where Alicia had been. He was eating a giant piece of chocolate cake. "And what happens at Alf's house stays at Alf's house."

Kit snorted. "So no telling Marian that you're cheating on your heart-healthy diet. Your secret is safe with me. Just don't go having any more heart attacks. Please."

"I'll do my best. I really miss lunches with you, kid," he said, taking a big bite of cake.

"I bet you do." Kit took one last look at all the papers Ryland had posted to the whiteboard, then sought the man out. He was packing up his laptops. "Thank you for coming to have lunch with us."

"I figured you could use a little morale boost," Ryland said. "We all heard what Navarro did."

"How?" Then she knew. "Duh. Baz."

Ryland didn't confirm or deny. "And while Navarro's technically right, it's not the best thing for the case. You're the best thing for the case."

Kit was touched. "I owe you several."

"No, you don't. But you only saw me here visiting with Alf and Kevin. Nothing more."

She mimed zipping her lips. "Drive safely back to the station. This guy is gunning for detectives for sure, but he might go after any cop on the case."

"Thought of that," Ryland said grimly. "I'm wearing a vest and I'll wear a tactical helmet until I'm back in the parking garage."

"I wish I'd thought to warn Alicia," Kit said with a frown.

"She knows," Ryland said. "Navarro's got a squad car parked outside the parking garage and one patrolling inside the garage at all times. He sent an email to the teams last night with the warnings and there were department meetings this morning to drive the point home. I think everyone's fully aware."

Kit tried not to be hurt that she'd been excluded from Navarro's communications, but it stung. "Good. I'm glad you all are being careful."

Ryland eyed her shrewdly. "Navarro isn't maliciously excluding you. Like I said, he's right. It is a conflict of interest. But you're the best detective he's got." He winced and glanced over his shoulder at Marshall and Ashton, who were glaring at him. "In the top four," he amended.

"Too late," Ashton said. "Don't even try, Ry."

Ryland shrugged. "I got fed. I don't need you anymore today, Alf. Later, guys."

Linda Vista, San Diego, California
Monday, January 30, 11:45 a.m.

Kit and Sam took the now-empty sofa in Alf Ashton's living room, both of them studying the other two detectives.

"How bad is it?" Kit asked. "Your injuries?"

"Alf's is worse," Marshall said. "We'll both be out for a few weeks. Desk duty when we come back. Just like you."

Kit scowled. "Desk duty."

"You'll survive," Ashton said. "At least you don't need crutches."

"At least you both can hold your own fork," Marshall said mournfully. "He got my right arm. I can't even play video games."

"You'll survive, too," Ashton said.

Kit was again aware of how lucky they'd been. "We all will."

"Thank the good Lord," Marshall's wife, Leslie, whispered.

"Amen," Stacey Ashton said fervently.

"Did you see the guy who shot you?" Sam asked.

Both men shook their heads. "He was in that damn brown Ford sedan with the hood of his jacket pulled low over his face," Marshall said.

"Also was wearing a surgical mask," Ashton added. "We know now that he's got gunshot wounds to his arm and leg. Hopefully that'll slow the asshole down. I don't like West, but I don't want him hurt. And Lennox is just a baby. I don't want her hurt, either."

"She's older than I was when I joined Homicide," Kit said with a frown.

"You were old at fifteen," Baz said, joining them with two plates of food. "Eat, Kit. Sam."

Kit stared at the sandwich on her plate. "What are we gonna do, guys?"

"For now, we're going to let West and Lennox work," Marshall said. "West isn't a great cop, but he is a cop."

"Why them?" Kit asked. "Why did Navarro assign them? He's got a dozen detectives. Connor is on disability, and now, so are we. But that leaves him six others besides West and Lennox. Why didn't he give this case to one of them?"

Marshall sighed. "He moved Wren's cold case to Seabrook and Paris. He couldn't give them Akiko's case because they, along with Daniels and Kowalsky, are dealing with fallout from the dead man's list," he said, referring to Kit's most recently closed homicide case. "That only leaves Singh and Villareal to deal with all new homicides, and Singh's wife is due any day now. I don't think Navarro wants to assign them anything big because Singh is taking paternity leave."

Kit felt ashamed. "I forgot that about Singh. Okay. So this case is big, but not the only one. I get it."

"Doesn't mean you're not allowed to be frustrated," Baz said. "Navarro's a good cop and a good leader, but he's got to follow the rules. Whether he wants to or not."

"And we broke the rules," Kit said with a sigh.

"I think most of us would have done the same," Ashton offered.

"And we knew you were going to do it," Marshall said. "We could have tried to stop you. But you're good at getting people to talk."

"That's mostly Sam," Kit said. "People like him."

Sam rubbed her back. "We're a team."

"Aw," Stacey said.

"Gag," Baz said.

Marshall laughed—then groaned. "Hurts to laugh."

"So what are you going to do, Kit?" Ashton asked seriously.

Kit glanced at Sam, who was watching her with a tender expression that made her feel warm and scared all at once. "I told you that I'd have your back," he said. "If Navarro fires me, I still have my practice and my work at New Horizons. If he fires you, that's a bigger deal."

"I know," she said. "But I still have to do this. The big questions—beyond who killed Mary Sherman—are where she went in LA, did Leo have a role in her death, why was the stalker following Dahlia, and who is the guy with size thirteen shoes?"

"And who is the second shooter?" Baz added. "Although I bet you're thinking the shoes are his."

"Crossed my mind," Kit said. "I wonder if his van was captured on any of the cameras in Mary's neighborhood."

"Who is Mary to Akiko?" Sam asked. "I know Akiko really wants to know that."

"We got a DNA sample from her yesterday morning," Marshall said.

Kit blinked. "I didn't know that."

Marshall nodded. "We went out to your parents' house after we interviewed Glenda Baker. Got a swab and submitted it, then stopped for a coffee near the station. We'd planned to go interview the victim's daughters next, but we got shot."

Once again, Kit was touched. "Thank you for getting that swab. There's some family connection. The resemblance between Mary and Akiko is too strong to be a coincidence."

"Why now?" Stacey asked, then blushed. "Sorry. I know enough of the details to be dangerous."

"It's fine," Kit said with a smile for Ashton's wife. "Why now for which thing?"

"For her reaching out to your sister."

"We wondered that, too. Mary lived in San Diego for at least twenty-four years. Knowing that Mary existed but didn't reach out, not in all those years that Akiko was in foster care... If Mary was Akiko's mother, why did she let her grow up with strangers?"

"She would have been fourteen when Akiko was born," Sam said. "If she was Akiko's mother, maybe she didn't have the resources to care for a baby. Maybe her family would have kicked her out. And then, later, maybe she thought that Leo would shun her if he knew. From everything the Sherman aunts and the twins said, she was a loving woman who wouldn't have abandoned Akiko to be cruel. There had to have been a reason she left her in that box at the firehouse."

"All possible. I think that's what I want to focus on now," Kit said. "Who is Mary to Akiko and why did she come forward now? And if it leads me to the man with the size thirteen shoes, then so be it."

Leslie was biting at her lip. She glanced at Marshall, who gave her a sad nod. "Go ahead," he said gently. "We're all friends. They'll understand."

"I..." Leslie exhaled. "I had a baby when I was a teenager

and chose adoption. I was assaulted and the thought of raising the child of my rapist . . ."

"Oh," Kit whispered.

"I'm not saying that that's what happened with Mary Sherman—if she is Akiko's mother," Leslie hastened to say. "But I knew I couldn't raise a baby. And I felt it was in the baby's best interest not to know that he was a child of rape. But I've never forgotten him. I will always wonder if he's okay. If he's had a good life. If I could find him now . . . well, I'd watch over him. But, unless he wanted to know me, I wouldn't try to contact him. Unless he was in some kind of danger or risky situation. Like if I found out that I had a genetic disease he needed to know about? I'd make sure he knew, even if I didn't have the courage to say, 'Hey there, I'm your mother and I gave you away.'"

"You didn't give him away," Marshall said. "You gave him an opportunity to have a better life. Not to grow up in that house you were forced to live in. You saved him from being abused, too."

Oh, Kit thought sadly. *Oh.*

"You made a courageous choice, Leslie," Sam said, his voice husky. "And that's valuable insight into Akiko's mother. Even if she wasn't Mary, her mother probably did what she thought was best for Akiko at the time."

"He's right," Kit said, reaching out to squeeze Leslie's hand because the woman looked like she needed it. Marshall's look of gratitude made it worth any discomfort Kit might have felt at touching someone she didn't know. But it really wasn't difficult at all. Leslie needed comfort and Kit was able to give it.

She might never be a touchy-feely person, but she could rise to the occasion.

"Whoever left Akiko in the box," Kit added, "put a photo of her mother in there with her, and 'Akiko' was printed on a scrap of paper and pinned to her blanket."

"It means 'bright child,'" Stacey said. "Or 'autumn child.' I looked it up."

"According to the firefighters who found her, she was a newborn, just a few days old. It was just a few days after the first day of fall," Kit said, releasing Leslie's hand.

"Were they good families?" Leslie asked, her voice tremulous. "Akiko's foster families, I mean."

"Most of them, yes," Kit said, unwilling to gloss over the truth. Leslie deserved more than a sanitized lie. As did Akiko. "The first few were good and only ended because of events out of the foster family's control. The first family moved overseas when she was two. Akiko lived with the second family for six years. But that foster mother got cancer, so she released Akiko back into the system. She died a year later. The husband was grief-stricken, but he always sent a birthday card to Akiko every year until she turned eighteen. They cared, but . . . life happens. She had a few more homes that were just okay, but her last home before she came to us was awful. She was fifteen and gorgeous. And I guess I don't need to say more."

"No," Leslie whispered. "Poor Akiko."

"But she made it to McKittrick House," Baz said. "I remember her first day. I was there to give Harlan an update on Wren when Akiko arrived with Betsy. She was scared but trying to hide it."

"And I wasn't welcoming," Kit admitted. "My sister Wren

had just been murdered, and I wasn't interested in a new roommate. Certainly not a new sister. But we came around. She's my family now. There are a lot of good foster homes and even more amazing adoptive homes, Leslie. It's my hope that your son has a family like I do." She tilted her head. "But you said something important, I think. That you'd contact him if he was in danger. Clearly Mary knew something that put her in danger, which is why she's dead. I think that's why she came forward now. I think it means that Akiko is also in danger, or Mary wouldn't have risked exposure."

"Maybe," Ashton allowed. "But Akiko wasn't shot, Kit. Only you were."

"True," Kit said. "And that's another question. Why only detectives? This shooter was specific. He could have shot Akiko on Saturday, and Sam was right next to me both times. It would have been collateral damage, but he didn't shoot at anyone but me—either time."

"I mean, I guess I should be thankful," Sam muttered. "But I'd rather it had been me."

"Aw," Stacey said.

Baz just sighed loudly.

"Stop it," Kit told him affectionately. "You're an old softie."

Baz lifted his chin. "I am *not* old."

"And the man with the size thirteen shoes?" Leslie asked, bringing them back on topic. "Was he on her home surveillance video?"

Marshall shook his head. "We checked. There were a number of points when the camera was deactivated, so we believe we know when he was there. None of those times fell during Mary's three trips to LA. We requested copies of the neighbors' surveillance footage at those times to see who was coming and going."

"So that's information West and Lennox will have," Kit said with a sigh. "I hope they can at least figure that out."

"West's not a great cop," Ashton said. "But he can do that much. Kevin and I have already told him to focus on that."

"Eat your lunch, Kit," Baz reminded her. "It's why you're here, right?"

"Right." Trying not to think about Detective West handling Akiko's case, Kit took a bite and listened as the conversation turned to more personal matters. Like doctors and surgeries and wound sizes, with Marshall and Ashton trying to one-up each other while their wives looked on with indulgent—and grateful—smiles.

Sam had gone silent, his mouth pinched. Kit lightly bumped her shoulder against his. "What's wrong? Because you're not okay."

"Still thinking about how close I came to losing you."

He looked at her then, and she could see the vulnerability in his green eyes. And the fear. And something else that she was too afraid to name. She knew it, deep in her heart, but . . .

Not yet. I can't. Not yet.

And he seemed to understand that because he smiled gently before stealing a cookie from her plate, making her laugh.

She'd laughed more in a few months with Sam than she had in years. It was strange. But nice.

She was about to scold him for the cookie theft when her cell phone buzzed in her pocket. She'd been checking every incoming call or text in case it was Navarro. He'd been so upset with her the day before for not taking his calls. It just meant wading through a shit ton of unwanted media calls.

"Hold my plate, please. It's my phone again." Doing everything one-handed was a pain in the ass, but at least she still had use of her dominant hand.

"Oh, it's Connor." The chatter around her ceased, everyone watching her. "Hey," she said when she'd brought the phone to her ear. "I'm at Ashton's house. What's up?"

"Who's there?" Connor asked, an edge of excitement in his voice.

She sat up straighter and told him who was in the room. "Do you want to be on speaker?"

"Hell yeah."

She obliged and everyone leaned forward in anticipation. "What do you have?"

"Dry eyes. I've been watching traffic cams for too many hours."

"And?" Kit demanded. "What did you find?"

"I know where Mary Sherman went in LA."

CHAPTER SEVEN

Linda Vista, San Diego, California
Monday, January 30, 12:05 p.m.

The energy spike in Ashton's living room was palpable.

Sam, on the other hand, sagged into his corner of the sofa. A lead. Finally. He felt like he'd been holding his breath ever since Kit had been shot the first time.

"No way," Kit said, her blue eyes sparkling. "Where did Mary go? Who did she see?"

"A PI."

Kit blinked, looking to Sam for . . . he wasn't sure what. He didn't think she was sure, either. But when her hand found his, he hung on tight. She was doing that more often, seeking him out. Instigating touch.

This seemed to be about grounding her. Giving her comfort.

All the things he was thrilled to be able to provide.

"A PI?" she echoed. "Why?"

"I dunno. That's on you to find out. You're the one who's mobile. I'm stuck in bed."

"Who's the PI, Connor?" Marshall asked.

"His name is Riccardo Nicchi. Goes by Ricky."

Ashton barked a laugh. "Ricky Nicchi? It rhymes? Really?"

"It does," Connor said. "But I don't think anyone's going to make fun of his name."

Sam googled the man on his phone, and his search revealed one Riccardo Nicchi in Los Angeles. "He's a PI, all right. And . . . jackpot." He turned his phone so that Kit could see Nicchi's photo, a group photo in which Nicchi towered over the other adults. "He's a big guy. Got to be six-four, maybe taller."

"I bet he's got big feet," Kit said thoughtfully.

"Maybe even size thirteen," Baz said with glee, staring at his own phone. "His website says that he is an expert marksman. Was in the Marines."

"The M40 rifle makes sense, then," Kit said. She studied Sam's phone screen rather than searching her own.

It was nice. Sam loved Kit's independence, but he found it satisfying when she let him help her, especially with things she was fully capable of doing herself. It was trust, something she did not give lightly.

Progress.

"M40s were the standard sniper rifle for the Marines until recently," Marshall told his wife.

Leslie gave him an irritated look. "I know. I looked it up when Sergeant Ryland put up all those pictures of bullet casings. I may not be a super detective like you guys, but I'm not stupid, Kevin."

Marshall grimaced. "Sorry, honey. Didn't mean to be a know-it-all."

"You're forgiven," Leslie said with a smirk.

Kit's lips twitched, but she didn't take her focus from Nicchi's website. "He looks familiar to me, but I can't place him."

"Like you've seen him before?" Baz asked.

"I don't know. But there's something in the back of my mind. I think I would have remembered meeting him. He's freaking huge."

"Maybe he's been following you," Sam said, managing to hold back the snarl that rose in his throat at the thought.

"Maybe. Or he was following the guy in the brown sedan who shot us. Maybe he's a good guy. Or maybe he's a bad guy who has a beef with another bad guy. This says he teaches self-defense and provides bodyguard services. I wonder who Mary wanted guarded—herself, Akiko, or Dahlia?"

"You think she knew that Dahlia was being stalked?" Sam asked in surprise. "I'd think she'd have stepped in if she'd been aware."

"You're probably right. May I?" She took his phone and scrolled through Nicchi's website. "He's got black belts in karate, Brazilian jiu-jitsu, and Krav Maga. This guy's a badass, if all his claims are true. We need to find out why Mary sought him out. Did she go to his office, Connor, or his house?"

"His office. I tracked her car up the 5, then used the street cams to track her to this guy's place and to the house where she stayed—not his house."

"She still could have been having an affair with him," Ashton said.

"Maybe," Connor allowed. "She was at his office from eight

in the morning till eight at night every day. At least her car was. She stayed in an Airbnb condo. I'll text you the address. It's owned by a corporation that doesn't seem to have any ties to Nicchi's personal protection business."

Kit was still scrolling through the PI's website. "Wait. Hold on just a minute. This is interesting. The school of karate that this guy has his black belt in is the same one that Akiko has hers in. It's called Shuri-ryū. It's not a common school in this area. I think there's one dojo in all of San Diego County and only one or two in LA. That's a legit connection."

"It is," Baz said. "Nice job, Kit."

"Hey!" Connor said, sounding outraged. "What about me?"

"Nice job, Connor," all the detectives chanted in unison.

"You guys suck," Connor said, but he was laughing. "Kit, are you going to mention this guy to Akiko?"

"Of course. But first I want to find out from Raisa and Dahlia Sherman what type of karate they studied. If it's the same school as Akiko's, then she may have met them. She's been studying at that dojo since she was five years old. She's ten years older than the twins, but their paths may have crossed. If she's met them without knowing that they're somehow connected . . . well, that's going to be a shock."

"Especially if Mary is her mother," Leslie said. "She has sisters that she never knew about. That's a huge deal."

Kit nodded grimly. "I know. Connor, this is amazing work, and I know you probably need to rest your eyes, but can you check to see if Mary went to this same place in October and November?"

"Already did and, yes, she did. Whatever she was doing, she'd been at it for several months."

"Unless she really was having an affair," Ashton said.

"It *is* possible," Kit said. "And we're going to find out if she was." She handed Sam back his phone. "I guess the question is, who is 'we'? Me and Sam and Baz? Or do we tell Navarro and let him give this lead to West and Lennox?"

"West and Lennox?" Connor demanded. *"They're* on the case now? What the actual hell?"

"I know," Kit said. "Believe me, I know. But Navarro's threatened to bring me in front of a disciplinary board if I continue investigating."

"It was intense yesterday," Sam said. "I don't know who's breathing down his neck, but it sounds like he might be forced to follow through."

Connor sighed. "If you give him this information, he's going to ask how you got it."

"I know," Kit said again. "That could implicate you, although you weren't ordered not to work on the case. I was. I need to think on this. Maybe talk to Mom and Pop and Akiko." One side of her mouth lifted as she met Sam's eyes. "And to Sam, of course."

"Awwww," Leslie and Stacey said together.

"Goddamned saps," Baz muttered, but his expression had softened.

Kit shook her head at them all. "I need to determine if Lennox and West are serious about solving this. They should have been working this angle already. If not, I want to know why. And if they haven't started working this angle, I will. Thanks, Connor. You're a hero."

"You're welcome," Connor said, uncharacteristically serious. "Don't get shot again, Kit. I know Sam has your back, but it's killing me that I don't."

"I'll be careful. And, who knows, I may let West and Lennox investigate."

Sam didn't think so. A shared glance with Baz showed that Kit's mentor didn't think so, either.

He'd better get his RAV4 gassed up and go home to pack an overnight bag. They were headed to LA. He only hoped Kit would be all right once the dust settled from whatever she decided to do.

Los Angeles, California
Monday, January 30, 5:15 p.m.

"Last chance to change your mind," Sam said as he parked in front of Ricky Nicchi's dojo. Nicchi's website said they had classes scheduled all evening, so hopefully he was still there.

Kit stared at the single-story brick building. Nicchi had bought the property shortly after being honorably discharged from the Marine Corps, ten years ago. He'd started his personal protection business—located in the building just next door—that same year.

He was forty-two years old, single, and regularly finished first or second in karate competitions worldwide. He was a native Californian and had been studying karate since he was ten years old.

Kit had gotten all of this from his dojo's website and social media presence, both of which featured a lot of photos of cute kids learning karate. There was very little on the bodyguard side of his business, which seemed more relevant to Mary Sherman.

"Is there any news of the white van from yesterday's shooting?" Kit asked.

"Nothing recent," Baz said. "Other than that the van's plates were stolen."

Which Baz had learned from Sergeant Ryland. Information continued to trickle in, but Kit felt like they were walking into this situation blind.

"No sign of the van in Nicchi's parking lot," Sam added, "but that's no surprise. The shooter in the sedan sprayed the van with bullets, so even if he got the windshield and the windows replaced, the vehicle's still going to need some bodywork."

She hadn't talked to Akiko or her father. Harlan had accompanied Akiko on her charter that morning, uneasy with his daughter being alone miles out to sea with a boat full of strangers. But Akiko still had a business to run, so she hadn't canceled the charter.

Akiko's first mate, Paolo, had gone with them, but Harlan was antsy. He'd also asked one of his older adopted sons, Anson, to accompany them, so at least Kit knew they'd be safe.

Anson had been a McKittrick House resident before Kit. He'd gone on to serve in the Army, then had started a security firm in Anaheim. His was not personal protection like Nicchi's firm. Anson specialized in electronic surveillance and alarms. He'd upgraded the McKittrick House's security system a few weeks before.

Kit implicitly trusted Anson to take care of her father and sister.

Since Harlan and Akiko were still out of cell phone range, Kit had talked her situation over with her mother. To investigate or not? As Kit expected, Betsy said the decision was entirely up to her.

At that point, Kit had been torn. She loved her job, but she loved her sister more.

Her decision had been made for her when one of Navarro's other detectives told Baz that West and Lennox hadn't done a single interview since Navarro had put them on the case. They'd been sitting on their asses, watching surveillance footage the whole damn day. Apparently, West was afraid he'd be shot next, which was why he was behaving so passively.

Kit had—without letting Navarro know what she knew—asked her boss if he'd consider assigning someone else to the case in addition to West and Lennox and he'd flatly said no. Even requesting a staffing change, he'd said, was proof that she was too biased. There were other murder investigations that were just as important as Mary Sherman's, and Kit was going to have to wait her turn.

Something was clearly off with Navarro. At any other time, she'd try to figure it out, to offer to help her boss. But this was Akiko's safety.

And mine. And Sam's. And Baz's.

"Does your grapevine have any info on the status of the DNA tests Marshall and Ashton requested before they got shot?" Kit asked Baz.

"They're being run today—Mary's, Akiko's, and the skin cells found under Mary's fingernails. Ryland said the crime lab hoped to have results by this evening. Ryland cashed in a few favors and got the tests moved to the front of the line."

Kit felt more than a little guilty about that. Other people's cases were also important. Maybe Navarro had a point.

But she couldn't worry about that right now. The throbbing in her arm was a reminder of what was at stake. Someone really didn't want the SDPD involved in this case.

"I'd prefer to know who Mary is to Akiko before we knock on this guy's door, but I suspect he knows we're here." She pointed to a camera over the front door. "We're not trying to hide who we are, driving up in Sam's SUV."

"Maybe we should have rented a car," Sam said.

Kit shook her head. "That makes us seem even more underhanded. We're here and I, for one, want to know why Mary spent four weeks here over the past few months and why Ricky Nicchi shot at our shooter."

"And if he wears size thirteen shoes," Sam added.

"That too." Kit got out of the car and stretched. They'd been in the car for four hours because traffic on the 5 had been even worse than normal. "Let's have a chat with Mr. Nicchi."

They didn't even have to knock on the door. It opened when they were halfway up the front walk, the space filling with a man so large that the top of his head nearly brushed the top of the doorframe.

He took one look at them and something flickered in his expression. Interest? Guilt?

It was hard to say, because it was gone far too quickly.

This guy's a pro.

Kit started to open her mouth but he shook his head. "I know who you are. We can't talk here."

Kit met his gaze without flinching, glad that they were separated by ten feet. Otherwise, she would have had to crane her neck to look up at him and she hated that.

"Then where?" she asked levelly.

"I have a secure office next door." He pulled the door closed and approached, his gait smooth and . . . elegant. Almost like he was dancing.

Akiko walked like that.

He stopped a foot from them and Kit had to stifle the urge to put her hand on the weapon holstered at her hip. He was careful not to loom, but he was still huge. And quietly lethal.

"I'm not armed," he said, holding his arms out to his sides.

"I don't think you need to be," Kit said.

He chuckled. "You'd be right. But bullets don't care what color your belt is."

Kit blinked and, beside her, Sam stiffened. Baz's indrawn breath was quiet, but she'd heard.

That was what Dahlia Sherman had said when she'd asked Glenda Baker's son to help her acquire a gun. It might be a coincidence. It might be a phrase used in dojos all over the country.

But it made Kit's gut uncomfortable, and she paid attention to her gut. "Lead on, Mr. Nicchi."

He did so, and a few minutes later they were seated in a nondescript office that was totally soundproofed.

"Can I get you something to drink?" he asked pleasantly. "You've been on the road for hours."

"Traffic's a bitch," Baz said mildly. "But I'm good."

"Same," Kit said.

Sam shook his head, saying nothing. It wasn't like him to be rude. Kit wished she could ask him what he was thinking, but she'd have to wait.

Nicchi frowned. "Suit yourselves. But for the record, I'm not planning to poison you." He took a seat and folded his hands on the table. "You may ask whatever you like, but I'll tell you up front that I won't be able to answer much."

"We're not here in an official capacity," Kit said.

"I know," Nicchi said. "In fact, a phone call from me might get you fired."

Kit lifted her brows. "You're well informed."

"It's my business to be. Ask your questions."

"All right. Why did Mary Sherman spend four weeks here between October and this past week?"

"Mary Sherman?"

Kit rolled her eyes. "I don't have time for games, Mr. Nicchi. You know exactly who Mary was. You know she's dead, and I'm betting those shoes left in her living room would fit your feet like Cinderella's slipper."

He chuckled again. "You're funny, Detective."

No, I'm really not. "Was Mary Sherman Akiko's mother?"

"No. She wasn't."

Kit didn't think he was lying. "Then who was she?"

"Her aunt," Sam murmured.

Nicchi looked reluctantly impressed. "The doctor's right. But I can confirm that without violating any client confidentiality as DNA testing will show that. I'm sure you've requested it."

"We have," Kit said. But if this was true, there was much about Mary Sherman that wasn't adding up. According to her daughters, Mary Sherman had been an only child. She'd been in foster care.

We need to find her foster family. Maybe they can provide some answers.

"Then who was Akiko's mother?" Baz asked. "Because there's no record of Mary Sherman having a sister."

"Records can be changed," Sam said quietly. "Names, places, new birth certificates. Or maybe Mary shared only one parent with her sibling, and they didn't have the same name. Isn't that true, Mr. Nicchi?"

Nicchi's eyes narrowed. "I wouldn't know about that."

Kit wondered what the hell Sam was talking about. "What *can* you tell us?"

"Not much."

"Were you having an affair with Mary Sherman?" Kit asked, annoyed that this man was making her dig for every scrap of information.

"No," he said, the word clipped. "She was my client. And that's all I can tell you."

"She's dead," Baz reasoned. "Don't you want to know who killed her?"

"I think he already knows," Sam said.

Nicchi's flinch was infinitesimal, but Kit saw it.

She agreed with Sam a hundred percent. Nicchi knew a whole lot more than he was telling, but she said nothing, waiting for what Sam would say next. She'd learned over the past months that Sam Reeves was incredibly good at reading people and getting past their defenses.

Sam let his statement sit for a moment before continuing, addressing Nicchi directly. "And if you'd been successful yesterday, Mary's killer would also be dead. But you weren't successful, Mr. Nicchi. You fired on the man in the hoodie from a few yards away with a sniper rifle, accurate to a thousand yards. A rifle you're extremely qualified to fire, if you haven't lied about your marksman credentials. Did you lie, Mr. Nicchi?"

Nicchi didn't blink. "No, I do not lie, Dr. Reeves."

"I didn't think so," Sam said. "So why isn't the shooter dead? I can only assume you hit him where you'd planned to."

Nicchi's expression became slightly mocking. "I can only assume you believe you have the answer. So why isn't he dead, Dr. Reeves?"

Sam only smiled. "You either wanted to send a message to whoever sent the shooter to Mary's house or you wanted the shooter to live so that the police would catch him and make him answer all the questions you're choosing not to."

Nicchi was clenching his teeth. Then he relaxed, his expression becoming as bland as Sam's. "Who do you think sent the shooter?"

"I don't know, but I think you do. Mary trusted you," Sam said, his tone becoming gently accusing. "She allowed you to come into her home. She turned her security system off so that you could come and go undetected. Her husband believes she was having an affair with you."

"Her husband is wrong," Nicchi said flatly. "About many things."

"He's an asshole," Kit said.

Nicchi nodded once. "On that we can agree. He didn't deserve her."

"Mary *trusted* you," Sam repeated. "She risked her husband's anger to come here. To see you. To spend a total of four weeks with you since October. Mr. Sherman might have divorced her over you."

"He wouldn't have," Nicchi said, a little too confidently. "She kept his space tidy, his meals hot, and his bed warm, when he bothered to join her there. He's lucky she didn't divorce him."

"Mary *trusted* you," Sam said once more. "Yet you sit here

and refuse to help us catch her killer—a killer you didn't finish off yourself. I have to wonder why."

Nicchi didn't move. Didn't blink. Didn't flinch. Didn't speak. Which was telling, Kit thought.

"You took a risk yourself," Kit said thoughtfully, "going to Ella Sherman's neighborhood to begin with. You knew there might be police there. Yet you went there and you fired shots, knowing you'd be captured by someone's security cameras. It's a wealthy neighborhood. Everyone has cameras."

"Detective, is there a question in there?"

"Eventually," Kit said with a smile. "See, I don't think you typically do risky things."

"I fly a plane," Nicchi said lightly. "That's risky."

"Different kind of risky. You run a business that is predicated on your clients' trust, like Dr. Reeves noted. You provide personal protection to vulnerable clients. You teach children karate. I don't think you'd just drive to San Diego to shoot at some guy randomly, and I don't think you'd do it without calculating all the possible consequences. The risk you took was worth it to you. Your silence right now is important."

"Still not hearing a question."

"What brought you to Ella Sherman's house yesterday?" Sam asked.

"I never said I was there, Dr. Reeves. In fact, I can provide proof that I wasn't."

Liar. She'd bet his alibi was someone who either owed him a favor or was in his personal circle. Someone who'd lie for him.

"Who are you protecting?" Baz asked.

And there it was again, Kit thought. That little flicker of something that was gone too quickly to analyze.

Nicchi *was* protecting someone—and that wasn't Mary.

Akiko. It only made sense. That had to be why Mary had contacted him to begin with. Anger began to burn in Kit's belly.

How dare this man keep secrets that affected her sister?

"Akiko," Sam murmured, following her train of thought.

Sam was good that way.

Kit let her anger flare. "She is my sister, Mr. Nicchi. I love her and I will do anything to protect her."

Nicchi was quiet for a long, long moment. Then he met Kit's eyes, his own cold and flinty. "Then walk away, Detective. You don't understand what's at stake here."

"Then make me understand." She enunciated every word. "Please."

It wasn't a nice "please." It was an angry "please."

A scared "please."

Because Nicchi had risked a lot to shoot Mary's killer.

He looked down at his hands, his posture tense. When he looked back up, she saw regret, but also determination. "If you leave this alone, if you walk away, your sister will be all right."

"I'm supposed to trust you?" Kit snapped.

"Yes."

"Mary did," Sam said. "Didn't end well for her."

Nicchi flinched then, and didn't try to hide it. "I know."

"Do you know my sister?" Kit demanded.

Nicchi shook his head. "Never met her."

Liar. She could hear the lie in his tone, in the way his voice shook just a little. In the way he met her eyes a little too defiantly as he said the words.

"Was Mary learning to protect herself?" Sam asked.

Kit glanced at Sam, grateful. She'd gotten sidetracked.

She'd let it get personal. She'd let her anger take over. Navarro was right to say she wasn't unbiased.

Kit was biased as hell.

Sam was, too, but he'd kept his cool.

Be like Sam.

Nicchi seemed to consider, then lifted a massive shoulder. "Yes."

"Martial arts?" Baz asked. "Or weapons?"

"Ask the doctor," Nicchi said dryly, but with a smidgen of respect. "He seems to know everything."

"No," Sam said, "but I know you're lying when you say you've never met Akiko."

Nicchi straightened, becoming even more physically intimidating. "That's unkind, Dr. Reeves. Accusing me of being a liar. I think we've talked long enough."

Sam glanced at Kit. "Are you done?"

Kit didn't think they'd get anything more out of Nicchi. "For now."

"I'm sorry you drove such a long way for not much information," Nicchi said, rising.

The three of them followed suit, ready to follow him out of the room.

"I think we got quite a bit of information," Baz said. "Thank you, Mr. Nicchi."

Nicchi looked condescendingly amused. "You're welcome, Detective Constantine."

"You don't seem worried about being identified as one of the shooters yesterday," Baz said. "Why is that?"

"Because you're not here officially. And because if my name gets reported to SDPD, Detective McKittrick will be the one to suffer, because she'll have to tell her boss how she got my name. My sources tell me that she'll likely lose her job. And, like I said, I have an alibi for those hours yesterday."

Kit leaned toward his desk, placing her hands on its surface. "You think you know me."

"You think you know me," Nicchi countered.

"Point," she allowed. "But you need to understand that I've already made my peace with whatever consequences I'll face for my actions. Akiko is my sister. My family. I can always have another career. I can't have another sister. Trust me. I've already lost one. I won't lose Akiko. So shore up your alibi, Mr. Nicchi. You haven't seen the last of us."

Nicchi looked a little rattled. "You'd risk your job?"

Kit didn't blink. "For Akiko? In a heartbeat."

With that, she turned to leave the room, Baz behind her.

But Sam didn't move, so she hovered at the door, waiting for him.

"She means it," Sam said. "One of her sisters was murdered when they were fifteen. That's why she became a cop. She risks her life to help people she's never even met. She'd definitely risk her job for her surviving sister." He gave the man his card. "If you change your mind, please call us. She won't rest until she finds out what you're trying to hide. She's already been shot once. I'd be very appreciative if she solves this quickly so she doesn't get shot again."

She knew that Sam respected her, but his words had her heart beating a little faster. He really did get her.

He met her in the doorway, resting his hand on her back. "You ready?" he asked.

"I am."

She headed for the front door but stopped because Baz was staring at a group of framed photos on the wall. She hadn't paid attention to the photos on their way in, too focused on Ricky Nicchi.

But now she focused, specifically on the photo of a much younger Ricky Nicchi, wearing a gi and standing next to an older Japanese man who also wore a gi. Nicchi looked to be about fifteen years old but already towered over the other man. They stood in a dojo, bodies rigid in a ready stance.

"Oh," she whispered, immediately recognizing both the older man and the dojo.

Baz glanced at her, his brows raised. "Am I right? I've seen him with Akiko, haven't I?"

"You have," Kit murmured. "Nice job, Baz."

Baz preened. "I'll meet you outside.

"Who is he?" Sam asked, looking over her shoulder.

"Kyoshi Ito. Akiko's sensei and mentor. She's been studying with him since she was five years old. He was Shihan Ito when I first met him at Akiko's black belt ceremony, but he was promoted to Kyoshi shortly afterward. He's a seventh-dan black belt and highly respected."

"Connections," Sam said. "Now we're finally getting somewhere."

"We are indeed." She looked over her shoulder to where Nicchi's hulking frame filled the doorway to the room where they'd met. "Please give Kyoshi Ito my regards."

Nicchi drew a deep breath, his expression carefully blank, but she could tell that he was unhappy that she'd seen the photo. "He's Hanshi Ito now. Eighth dan."

"Promoted again," Kit said evenly, but she was fuming

inside. "So noted. Mr. Nicchi, the next time I ask if you know my sister, don't you fucking lie to me again."

She walked out before she lost her temper.

What a prick. Flat-out lying.

She and Sam found Baz near the RAV4, tapping on his phone. "What are you doing?" she asked.

"Pulling up Ito's home address. I figure he's the next stop."

Kit looked grim. "You figure right. Let's pay the good sensei a visit. Back to San Diego we go."

"Nope," Baz said. "He's got a condo not even a mile from here. And take a look at the address."

Kit did so, and another piece of the puzzle clicked. "That's the address where Mary Sherman stayed when she came to LA. Let's get over there before Nicchi warns him to run."

CHAPTER EIGHT

Los Angeles, California
Monday, January 30, 6:30 p.m.

"Not a bad place," Sam said as they entered the condo building where Edwin Ito lived. "It's older, but not too run-down."

Kit said nothing. Her scowl was one of the more impressive ones that Sam had seen on her face.

"Are you okay, Kit?" Baz asked.

"Yeah. Still mad as hell that Nicchi was such a bald-faced liar."

"Well, take a breath, kid. You don't want to knock on Ito's door looking like that."

"You're right." She drew a breath, her shoulders visibly lowering. They'd been crunched almost to her ears.

"That's the way," Baz soothed.

"What did you find out about Ito?" Sam asked.

"Not a lot," Baz said. "I didn't have time to do an in-depth search. He's seventy-six years old. He owns this whole building, plus two properties in San Diego—a house and his dojo. He's got almost no debt except for a small mortgage on this building, nothing substantial."

"He doesn't own the dojo here in LA?" Sam asked.

"No. He sold it to Nicchi ten years ago. This might be the most important fact, though: he was born in Los Angeles but moved to San Diego thirty-two years ago."

"The year Akiko was born," Kit said quietly. "Not a coincidence."

Sam had to agree.

"I checked the website for Ito's dojo in San Diego," she added. "Guess whose photos are there as black belts?"

"The Sherman twins?" Baz asked.

She nodded grimly. "Yeah. It's all coming together, but I still don't know how."

"You'll figure it out." Sam pressed his palm to her lower back, gratified when she leaned into him. "We'll figure it out together."

The elevator doors opened and the three of them walked inside, their conversation stilling.

"Thank you," she murmured as the elevator rose. "For coming with me."

"Couldn't have stopped me," he murmured back.

"You guys are just doing this on purpose now, aren't you?" Baz grumbled.

Kit chuckled, and Sam was grateful that Baz had gotten her to smile at least.

"Suck it up, old man," she said. Then the elevator doors opened and Kit's chuckle evaporated. "Look," she muttered, pointing up at the camera in the corner of the hallway.

It was smashed, pieces of broken plastic littering the floor.

That wasn't good. Sam steeled himself for what they'd find.

Kit had one hand on the weapon at her hip when she knocked on the door, then swore when the door moved, opening an inch before swinging back to its original position.

It hadn't been closed.

And, on closer inspection, Sam could see that the door had been forced open. Someone had used a screwdriver or something similar.

"I'll call 911," he said quietly.

"Thank you." Kit pulled on a pair of disposable gloves and gave the door another nudge, enough so that it opened fully. She sighed heavily. "Dammit."

Hanshi Edwin Ito lay on the floor, his face and head covered in blood. Blood pooled on the carpet and one of the man's legs was bent at an unnatural angle that made Sam wince. His leg was clearly broken.

"Cover me, Baz," Kit said, giving him the weapon in her hip holster. "I need to see if he's still alive."

She and Baz entered Ito's living room, Baz staying near the front door with his eyes on the hall that went to the bedrooms in the back while Kit crouched by Ito's body, taking care to touch only his throat. She looked up, startled. "He's still alive. Sam, have 911 send an ambulance. Tell them his condo has been thoroughly searched as well. It's a mess. Mr. Ito? Can you hear me?"

Sam was talking to the operator when he saw Kit lean

down, her ear to the man's mouth. When she straightened, she was frowning.

"Oh my God!" a man shouted behind them.

Sam spun around to see Ricky Nicchi bounding out of the elevator, his expression no longer blank and controlled. The man was thoroughly panicked.

"Hanshi!" he yelled. "Hanshi!"

Sam grabbed his arm, thinking the big man would shake him off like a bug, but Nicchi stopped and stared at Sam, his eyes wide and shiny.

It was as if the unflappable Marine had become a small boy. "Is he dead?"

"Kit says he's alive. I've got an ambulance coming. You need to calm down, Nicchi. You're no good to him like this."

Nicchi sucked in several breaths, forcing himself to calm. "I know. It's just . . ."

"He's more than a teacher to you, isn't he?"

"Yeah." Nicchi swallowed hard. "I tried to call him and he wasn't answering. He always answers. *Motherfuckers.* They hurt him."

They certainly had.

Sam wondered who "they" were. He wondered if Nicchi would be more forthcoming now. But he was conscious of the 911 operator listening, so he kept his questions to himself.

"I've got 911 on the line," Sam said.

Nicchi nodded then drew a few more deep breaths and entered the condo, his gait even and smooth.

"Don't touch anything," Kit said sharply.

"I won't." Nicchi crouched beside his teacher and stroked

the older man's face tenderly. "I'm here, Hanshi. Please hold on. Please don't die."

Kit's expression softened. "He's breathing evenly. Pulse is in the normal range. He was conscious for about thirty seconds but then slipped under again."

Nicchi met her eyes over Ito's limp form. "Did he say anything?"

Kit glanced at Sam, then back at Nicchi. "Just asked for help."

Well, Sam thought, that wasn't true. He knew Kit well enough by now to know when she was lying. He wondered if it was the open line to 911 or her unwillingness to share with Nicchi.

The condo truly was a mess. Books had been pulled from the shelves, sofa cushions ripped apart. The kitchen was visible, separated from the living room by a counter. The cabinet doors were open, the shelves empty. He figured they'd find broken plates and crockery on the floor.

Whoever had done it had not tried to hide their search.

Kit pointed to a trophy that lay on the floor, covered in blood. "I think that's what they hit him with, but he's got defensive wounds. When did you last speak to him?"

"This morning. He asked about Mary's funeral arrangements."

Kit eyed a suitcase sitting just inside Ito's front door. "He was planning to go?"

Nicchi only nodded and said no more.

"How long has he owned this condo?" she asked.

"For nearly fifty years."

Kit blinked at him. "He's kept two residences for that long?"

Nicchi nodded, then leaned down. "Hanshi? Please wake up."

But Ito wasn't stirring. He continued to breathe steadily but remained unconscious. Which was probably merciful, Sam thought. The pain from that broken leg had to be excruciating.

"Does he have next of kin?" Kit asked. "Who should we call?"

"Me," Nicchi said. "I'm his emergency contact. I have his power of attorney."

Kit studied Nicchi before nodding. "All right. I need to call my sister. I don't want her here. I don't think she's safe here. But if she finds out that I knew Ito was hurt and didn't tell her . . . well, she might not forgive that. So we'll have to keep her safe. She'll want to sit with him in the hospital."

Nicchi sighed. "I guess she will."

"You will talk to me later, won't you?" Kit asked.

Nicchi closed his eyes. "Yes. I'll talk to you. Later."

The elevator doors opened and a pair of medics appeared with a gurney. Sam ended his call with 911 and stepped aside.

Kit and Baz joined him, Baz earning a glare from the medics for the gun in his hand. Baz returned Kit's weapon to her and she reholstered it.

"Where will you take him?" Kit asked the medics.

"County," one of them said. "Cops were right behind us. You need to stay and give your statements."

"Of course," Kit said. "We planned to."

"But not me," Nicchi said. "I'm coming with him in the ambulance."

"Who are you to the patient?" one of the medics asked.

Nicchi looked straight at Kit, as if challenging her. "I'm his son."

Kit pursed her lips but nodded. "We'll catch up with you at the hospital."

"You'll have to ride up front with me," the medic said. "Come on."

They stood with Baz as the medics pushed Ito into the elevator. It was immediately clear that, with the gurney, there was no room in the elevator for Nicchi, too.

Nicchi started to head to the stairwell but paused next to Kit. "Thanks," he whispered. "I'll tell them we were talking about self-defense classes for your doctor's teen shelter."

Then he ran, taking the stairs to the lobby two at a time.

"He's going to protect your job," Baz said softly.

Kit hadn't looked away from the path Nicchi had taken. "I know. But then I'll be beholden to him. I'm not sure I want that."

"Neither am I," Sam said. "Navarro won't believe it anyway."

Kit turned, smiling up at him wryly. "There's that, too."

Sam didn't know how much time they had before the cops showed up and he needed to know. "What did he say to you? Ito?"

Kit frowned, troubled. "'Tell her I'm sorry.'"

Los Angeles, California

Monday, January 30, 7:45 p.m.

"So why are you here?"

Kit forced a smile for the LAPD detective. Once she'd given

their names to the officers who'd responded to the 911 call, Kit, Sam, and Baz had been nicely asked not to leave.

Detectives Burroughs and Desoto had shown up about forty-five minutes later. Burroughs was older, somewhere in his mid to late fifties. Desoto appeared to be in his early forties. Both were eyeing her suspiciously.

Burroughs had asked the question, his tone terse.

Kit couldn't blame him. She, Sam, and Baz were encroaching on their turf and hadn't given them a courtesy heads-up of their visit. Not that she'd planned to.

She didn't plan on telling them everything now. Not until she knew who she could trust. Right now, she could only trust Sam and Baz. Marshall, Ashton, and Connor as well, but she'd keep their names out of this as long as she could.

That she hadn't yet called Navarro unsettled her. That she didn't include him in her circle of trust unsettled her even more.

"I assume you've looked us up," Kit said.

Burroughs nodded. Desoto just tilted his head, waiting.

"You know I was shot on Saturday."

"And shot *at* yesterday," Desoto said.

Beside her, Sam tensed, just as he did every time he thought of her being hurt.

"Yes," she said. "That's true, too. It started when a woman called my sister, claiming to have known her mother."

Burroughs's brows lifted. "Your sister's mother. Not your mother, too?"

"No. We're adopted. We both grew up in the system. My sister never knew her mother and was curious, so we visited the woman who called, only to find she'd been murdered very recently. Like, an hour before our arrival."

"Which was when you were shot," Burroughs said. "Get to the point, Detective McKittrick. Why are you here?"

"Because we don't know who the woman is to my sister. My sister studied karate with Mr. Ito for many years, and they are very close. We came to make sure he knew what was going on."

Neither detective looked convinced in the slightest. "You came all this way," Burroughs said, "to update him."

"And to see if he knew the victim. The woman's daughters also studied karate in Mr. Ito's dojo in San Diego."

"And to ask who she was to your sister?" Desoto asked.

Kit nodded once. "I hoped he'd know. But when we got here, we found him beaten and unconscious."

"He didn't tell you anything?"

Tell her I'm sorry. But that was for Akiko's ears. Until she knew what was going on, she was keeping that to herself.

She shook her head. "No."

Desoto frowned. "And this other guy who showed up. This . . ." He checked his notes. "Riccardo Nicchi. Who's he?"

"He said he was Mr. Ito's son," Baz said.

Burroughs's brows went up again. "We got his photo from the DMV database. He does not look like Mr. Ito's son."

"Well, my sister Akiko doesn't look like me, either," Kit said, annoyed.

Sam cleared his throat. "He seemed very upset when he arrived. He behaved like a son seeing a parent injured."

Kit calmed herself. She'd allowed the detective to get under her skin, something she rarely did. But this was personal. Navarro had a point, she supposed. She was grateful to Sam for redirecting Burroughs's attention to himself, giving Kit a moment to breathe.

"Dr. Sam Reeves," Desoto said. "You're their shrink."

Sam nodded. "I am. I don't know if Mr. Nicchi is Mr. Ito's legal son or if their relationship is more informal, but his reaction seemed genuine."

Burroughs turned back to Kit. "You didn't know Ito had a son?"

"No, I didn't," she answered truthfully. "I've only known Mr. Ito through my sister. My exposure to him has been limited to the times I've visited the dojo, like when she got a belt promotion. I wasn't aware that Mr. Ito had children. But I have no reason to doubt Mr. Nicchi's word."

No reason other than that the man had blatantly lied about knowing Akiko, but again, she kept that to herself. There were too many things she didn't know.

"Did you see anyone leaving the building as you came in?" Desoto asked.

All three of them shook their heads.

"And the camera was broken when we arrived," Baz added, pointing up at the busted device.

"So is the camera at the front door," Desoto said. "Good thing the camera in the building across the street was functional."

Kit's gaze abruptly lifted to meet Desoto's. "Did you see who did this?"

"We got an image, yeah." Desoto regarded her for a long moment. "Who would you guess did this, if you had to guess?"

Kit felt like they were dancing around each other. "From what I've been told about the case, the main suspect is a man wearing a hoodie. Approximately five-seven and maybe a hundred thirty pounds. He was seen leaving the murder victim's house on Saturday. Whether he was seen yesterday when I was shot at again would need to be verified with SDPD." Because she wasn't supposed to know that.

Keeping her story straight was becoming exhausting. *I could never be a criminal. Too many secrets to juggle.*

Desoto studied her for a long moment and Kit fought not to squirm.

"Are you investigating the murder?" he asked directly.

"I'm not allowed to be," Kit said simply.

Burroughs rolled his eyes. "That's not an answer, Detective."

"It's the best one I can give you. If I told you that I didn't want to catch Mary Sherman's killer, I'd be lying. But I'm also here on behalf of my sister. She needs to know who the victim was to her. If you didn't grow up in foster care, never knowing your parents, you wouldn't understand."

"That's fair," Desoto murmured. "We have to report your presence to your lieutenant."

"I know." Kit knew procedure. "Can you tell me if SDPD's suspect was seen leaving this building?"

Burroughs and Desoto shared a long glance. Burroughs shrugged.

Desoto nodded. "Surveillance video shows an individual who matches your description leaving the premises."

"Okay. I don't know why he came here," she said honestly. "I don't know what Mr. Ito has to do with any of this, other than being a sensei to my sister and the victim's daughters. That's the truth."

"You staying in LA?" Burroughs asked.

"We'd planned to wait at the hospital," Sam said. "Detective McKittrick has called her sister to inform her of Mr. Ito's injuries. She's on her way from San Diego."

Kit had actually told her father. She wasn't sure she could talk to Akiko at the moment. Her sister would want answers that Kit couldn't provide—yet.

"Are we free to go?" she asked, keeping her tone respectful.

Burroughs jerked a nod. "Let us know when you head back home, okay?"

"Of course." Kit took a final look at Ito's broken door, at the mess left behind by whoever had tossed his condo. "Someone was searching for something. They also searched Mary Sherman's house, but tried to hide that they had. If you find what they were looking for, can you let SDPD know?"

"Of course, Detective," Desoto said. "Give us your number so we can call with questions."

Kit gave him her card. "We'll be at the hospital."

Los Angeles, California
Monday, January 30, 10:40 p.m.

"Kitty-Cat?"

Kit jerked awake at the sound of her father's voice. He and Akiko had finally arrived at the hospital waiting room. Akiko was pale and trembling. Harlan had his arm around her, holding her up.

Kit struggled to her feet, sucking in a breath when a pain shot up her arm. She kept forgetting not to put weight on the damn thing. She kept it quiet, though, trying not to wake Sam. Baz was nowhere to be seen.

Neither was Nicchi, which was a good bit more concerning. He'd apparently left the hospital three hours before, after giving the intake nurse Ito's insurance information. He'd been gone by the time they'd arrived.

"Baz went to get coffee," Harlan said. "He's been watching over you so that you could sleep. Said now that I was here, he was getting a caffeine fix."

Kit had to smile at that. "Not a surprise." Then she opened her arms to Akiko, who fell into her embrace, holding Kit so close that she had trouble breathing.

But she could breathe later. Akiko needed her now.

"He was still in surgery before I fell asleep," Kit murmured. "That was a half hour ago. But there's no next of kin here right now, so we may not be able to get information."

"I'm an emergency contact," Akiko said.

Kit reared back and stared. "You are?"

Akiko nodded. "I have been for years."

"Why?" Kit asked, trying not to sound unkind. She knew they were close, but she hadn't realized they were that close.

"Hanshi's been my sensei for most of my life, Kit. He was my father figure before Pop came along. Hanshi still considers me to be a daughter. I was there for him when he got sick a long time ago. He gave me medical power of attorney. I scanned a copy of the document and I have it on my phone."

Kit glanced at her father over Akiko's shoulder. He seemed as surprised as Kit was.

"When did he sign the paper?" Kit asked, wondering if she knew that Nicchi also had power of attorney.

"When I turned twenty-one. You have some explaining to do, Kit. How did Hanshi get hurt? Did he fall? And why are you, Sam, and Baz here? How does this connect to the case?"

Because all Kit had told Harlan was that Ito was severely injured and that Akiko needed to come to LA immediately. Akiko had called her, begging for more information, but Kit had stood firm. They'd discuss it in person.

Mainly because Kit had hoped to have gotten answers from Nicchi but the bastard had probably skipped town. Now Kit had to tell the story without his answers.

Either way, Akiko was going to be devastated. And confused.

"I know you need answers. I'll tell you what I know, but can we wait until Baz comes back with coffee?" Because every minute she could delay was a minute that Nicchi might come back.

Akiko frowned but nodded. "Okay. Pop, are you okay?"

Because Harlan was looking around the room as if expecting an attack.

He might not be wrong, Kit thought grimly.

Harlan kissed the top of Akiko's head. "I'm fine. Just . . . twitchy. This feels wrong."

Because it is. Kit couldn't dispute her father's words, so she sat next to Sam, gently jostling his shoulder. "Sam?"

He woke with a jerk and a gasp, looking around much like Harlan had.

This couldn't go on. Her family was afraid.

"Pop, who's staying with Mom and the girls?" she asked. Not that she knew if they were in immediate danger. But she didn't *not* know that, either.

"Anson," Harlan said. "He said he could stay overnight. When we leave here, we can crash at his house. I have a key. It's only about forty-five minutes away."

"I remember. I haven't been to Anson's house in years. Does he still have that mean cat?" she added lightly, hoping to get Akiko to smile.

"That cat isn't mean," Akiko said. "She's sensitive."

"She's mean," Kit told Sam. "Hisses at everyone."

"She hisses at Kit and only Kit," Akiko said then exhaled. "I need to show my power of attorney form to the nurse. I'll be back."

"Not alone," Kit said, moving too quickly, which sent another jolt of pain through her arm. "Dammit."

Harlan's sigh was long-suffering. "Mom knew you wouldn't be taking any painkillers. I brought some. And I asked Baz to bring some food from the vending machine so the pills don't eat through your stomach lining. Let's go see the nurse. Sam, will you wait here for Baz?"

Sam didn't look pleased at being left behind, but he nodded.

Kit impulsively pressed a kiss to Sam's cheek, now scratchy with dark scruff. His frown of consternation quickly became a sweet smile.

"We'll be right back," she said. "Don't drink my coffee."

"Wouldn't dream of it," Sam said dryly.

Harlan gave her a look of approval before offering an arm

to both his daughters. Kit linked her good arm through his, resting her head on his shoulder for a moment.

"You're okay?" he murmured.

"Yeah. Confused, but physically fine. Akiko, do you know a man named Riccardo Nicchi?"

"Ricky Nicchi?" Akiko asked, and Harlan snorted a laugh.

"Ricky Nicchi?" he repeated. "That's his real name?"

"Don't laugh too hard," Kit muttered. "Fucker's huge."

Akiko peered at her around Harlan. "Why is he a fucker and why are you asking about Ricky?"

"Do you know him?" Kit pressed.

"I know of him. I don't think we've ever been in the same class or anything. He's about ten years older than me. Another of Hanshi's kids. Studied on a scholarship, just like me, but in the LA dojo. He joined the Army, I think, when I was still little."

"Marine Corps," Kit corrected, making Akiko scowl.

"How do you know him?" Akiko demanded.

"I'll tell you, I promise. Just tell me first what you know about him."

"I swear to God, Kit, you make me crazy."

"I know. Indulge me, please."

Akiko huffed impatiently. "Like I said, he was one of Hanshi's scholarship students. From what I understand, he was about ten years old when he started. He'd progressed to the upper levels when I entered the program as a white belt. He'd come and teach classes at the San Diego dojo sometimes, when he was visiting his brother, but never my classes. He was always one of Hanshi's favorites, or so the other students said. I think he lived with Hanshi for a while, before he went away to the military, but that's rumor. I asked Hanshi once and he said that wasn't my business. He said it nicely, but I got the message. I never asked again."

Kit wished that Akiko had asked again. Kit wished Akiko had asked a lot of questions. But for the life of her, Kit didn't know what those questions should have been.

"Okay. So . . . before we get to the nurses' station, you need to know that Nicchi is also your Hanshi's emergency contact and also has medical power of attorney."

Akiko didn't blink. "Okay."

"Okay?"

"Okay. It's Hanshi's business who he signs authority to. Not mine."

Kit did blink. Her arm hurt and her head hurt and she hoped Baz brought back a freaking sandwich because she was starving and starting to get hangry.

"What?" Akiko asked.

"I guess I've never understood your deference to Ito."

Akiko's brows shot up. *"Deference?"*

"Tread carefully, Kitty-Cat," Harlan murmured. "I don't want to literally be in the line of fire."

Kit's lips twitched and so did Akiko's. Harlan had always known how to defuse their arguments.

"It's just . . ." Kit searched for the words to explain. "You're brave and confident and independent and so damn competent at everything. But if Ito says to do something or not to do something, you obey him."

Harlan frowned. "He's never asked Akiko to do anything dangerous or inappropriate. Has he, Akiko?"

"Never. It's always been things that were in my best

interest. You remember that guy who asked me to prom and Hanshi said no? I was upset."

"You cried so hard," Kit remembered. "I wanted to smack him, but he could break all my bones with his pinkie finger."

"So can I," Akiko said, and it was only mostly in jest.

"Understood," Kit said. "So, the prom boy?"

"Hanshi was right. That kid was a drug addict. He got arrested on prom night and so did his date. Hanshi said no when things would hurt me."

Kit wondered how Ito had known the boy was an addict. She hadn't suspected a thing, and back then she'd suspected everyone of something.

"Maybe it's a martial arts thing," she said.

"It is," Akiko agreed. "I have a respect for hierarchy that you didn't have."

"Still don't," Harlan drawled, and Kit winced.

"Which is going to get my ass in trouble," she grumbled, because it was all true. She'd never been good at respecting authority when she didn't agree with the reasons behind an order. And sometimes when she did.

"We're going to talk about that, too, aren't we?" Akiko said, her tone becoming ominous. "When Baz comes back with coffee."

"Yeah." Kit sighed heavily. "We are. Oh look. Here's the nurses' station. Go do your thing, Akiko."

Harlan snorted. "So subtle."

"I know," Kit said fondly. "Which is why you love me."

"Well, I love you for enough other reasons that your lack of subtlety isn't a problem."

Kit laid her head on his shoulder again. "Love you, too, Pop."

Harlan waited until Akiko was at the counter. "What's going on, Kit?"

"I wish I knew. I really wish I knew."

CHAPTER NINE

Los Angeles, California
Monday, January 30, 11:10 p.m.

Both Akiko and Harlan listened quietly as Kit told them what they'd learned. Which didn't take long because they still didn't know all that much.

Especially since Ricky Nicchi still had not shown his face.

They'd returned to the waiting room, where a doctor came out to tell them that Ito was out of surgery but his condition was critical. One of those "the next twenty-four hours will tell" situations. They were waiting for a nurse to take Akiko to see him once he was out of recovery and in an ICU room.

But he was alive, and knowing this had given Akiko the ability to focus on the details as Kit told her everything that she knew.

When Kit was finished, Akiko drew a breath and let it out.

"Let me get this straight. You disobeyed a direct order from Navarro and continued investigating."

"Yes," Kit said. "Because—"

Akiko held up one hand. "I'm not finished. Connor also investigated without permission and found out where Mary Sherman went during the two weeks before her murder."

"Actually," Kit said, "it was a total of four weeks since October."

Akiko's dark eyes flashed with temper. "Fine. Four weeks. And instead of telling Navarro what you'd found, you three got in Sam's SUV and drove to LA to continue investigating."

Kit opened her mouth, then closed it again.

"Well?" Akiko asked sharply.

"I don't know if you want me to talk or not."

Akiko closed her eyes as she breathed deeply. "Yes or no, Kit?"

"Yes, of course. Obviously. We're here."

Akiko glared at her. "You went straight to a stranger's place of business, a stranger who you believed to have been involved in yesterday's shooting. Although I can't believe that Nicchi, Hanshi's pupil, was shooting at you."

"Nicchi didn't shoot at *me*," she said logically, then winced when Akiko clenched her teeth. "Yes. We did that. We went to his place of business."

"Without requesting backup."

Kit sighed. "Yes."

"And then you found that Nicchi was involved with *both* Mary Sherman and Hanshi Ito. *My* Hanshi Ito. Who I've known since I was five years old."

"Yes. Nicchi denied being romantically involved with

Mary, just claimed she was a client. He said Ito was his father. I assume he meant it in a symbolic way because there are no records legally tying him and Ito together. I don't know about Ito and Mary."

"Kit," Akiko hissed.

"What?" Kit snapped. "I'm answering your goddamn questions."

"You didn't think to ask for *backup* when you went to see Hanshi?"

"No!" Kit cried. "Why would we? I know him. You know him. You trust him. He's seventy-six years old. I didn't consider him a threat."

"Yet when you arrived, he'd been beaten nearly to death, so there clearly was a threat."

Kit sighed again. "Yes."

"Without backup."

"Yes," Kit said. "I'm sensing a theme here."

"Kit," Harlan cautioned. "Cut the sarcasm. It's not helping."

She folded her arms over her chest. "Fine."

"God," Baz muttered. "It's like they're fifteen again."

"Tell me about it," Harlan said, but it was with the exaggerated calm that meant he was actually furious. "Akiko is angry that you put yourself in danger, Kit. And, if I'm being very honest, so am I. You've been shot at twice, told to step away from this case, but instead of complying, you plunge headlong into a situation that could have turned deadly."

Kit's cheeks heated. "Fine. When you put it like that."

Akiko pressed her fingertips to her temples. "Is that all?"

Kit looked to Sam and Baz. "Is it?"

Sam shook his head. "You forgot the part where we asked

Nicchi if Mary was Akiko's mother and he confirmed that she was Akiko's aunt."

Akiko sucked in a small gasp. "My aunt?"

"Yes," Kit said gently. "And I hadn't forgotten that. I didn't want to tell you until we checked it out because I don't trust Nicchi as far as I can throw him. Which is, like, nothing because he's fucking huge." She sent Sam a mild glare, but he only shrugged.

"You're not helping her by keeping secrets."

Baz looked uncomfortable. "Sorry, kid, but I'm with him. You can't protect everyone. Harlan, we should have called for backup. I take responsibility for that."

"I don't blame you, Baz. I don't blame Kit, either. I understand that you didn't feel threatened, but . . . next time, just call for backup."

Baz nodded once. "I promise. Kit?"

But Kit was only half listening. Her attention was on Akiko, who looked stunned.

"My aunt," Akiko said quietly. "I didn't want to get my hopes up, but it's true. I have a family." Then she flinched, abruptly shifting her gaze to Harlan. "Pop, I don't mean—"

Harlan wrapped his arm around her shoulders. "I know what you mean, honey. And Mom and I will support you, however you choose to use this information."

"Thank you." Squaring her shoulders, she turned to Kit. "Is my mother dead?"

"I don't know," Kit said. "Nicchi only admitted the aunt detail because he said we'd figure it out from the DNA anyway. He didn't say much of anything else."

"Were the size thirteen shoes his?"

"We think so." Kit blew out a breath. "Look, I wanted to have actual answers for you, but all I have are more questions."

"I know that you wanted answers for me. And I love you for that."

Kit winced. "But?"

"But I'd rather be in the dark forever than have you risk your life for me. Why didn't you let those other detectives follow up? Lennox and West?"

"Because they refuse to leave the precinct," Kit said angrily. "They're afraid they'll get shot." She sighed. "And that just proved your point, didn't it?"

"It sure did. And even if this guy in a hoodie doesn't kill you, you're going to get fired. You've wanted to be a cop since I met you. You're a good cop. You care about the victims and their families. If you lose your job, who will stand for the dead?"

Kit took Akiko's hand. It was cold and trembling. "I can stand for the dead in a lot of different ways. I don't have to be a cop." But the words stuck in her throat. She *did* have to be a cop. She didn't know anything else. But she'd figure it out. "You are my priority. Stopping whoever killed your aunt is my priority, because I believe she contacted you because you're in danger."

"But nobody's shooting at me, Kit!" Tears filled Akiko's dark eyes. "They're shooting at you!"

"And they nearly killed your sensei. They may not be shooting at you, but you're involved somehow, and I don't like it."

"Same," Sam said quietly.

"Ditto," Baz added. "Akiko, you've made some valid points.

We should have requested backup. And Kit might get fired. But something is going on with Navarro, something we're not privy to. He's insisting on putting the worst detectives in his department on this case. If I were in Kit's shoes, I'd do the same thing she did."

"Same," Sam repeated. "There's one other thing that I haven't mentioned, even to Kit. We got sidetracked with Hanshi Ito."

Kit's brows went up. "What?"

"You said that you felt like you'd seen Nicchi before, that he seemed familiar."

"Right. Did you think so, too?"

"Not until we were in his office. He's got a photo on his phone—his wallpaper. It lit up when we first got there, before he turned it over. It was Nicchi and Paolo."

Harlan held up a hand. "Wait. You mean Paolo Feliciano? Akiko's first mate?"

Kit blinked, processing the information. And then she saw it. It was their eyes. And their olive skin tone. And the way their mouths set when they were annoyed. "That's why he seemed familiar. Damn, Sam. They could be brothers."

"That's what I thought," Sam said.

"Nice job, Sammy," Baz praised.

But Akiko didn't look concerned. "They are brothers. Half brothers, I think. Same mother, different fathers. I've always known that. I don't know Ricky, but Paolo and I have been friends since we were in elementary school. He's been working for me since I bought the boat."

He'd been Akiko's first mate from the day she'd started her charter fishing business, five years ago.

"What exactly is going on here, Kit? How did Nicchi know Mary Sherman? How did Hanshi know her? And Paolo? Did he know her, too? Are they all connected?"

"I'm not sure about Paolo, but I'm nearly certain that Ito, Nicchi, and Mary Sherman are connected," Kit said grimly. "We need to get some answers. Nicchi promised to give us some, but then he disappeared. I'm hoping Ito regains consciousness soon so he can tell us."

Akiko looked up at Harlan. "Pop? Why would Hanshi know Mary Sherman? And if she was my aunt, why did he not tell me?"

"Maybe he didn't know or, if he did, it was only recently. We will figure it out, Akiko. I promise. How can we find this Nicchi person?"

"We have his home address," Kit said. "We'll start looking for him when we leave here."

Harlan tightened his hold on Akiko. "Kit, what did the police say when they arrived at Ito's apartment?"

"Not much. Someone broke into his place. The camera in the hallway was busted, but they got an image of someone leaving his building that fits the description of Mary's killer."

"So they are connected," Harlan said, jaw tense.

Kit shrugged. "I'm assuming so. He used a crowbar or a screwdriver or something like that to get through the door. It's an older building, so that wouldn't have been hard to do. Property records show the building being built in the 1940s. Ito's owned the whole building for nearly fifty years."

"Who did you tell the cops you were?" Harlan asked. "And why did you say you were there?"

"I introduced us with our real names, said we were from

San Diego, told them our roles in SDPD, and said we were visiting Ito because he knew my sister as well as the daughters of the victim. And that I was hoping he knew whether Mary was Akiko's mother. All one hundred percent true."

"Kit," Harlan groaned. "Navarro's going to have your head on a platter when he finds out that Connor located Nicchi."

"Probably," she agreed, but she wasn't allowing herself to think about that. She'd made her choice. She'd live with the consequences. Especially since Detective West was a fucking wuss who was afraid to leave the precinct, much less investigate this case. "I didn't lie. I just didn't tell them the whole truth. I wanted to get answers from Nicchi first. Ito cares about Akiko. I know he does. Nicchi cares about Ito. I know he does. His reaction at seeing Ito unconscious was genuine."

"I agree," Sam said. "He was devastated."

"He could have been faking it," Harlan said.

"Maybe." Though Kit didn't think so. "But if Akiko was in danger, which we believe is why Mary made contact, why didn't they come straight out and tell her? Why didn't they go to the police?"

Harlan frowned. "Are you thinking cops are involved?"

Kit shook her head hard. "I didn't say that. But until I know who I can trust and who has Akiko's best interest at heart, I'm not volunteering information. That's not negotiable."

Harlan sighed. "I see your point. Will you tell Navarro?"

"I'd planned to once I got answers from Nicchi." Kit brushed a hand down Akiko's arm. Her sister looked so defeated, it broke Kit's heart. The man Akiko had trusted had been hiding at least one secret. How many more were there? "Hey," she murmured. "Your Hanshi did regain consciousness for a few moments. He said, 'Tell her I'm sorry.' I think he meant you."

Akiko wiped at her eyes. "Sorry for what?"

"Akiko McKittrick?"

As one, they turned to the door where a nurse stood, smiling gently.

Akiko stood. "That's me. Is he okay?"

"He's in the ICU. Still unconscious, but you can see him now. Just you and one other person."

Akiko looked from Harlan to Kit.

"Take Kit," Harlan said. "If he wakes up, she'll know the questions to ask."

Akiko tugged Kit to her feet. "Let's go."

Kit gripped Akiko's hand as they followed the nurse. "I'm sorry, too," she whispered. "I didn't mean to keep things from you."

"Yeah, you did. And I understand why. But I swear that if you risk your life again for me, I'll take care of you myself."

"I can't promise that I won't. Y'know. Risk . . . stuff." *My life.* Because she would risk her life again for her sister. In a heartbeat.

"I know. But I can't promise that I won't lock you in a bulletproof closet."

The nurse paused, glancing over her shoulder. "Um . . . I feel like I should report something."

"She's my sister," Akiko said. "And she's a cop. She takes risks that she shouldn't and she's going to get herself killed."

"Ah." The nurse nodded. "My husband is a cop. I know exactly what you mean."

"We're okay?" Kit asked Akiko.

"We're always okay," Akiko said. "But don't get killed. I can't do this without you. Any of it. I need my sister and I need her alive. I love you." Her voice broke. "Don't get killed."

"I love you, too. I'll be more careful. I promise. But I'm not letting this go."

Akiko seemed to brace herself. "What are you going to do next?"

"Find Ricky Nicchi. Talk to Paolo. Investigate the hell out of Ito. Find out what the hell is going on."

Los Angeles, California
Tuesday, January 31, 1:15 a.m.

"I didn't think he'd be here," Kit said as they walked away from Ricky Nicchi's front door.

"Me either." Baz wore a weary scowl. "But I'd hoped."

Sam unlocked his SUV, studying Baz as the older man slid into the back seat. Baz was looking pale, with dark circles under his eyes. He needed to rest.

We all do. "We need to call it a night, guys." He got behind the wheel and closed his eyes. "I don't know about you, but I'm beat."

"Same," Baz murmured. "Nicchi's not at his house or his dojo and he didn't go back to Ito's condo."

Because the three of them had gone back and asked Ito's neighbors. No one had seen Ricky Nicchi since Ito had been transported to the hospital, although Ricky was known to nearly everyone in the building. It seemed he was a frequent visitor to Ito's condo.

Sam started his SUV. "I honestly thought he'd come back to the hospital to sit with Ito. I hate to think he was faking his shock and devastation at seeing the old man hurt, but now that might be a possibility."

"I believed him, too," Kit said. "And I don't have his cell phone number to call. The nurse at the desk wouldn't give it to me. She said they'd called him with an update on Ito's condition but had to leave a message. That's all they can do. Drop me off at the hospital. I'll stay with Akiko tonight and Pop can sleep at Anson's house with you two."

"Nope," Sam said, typing Anson McKittrick's address into his GPS. "Already talked to your father and he said you're to get a good night's sleep. He knew you'd want to spend the night with Akiko and he said, and I quote, 'I'm not gonna be chasing the bad guys. Kit is and she needs to be rested.'"

Kit sighed. "Dammit. Ganging up on me."

"Poor you," Sam said, amused. "Too many people care about you."

She made a face at him. "Ha ha." And then she groaned as she stared down at her buzzing phone. "It's Navarro."

"Surprised it took him this long," Baz said. "Better answer it. Rip that Band-Aid off."

Sam put the SUV back into park. "We'll wait."

Kit hit accept, putting her phone on speaker. "Sir."

"Sir, she says." Navarro sounded angry. "Sir, like she's got respect for me or something."

"I do."

"You do not!" Navarro's tone was more than angry. There was a tension that Sam hadn't heard before. "We *discussed* this, Kit. We *agreed*. No more investigating this case."

"You commanded and I told you that I'd do what I thought was right," Kit said levelly. "And since the two detectives on the case haven't left the precinct because they're afraid they'll get shot, I decided that the right thing to do was to protect my family."

Sam was proud of her. Her jaw was tight, but she'd kept her tone far more professional than Navarro's.

Navarro sighed. "This place is a fucking gossip mill."

"This is true." Kit bit at her lip. "What have you heard?"

"From my end? Nothing. From the LAPD? That two of my detectives and my police psychologist were on the scene of a brutal beating that left a man unconscious. Care to explain?"

For a moment, Sam thought she'd say no. But she squared her shoulders as if Navarro were right in front of her. "We arrived at the home of Akiko's sensei, the man who's been her karate master from the time she was five years old. The door had been forced open and he was lying on the floor, beaten and unconscious. I entered the premises to see if he was still alive. He was, so we called an ambulance and the police, and that was that."

She hadn't mentioned Ricky Nicchi, Sam noticed.

Baz had lifted his brows at the omission as well.

"And what brought you to this karate master's residence?"

"We were looking for connections. Mary Sherman's daughters studied karate at the same dojo as Akiko."

Another long beat of silence. "You're trying to tell me that on the basis of a very, very nebulous connection, the three of you drove to LA?"

"Not nebulous, sir. Edwin Ito is a common denominator."

That, Sam had to admit, was pretty damn brilliant. She

hadn't lied to Navarro or the LAPD detectives. Exactly. And she'd protected Connor, who'd found the Nicchi connection.

Of course, when Navarro found out about Ricky Nicchi, there'd be hell to pay.

"I see. And how is Ito?"

"Still unconscious. Akiko is with him. She has his medical power of attorney."

Navarro made a noise of surprise. "Really?"

"I was surprised, too, but she said she's had it since she was twenty-one."

"They're close, then."

"They are. Up until she came to McKittrick House, he was the one steady person in her life. Do . . . do you have any updates?"

"There was another man in the victim's condo—a Riccardo Nicchi."

"Yes, we met him."

Whoa. She was cool as a cucumber.

"Why was he there?"

"He said he'd called Ito and the man hadn't answered. He told the medics that he was Ito's son."

Again, all true.

"And," Kit added, "he's a big guy. Big feet."

Sam grinned, shaking his head. She'd found a way to kind of tell the truth.

"The shoes found in Mrs. Sherman's living room?" Navarro asked.

"I believe so, yes. But he went to the hospital in the ambulance with Ito and disappeared. We just left his house and he's not home."

"I see. So you're still investigating."

"I am. Sir. Have Lennox and West left the precinct?"

"They have." He drew a breath. "To go home for the night."

"Goddammit," Kit whispered. "I don't understand, sir. I get why not me. But why not someone else? Somebody qualified?"

Then she tilted her head. Sam knew that expression. She'd just figured something out. And by the set of her mouth, she didn't like it. "Are you getting pressure from the higher-ups? Is that what this is? That I have to be shown that I'm not more important than anyone else?" Her voice rose a half octave. "That I should have to deal with incompetence like any other victim's family?"

"Detective," Navarro snapped.

"Well?" Kit demanded. "Is that the case? If so, tell me straight out. I might not be special when it comes to this case versus the others we're all working on, but I feel like I deserve the truth. Sir."

"You make 'sir' into a slur."

Kit swallowed and she met Sam's gaze, her eyes filled with tears. Because Navarro's non-answer was answer enough. "Don't change the subject. Sir."

"We can't look like we're playing favorites," Navarro said stiffly.

"I see," Kit whispered, then cleared her throat. "That your detectives are getting shot at doesn't move the needle at all?"

"It does. Of course it does. But it's also made us all cognizant of the risk."

"So you approve of the fact that Lennox and West just

camped out at their desks all day and didn't go interview a single witness?"

"No, but it's an understandable fear. As you well know."

"Yet I'm out here asking questions." Her voice had gone cold. "As I would be for anyone else."

"I know," Navarro said quietly.

Sam held out his hand and she took it, squeezing hard enough that he had to hide a wince.

"I'll be going now, sir. We're tired and we're going to get some sleep."

"Where will you be?" he asked.

"At my brother Anson's house. He lives in Anaheim. I can send you the address if you don't believe me."

"Goddammit, Kit," Navarro muttered.

"Good night, sir." She ended the call and blew out a breath. "Well. Guess I know where I stand."

"I'm sorry," Sam murmured.

She braved a smile. "I know. Let's go. My eyes won't stop leaking."

Baz leaned forward and gripped her shoulder. "He's being an ass."

She covered Baz's hand with hers, so that she held on to both of them. "He really is."

Sam put the car in gear and pulled into the street. He didn't know what else to say, but he could be there for her. And for now, that seemed to be enough. She hadn't let go of either of their hands and, for Kit, that was telling.

Then her phone rang again.

"I don't recognize the number," she said. "Maybe it's Nicchi."

She let go of Baz's hand and hit accept, once again putting it on speaker. "Detective McKittrick."

"I have DNA results," Navarro blurted out.

Sam immediately pulled into a gas station parking lot. "And?" he asked, because Kit was staring at her phone like it was a grenade.

"Did you call me from a burner phone, sir?" she asked, looking dumbfounded.

"I did. I've been working this case, too, Kit. And if you tell anyone I called you, I'll call you a liar."

"Understood, sir. What did the DNA results say?"

"Mary Sherman was Akiko's maternal aunt."

She made a disappointed face. "Was that all?"

"No. The DNA came back on the skin cells found under the victim's fingernails."

Kit sucked in a breath. "Is the shooter related to Mary Sherman?"

"No. He's related to Akiko."

Kit turned slowly to stare at Sam, who was staring back, glad he'd pulled over.

He hadn't expected that.

Neither had Kit.

"Holy shit," Baz muttered, and then he raised his voice so that Navarro could hear him. "How are they related, Navarro?"

"He's Akiko's half brother. On her father's side."

"Oh," Kit breathed, blue eyes wide and shocked. "Oh my God."

CHAPTER TEN

Los Angeles, California
Tuesday, January 31, 2:30 a.m.

Akiko slowly stood when Kit reentered Ito's ICU room. "I thought you all were going to Anson's to sleep."

Kit was dreading this conversation and she was sure it showed on her face.

Staying seated next to Akiko's chair, Harlan studied Kit carefully. "What's happened, Kitty-Cat?"

Kit gestured to Ito. "Any change?"

"Kit," Akiko bit out. "Answer us."

"I will. But not here. Can you come back to the waiting room? I got one of the nurses to give us a private area. We need to talk."

Akiko shook her head stubbornly. "I'm not leaving him."

Harlan rose, putting his arm around Akiko's shoulders.

"Let's hear what's happened, then we'll come back. This won't take long, will it, Kit?"

"No. Let's go. Sam and Baz are waiting for us."

Baz was, at least. "Sam went to get coffee," Baz said when they got to the private conference room. "He asked you to wait until he gets back."

"I'm back," Sam said, following them in. "I got waiting room coffee, so it'll be fuel only." He grimaced. "Smells like it's been cooking for a while."

"Right now I don't even care," Kit said gratefully. She took a sip and made a face. "Wow. Okay, Akiko. We've found out a few things. First, there's still no sign of Ricky Nicchi. He's not at his house or his dojo and he didn't return to Ito's apartment, either. He's important, because he's got answers. I've got information, but no answers." She drew a breath and gripped Sam's hand under the table. "Mary Sherman was your aunt. The DNA has confirmed it."

Akiko swallowed. "We knew that already."

"We did," Sam said in that kind way he had, "but now it's official. You have cousins. Twins. Raisa and Dahlia. They're black belts, just like you. Studied at Ito's San Diego dojo."

"I must have met them at some point," Akiko said numbly. "I used to teach the little ones. But I'd remember twins."

"Fraternal," Kit said. "They look nothing like each other. They don't even look like sisters."

"They're pretty badass," Baz added.

"Do they want to meet me?"

"Eventually, yes, but not right now," Kit said honestly. "They're still grieving. They're currently in a safe house."

"Because someone shot at the house where they were staying. But not at them."

"We assume," Kit said, measuring her words, then shrugged her hesitation away. Akiko needed to know. And so did the twins. "The shooter has been stalking Dahlia at her university. Never got close enough to touch her and never made an aggressive move, but it was enough to rattle Dahlia. And, like Baz said, she's badass. I don't think she rattles easily."

"I'd like to meet them," Akiko said. "When they're willing."

"I'll follow up with them," Kit promised.

"Is that it?" Harlan asked.

Kit shook her head. "That was the good news." She briefly closed her eyes, opening them when Akiko huffed angrily.

"Just tell me, Kit."

Kit met her eyes. "Mary Sherman fought her attacker. She had his skin under her nails. The DNA came back on him, too. He's also related to you, Akiko. He's your half brother."

Akiko's eyes widened in shock. "My what?"

"Your half brother," Sam repeated, his tone so very gentle. "Through your biological father."

Akiko's mouth opened, but no words came out.

Harlan cleared his throat. "Do you have a name for this half brother?"

"Not yet," Kit said. "They're checking him against the criminal DNA database. That could take another day or two. If we're lucky, there'll be a hit. But he'd have to have been convicted of a crime."

"How did you get this information?" Harlan asked.

"From Navarro. He's also working the case. Personally."

"Because the lead detectives are too afraid to leave the precinct?" Harlan asked, reading between the lines as skillfully as he usually did.

Kit nodded. "Basically, yes. For now, I needed you to know that the shooter is a blood relation, Akiko. You are the central piece to this puzzle. You need to be careful."

Akiko appeared dazed. "But he didn't shoot at me. Just you."

"For now." Kit hated to hurt her. "But that doesn't mean that they don't have sinister plans for you. They killed Mary Sherman before she could talk to you."

"Maybe Mary Sherman was the bad guy," Harlan said. "Maybe she planned to harm Akiko and the shooter saved her." He shook his head. "But he shot you. And then Marshall and Ashton."

"Exactly." Kit leaned across the table, setting her hand in front of Akiko, who immediately took it. "We need to find Nicchi. Do you think Paolo can help us? Nicchi knows stuff that he's not telling us and I don't know why. I thought he'd spill after Ito was attacked, but we can't find him. Can you call Paolo?"

"Yes. He's probably asleep, but he's a light sleeper, so . . ." She took her phone from her pocket with hands that visibly shook. "I'll just . . ." She trailed away, staring at her phone, looking so lost it broke Kit's heart.

I'm an asshole, Kit thought. Dropping a bomb like that without even a hug. Akiko liked hugs. Needed them, even.

Kit gave Sam's hand a final squeeze before letting him go and moving her chair next to Akiko's. She wrapped her arms around her sister's shoulders. "I'm sorry," she whispered. "I'm so sorry. I don't know what else to say."

Akiko pressed her face into Kit's shoulder, her body shaking.

"Who am I? I have a half brother who killed my aunt. And tried to kill you. Twice. Who even am I?"

Kit *could* answer that question, goddammit.

"You're Akiko McKittrick," she said fiercely. "And you are *amazing*. You have the best heart." Her voice broke a little. "You love everyone, even me, even when I probably don't deserve it. You're Harlan and Betsy McKittrick's daughter and they're *proud* of you. You're sister to Rita and Tiffany and Emma. And Dawn and Amy and Stephie. And Anson and Mateo and all the others. And especially to me. You're smart and capable. You run a business that brings people joy and adventure. You could break me in half with your pinkie, but you never would," she added lightly, then drew a breath that hurt her chest. "We love you. *That's* who you are."

Akiko broke into a sob. "Kit."

"I know." Kit rubbed her sister's back, embarrassed at her outburst. "Too much, huh?"

"Just right," Akiko whispered. "I'm so confused."

"I know. It's a big deal, finding your family. I mean, I guess it is." Because she had no idea who her family was. She'd never really wanted to. "You're allowed to feel however you feel."

Kit chanced a glance at Harlan to find him wiping his cheeks, but his smile was electric. He rested his big hand on Kit's head, then Akiko's, but said nothing. He didn't have to.

He's proud of me, too. She always knew he was, but it was in moments like this that it really hit her. She'd come a long, long way since she and Wren had hidden in his barn.

Her gaze moved to Sam, who gave her a nod of approval, his expression soft. "Nicely done," he said quietly. And that his approval meant as much as Harlan's? It was a little terrifying.

"Goddammit," Baz muttered, because he was wiping his eyes, too. "I liked you better when you were snarky and sarcastic."

"Liar," Kit said affectionately. She kissed Akiko's temple. "You're going to be okay. I promise."

Akiko shuddered out a breath. "You can't promise that."

"Watch me." It was a vow, and Kit was one hundred percent serious. "You *will* be okay. I can't promise that Ito will be okay. I don't know what he knows, and he can't tell us until he wakes up."

"*If* he wakes up," Akiko muttered.

"If," Kit allowed. "I might be super pissed at him when we find out what secrets he's been keeping, but he was there for you before we could be and . . . well, I'll always be grateful for that."

Akiko nodded then pulled away, wiping her face with the sleeves of the sweatshirt she wore. "You're wrong, you know. You always deserve it."

Kit frowned. "Deserve what?"

"You said that I love you, even when you probably don't deserve it. But you always deserve it. You always have."

Kit sniffled, determined not to cry. Not in front of all these people. Although, if she couldn't cry in front of the people she trusted most, who could she cry in front of?

Still. They had work to do. "Thank you," she whispered. "Now call Paolo."

"You're welcome. And okay, fine. I'll call him."

Her hand still trembled when she picked up her phone, but not as much, so Kit would take that as a win.

Akiko put the phone on speaker after dialing. "He won't be

nice if I wake him." Then she frowned as Paolo's phone began to ring. "Or he might be awake, but without cell service. If he doesn't pick up, I'll try the sat phone."

"Where did he go?" Kit asked in surprise. "Did he go out on your boat?"

"He might have," Akiko said, then sighed when she got the beep at the end of his recorded greeting. "Paolo, it's me. Call me. It's urgent." She ended the call. "I don't know how else to reach him at this hour. His hangouts are all closed."

"Kit," Sam said before Kit could ask her sister another question. "Nicchi's back."

Kit turned in her chair. Ricky Nicchi stood outside the door, visible through a tall, skinny window. She beckoned him to enter.

When he did, there was no need for him to duck under the doorframe. His head was bowed low, his shoulders sagging.

"Come in," Kit said. "Meet my sister who you claimed not to know."

Akiko stared at Nicchi in surprise. "You told her you didn't know me?"

"We've never met," Nicchi said defensively.

"True, but you have to have known who I was. Ito had to have told you about me. He told me about you. Paolo has worked with me for five years. You know who I am."

Nicchi carefully lowered himself into one of the chairs. "Okay. You have questions. I have questions, too, and also some answers. But first, Akiko, have you talked to Paolo at all today?"

"I just left him a voicemail. Other than that, not since this afternoon when we docked. He helped the customers clean their fish, did his part of the cleanup, and he left. He said he had somewhere to go, but didn't say where."

"What time was that?" Nicchi asked, desperation in his eyes.

Akiko glanced at Harlan. "Four o'clock?"

"That's about right," Harlan said. "Is Paolo missing?"

"I haven't been able to get in touch with him." Nicchi rubbed his face wearily. "I called everywhere that he hangs out. Called all his friends."

"That's where you were all this time?" Baz asked sharply.

"Yes."

"But you weren't making those calls from home," Sam said. "We checked your house."

"I know. I have cameras and they alerted me when you stepped onto my property—at home and the dojo."

"Then where were you?" Kit asked, trying not to make it sound like a demand. Clearly she was unsuccessful, because Nicchi bristled.

"None of your business, Detective."

Akiko raised a hand. "It *is* our business. You're the guy with the size thirteen shoes. You were in Mary Sherman's house—*my aunt's* house—sometime before we found her body. Are you also the man who shot the shooter who tried to kill my sister?"

Nicchi scowled. "I'm not answering that."

Akiko rolled her eyes. "You are, then. Did Hanshi know Mary Sherman?"

Nicchi hesitated, then exhaled. "Yes."

Akiko nodded. "Thank you for that truth. How did he know her?"

"That's not my story to tell. You'll have to ask Hanshi."

"He isn't waking up," Akiko said quietly.

"He will." Nicchi was trying to sound sure, but he didn't pull it off. "He has to. Right now, I'm more worried about Paolo."

Kit frowned. "Does the shooter know who you are? Will he go after Paolo?"

"I don't know," Nicchi said. "I don't know if he knows who I am."

Lie, Kit thought. Although why he'd lie, she wasn't quite sure. Yet.

"But you know who he is," Akiko said quietly.

Nicchi shook his head. "I do not."

Kit didn't believe that, either. "How did you know to be in front of Ella Sherman's house?"

"Because I was afraid he'd go after Mary's daughters. Can you try Paolo again, Akiko? He'll be more likely to pick up for you than me."

Akiko regarded him soberly. "Is Paolo angry with you?"

"I don't know," Nicchi admitted. "We had words. He asked to borrow money and I said yes, until I heard how much. He wouldn't tell me why he needed it."

"How much?" Kit asked, not liking where this was going.

"Twenty grand."

Akiko gasped. "Why would Paolo ask for that much money?"

Nicchi shrugged wearily. "Like I said, he wouldn't say."

"When was this?" Sam asked.

"October."

"When Mary first started going to LA," Sam said.

Nicchi sighed. "Yeah. But the two have nothing to do with each other. Of that I'm certain."

Akiko brought up her phone's contacts list. "I guess that explains why he wanted to do his own charter runs."

"Wait," Nicchi said sharply. "What do you mean, he's doing his own charter runs?"

"He asked if he could rent my boat to take out his own charters. To build up the business with overnights. We do a few, but he wants to do more. We can charge more for them and he said he wanted to be the one to do them. I rent him the boat and I get both the rent money and a portion of his profits."

"Now I'm more worried," Nicchi said. "Why does he need more money? You've always paid him well."

"I don't know. Let me try the sat phone. I didn't think he was going out tonight, since we did a run earlier today, but I can try calling." Akiko tapped the contact and put her phone on speaker. It rang and rang before going to voicemail. "Paolo, it's Akiko. You need to call me ASAP. Hanshi's hurt and it's bad. Call me." She ended the call.

"You didn't tell him that I'm here, too," Nicchi noted.

"No, I didn't. If he's mad at you, he won't call me back if I said you were here with me." She glanced at Kit. "Paolo can be a petulant little bitch when he's angry."

Nicchi sighed. "He really can be. He's impulsive and too carefree. I keep bugging him to settle down, but he says he likes his life."

"He is a bit of a bohemian," Akiko agreed. "Do you know my half brother?"

Kit wanted to grin because Nicchi visibly startled. Akiko was good at this.

"No," he said when he'd pulled his reaction back behind his mask of indifference.

Liar, Kit thought.

"Do you know my father?" Akiko asked.

"No."

Liar.

Akiko studied him. "Do you at least know his name?"

Akiko really was good at this. That was a subtle nuance.

Nicchi shook his head. "You have to ask Hanshi."

"And if he never wakes up?" Kit asked sharply, annoyed at the man all over again. "I'm sorry, Akiko." Because her sister had whimpered. "I want him to wake up, both to get answers and because you love him. But if he does not, is Nicchi here going to man up and answer our fucking questions?"

"Yes," Nicchi said grimly. "I will. But out of respect for Hanshi Ito, I need to wait."

"Fucking respect," Kit snapped. "I don't share the respect. Because he hid secrets from my sister. Who I love. Who I will protect down to my last breath."

"So will he," Nicchi snapped back, then grimaced. "I can't believe I fell for that. Kudos, Detective. You got me to tell you something."

"Ito is protecting her?" Harlan asked. "Not hurting her?"

"He'd rather die than hurt her," Nicchi said and Kit was surprised at the bitterness in his tone. "Trust me on that."

"I do," Kit said. "I probably shouldn't, but I do. How long will you give Ito to wake up? A day? A week?"

Nicchi closed his eyes. "If he doesn't wake up in the next twenty-four hours, I'll tell you."

And then a nurse knocked on the door and upended everything. "Mr. Ito is awake and asking for Akiko."

Nicchi lurched to his feet. "I need to see him, too."

"After he answers Akiko's questions," Kit said firmly. "Don't push me, Mr. Nicchi. I'll call LAPD so fast your head will spin, and I don't care if I get fired for being involved."

Nicchi glared at her. "I'm starting to believe that."

"She's as serious as a heart attack," Baz said.

Kit snorted in surprise. "Shut up, old man. It's still too soon for heart attack jokes. Akiko, you can take Pop if you want to, or I'll go with you."

"I'll go with her," Nicchi insisted, but Akiko merely shook her head.

"My sister goes with me," Akiko said, taking Kit's hand. "You'll get your turn soon, Ricky. Come on, Kit. Let's get some answers."

Los Angeles, California
Tuesday, January 31, 3:05 a.m.

Edwin Ito's gaze latched onto Akiko as soon as she and Kit entered his room. He was awake, but barely. His head was bandaged and his leg was in a cast, its outline clearly visible beneath the thin blanket that covered him.

Akiko sank into the chair, not taking her eyes off Ito's face. "Hanshi?"

She sounded like a small child, and Kit's heart squeezed. She couldn't even imagine what was going through her sister's mind, so she sat in the chair beside her and held her hand.

"Akiko," said Ito quietly. "You came."

"Of course I did." Akiko gave Kit's hand a grateful squeeze before letting go and covering Ito's hand. "I have questions."

"I imagine you do," he said wearily. He glanced at Kit. "You were there. In my condo. How?"

"We tracked Ricky Nicchi to LA," Kit said. "He shot the shooter who'd shot me and two of my colleagues. So we wanted to ask him a few questions. He didn't answer anything, though."

"I don't suppose he did."

"But we saw a photo on the wall of his office. It was the two of you. I recognized you from all the belt ceremonies I've attended for Akiko. We immediately went to your condo and . . . there you were."

"There I was. Thank you for assisting me."

"You're welcome. You owe Akiko some answers."

He closed his eyes. "What do you know?"

"Mary Sherman is dead. DNA shows that her killer is Akiko's half brother on her father's side. Mary Sherman is her aunt on her mother's side. You knew this and you kept it from her. Ricky Nicchi shot Mary's killer but didn't kill him. Just wounded him. Ricky had been visiting Mary in her San Diego home while her husband was at work. The killer was stalking Dahlia Sherman at her university."

Ito's eyes flew open. "What? Is Dahlia okay?"

Kit nodded. "Dahlia is okay. She's in a safe house."

Ito settled back into his pillow. "Good. You know a great deal, Detective."

"I beg to differ, sir. We barely know anything. Who are you to Akiko? Who are you to Mary? Why didn't you tell Akiko she had a family?"

"To protect her."

"From?" Kit asked.

"Danger."

Kit leaned forward in her chair. "And?"

Ito sighed. "It is a long story."

"We have time," Kit said flatly. "What kind of danger? How do I protect her?"

Ito's lips curved slightly. "You are a good protector, Detective. I am confident you'll take care of her when I am gone."

"Well, don't go yet," Kit said tartly. "Answers first."

Akiko gasped. "Kit!"

Ito chuckled, but it turned into a cough. Akiko gave him a sip of water and stroked his face tenderly. "Settle, Hanshi. It'll be okay."

He closed his eyes again, his breathing labored. "Mary Sherman's real name was Himari."

"Mari," Kit murmured, remembering what Leo Sherman had told them. "You talked to her on the street once. She was coming out of a restaurant with her fiancé. You called her Mari and she was upset with you."

"Oh right," Akiko whispered. "I'd forgotten that Leo told us that."

"She was right to be upset," Ito said. "I was careless and could have jeopardized her life by using her given name."

"I'm sorry," Kit said. "I interrupted you. You were talking about Himari."

"Himari had two siblings, twins who were three years older. Ichiro and his sister, Minako. We called her Minnie."

"Minako," Akiko breathed. "My mother."

"Your mother." He opened his eyes and smiled at Akiko. "You resemble her and Mari. The first time I met you, you were five years old. Such a sweet little face. I wanted to take you home with me. You looked just like Minnie at the same age."

Oh no, Kit thought. She had a feeling she knew where this was going. Ito's explanation better be very good. He'd kept more than one secret from Akiko. If he'd known Minnie when she was Akiko's age . . .

"Did you know I was Minnie's daughter?" Akiko demanded.

"Yes," Ito said, so quietly that it was almost inaudible.

"Then why didn't you take me home with you?" Akiko asked brokenly. "Why didn't you adopt me? Why did you leave me in foster care all those years?"

"Too dangerous," he said. "I'm sorry that you had to pay for my choices."

"What does 'too dangerous' mean?" Akiko asked, then frowned. "Wait. You knew my mother when she was five years old? Who are you to her?"

Kit drew a breath, wondering how Ito would answer. If he would tell the truth.

"I was her father."

Akiko gasped quietly. "What?" She released Ito's hand when he said no more. "You're my . . . my grandfather?" She whisper-shouted the final word and Ito winced.

"Yes."

"You . . . left me there. In foster care." Akiko drew a breath through her nose, her nostrils flaring. "I'm so angry right now."

"I know," he said. "And you've every right to be angry." He sighed. "I've made too many mistakes in my life. And you've paid for them."

Tears rolled down Akiko's cheeks. "But . . . why?"

"What danger is my sister in?" Kit asked coldly. Because

whatever Ito, Mary Sherman, and Nicchi had been up to, it had culminated in Mary's murder.

Mary. Himari. His daughter.

"I'm sorry," Kit added softly, not regretting her question, but she did regret the tone she'd used. "You've just lost your daughter. I'm sorry that I couldn't get to her in time."

"She died alone." Ito began to breathe heavily. "Alone and frightened. And knowing—"

He gasped suddenly and all the machines started beeping.

"Hanshi!" Akiko cried.

Kit ran to the door, but a nurse pushed past her, running to Ito's bedside.

"You two have to leave."

"No," Akiko begged. "Please. He's my grandfather."

The nurse was preparing a shot for his IV. "Go *now*."

Kit grabbed Akiko's arm and gently led her away as several more medical professionals rushed into the room. "Come on, honey. We'll wait outside."

Akiko tugged her arm free, turning back to look at him. "Hanshi," she whispered.

"I know, honey. Come with me." Kit put her arm around Akiko's shoulders and steered them into the hall.

And they waited.

"Should we tell Ricky?" Akiko asked.

"Let's see if we can get a status update before we do that."

Akiko nodded and rested her head on Kit's shoulder. Kit stroked her hair and said nothing, because what could she say?

Akiko had found her grandfather—who'd been there all along.

She'd found her aunt, but too late to have a relationship.

And Ito hadn't told them who her father was. Who Mary's killer was.

He hadn't told them who'd attacked him.

I should have asked better questions. But she hadn't been thinking like a cop. She'd been thinking like a sister.

After about ten minutes a doctor came out, looking harried. "We've stabilized him. No more conversations that upset him."

"Okay," Kit agreed. "Can she sit with him?"

"Not yet. He needs rest."

Kit took one look at the tears on Akiko's face and turned to the doctor. "She just found out that the man she's believed to be her karate sensei for twenty-seven years is really her grandfather."

"Oh. Wow." The doctor blinked. "Well, that doesn't change his condition, Miss . . . ?"

"McKittrick," Kit supplied. "We're sisters."

The doctor appeared to be digesting this. "Adoptive sisters, obviously."

"Still sisters," Kit said calmly, although she wanted to snark. "If she promises not to talk to him, can she sit with him?"

The doctor sighed. "Come back in a half hour, okay? If his condition changes, we'll come to the waiting room and get you."

"Okay," Akiko whispered. "I'll be back."

Kit pulled her close. "Let's give the others an update."

CHAPTER ELEVEN

**Anaheim, California
Tuesday, January 31, 4:45 a.m.**

Sam punched in the gate code as Kit rattled off the numbers. He was impressed. Kit's brother Anson had a very nice house.

"I think he could host a McKittrick family reunion," he muttered as he drove up the long driveway.

Kit's laugh was weary. "I haven't been here in a few years. I forgot how huge it was."

"I need to ask Anson for a job," Baz said from the back seat. "The security business pays a helluva lot better than my pension."

Kit turned around to look at her former partner. "Would you? Get another job?"

"Maybe. I've been bored. Marian wants to travel and go on cruises and that's fine for her, but not for me. I need to be productive. This is the most fun I've had in a long time."

"We need to talk about your definition of fun," Sam said darkly, because he wasn't having any fun at all. His head hurt.

Even worse, his heart hurt, the memory of Akiko's shock seared into his mind.

Her half brother had tried to kill Kit. Twice. He'd killed her aunt. It was mind-blowing.

But even more of a shock had been learning Ito's true identity. Edwin Ito was Akiko's grandfather. The man had been the one rock in her life until she'd arrived at Harlan and Betsy's house, had been her mentor since she was five years old. For twenty-seven years he'd kept a life-changing secret from Akiko, and she was understandably hurt and angry.

Unfortunately, all the revealed secrets had raised so many more questions.

"Well, you know what I mean." Baz sighed. "Not fun. But . . . I'm feeling . . ."

"Alive?" Kit asked, clearly understanding Baz's point.

"Something like that. But I don't want to feel alive at Akiko's expense."

"I know," Kit said with a sigh of her own. "I shouldn't have left her alone."

None of them had wanted to leave Akiko after she'd been hit with so many bombshells that evening. But she'd insisted. She'd sit at Ito's bedside until he woke up. Harlan had stayed with her.

It probably should have been Ricky Nicchi joining her at Ito's bedside, but the bastard had disappeared once again.

Nicchi had been sitting with them in the private conference room they'd been given, listening to Kit's grim retelling of Ito's story so far.

They could assume Minako was dead, because Ito had said he "was" her father, but *how* had she died?

What had happened to the twin brother, Ichiro? Was he still alive?

Who was Akiko's half brother?

Who was her biological father?

Once they'd recovered from their shock, they'd turned to Nicchi for more answers—why had Ito kept his identity a secret? What was the "danger" he was so afraid of?

But Nicchi's chair had been empty.

Fucker was like a silent ninja. Nobody that big should be able to move so stealthily.

Asshole.

Sam pulled into one of the parking spots in front of Anson's house. "Harlan's with her. And your brother's sent one of his employees to stand watch outside the ICU." Anson himself would stay with Betsy and their current fosters. Just in case.

Sam wanted to think that it was paranoid to worry that whoever had shot Kit would attack McKittrick House, but unfortunately, it was quite possible. Akiko was at the center of this case, and the danger Ito feared—whatever it was—was quite real.

Ito's injuries were proof of that.

Sam turned off the engine but didn't move, his mind whirling. Kit sat staring up at the house, her expression a mix of exhaustion, anger, and fear.

He hated seeing fear on her face. She was courage personified—unless her family was in danger. He didn't know what to say to her.

So he'd be there for her. He took her hand, and she glanced

at him, her lips quivering up into a sad smile. "This is all so wrong."

"It is," Sam agreed. "Why didn't Ito immediately contact Akiko after hearing that Mary was dead?"

She blinked slowly and he could see the gears of her mind start to turn. "That's a damn good question. He was going somewhere. He had a suitcase in his apartment."

"I'd hope he was going to Akiko," Baz said. "It's what I would have done under the circumstances, but then again, I'd never have kept such a secret from my granddaughter." He opened the back door of the RAV4 with a groan. "Nicchi is a secretive SOB. I'm still not sure that he's a good guy."

"You and me both," Sam said. "Let's go inside. Baz is about to fall down."

"You're not doing much better, kiddo." Baz's sneer was indignant.

Sam chuckled. "You're right. I need to sleep."

Kit looked apologetic. "I'm sor—"

"Be quiet," Sam ordered softly. "I'm exactly where I want to be. Well, on a soft mattress is exactly where I want to be right now, but you get my meaning."

She smiled at him. "I do. Thank you." She opened her own door and made a small sound of discomfort. "My arm hurts like a bitch."

Sam got out of the SUV, grabbed the overnight bags they'd brought with them, and rushed to her side to help her get out. "Harlan gave me the painkillers the doctor prescribed."

"Not taking them. They'll make me sleep."

"You *need* to sleep, Kit," Sam said.

"Give it up," Baz said, groaning again. He shouldered his

own bag. "She's more stubborn than both of us put together, Sammy."

"Which is why I also got over-the-counter meds. Anson told your father that there are ice packs in his freezer. I'll get you situated." Sam gently put his arm around her shoulders, content when she leaned into him. "Come on. Let's get some rest."

She let him guide her into the house. "Hungry?" she asked, veering left from the foyer.

Sam followed her lead. "I could eat something."

"Harlan said we'll find deli meat in the fridge," Baz said. "I'll make us some sandwiches."

The three of them ate in exhausted silence, and a half hour later Baz had already taken himself to bed, choosing one of the many guest rooms.

Sam wasn't sure what Kit wanted to do, so he pushed his plate away and tipped her chin up so that he could see her eyes. They were more expressive when she was tired. She didn't have the energy to maintain her walls.

He liked her like this, all soft and vulnerable, even though he hated the reason behind her weariness.

"Where do you want me to sleep?" he asked quietly.

She blushed, such a pretty sight. "I . . ." She closed her eyes. "I can't . . . I'm not ready yet."

He grinned, despite himself. "I didn't think you were, but I appreciate that that's where your mind went."

She opened her eyes and he saw embarrassed amusement. "You don't have to be so happy about it."

His grin widened. "Oh, I think I do." He kissed her forehead. "But, when you're ready, I want to do it right. Not when you're so exhausted. And not in your brother's house."

She laughed quietly. "Same. Thank you."

"For?"

"Being so patient with me."

"I've got all the time in the world when it comes to you."

Her blush deepened. "The things you say."

"Only the truth. Now, back to my question. Where do you want me to sleep? I can take a room next to yours or we can share. I don't want you to be alone."

Vulnerability replaced the embarrassment. "Me either. We can share."

He rose and extended his hand. "Come on. It'll be dawn soon."

He led her to the second bedroom they came to after climbing the stairs. Baz was already snoring in the first room.

Sam kept going. "Let's put a few walls between us and the snoring."

"Deal." She quickened her pace, stopping at the fourth room. "This is my favorite room. Nice soft mattress. Pretty quilt on the bed. Mom made it."

Sam didn't care about the decor. The soft mattress beckoned, and in a few minutes, they were both changed into sweats. Sam exhaled as he settled into the mattress, then held out his arm. "Just want to hold you."

She obliged, turning off the light before snuggling up against him, her back to his chest. They hadn't pulled the window shade, and the moonlight was bright. But Sam was too tired to get up and pull the shade down. He was pretty sure he'd regret that when the sun came up, but he didn't think his body could move. Plus, he held Kit in his arms.

"Thank you," she whispered.

He kissed the back of her neck, his body waking up at her nearness. "Stop thanking me. I'm in this for the long haul, Kit. I've told you that."

"I guess . . ." Her voice was small in the darkness. "I know. But it's hard for me to . . ."

"To trust me?" That hurt, he wasn't going to lie. But he'd get over it. She was here. With him. That was trust enough for now.

"No." She rolled over, meeting his gaze in the moonlight. "I *trust* you, Sam Reeves. More than anyone else. I wouldn't be here otherwise. I wouldn't have let you near my family otherwise. It's just hard to believe you want to be here. With me. I still don't understand why you want me."

That hurt even more than thinking she didn't trust him yet. She truly didn't see herself the way others saw her. The way he saw her. He cupped her cheek. "You don't have to understand it. Just accept it."

Her smile was wry. "Easier said than done."

"Then accept it for tonight."

She bit her lip, but nodded. "Okay." She rolled back to her side and snuggled into him again. Then froze when her butt brushed up against the erection he was powerless to subdue. "Oh."

He chuckled into her hair. He loved her hair, loved when she let it down like this. He loved Snarky Kit, but when she was like this, soft and open, her walls down . . . This was nice, too. "I can't help it. I'm like this a lot around you. Nothing for you to worry about. I can wait, Kit."

She said nothing, but she didn't fall asleep. He could tell. He could almost hear her mind whirling, which was no surprise. His was, too.

"Want to talk about it?" he murmured.

"I don't know."

Not a "no" then. "Questions about the case?"

"Well, yeah. That too."

He kissed her neck again and felt her relax a fraction. "Talk to me, Kit."

"Akiko always wondered about her mother."

"Okay." He was afraid he knew where she was going with this. He didn't know what to say. "Did you?"

"No. I didn't care."

He hummed sleepily. "Don't believe that."

She sighed. "Someone cared enough to put her name on a piece of paper and pin it to her blanket. They wanted her to have a name."

"Who named you Katherine?"

Katherine Matthews had been her name before she'd arrived at McKittrick House all those years ago. He knew that it was Harlan who'd started calling her Kit. He wasn't sure why, though.

"My first social worker, or so the story goes. By the time I was old enough to comprehend, I'd already been in four foster homes. I was not an easy baby, apparently."

"Sick?"

"Irritable."

"That tracks," he said lightly.

She laughed, swatting him on the leg. "I'd be mad, but you're right." She was quiet for a long moment. Just when he thought she'd gone to sleep, she said, "My file says I was found in a pile of trash."

His erection abruptly softened as tears stung his eyes. "Oh."

"Yeah. Oh. I was a few months old and screaming at the top of my lungs in a dirty alley in the city. Someone heard me and called the cops. There was no note, no name tag. No photo of my mother. Just a pile of trash."

He'd wondered about the circumstances of her birth many times, but had never asked. Maybe because he'd been afraid of exactly this.

"Had a few families consider adopting me," she went on. "But something always happened. Akiko's first two foster families were good people who would have adopted her, but things happened out of their control. One family moved out of the country and the other foster mother got cancer and died. But with me . . . well, no one wanted to keep me. I was unruly, and I screamed a lot. When I learned to talk, I was mouthy and disrespectful. When I learned to walk, I was hell on wheels. By the time Akiko was five years old, Ito had come along and was mentoring her. By the time I was five, I'd been in six foster homes and knew that no one would ever want me."

"Kit," he whispered, tightening his hold on her, unwilling to let her go.

She patted his hand. "It's just a fact, Sam. But . . . I wanted you to understand. Letting people in is hard."

But she was letting him in. He blinked, his tears sliding down his cheeks and into her hair. "I want to go back in time and hit some people. But I don't know who to hit."

Her laugh was wet. "Same. And Mom and Pop feel the same way. They feel that way for every kid who passes through their doors. I got so lucky."

"The universe owed you a boon."

"Maybe. Maybe it was destiny. Maybe it was dumb luck.

But I always knew that no one would want me. Took me years to believe that Mom and Pop did."

"They love you." *So do I.* But she wasn't ready to hear that yet.

"Oh, I know. It was Akiko who helped me see that. She was always so much more willing to trust than I was. Than I still am."

He held her tighter.

She patted his hand again. "It's okay, Sam. I survived. Then I thrived. Harlan McKittrick was the first man I ever trusted. Baz was the second." She hesitated. "You're the third."

His chest hurt. "You honor me."

"I tell the truth."

Another thing he loved about her. What you saw with Kit was what you got. "You still honor me."

She sighed. "When I first met Akiko, she was almost a black belt. Ito was making her wait until she was sixteen to test. I remember meeting him and being so jealous. I was jealous of Akiko anyway. She was sweet and funny. Pretty and talented. Everyone loved her. I was prickly and angry and . . . well, Mom and Pop loved me but I didn't believe that yet. I remember that Ito looked at her like she hung the moon and stars. It seemed fishy to me then. I suspected him."

"Of being abusive?"

"Yes. Nice men aren't supposed to look at a teenager that way. She and I fought about it. She told me that her Shihan—this was a few promotions back and he was Shihan then—that he would never hurt her that way. I didn't believe her. He seemed off to me."

"You were right. He was hiding some big secrets."

"Yeah, I see that now. But I realized I was hurting her with my suspicions, that she was capable of defending herself, so I stopped accusing him."

"But you never stopped suspecting him."

"Not really. Eventually, I accepted that my suspicion was rooted in jealousy. I wasn't proud of myself for that."

"You loved her. You still do."

"With all my heart, as twisted as it was."

Sam's chest hurt again. "Your heart is not twisted. Then or now. It's a big heart and you guarded it because you didn't want to be hurt. That's human nature, Kit."

"You're kind."

"I tell the truth."

She chuckled. "Throwing my words back at me. Nicely done." She settled a little more, linking their fingers together over her stomach, and some of the pain in Sam's chest eased. He couldn't change what she'd been through, but he could make sure she understood what she meant to those who loved her.

"Thank you," he murmured.

She made a contented sound as she relaxed into him. "I wonder how Ito knew where she was. In the foster system, I mean. He had to have known because he chose her to receive a scholarship to his dojo."

"Good point."

"I wonder who left her in that box on the fire station stoop—Himari or Minako."

"Mary or Minnie."

"Yes. Ito had to have gotten some kind of permission for Akiko to attend his dojo. Either from social services or from her foster parent at the time. Maybe both."

"I don't know what the rules were back then," Sam admitted. "Why are you wondering about this?"

"Because if Ito dies, we have no way of reconstructing all those years he mentored Akiko, when she was all alone except for him. I want to reconstruct those years. I want to know what the danger was. Why he didn't adopt her. He's her grandfather. He could have established his custodial right, but he didn't. And he said it was because of the 'danger.' Danger that's clearly come to fruition."

"We could ask around at social services. Or ask the foster family who had custody of her when she was five."

"The mother died, but the father might still be alive."

Sam didn't think it mattered to the case, but this mattered to Kit because it would matter to Akiko. Especially if Ito didn't make it.

"We can make some calls once we've slept."

"Thank you, Sam. For being here. You always know how to make me feel better."

Because I love you. "You're welcome. Sleep now."

"Don't let me go," she whispered.

"Never," he whispered back, but she'd already slipped into sleep.

Anaheim, California
Tuesday, January 31, 11:15 a.m.

Sam was frying bacon in Anson's kitchen when Harlan came in and slumped into a chair at the table. Harlan was looking . . . old, which left Sam feeling unsettled.

Sam moved the bacon from the pan to a plate before pouring Harlan a cup of coffee. "You don't look okay. I'm not even going to ask if you are."

Harlan sipped his coffee. "I hate seeing my kids hurting. It's awful."

Sam got himself a cup of coffee and joined Harlan at the table. "Did Ito die?"

"No. Still unconscious. Never woke up after those few moments he talked to Kit and Akiko last night."

"Prognosis?"

Harlan shrugged helplessly. "Not good. But he's holding on. Anson promised to have one person on guard outside the ICU for the next few days. They have no jurisdiction or authority, so they're working with hospital security in case someone does come after Ito. The cops came and went a few times, but they aren't a constant presence."

"At least he's protected. Where's Akiko?"

"Kit's tucking her into bed. I got us some food from a drive-through when we left the hospital." He sniffed appreciatively. "But I'll take some bacon. I'm still hungry."

"And an omelet?"

"I knew I liked you."

Sam smiled and got busy. "I take it that Ricky Nicchi never came back."

"He did not."

"Asshole."

"I agree."

"Next time I see him, I'm tackling him and tying him up so that we can call the cops. He knows so much more than he's admitting."

"Again, I agree, but who are you going to get to help you tackle him? He's kind of huge."

"Yeah," Sam grumbled. "Everyone I'd ask is incapacitated at the moment. Connor would have been my first choice, but he's recuperating. Marshall and Ashton are out, too. Maybe Kit can help me. She's good at takedowns."

"Akiko taught her that."

"She told me that. Kit was wondering about something last night and I think she's right. She wants to track Ito's movements over the years so that she can figure out what this danger is to Akiko—you know, in case he never wakes up."

Harlan sighed. "I think that's wise. Where does she want to start?"

Sam had been mulling it ever since he'd woken up. "I'd start with the social worker who handled Akiko's case when she was five years old."

"I don't know who that was. I only know the social worker who placed her with us."

"I'll start with her, then. The first social worker's name should be in Akiko's file. I'll probably need her to sign a release or something to get it. How did Akiko come to McKittrick House?"

"Betsy and I got a call from the social worker who took over Kit's case after her former social worker was fired."

Sam nodded. "She told me about that, too. How her previous social worker made her look like a 'little psycho' for defending herself against predatory foster fathers."

Harlan made a low sound in his throat, almost a growl. "I wanted to kill those men with my bare hands. Both of them.

Trying to touch my Kit. Trying to touch any of the children under our care."

Sam agreed with him wholeheartedly. "She told me that a new social worker believed her. That the men who tried to hurt her were finally punished."

"Not enough," Harlan grunted. "But that's water under the bridge. They're both dead now."

Sam turned from the stove, surprised. "How?"

Harlan lifted his brows. "Well, *I* didn't do it."

"I didn't think you did." Mostly. "Kit didn't tell me they were dead."

"She might not know. I think she's put it behind her, but I've kept up with them. One of them ended up in prison, where he was beaten to death."

"Good," Sam said viciously, taking out his anger on the vegetables he was chopping for the omelet. *Die, bell peppers, die.*

"Like I said, I knew I liked you. The other had an aneurysm or something. Didn't suffer."

"Too bad."

"I agree." Harlan took out his phone and tapped the screen. "I just sent you the contact info for the social worker who placed Akiko with us. Wren had been gone for a few months and we hadn't filled her bed. We . . ." He sighed. "We couldn't."

Sam heard the sorrow in Harlan's voice. All these years later, he still mourned Wren, the girl he hadn't been able to save. "I understand."

"Then Kit's social worker called and said she had a girl who needed a home. She was Kit's age—and Wren's age, of course—and was in a bad place. She was a skilled martial artist who had used her skill to defend herself against a predatory foster father. Same story, different day. So many good foster parents out there, but the bad ones are the ones people remember."

Sam whipped the eggs and poured them into the pan. "I think every person who's been through McKittrick House remembers you. You've made a difference in so many lives."

Harlan's smile was fond. "Thank you, Sam. That's all Betsy and I set out to do. Make a difference. Anyway, the social worker told me about this girl, Akiko. That she'd really hurt her foster father. The social worker had convinced the man not to press charges, but she had no proof of the man's wrongdoing other than Akiko's word. She believed Akiko and was investigating the foster father but wanted her somewhere safe in the meantime. She'd held off calling us for any placements because we were still grieving Wren, but Betsy and I agreed it was time. We said yes to Akiko's placement with us. The only special request was that we provide her with transportation to her dojo in the city once a week. That was no issue and Akiko settled in quickly. Well, except the feud she had with Kit."

"Kit said she wasn't ready for another roommate."

"Kit wouldn't have ever been ready. She was . . . well, less than kind to Akiko at the beginning."

"She told me."

"Really? Well, they worked it out and the two of them became thick as thieves. And when Akiko got her driver's license, we gave her car privileges so she could take herself to the dojo. Kit always went with her, though."

Sam glanced over his shoulder in surprise. "Kit studied

with her? I know Akiko's shown her a few moves, but I didn't realize Kit had been a student."

Harlan chuckled. "Not a student. Not a formal one, anyway. Kit wasn't a fan of the discipline Ito required of his students. She chafed at it. Couldn't take the bowing. She'd take Akiko and watch her like a hawk."

"Ah. Making sure she stayed safe. Because of Wren."

"She's not all that difficult to figure out," Harlan said.

Sam plated the omelet and slid it in front of Harlan, then sat at the table to finish his coffee. Sam, Kit, and Baz had already eaten. Baz was on the phone with his wife, trying not to land in the doghouse for his part in Kit's off-the-record investigation. Seemed like neither she nor Baz did well with authority. "I've always wondered why Kit joined the Coast Guard. That required discipline."

"Well, sure. But that was the military and she accepted that. Plus she wanted the money for school, so she swallowed her natural urge to buck authority."

Sam thought of Navarro, of the mess Kit had found herself in. "I think that her inclination to fight authority is a factor in Navarro's behavior right now."

"You could be right. But Kit's a damn fine cop. She has the highest percentage of closed cases in Navarro's department. They won't fire her, but they can make her life difficult. She's going to need to meet with Navarro, bring him up to speed. Especially since she hasn't told Navarro that Nicchi shot the shooter outside Ella Sherman's house on Sunday."

Sam winced. That conversation wasn't going to go well. "I told her that I'd go with her. She plans to do that today."

"Good. On both things. When will you see Navarro?"

"I don't know. Probably after we contact this social worker. We also want to track down Paolo. Did he ever call Akiko back?"

"No, and she's worried about him. It's not like him to ghost her. He'd mentioned a charter this morning, but her boat's remained docked. She had to deal with issuing refunds to a number of very angry customers."

"Paolo disappears at the same time that Ito is beaten? I don't like it."

"Neither do I. My bet is that Ricky Nicchi is off searching for his brother. I dislike the man for not sharing what he knows—especially because it puts Akiko in danger—but he's got to be feeling stressed. Mary is murdered, Ito is beaten, and Paolo disappears? That's a lot."

Sam knew he should feel sorry for Nicchi, but he really didn't. "Why isn't he telling us what's happening? None of this 'it's Hanshi's story to tell' bullshit. What is this guy hiding?"

Kit came into the kitchen, her phone at her ear. "He's not the only one hiding something. I'm putting you on speaker, Connor. Sam and my dad are here."

"Hey, guys," Connor said. "I reviewed the traffic cams again and guess who else went to Nicchi's address?"

"Just tell us, Connor," Harlan said wearily. "I'm too tired for guessing games."

"I'm sorry, sir," Connor said, sounding contrite. "Leo Sherman."

Sam blinked. "Wait, what? Mary's husband followed her to LA?"

"Yes," Connor confirmed. "In December."

Sam met Kit's gaze. "That's very interesting."

"Isn't it?" Her eyes were sharp and calculating. "I think we need to pay the good doctor another visit."

"Tell Navarro everything first," Harlan said. "Please."

"Okay, Pop." Kit blew out a breath. "But I'll have to make something up about who got the information that led us to Nicchi. I'm not throwing Connor under the bus."

"He's going to figure out that it was me," Connor said. "He never told me not to help you. Easier to ask for forgiveness than permission."

Sam would bet that Connor hadn't studied martial arts, either. Connor, Kit, and Baz were like Wild West gunslingers. "This is going to be fun."

"It's past time," Harlan said.

"I know." Kit sighed. "I better start working on my résumé."

Sam reached for her hand and squeezed it. "He's not going to fire you. You might get demoted, though."

For a moment Kit looked unbearably sad, and then she squared her shoulders, a mutinous set to her jaw. "Then I might as well make it worth the punishment."

Harlan groaned. "Kit. Just . . . wear a vest. Please."

She kissed Harlan's cheek. "Will do. I promise."

But a vest wouldn't have protected her if the shooter had been a little more accurate on Sunday at Ella's house. It would have been a headshot and she wouldn't have survived it. That the shooter hadn't succeeded on Sunday was due to Nicchi's interference.

Sam's irritation at the man lessened dramatically. Nicchi had saved Kit's life. Sam would have to cut him a little slack.

But only a little.

"You ready to go back to San Diego?" Sam asked.

"I am. Let me get Baz. Marian found out about his involvement and called him from the Panama Canal. He's still groveling. Gotta go, Connor. Thanks for the intel."

She ended the call and left the kitchen, leaving Harlan and Sam alone.

"Go to bed, Harlan. You're no good to anyone if you keel over."

"I think I will." Harlan rose, then swayed on his feet. "Keep me updated, please. Kit forgets sometimes."

"I promise."

CHAPTER TWELVE

San Diego, California
Tuesday, January 31, 3:30 p.m.

Reynaldo Navarro was in his office. Kit had hoped that he wouldn't be so that she could put this meeting off for a little while longer. It was childish, she knew, but she was dreading this.

Sam held her right hand tightly and her left arm was throbbing, so she didn't wave at the other homicide detectives as they greeted her. She just nodded and tried to smile instead.

"Healing" was her reply when the others asked about her arm.

"It'll be okay," Baz murmured behind her.

She hoped he was right, because for all her bravado, she was scared. She didn't want to lose her job.

She wanted to be a cop. It was all she'd ever wanted to be.

But then she saw Alan West at his desk, staring at her coolly as she walked by. He had a bunch of papers spread all over his desk and a food delivery bag. She could see the receipt stapled to the bag.

He hadn't gone out for lunch.

She wondered if he'd stayed inside for a third day.

Detective Meghan Lennox turned around in her chair to look at Kit, and Kit thought she saw regret in the woman's eyes. Lennox was a few years younger than Kit, and she was new to Homicide. She struck Kit as shy and unsure—a bad combination for a detective. The current expression on Lennox's face served to underscore Kit's opinion.

Lennox started to rise, but her partner cleared his throat and she aborted the movement. She nodded once and Kit could only nod back.

It wasn't Lennox's fault that she'd been stuck with Alan West. But when Kit had been stuck with him, she'd shown initiative. She'd gone out and worked the case on her own. She hadn't let West tell her what to do.

But she's not you.

No, Lennox wasn't. But she was responsible for catching the man who'd killed Akiko's aunt. And so far, it didn't appear that the team of West and Lennox had come up with anything useful.

Sam squeezed her hand before letting it go as they got to Navarro's office door. "I've got your back," he whispered.

"Thanks." But that wouldn't be enough to keep her job if Navarro went through with his threat.

Navarro waved them in and she entered, feeling like she was heading for a firing squad.

Baz closed the door behind them. "Hi."

Navarro's laugh was more like a bark. "Hi, yourself. You all might as well sit down. I'm not going to like this, am I?"

Kit braced herself as she sat. "Probably no more than I'm going to like it."

"You've been investigating," Navarro said.

"I have been. I have some things to share. Things I should have shared before."

"No," Navarro drawled sarcastically. "Really?"

"No need for the attitude, Rey," Baz said quietly. "She's nervous enough as it is."

"Then Detective McKittrick shouldn't have gone off on her own."

"Has West left the building today?" Sam asked.

Navarro glanced out his office window to West's desk. "Yes. He and Lennox went to the hospital to interview Leo Sherman."

Well, that was something at least.

"Because you yelled at him?" Baz asked.

Navarro narrowed his eyes. "Why are you here, Constantine?"

Ouch. Kit winced at the slight. Baz had called Navarro by his first name, but Navarro was sticking to last names.

"I've been . . . providing my expertise," Baz said. "We've found out more than West and Lennox have, I can guarantee you that."

"I assume that you know more than you told me last night when I called you with information that you had no right to, but that I shared out of respect."

Kit sighed. He had shared the DNA results with her and she hadn't reciprocated. She'd betrayed his trust and it was now time to pay the piper.

She just hoped the price wouldn't be too high. "Riccardo Nicchi is the other shooter," she said, wanting to get this over with. "He shot Akiko's half brother in front of Ella Sherman's house. He is the owner of the size thirteen shoes found in Mary Sherman's living room. He was the visitor when her security system was deactivated. His office in LA was Mary Sherman's destination for all three trips. He is close to Edwin Ito. Like a son. He is also the half brother of Paolo Feliciano, Akiko's first mate on her fishing charter boat. They have different fathers, different last names. Paolo is currently missing."

Navarro didn't react, his expression unreadable. "Anything else?"

"Oh right." Yes, there was one more thing. She should have led with it. "Edwin Ito was Mary Sherman's biological father. And Akiko's grandfather."

Navarro's mask gave way to shock. "Wow."

"Yeah." She glanced from Sam to Baz. "Did I forget anything?"

"I think you covered it," Sam murmured.

Navarro folded his hands on his desk. "You have been busy. Who's been feeding you information on the case status?"

"I'm not gonna say, sir." There was no way she was throwing anyone under the bus. Not Connor, not Sergeant Ryland, not Marshall or Ashton.

Navarro clenched his jaw. "I'm disappointed but not surprised." He took a single sheet of paper from his desk drawer and slid it across the table to Kit.

Kit swallowed, the roiling in her stomach becoming a rigorous churning as she read it. "I'm being suspended?"

Navarro's shoulders sagged, his eyes weary and sad. "Yes. With pay. Your union rep will update you regarding your hearing."

"Okay. Will you take my badge?" Her service weapon belonged to her. They'd already taken the one issued by the department back on Saturday, after she, Sam, and Akiko had discovered Mary's body.

"No. But I swear to God, if you keep investigating, I'll declare you unfit for service."

Kit couldn't control her gasp. She wanted to say something, anything, but no words would come.

"Don't make me do that," Navarro said quietly. "Because of your relationship, Sam won't be able to declare you fit, if you're already thinking of a way to get around it."

She wasn't. She wasn't thinking at all. Being declared unfit was . . . well, unthinkable.

"Lieutenant," Sam started, but Navarro waved him to silence.

"Don't, Dr. Reeves. She knew the risks. So did you, yet you supported her insubordination. She's left me no choice." He put a pen on top of the suspension paperwork. "Detective McKittrick, read this and sign it. It's not an admission of guilt, only an acknowledgment that I've explained the process to you."

She read it once, then twice, the words not sinking in.

Despite knowing this was a possibility, she really hadn't considered how she'd respond if it happened. Part of her, she realized, had assumed Navarro wouldn't follow through on his warning.

Because, on some level, she and Navarro had become . . . well, not friends. But at least friendly.

She'd allowed him in. Let down her walls and let herself trust him.

That's not fair. He's only doing his job.

And she'd only been doing hers.

Not true. You were doing West's and Lennox's jobs.

Because they refused to.

"Detective?" Navarro pressed. "Is there a problem?"

Yes. So many problems. She picked up the pen, her hands shaking. Gritting her teeth, she signed the paper and lurched to her feet.

Do not throw up. Do not.

Sam rose slowly, his shoulder brushing hers. "Do you want to suspend me, too?"

Navarro's jaw clenched. "No."

Baz stood. "Reynaldo. Don't do this."

Navarro's gaze jerked to Baz. "Do you think I want to? She's given me no choice. She knew the rules and she broke them. She disobeyed a direct order."

Kit blindly reached for Sam's hand. It was there, of course, enveloping hers. He was warm, strong. Safe.

She lifted her chin. "And I'd do it again. Sir."

Navarro closed his eyes. "I know. And in your position, I might even do the same. But you leave me no choice, McKittrick."

McKittrick. Not Kit. Not even Detective.

"My sister is at the heart of this, and West and Lennox aren't properly investigating. You know it and I know it. Every detective out there knows it. I don't know who's pulling the strings here, Lieutenant, but this isn't you. You're fair and you do the right thing, even when it's the hard thing. I learned that from you."

Baz sighed. "She's got you there, Rey."

"Be quiet, Baz. Please." Navarro met Kit's gaze. "I gave you information last night. I expected you to do the same."

"You gave me information," she agreed, "and it was shocking. I took the time to process. I'm here now."

"Doesn't change anything. You still disobeyed a direct order. You can't choose which orders to obey and which to ignore. We'll be contacting you regarding the suspension. In the meantime, don't get yourself killed."

She went to his office door, then paused, her hand on the doorknob. "I suppose that West and Lennox interviewed Leo Sherman because they found out that he followed Mary to LA." Navarro's barely audible gasp had her turning to face her lieutenant. He was staring at her. "So they didn't know," she murmured.

"How did you know?"

"Studied the traffic cams. Followed his black Audi. Why did they interview him, then, if they didn't know that?"

Navarro hesitated, then shrugged. "He spoke to his wife several times. We have his phone records. We wanted to listen to his voicemails from his wife, but he refused to give us his phone, so we're getting a subpoena. Who studied the traffic cams? I want a name."

"I'm not going to give you one. I mean, I'm already suspended, right?"

Navarro nodded woodenly. "So you are. Thank you for that information."

She opened the door and walked away, acutely aware of every eye in the bullpen following her movement. Sam and Baz trailed her, but she didn't look back. She needed to get to the restroom.

Now.

She barely made it in time, her stomach heaving as she leaned over the toilet. Everything she'd eaten that day was violently expelled. She gagged, her eyes stinging.

She flushed the toilet and went to the sink to wash her face and rinse her mouth. *I don't have time for this. I have work to do.*

Slowly she straightened, staring at her reflection. She looked hollowed out. Haunted.

Sad.

Which was fair. She was all those things.

A figure edged into the reflection and she jumped, spinning around. "Lennox."

"Kit."

"What do you need, Detective?"

Lennox fidgeted with a button on her blazer. She was taller than Kit, her dark hair cut in a stylish bob. She'd come from the robbery unit, where she'd built a solid service record. That she'd been paired with West was a shame. "I'm sorry. I . . . He's a difficult partner."

Kit smiled wryly. "I know. Everyone knows that."

"You deserve better. Your family deserves better."

"We do. Thank you." She started to walk around Lennox.

"Wait. Please."

Kit stopped, cursing inwardly. "What do you need, Detective?" she asked again.

"Help. I need help. West won't investigate. Says that there's no way he's going to let himself get shot with only three months to go till his retirement."

"I believe that."

Lennox lifted her chin and, for a moment, Kit was reminded of herself as a rookie homicide detective. "I interviewed Leo Sherman on my own."

Kit frowned. "Navarro said West left the building."

"He did, but he wouldn't leave the car. So I went into Sherman's hotel next to the hospital and interviewed him. He repeated that he didn't know where his wife went. He admitted that he'd received voicemails from her but refused to hand over his phone. Said he had patient information stored on it and it would be a breach of confidentiality."

Kit leaned against the counter. "But?"

"He was lying. I don't know what the truth is, but I'm positive Leo Sherman was lying. He knows where his wife went. I've requested a subpoena for his phone, but it'll take a while. We'll probably have to use a third party to review its contents to protect his patients."

Kit was reluctantly impressed. "You're right. He was lying. I just got finished telling Navarro that Leo followed his wife to LA. He knows exactly where she went."

Lennox's eyes sharpened. There was an intelligence there that gave Kit a little hope that the detective would be an asset to the department.

"How do you know?"

"Traffic cams, all the way up the 5."

One side of Lennox's mouth lifted in a sardonic smile.

"West has been reviewing traffic cam footage for days. It's all he does. Says determining where the victim went in the two weeks before her death will be a key to cracking the case."

"Well, he's right about that, but he's clearly not as good as the person I had checking the traffic cams. They found it in a day."

"Shocking," Lennox deadpanned. "Where did she go?"

"To a karate dojo owned by a guy named Riccardo Nicchi."

"Thank you, Detective. I'm going to interview Leo Sherman again. I'd appreciate any help you can provide."

"I can't go with you. I'm suspended."

Lennox blinked. *"Shit."*

"That's pretty accurate. Look, you seem . . . nice. I don't want to get you suspended, too, especially if you're willing to work around West. That's why he hates me, by the way. I worked around him years ago. He doesn't like that."

"I don't really care," Lennox countered. "And he's retiring in three months anyway. But I want to do this right and he's supposed to be my training partner. You asked me what I needed and what I need is help. I know you can't go with me, but would you be willing to listen in when I interview Leo again?"

It was Kit's turn to blink. "You're offering to wear a wire?"

"Sure. Look, I know Sherman's lying, and I'm normally good at sussing out the lies from the truth, but I think this guy is really good."

"He is. I almost believed him the time he came to my house to speak to me."

Lennox's eyes widened. "He came to your house? I didn't know that."

"He did. That's when we realized that Akiko had to be related to Mary Sherman. Leo looked like he'd seen a ghost when Akiko walked into the room. I don't think he faked that reaction. Neither does Sam Reeves."

Lennox tilted her head. "Is Sam suspended?"

Ah. Kit saw where she was going. "He's not. Just me."

"Would he come with me to interview Leo Sherman?"

"Let's go find out."

San Diego, California
Tuesday, January 31, 4:55 p.m.

This had not been on his bingo card for the day, Sam thought.

He and Meghan Lennox walked through the building that housed Leo Sherman's private practice. Both of them wore earpieces, and an app on Sam's cell phone was their transmitter. Kit and Baz waited in Sam's RAV4, ready to listen and provide commentary once he and Lennox started interviewing Leo.

Sam wasn't sure if he could trust Detective Lennox, but he really wanted to. She'd been respectful to Kit—at least on the surface—but Sam could envision half a dozen ways she could hang Kit up and leave her to dry.

Kit was already suspended, however, and for that, Sam wanted to hurt Navarro. Sure, the man had simply been "doing his job," but there must have been other ways he could have made his point.

"Do you want to take the lead," Sam asked, "or should I?"

"I've already been here once today. Why don't you give it a go?"

"Okay." They'd reached Leo's office door. "Let's do this."

Sam and Lennox barreled past Leo's receptionist, Lennox flashing her badge at the woman when she tried to stop them. The receptionist shouted after them, then ran to her phone, no doubt calling her boss. Lennox didn't look back, didn't apologize.

In that way, the detective was very much like Kit—confident and a little brash. But she wasn't afraid to ask for help. So . . . not like Kit at all in that respect.

Lennox rapped on Leo's door. "SDPD, Dr. Sherman. Open up."

The doctor opened the door, his scowl impressive. "Detective Lennox, what are you doing back—" He stopped when he saw Sam. "Dr. Reeves, isn't it? I didn't expect to see you."

"We have a few more questions for you," Sam said mildly, even though he felt far from mild. This man had followed his wife to LA, then lied about knowing where she'd gone. Clearly, his priorities were not in bringing Mary's killer to justice.

What Leo's priorities were was what they were here to discover.

Lennox had run full financials on the surgeon. He wasn't in obvious debt. His credit score was phenomenal. He owned the home in which his wife had died as well as the homes in which his sisters lived.

He made a good living as a cardiac surgeon and, even though online reviews described him as an "asshole with a God complex," he *had* saved their lives, and those patients were begrudgingly grateful.

Expression blank, Leo invited them in. "I thought I told you to get a court order for my phone."

"That request is in process," Lennox said, her smile easy and friendly as she and Sam sat in the guest chairs in front of Leo's massive desk. "But something else has come to our attention. Thus, more questions. Dr. Reeves, you have the floor."

Sam studied the surgeon, conscious of Kit listening. "You're looking a little haggard, Dr. Sherman. Are you sleeping well?"

Now Kit would know what he looked like, too.

"Don't insult my intelligence by pretending you care, Dr. Reeves. What do you want?"

Sam leaned forward, capturing the man's stubborn gaze. "Where did your wife go in LA?"

Leo blinked. "I already told you. I don't know."

"Yes, that's what you told us—Detective McKittrick and me. Now, how about the truth?"

Leo bristled. "Please leave."

Sam didn't move. "Have you loaned your car to anyone recently?"

"No." Panic flickered in the surgeon's eyes. "Why do you ask?"

On his phone, Sam brought up the photo that Kit had requested from Nicchi's dojo—a photo taken from their own security feed clearly showing Leo's black Audi parked in front. His license plate was crisp and readable.

Nicchi had, apparently, been taking calls from his coworkers. It was only Kit who he was avoiding. When the dojo's receptionist had asked his permission to provide the photo, he'd immediately given it.

So Ricky Nicchi wasn't a complete asshole, Sam thought. "Do you recognize this car, Dr. Sherman?"

Leo paled. "What is this about?"

"Well," Sam said in his friendliest tone, "it appears that this is about me telling you that you're a liar. Now, I'll ask you again. Where did your wife go when she went to LA?"

Leo swallowed. "Why ask me if you already knew?"

"Because I really don't like liars."

"So you caught me. I followed her, all right? I wanted to prove that she was cheating."

"And did you?" Sam asked.

"To myself, yes. Would it have held up in court? Probably not. Did I catch her in bed with the guy? No. But she went to his place of business every day. She stayed in his condo. She was cheating. I'm certain, and that's enough for me."

But Mary hadn't stayed with Nicchi.

She'd stayed in the same building where Ito had lived for fifty years. The building Ito owned.

"I suppose it's possible that she cheated," Sam allowed. "But knowing where she went might have helped us find out who killed her—if you'd told us the truth. I assume you *do* want to find out who killed her?"

Leo looked away. "Of course I do."

Sam put his phone away. "I really hope you're better at surgery than you are at lying."

Leo glared at him. "What's that supposed to mean?"

"It means that I don't believe you care enough about your wife to want to catch her killer. You must have been angry when you followed her to LA."

Leo's cheeks reddened, the color stark against his pale face. "Fine," he snarled. "I was angry, all right? Any husband would have been. I didn't kill her, but discovering that she was cheating makes me look like I had motive."

"You have an alibi," Sam said logically.

Leo rolled his eyes. "Right, like you haven't considered that I paid someone to do it."

Sam raised his brows. "Did you?"

"No!" Leo dragged shaking hands down his face. "Fucking hell. This is a nightmare."

"It is," Sam agreed. "For your daughters. And especially for your deceased wife. Someone broke into your home, sir, and shot her in the head."

Leo glared again. "I know that. And I know that this has been a nightmare for my daughters. How the hell am I supposed to tell them that she brought this on herself? They're going to hate me even more than they already do."

"Why do they hate you?" Lennox asked quietly.

Leo whipped around to meet her gaze. "They say I work too much."

Sam sighed loudly. "Lying again."

"I figured that out for myself," Lennox said dryly. "I think your daughters know that you cheated on your wife for years."

Leo ground his teeth. "That doesn't mean I killed her."

"Never said it did," Lennox said. "You're the one who said they hated you. I thought maybe there were other reasons."

"They all said I worked too much. Mary too. Like they'd have the lifestyle they were used to if I didn't. Nobody appreciates the breadwinner. They just take, take, take and constantly complain."

Leo had gotten himself worked up thanks to Lennox's distraction, ranting about his ungrateful family and how hard he worked.

Lennox had distracted him on purpose, to derail his thinking.

Smart.

"How did Mary bring this on herself?" Sam asked.

Leo stopped mid-rant and stared at him. "What?"

"You said that your wife brought this on herself. How?"

"Those . . . men. The ones she was with. They're mixed up in shady shit."

Now they could be getting somewhere. If Leo was right, if Nicchi was mixed up in shady shit, that could explain why the man was so unwilling to come clean to the police.

Everyone wanted to assume Mary had Akiko's best interests at heart because she'd been a blood relation, but what if she hadn't? What if she hadn't been the nice woman her daughters believed her to be? What if she'd been involved in something illegal?

"Which men?" Sam asked. "How many?"

Leo's nostrils flared. "Three. Two Japanese, one Italian. One of the Japanese men was Edwin Ito. I knew him from my daughters' dojo when they were growing up."

Nicchi hadn't mentioned a third man. *What the fuck, Ricky? What are you hiding?* "Was he the man you remembered talking to your wife all those years ago? Before you got married?"

Leo's body sagged. "Yes."

"So you lied about that, too," Sam said. "You told Detective McKittrick that you didn't know who the man was. But you did."

"He was always around, but . . . sneaky. Like he didn't want to be seen. He'd come to the dojo to watch my daughters, even though he wasn't their sensei. He just owned the dojo. They were so small at the time. It was disgusting. He'd watch Mary, too. All the time." He closed his eyes, his words bitter. "I think he believed he was being discreet, but I saw. At least I know that Dahlia and Raisa are mine. I did a paternity test years ago."

Sam said nothing for a long moment, waiting for Leo to open his eyes.

Leo finally did, only to narrow them in anger. "You think I imagined that Ito was interested in my wife? Well, fuck you, Dr. Reeves. You are a terrible psychologist."

"I don't think you imagined it," Sam said, gentling his tone.

Leo sucked in a startled breath. "You don't?"

"No. I think Ito did watch your wife and daughters, but not for the reason you think." At least Sam hoped not. "Ito is Mary's father."

Leo's face went slack in shock. "What?"

Sam heard Kit's voice in his ear, quiet and calm. "He didn't know, did he?"

Sam wasn't certain, but he didn't think that Leo had even suspected it. "You didn't know," Sam said softly, answering Kit.

Leo shook his head. "No," he whispered. "I didn't."

"He's a lot older than your wife," Lennox observed, sounding skeptical. "Did it ever enter your mind that they weren't having an affair, that it was something else?"

"No. She married me—I figured she just liked older men. Do my daughters know?"

Sam shook his head. "Not yet. Ito was attacked in his own home yesterday. He was beaten nearly to death. He's in the ICU in LA."

"Oh." Leo seemed genuinely shocked. "I didn't know."

Kit murmured, "Ask him about the other man."

Sam would, but in a minute. "You speak Japanese, at least a little bit. Did you ever overhear any other conversations between them?"

Leo shook his head numbly. "I never saw them speak, except for that one time on the street. He'd come into the dojo, watch Mary and my daughters, and then leave. When I saw Mary with him in LA, when I followed her there, I thought it was proof. I thought for years that they'd been having an affair."

"Why did you stay with her all these years if you thought she was cheating with Edwin Ito?" Lennox asked.

Leo looked down at his desk. "If I'd divorced her with no proof, she'd get a lot more of my money. We had a prenup. But the PIs I hired over the years were never able to find anything incriminating. She mostly worked and took care of the house and the children. Went to an occasional garden club meeting."

Oh wow. Sam had to struggle to keep his true feelings hidden. It all had come down to money. Leo truly was an asshole. "Why did you follow her yourself this time? Why not have the PI do it?"

"I figured the PI was lazy. Just charging me for the time he sat on his ass and watched TV. After the first trip to LA—after she lied and told me she'd gone to a training class—I put a tracker on her car. I knew after the second trip where she'd gone. I followed her the third time and saw her with Ito."

Lennox pulled a small notebook from her pocket. "And the two other men? Can you describe them?"

"One was her age. Italian, like I said. I think he works at the dojo because he was always walking around in a gi."

"Name?" Lennox asked, as if she didn't know it already.

She did, because Kit had told her, but there might be another Italian guy walking around LA in a gi.

"Riccardo Nicchi. He owns the dojo now. Ito sold it to him."

She wrote it down. "And the other man?"

"I don't know who he was, but he looked . . . sinister."

Sinister. That was the word Dahlia Sherman had used to describe her stalker. "What did he look like?" Sam asked, furious that Nicchi had withheld this information. It was difficult not to let his anger show.

Sonofabitch.

"Older. Taller than Ito, but shorter than Nicchi. Looked about Ito's age, but I only saw him from a distance."

Not the man who'd stalked Dahlia and murdered Mary. He was much younger than Ito.

"Ask for the photos he took of these men," Kit instructed through the earpiece. "Because I know he did. He would have wanted proof so that his divorce attorney could invalidate the prenup."

Good point. "I'd like to see the photos you took while you were in LA," Sam said.

Leo opened his mouth, most likely to lie, but Lennox shut him down.

"Don't even try it, Dr. Sherman," she said. "We know you took them. You would have needed proof to invalidate your prenup."

Leo scowled. "Fine. Give me your phone numbers and I'll send everything I took."

They did and a moment later, Sam was staring at the third man Mary had met with in LA. He forwarded it to Kit, then zoomed in on the man's face. It was shrouded in shadow, turned just enough that the only usable details were his buzz cut and heavy, dark-rimmed glasses.

Nicchi had a lot more questions to answer.

"What seemed sinister about him?" Sam asked.

"It was the way the others treated him. The big guy, Nicchi, kind of . . . Well, he didn't cower. But he stood back and kept himself . . . ready? Like if the guy tried anything he'd attack."

"Interesting," said Lennox. "How did Ito act toward him?"

"He wasn't afraid of him, I don't think. I only saw them together once. They were standing in front of the dojo, talking. They'd been inside and had all come out together."

"And Mary?" Sam asked. "How did she seem?"

"Worried. She kept looking over her shoulder. I thought she'd seen me, but she looked right past me. She was watching for something or someone else."

"And the men being into some 'shady shit'?" Sam asked. "What made you think that?"

"Look at the second photo."

Ah. The second photo showed the other Japanese guy pulling an envelope from his coat pocket. The third photo showed Nicchi sliding the envelope up the sleeve of his gi. Seemed to be the right size envelope for cash.

That did look shady, Sam had to admit. "Did they all leave together? In the same car?"

"No. Mary and Ito got into her car, Nicchi went back into the dojo, and the other guy walked down the block. He might have caught a cab. I don't know. I followed Mary and Ito back to his condo." He exhaled heavily. "Ito was her father? For real?"

"He says so," Lennox said. "We'll double-check with DNA, of course."

"Why wouldn't she tell me? Why keep it a secret?"

"Good questions," Sam said. "We're going to find out."

Lennox nodded. "We are. Dr. Sherman, we'd like to put you into protective custody. Whoever attacked Edwin Ito tried very hard to kill him. Your daughter has been stalked and your wife murdered. Will you go to a safe house?"

"No." Leo shook his head hard. "Absolutely not. I'll be fine. I have too much work to do to be cooped up in a safe house."

Lennox rose. "If you think of anything else, let me know."

Sam gave Leo one of his cards. "Call if you remember anything else. Or if you get shot at. Or stalked."

Leo took the card, an angry sneer twisting his mouth. "Sure."

"Lovely man," Lennox muttered when they'd cleared Leo's receptionist and were standing by the elevator.

"Hard to feel sorry for—" Sam paused when his phone buzzed in his hand. Then he groaned quietly when he saw the caller ID.

He'd lost track of time. He'd lost track of *days*.

He checked his phone for the date. Of course it was Tuesday.

"I have to take this, Kit," he said so that she knew what was happening. Then he hit accept and put the phone to his ear. "Hi, Mom."

"Sam? We're here, but you're not answering your door, and Siggy's not barking. Where are you, son?"

Sam sighed. "It's kind of a long story. I'll be there soon."

"*We*," his mother corrected. "You promised to bring Kit so that we can meet her."

"Oh my God," Kit whispered into his earpiece. "Oh my God."

Sam sighed again. "I'll be there soon," he said again. "We'll come to your condo."

Because his parents rented a condo in his building for when they visited him from Scottsdale. He'd been afraid they'd move in permanently, but they were amazing about giving him space. Plus, his father's recent stroke hadn't allowed them to travel the way they used to. This was their first trip since December.

"All right. We'll be waiting."

"Bye, Mom."

Lennox lifted her brows, because she could hear Kit's frantic whispers, too.

"My parents are visiting," he explained. "They want to meet Kit."

Lennox bit her lip to keep from smiling. "You'll be fine, Kit. I'm sure they'll love you."

"Oh my God," Kit groaned, her terror crystal clear.

Sam hit the button for the elevator. "It's not like they're serial killers, Kit."

She groaned again. "I wish they were."

CHAPTER THIRTEEN

San Diego, California
Tuesday, January 31, 6:10 p.m.

"I need to work," Kit said as Sam tugged her out of the elevator on his parents' floor of their building. Her voice was thin and high, far from normal for his confident detective. "I have to find Nicchi and Paolo. I have to find out who the second Japanese man was and what was in the envelope that he gave to Nicchi. I don't have time to see your folks right now. Maybe later."

Sam stopped in the hallway. "Kit," he said softly, tipping up her chin so that she met his eyes. She looked as terrified as she sounded. "Why are you scared of my parents?"

She swallowed hard, looking lost and . . . young. "I'm not."

He waited silently.

She sighed. "Okay, I am. I haven't been this scared in months."

"You were shot three days ago," he said dryly.

"I said what I said."

"What scared you months ago?"

Her eyes closed. "You. Getting close to you."

Which was exactly what he'd expected her to say. "Kit." He let go of her hand and cupped her face, knowing he'd done the right thing when she leaned into his touch. This woman was touch-starved, and he was afraid to give her too much too quickly. It would send her running, and that was the last thing he wanted her to do.

He kissed her then, keeping it chaste even though he wanted so much more. *Patience.* He had to have patience.

She was worth it.

And, as he kissed her, he could feel her tension ebb. She hummed quietly when he pulled back just far enough to see her eyes when they opened.

"You always know the right thing to say," she murmured.

He smiled. "I didn't say anything."

"Not with words. You're good at both, though." She dropped her head, her forehead resting on his chest. "What if they don't like me?"

"They will."

"And if they don't?"

"Then I'll still like you."

Her snort of laughter was unladylike and so very Kit. "You're the cheesiest man." She heaved a heavy sigh. "This is important. *They* are important. They love you and always have. Mom and Pop love me, I know that. But I didn't have the same childhood you did. It messed me up, Sam. Made me suspicious and sometimes even . . . mean. But you grew up secure. You're never mean. You're . . . perfect."

His heart hurt. That she could think herself mean when she had the biggest heart of anyone he knew. But she wasn't ready to address that truth yet. "I am not perfect."

She looked up, her eyes bright with unshed tears that shocked him. "You are. Everyone says so. And I'm just . . . me."

He touched the edges of her eyes with his fingertips, gathering her tears before they had a chance to fall. "I like you." *I love you.* "Just you." He kissed her again, gratified when she melted into him. "You're going to be scared until you get this over with, just like our first date. And our second."

She hiccupped a laugh. "And the third."

"Which was, mercifully, homicide-free." A week ago, they'd gone to a movie that he hadn't paid attention to. He'd had eyes only for her. Then he'd made her dinner, and they'd snuggled on his sofa. There was kissing, but nothing more. She was the strongest woman he knew—and at the same time, the most fragile.

She was a gift, and he'd take his time showing her how he saw her.

She smiled, a tremulous thing. "Full disclosure, I wished for a dead body or two. All three times."

He smiled. "I know you did. Time to rip off the Band-Aid, Kitty-Cat."

She rose on her tiptoes to kiss his cheek. "I'm ready now. Thank you for always knowing what I need, even when I don't."

She turned to the door, leaving him stunned in the best of ways. Suddenly she was calm, and he was the nervous one.

Not because he thought his parents would be anything but kind to her. They were wonderful people.

But because, like Kit said, this *was* important.

He wanted the people he loved to like each other.

His mother opened the door before they could knock. She had a soft look on her face that could only mean she'd been watching them through the peephole. She'd seen the kisses. And Kit's tears.

Sam hoped Kit didn't figure that out.

Beside him, Kit made a face and gestured to the elevator. "Sorry. I was nervous."

So she knew she'd been seen. *Fantastic.*

"I understand," his mother said, taking Kit's hand. "Betsy warned me that you might be a little nervous."

Kit glanced up at Sam sharply before returning her attention to his mother. "You know my mother?"

Ann Reeves smiled, as if unaware she'd waded into a lake filled with alligators. "Of course. We've been talking for a few months now."

"I . . ." Kit shook her head. "I did not know that."

"Well, you do now." Ann tugged Kit into the living room. "Clearly I did not teach my son manners. I'm Ann, Sam's mom."

Kit smiled at her. "I figured that out. And he has very nice manners, so you shouldn't worry. I'm Kit, but I think you figured that out, too."

"Welcome, Kit. We've been waiting to meet you for a long time."

"Oh." Kit glanced up at Sam again, and he was relieved to see humor dancing in her eyes. "So no pressure."

"None at all," Sam replied.

He followed her into his parents' condo and closed the door, breathing in the aroma of something delicious. Beef stir-fry, maybe. Whatever it was, either his father had made it or they'd ordered in.

He hadn't been kidding when he told Kit that his mother didn't cook. Unlike Kit, who could probably cook if she cared enough to try, his mother continually tried and failed.

His father was coming to his feet, his smile quiet but broad. "I'm Bill," he said to Kit. "I'd hug you, but I hear you're not comfortable with that, so I won't. But know that I would if you'd let me."

Kit chuckled and, squaring her shoulders, held out her arms to his father. "Consider this consent."

His father folded her into his arms and winked at Sam over her head. "See? We can play nice, Sammy." He let Kit go quickly and Kit exhaled. "Thank you," he added quietly. "But you really don't have to be anyone but yourself with us."

"New me," she said. "I'm trying. But since you talk to my mother regularly, you probably know that."

Ann grinned. "Yep. Come, sit down. Let's chat for just a minute. I know you're working on a big case."

Kit sat on the sofa next to his father. "My mother told you?"

"We talked about it," Ann said, taking the chair she always sat in. It was the same brand, model, and color of the chair she had in Scottsdale. His mother knew what she liked. "I called her when I saw it on the news. Internet, you know."

Kit looked at Sam, who'd sat beside her on the sofa. "We made the news?"

He wasn't surprised that she didn't know. She tended not to pay attention to the media unless they could be useful to her on a case. "You got shot, Kit. What did you think would happen?"

"What do they know?" she asked Ann.

His mother began counting on her fingers. "That you were paying a visit to Mary Sherman with your sister Akiko and your 'boyfriend.'" She used air quotes to emphasize the word, looking very pleased. "That you got shot, and then two other detectives were shot and hospitalized, and you got shot at a *second* time. Oh, and that there was a shootout in the street and that both shooters have eluded the SDPD. Is that all, Bill?"

"I'd say you have it covered, dear."

"There was no mention of Akiko's relationship with Mary Sherman?"

Ann shook her head, a flicker of surprise her only outward acknowledgment of Kit's question. "And your mother didn't tell me. I didn't ask, either. I only called to see how she was doing and ask if we could help. It seemed . . . painful for her."

"Oh." Kit looked up at Sam. "My mother's hurting?"

"For Akiko, I think," Sam said. "Not because it involves her bio family."

"The victim was Akiko's biological aunt," Kit explained. "It's been a difficult time, learning about her past. About family she didn't know she had."

Bill patted Kit's shoulder. "And for you, too, I'd imagine. Must be hard to see your sister upset and confused."

Kit smiled at his father. "Sam comes by his empathy honestly." She turned that smile on his mother. "From both of you. Thank you for checking on my mother."

"You're very welcome." Ann took out her phone and began to scroll. "Here's the article, if you— Oh." She frowned. "Here's a new one. I, um, I don't think you're going to like this one. It says you were suspended."

Kit scowled. "I was." She held out her hand. "May I?"

Ann gave it over without a second thought. "I'm sorry that I mentioned it."

"It's true, so don't be. Better to know what's being said, I guess." Kit's scowl deepened when she saw the screen. She tilted it so that Sam could read it.

He put his arm around her shoulders, wanting to punch someone when he saw the byline. "Tamsin Kavanaugh."

Or *Tamsin Fucking Kavanaugh*, as Kit had renamed her. But his mother didn't like it when he swore, so he full-named the reporter only in his mind.

"Of course it'd be her," Kit said quietly.

"Not your favorite reporter, eh?" Bill said.

That was putting it mildly. The reporter had some kind of bone to pick with Kit because she wouldn't give her exclusives. *As if.*

"She's kind of obsessed with me," Kit said. "Sometimes she follows me when she needs a story."

The woman was a menace. "How did she find out you were suspended?" Sam read on and growled. "She cites someone inside the SDPD as her source. Who told her?"

"My bet's on West. He looked very happy when I came out of Navarro's office. Oh, and look. An update to the article. You have a new partner since I've been 'kicked to the curb.' That didn't take her long. She followed us to Leo Sherman's office."

Kavanaugh had posted a photo of Sam opening the door for Detective Lennox as they'd entered the surgeon's office, sounding almost gleeful that Kit had been "kicked to the curb" and wondering if that meant their personal relationship was also "dead on arrival."

"She's exposed Lennox's secret," he said, ignoring Kavanaugh's musings about his and Kit's relationship. "West now knows she went behind his back. I hope that doesn't backfire on her. West could make her life rough."

"West should leave his damn desk," Kit muttered. "At least Lennox has a spine." She read on, her brow creasing in a frown. "Wait. Here's a third article, and it just went up on the newspaper's website." She lurched to her feet, his mother's cell phone still clutched in her hand. "She says that Leo Sherman left his office right after we drove away. That he went straight to a home owned by a Laurette Curry but was turned away at the door by police officers who stated the home was a crime scene. Tamsin F— I mean, Effing Kavanaugh says 'her sources' tell her that it's a murder scene. Who is Laurette Curry?" She returned his mother's phone to her, then pulled her own from her pocket and began furiously typing. "Laurette Curry has a Facebook page—oh, and guess who's in her photos, all cozy over candlelit dinners?"

"Leo Effing Sherman?" Ann asked brightly.

Sam let out a surprised laugh. "Mom."

Kit spared a moment to grin at his mother. "Right in one." Her grin morphed back into a frown. "This is Leo's mistress of the moment. Why is she dead?"

"This is so exciting," Ann said, her hands clasped together.

"Better than TV," Bill agreed. "What are you going to do?"

Sam rose, kissed his mother's cheek, and gave his father a hug. "We're going to Laurette Curry's house."

Kit looked from Sam to his parents uncertainly. "They just got here. Should you stay?"

Sam rolled his eyes. "Like I'm going to let you out of my sight."

She narrowed her eyes. "I don't need a babysitter." Then she shrugged. "But if Lennox is there, you can go into the crime scene with her. Unlike me, since I've been kicked to the curb. So let's go."

Sam chuckled. "I'm so happy to have a use. Mom, Dad, we'll be back as soon as we can. I've got lots of food in my fridge upstairs. Help yourselves."

"We ordered Thai stir-fry," Ann said, walking them to the door. "We're good, son."

"I bought stuff you can just warm up, Mom. Gotta run." Because Kit was already at the elevator, staring at her phone. "Love you."

"Love you, too," Ann called after him. "Nice to finally meet you, Kit!"

Kit looked up and smiled. "Same, ma'am. I won't keep him too long."

Sam hoped she'd keep him forever.

San Diego, California
Tuesday, January 31, 7:00 p.m.

"So what do you know?" Sam asked as they turned onto the street where Laurette Curry owned a single-story rambler. It was a nice neighborhood. Middle-class, tidy.

And nosy. All the neighbors were out on their front lawns, watching the action unfold. The CSU van was parked in front of Curry's house, the street lined with police cars.

The victim's house was completely dark—the power had been turned off, just like at Mary's house. Sam could see flashes of light inside as SDPD moved around with Maglites.

Kit looked up from her phone to glance at the gathering crowd, then refocused on the notes she'd been taking as they drove. "Laurette Curry, white female, thirty-four years old. She's a surgical nurse, works in the hospital where Leo has privileges. Curry was behind on all her credit cards. She paid off her cards in full and caught up with her mortgage in October."

"Lots of stuff happening in October," Sam observed.

"True enough. Total amount she paid to creditors was around fifteen grand."

"I wonder what she did to earn it. Oh." He parked and pointed to a black sedan. "Lennox is here. But not West."

"I'm wondering if he's behaving like this because he's trying to get them to give him a package to retire before his due date. They won't fire him. That's way too much paperwork for only three months."

Sam wondered if West had a more nefarious intent. If he didn't go out to investigate, he knew Kit would. Putting a target on her back. "Nobody's seen the shooter in days. Unless he's been here."

"Let's find out." Kit got out before he could open her door. "Lennox!"

Detective Lennox turned around and frowned. "How did

you know about this? Have you been listening to the police radio?"

"I don't need to." Kit held out her phone. "Tamsin Kavanaugh's already been here."

Lennox shook her head. "Tamsin Fucking Kavanaugh."

Kit's lips twitched. "You've got promise."

Sam looked around, nervous for Kit to be in the open like this. "Where is Leo Sherman?"

"In that cruiser." Lennox pointed at the middle police car in the row. "I'll talk to him when we're done. Detective McKittrick, you should probably wait in the car. Sorry."

"It's okay. Can Sam go in with you?"

"Nobody's told me otherwise. Where's Constantine?"

"He went home," Kit said. "Needed a nap." She handed Sam her Maglite. "You're going to need this inside the house."

"Thank you. How long has the victim been in there?" he asked Lennox.

"Could be as much as a few days, from what I've been told. ME hasn't arrived yet to give us an estimate. The smell isn't too bad, though."

Sam was glad to hear that, because he hated dead-body odor. Not that anyone liked it. He took a handkerchief from his pocket, just in case his definition of "not that bad" differed from Lennox's. He'd started carrying a handkerchief a few weeks before, after walking into a murder scene with Kit and Connor. The victims had been dead for close to a week and he'd nearly vomited right there at the scene. He covered his nose with the handkerchief. "Let's go."

He looked over his shoulder to see Kit getting back into his

RAV4. He hated that she'd been sidelined, but he had no doubt she'd be making good use of her time, digging into Laurette Curry's background, her friends, her hobbies, anything that might provide a link to whoever had killed her.

"She was last seen on Sunday evening when she reported into work," Lennox said, handing him a pair of booties to cover his shoes. He actually carried those in his SUV now, too, but accepted the ones she gave him with a nod of thanks.

"Who called it in?"

"Her neighbor. Her dogs were howling this morning and it appeared that they'd been outside all night. The victim never left her dogs out all night, especially with it being so cold, so they knew something was wrong. The woman knew where the victim kept her extra house key and let herself in. She was shaken and nearly hysterical according to the first responder."

"I understand that. Finding dead bodies is hard."

"I guess you've had some experience with that in recent months." She showed her badge to the first responders, who allowed them to enter Laurette's home, and then aimed her flashlight throughout the room.

The room had been ransacked, just as Ito's had been. Someone had been searching for something and hadn't bothered to cover their tracks.

The beam of Lennox's flashlight halted. "Meet Laurette Curry."

The victim was lying on the living room floor, a bullet hole in her forehead. "Just like Mary Sherman," Sam murmured, putting his handkerchief away. She hadn't been dead long enough to start stinking, at least. "Did he disable her alarm system like he did Mary's?"

"Not sure yet, but given the power's out, that's a good guess. It looks like he missed his first shot. There's a bullet hole in Miss Curry's living room wall, a second in her back, and a third in her brain."

"It makes sense that he shot the wall first. His aim's been off." *Thank God.* Kit might be dead, otherwise.

"I know. The man who shot Mary has received some injuries. Shot in the arm by Alf Ashton on Sunday and in the leg by someone later the same day."

"Bad day for the shooter," Sam said.

Lennox looked amused. "Good day for Riccardo Nicchi, though."

Sam sighed. "Maybe not. I don't know if Nicchi meant to hit him in the leg or not. My best guess is that, based on his marksman skill and the distance from which he was shooting, he hit the shooter where he intended to. But we can't find Nicchi. Have you?"

"Not yet. Navarro put out a BOLO on him after Kit told him that Nicchi was the second shooter. I wish she'd told him sooner. We might have him in custody now. But he's had a lot of time to run."

I wish you and your partner had done your jobs sooner, Sam thought. But Lennox was here now and that was important. So he said nothing at all.

Lennox gave him a sharp look then shrugged. "I know what you're thinking and you're not wrong."

Sam still said nothing. His loyalty lay with Kit, but he appreciated Lennox acknowledging his unspoken point. He turned a slow circle, taking in the living room. Kit would want to know.

"Where's the cat?" he asked, pointing at the cat tree in the corner.

"Shut in the bathroom," one of the first-responding officers said. "But we didn't put it in there."

Sam carefully stepped up to the body, noting the bloody paw prints on the cream-colored carpet in the beam of his borrowed flashlight. "The cat was out when she was killed. Someone stashed it in the bathroom afterward."

"Yep," Lennox said. "I wonder who put the dogs out, the victim or her killer?"

"Camera footage?" Sam asked.

Sergeant Ryland came into the living room from the kitchen. "She didn't have a security system, but I counted three Ring cameras as I drove up the street. We'll ask for their footage. We'll also examine the cat for trace evidence. If her killer picked up the animal to put it in the bathroom, there may be something in the fur."

Lennox turned back to the body. "He shot her in the back then rolled her over to shoot her in the head."

"The ME will dig the bullets out of the victim. Then we can run ballistics, depending on the condition of the bullets. We'll compare to the bullets that killed Mary Sherman and the ones that hit Kit, Ashton, and Marshall. I'll let you know as soon as I hear something."

"Did he leave anything obvious behind?" Lennox asked.

"Nothing that jumps out and says, 'Hey, I'm the killer,'" Ryland deadpanned. "We'll let you know, Detective. You should take a look at her bedroom, though. It's . . . a sight."

Sam followed Lennox into the victim's bedroom. And stopped short as Lennox's flashlight illuminated the wall.

"Holy shit," he breathed, horrified.

"Yeah," Lennox agreed, sounding as stunned as he felt.

Because covering part of a wall were six photos of Akiko McKittrick. Six distinct poses and backgrounds.

"What the hell?" he whispered.

"Someone needs to warn Kit, so she can warn Akiko," Ryland said from behind them.

Sam nodded. "I will. And the McKittricks have protection there at the hospital in LA." Because Akiko refused to leave Edwin Ito. "Just . . . how?"

"And why?" Lennox added. "Why would Leo Sherman's mistress have all these photos of Akiko?"

"All of the photos were taken on Akiko's boat," Sam said, recognizing the background details. "Two of them were taken recently. Kit gave her that coat for Christmas."

"Good to know." Lennox's expression was grim. "Any other rooms have photos like this?"

"No," Ryland said. "Only this one. We'll go over every square inch. Make sure Kit knows that, too."

Sam gave Ryland a tight smile. "She knows you'll do everything you can and she appreciates it. I promise."

Ryland nodded. "I went on Akiko's boat once. It was a department party. She's a nice woman. I hate that this is happening to her."

"Me too," Sam said softly, his gut churning. "Someone who went on Akiko's boat took these photos. You should get her charter records, Detective Lennox. Check out everyone who's sailed with her."

"Already planned to. Sergeant Ryland, can you walk me through the crime scene?"

Ryland looked surprised, but he agreed and the two of them walked from the room, leaving Sam alone. Alone with all the photos of Akiko, which Kit would want to see.

Sam huffed a laugh. Lennox was giving him the time and space to record the scene for Kit. As he used his cell phone to photograph the walls, he decided that he liked the woman.

He almost dropped his phone when it buzzed in his hands.

Oh. It was Ricky Nicchi. "Hey."

"You gotta come," Nicchi said, and his voice sounded thick. He was crying.

"What's wrong?"

"It's Paolo. I f-f-found him. Please come."

Sam looked over his shoulder. He was alone. "Is he alive?"

Nicchi's voice broke on a sob. "No. Hurry."

Shit, shit, shit. First these photos of Akiko on her boat, and now Paolo? *Shit.*

He needed to tell Lennox. But he found himself reluctant to do so. He wanted a moment alone with Nicchi because he wanted answers that he might not get if the man was hauled away by SDPD before he could get there. "Text me the address. I'm on my way." Sam rushed to the living room, waving at the others. "I need to go. Call me if you need me, okay? Thank you."

Ryland and Lennox waved back, and Sam gathered his composure before leaving the house. If Tamsin Fucking Kavanaugh was still out there watching, he didn't want to give her any more fodder for her newspaper.

He had his hand on the doorknob when his phone buzzed again. It was Kit. "I'm on my way out," he said when he answered.

"Good. Baz called. He was supposed to be resting, but he

went to sit in front of Paolo's house, waiting for him to come home. Instead, Nicchi went inside."

"I'll be out in a minute." He ended the call, drew a deep breath, then calmly walked to his RAV4, saying nothing to Kit until he was in the driver's seat with the door locked. "Don't say a word."

He started the engine, drove out of Laurette Curry's neighborhood, then pulled into the first gas station he came to. Kit had been watching him, her gaze sharp, but she'd said nothing.

Sam exhaled. "I didn't know if Kavanaugh was still around and what kind of listening device she might have. We need to talk."

"We need to get to Paolo's house. Nicchi is there."

"Paolo's dead. Nicchi called me."

Kit sucked in a breath. "Goddammit."

"That's not all." He checked for Nicchi's text, memorizing the address. He knew about where it was, so he could start driving while Kit processed what he was about to show her. He handed Kit his phone. "This is the dead woman's bedroom."

Kit's gasp filled the quiet of his SUV as all the color drained from her face. "What the fuck? Sam?"

"I know."

Kit was staring in horror at his phone, just as he'd known she would. "Why?"

"We'll find out. Lennox knows to check Akiko's passenger lists since Christmas." He put the SUV in gear and headed toward Paolo's address.

"Christmas?" Kit sounded detached. Numb.

"The coat she's wearing," he said gently. "You want me to call your father?"

"Yes," she whispered. "Please."

Sam pushed the button for his hands-free to place the call to Harlan McKittrick, then abruptly changed his mind and dialed Baz. "It's Sam. You're at Paolo's?"

"Yeah," Baz said. "Nicchi showed up here about five minutes ago. I should call it in since there's a BOLO for him, but I wanted to give you two a moment to talk to him first."

"He called me. Paolo's dead. We're on our way." Sam ended the call and dialed Harlan. "Hey. It's Sam."

CHAPTER FOURTEEN

San Diego, California
Tuesday, January 31, 7:40 p.m.

Baz was waiting for them outside Paolo's house.

"Nicchi's inside," he said. "This isn't good, guys."

It was a nice place, nicer than the house Akiko owned, and Kit wondered how Paolo afforded it. Maybe he couldn't. Maybe that was why he wanted to run his own charters in addition to being Akiko's first mate.

Kit couldn't put aside the image of Akiko's photos on a dead woman's bedroom wall. *What the hell is going on?*

Focus. "Didn't think it would be good," she murmured. "Paolo being dead and all."

Baz frowned at her, his concern obvious. "We're going to figure this out. In the meantime, Akiko will have twenty-four-hour protection. Right, Sam?"

"Yes. I talked to Harlan, and Anson's assigned some of his

employees to accompany them everywhere. He doesn't run a bodyguard company like Nicchi does, but most of his guys are former law enforcement or military or both." He cupped Kit's face in both hands. "Harlan and Akiko are safe."

"I know." She leaned into his touch, his hands warm. He'd made sure that Harlan was aware of the newest threat to Akiko, and then he'd called Baz to update him as well.

Sam had been thorough and authoritative. *And here.* Above everything else, he was here, at her side. She rested her forehead on his chest. He wasn't big and brawny like Ricky Nicchi, but she felt far safer with Sam Reeves than she'd felt with any other man.

Maybe even her father. That was a startling thought. When had Sam become so completely . . . everything?

"Thank you," she whispered. "For not leaving me."

"Never," he whispered back. "I told you, you're stuck with me. Now, we need to go inside. I don't like you being out here in the open. Let's go check on Nicchi."

"I haven't been inside yet," Baz said as he led them up Paolo's sidewalk. "I don't want to call this in until you've had a chance to talk to Nicchi, so me staying outside means I have plausible deniability." He rapped on the door, then pushed the door open when Nicchi didn't answer. "Nicchi? It's Constantine, McKittrick, and Reeves."

"Come." The word was rough and broken and Kit's heart hurt.

Riccardo Nicchi might have been a tough guy, but his heart was breaking, and Kit knew what that felt like. She knew the pain of losing a sibling to murder.

"Ricky?" she called softly. "Where are you?"

"Kitchen."

She walked carefully through the house, noticing the mess. Everything was upended, drawers emptied, sofa cushions sliced to shreds.

Just like in Ito's condo and in Mary's house, someone had been looking for something.

She wondered if they'd found it.

Nicchi was sitting at the kitchen table, his face in his hands. Kit touched his shoulder gently. Briefly. "I'm sorry, Ricky."

Nicchi nodded. "He's in the pantry."

Kit pulled on a pair of gloves and opened the pantry door. And grimaced.

"Oh, Paolo," she whispered. *What did they do to you?*

Paolo had been beaten severely. If she hadn't known him for years, she might not have recognized his face. That probably hadn't killed him, though.

The cause of death was most likely the bullet hole in his forehead. Just like with Mary Sherman. And Laurette Curry.

But the beating was more reminiscent of Edwin Ito. She backed out of the pantry and closed the door. "We need to call this in, Ricky."

"I know."

Sam had a hand on his shoulder and Baz was standing at the back door, staring out into the backyard.

"Kit," Baz said. "Come here."

She did, taking her place at his side. "What?"

"That shed out there. The door's been forced open."

"It's empty," Nicchi said dully. "I already checked. Smells like gun oil."

"Did Paolo own a gun?" Kit asked.

"Of course he did. Carried it, too. Every time he went out with your sister on a charter. She never knew."

Kit sighed. "He was protecting her."

"Yeah."

She moved to the table, leaning her hip against it. "What was someone looking for in his living room?"

Nicchi shook his head. "I don't know."

"You think he got mixed up in something?" Sam asked her.

"Yeah. And that he wanted to do night runs on Akiko's boat doesn't bode well."

"I didn't know about the night runs," Nicchi said. "Not until your sister mentioned it at the hospital, early this morning."

"We need to call this in, but before we do, I need some answers, Ricky. Your brother is dead, and so is Leo Sherman's mistress."

Nicchi closed his eyes. "Why?"

"I don't know," Kit said. "But in her bedroom were photos of Akiko, tacked to the wall."

Nicchi's eyes opened and they were filled with quiet fear. "Why?"

"Don't know. But we do know that there was a third man in your little meeting with Mary Sherman. Who was he?"

Shock flickered in Nicchi's dark eyes before they went expressionless and cold. "I don't know what you're talking about."

His mouth tightening into a grim line, Sam dropped his hand from Nicchi's shoulder. "Liar," he said quietly.

"I don't know," Nicchi repeated. "Call me a liar all you want, but I do not know."

Kit's temper snapped. "Listen, you sonofabitch. You *do* know and you *will* tell me."

Nicchi's eyes narrowed. "Or what, Detective? Can I still call you that? Seeing as how you're suspended?"

Kit wanted to hurt him. Wanted to claw his eyes out. But then she stopped herself.

That's what he wants. He wanted her to lose her temper. Because Nicchi was very good at distraction and redirection. So she drew a breath, took out her phone, and dialed Meghan Lennox.

"We have another body," Kit said when the woman picked up. "Paolo Feliciano. He's Riccardo Nicchi's brother."

"What?" Lennox demanded. "How did he die?"

"Bullet to the head after he was beaten severely."

Nicchi made a wounded noise. Kit had to steel herself to continue, because the part of her that still mourned Wren wanted to comfort him.

"Someone was searching for something," she added. "Nicchi claims not to know what that was."

"I don't," Nicchi said between clenched teeth.

"He *also* says he doesn't know the third man who was with Mary Sherman, so I don't believe anything he says."

Rage transformed Nicchi's face and Kit felt a moment of true fear. She was armed, but he was huge.

"Don't even think about it," Baz said quietly. He'd pressed the muzzle of his gun to the back of Nicchi's head. "I will blow your fucking head off if you lift one single finger to hurt her."

Sam took a few steps back, whirling to face the front door. "Someone's—"

The door opened and a man Kit had never seen sauntered in like he owned the place. He held a badge in one hand and a gun in the other.

"Special Agent Brewer, ATF," he announced. "Stand down, Constantine."

Baz didn't move a muscle. "Get his badge number and call him in to Navarro," he told Kit. "I'm not letting Nicchi go until I know this guy is legit."

"I want to see a warrant," Kit said, then snatched it from the special agent's hand when he produced it.

"McKittrick?" Lennox demanded and Kit startled. She'd forgotten she was on the phone. "Kit? Are you okay?"

"I am. But we have a new wrinkle. A guy claiming to be ATF just showed up. He's got a warrant. It looks official."

Lennox whistled. "Wow. You don't do things halfway, do you?"

Kit had the absurd urge to laugh. "I guess not."

"Who is that?" Brewer asked with a frown.

"Detective Lennox, SDPD," Kit said. "She's primary on this case."

"I thought Alan West was primary," Brewer said.

"He's my partner," Lennox said. "Why would you know that?"

Brewer pursed his lips.

"He's not going to tell us," Kit told Lennox. "I'm going to keep you on the line, on speaker, so you can bear witness. And then I'm going to use Sam's phone to call Navarro."

Sam held out his phone. He'd already dialed Navarro's number and had it on speaker.

"Dr. Reeves," Navarro said. "Why are you calling me?"

Kit sighed. "He's with me and Baz."

Navarro sighed as well. "Of course he is. Why are you calling me, McKittrick? You're on suspension."

"I am aware." *And I'll be on double-triple suspension after this.* "Long story short, Paolo Feliciano is dead, we're here in his house with Ricky Nicchi who claims not to know who the third man with Mary Sherman was, and now we have some guy named Brewer who claims to be ATF. He just arrived, he has a gun, and he's telling us to stand down."

"Don't move," Navarro growled. "Do not move a fucking muscle. One of you assholes text me the address and the ATF agent's badge number. I'm on my way."

"I've already called Lennox," Kit said. "She's on her way as well."

"Then we'll have a fucking party," Navarro said sarcastically and ended the call.

"Your life is so much fun," Lennox said through the speaker. "What's your badge number, Special Agent Brewer?"

Brewer hadn't lowered his gun. He recited his badge number and Kit noted it in her phone.

"I'll have him checked out on my way over there," Lennox said. "Just . . . sit tight."

Kit rolled her eyes. "We're not going anywhere, right, Nicchi?"

Nicchi closed his eyes again and clenched his massive fists on the tabletop. "Why are you here, Special Agent Brewer?"

"Looking for Paolo, but I understand I'm too late."

"Fuck off," Nicchi snarled.

"Temper, temper," Brewer said. "Your brother was smuggling guns on that boat he works on. Or he was attempting to. He made a run last night, but no guns changed hands."

Kit managed not to visibly react, but her gut was suddenly churning. *Paolo was using Akiko's boat to smuggle guns?* He'd dragged Akiko into his mess, and now he was dead for his trouble. He'd put Akiko in danger. *Sonofabitch.*

"I think the guns are gone," Kit said calmly. "Nicchi here says the shed smells like gun oil, but it's empty."

The so-called agent swore softly.

Kit studied him. "Why are you here *now*, Special Agent Brewer? Why today?"

Brewer shook his head. "Need-to-know, Detective."

Kit wanted to hit him, too. "For fuck's sake," she muttered. "Can you tell me if he used my sister's boat to successfully smuggle guns at any time?"

"We don't believe so."

"At least there's that. Is my sister safe?"

"Yes. We've got an agent watching her at the hospital in LA."

"Why?" Kit demanded.

"We wanted to see if anyone involved approached her."

Kit frowned down at Nicchi. "Is that what you're hiding? The identity of a weapons smuggler?"

Nicchi shook his head, looking as exhausted as Kit felt. "No."

"But you're not surprised," Sam noted.

Nicchi tensed. And said nothing. Which was answer enough.

Baz's gun remained pressed to the back of Nicchi's head. "I'm really starting to hate this guy," he muttered.

"Join the club," Kit said.

"I'm not trying to hurt your sister," Nicchi said stonily.

"Well, you're not trying to help her," Kit snapped.

"Children, children," Brewer cautioned.

Kit glared at the special agent. "You're not on my happy list, either."

"Don't care," Brewer drawled. "Just here to do my job."

"So am I," Lennox said from the speaker, startling Kit yet again. "Sorry, guys, I muted myself while I checked into Brewer. His badge number is legit and I'm texting you a photo of his face so you can be sure."

"Thank you," Kit said. "I appreciate it."

"No problem," Lennox said. "Is he the guy you're talking to?"

Kit looked at the photo attached to Lennox's incoming text, then held her phone up to Brewer's face. He smiled sweetly. Almost mockingly.

Kit rolled her eyes. She did not have the patience for an interagency pissing match. "It's him. You can put your gun away, Baz."

Baz lowered his gun but deliberately did not reholster it, and Kit loved him for that.

Sam was watching Brewer, who still had his gun trained on them. "You said you were looking for Paolo?"

"Not anymore. I heard you all say that he was dead when you were standing outside."

Kit winced. They shouldn't have been discussing a dead body out in front of Paolo's house. "We are clearly not at the top of our game."

Brewer looked mildly sympathetic. He would have looked more sympathetic were he not still holding a gun on them. "I've heard. Getting shot at will do that to you. Been there myself."

"Why are you still holding a gun on us?" she asked.

"I don't want anyone to make any sudden moves. Especially not Nicchi here, since he's wanted for a shooting."

Nicchi lifted his head to stare at Kit. "You don't have a shred of evidence to prove that."

"No, we don't," Kit agreed. "But no one has searched your house yet. That M40 you used on the shooter isn't available just anywhere. I kind of doubt you just threw it away. When Lennox gets here, she'll arrest you and you can call an attorney. You know the drill, Ricky." She turned back to Brewer. "But why are you holding a gun on *us*?" She gestured to Sam, Baz, and herself.

"Because you're rogue, McKittrick, and unpredictable. I don't want you touching any evidence. My partner's on his way. We'll take over this crime scene."

"My boss is also on his way," Lennox said. "You all can duel at dawn over the crime scene. Please don't let him touch anything, Kit. Not until we get there."

"I'm not sure we can stop him," Kit said, feeling helpless.

"You can't," Brewer said, rather smugly.

She started to say something snarky when Sam spoke in that calm voice that grounded her.

"If you knew that Paolo was trying to smuggle guns last night," he said, "why didn't you arrest him then? I assume you knew he had the guns on Akiko's boat. Why let him get away?"

Brewer frowned. "He gave us the slip."

"He was right here in his house. You had to have checked." Sam's tone was reasonable and calm, but Kit knew him well enough to know he was going somewhere with his line of questioning. "You might even have been listening in on his phone calls. If you knew he possessed illegal guns, you had enough for a phone tap warrant."

"We did check," Brewer claimed. "He was alive this morning."

"Why didn't you come here earlier?" Sam asked.

"Yeah," Nicchi said bitterly. "Like *before* he was murdered?"

Brewer seemed genuinely regretful. "I wish I had."

Probably because he'd just lost a suspect.

Oh. Now she understood where Sam was going.

"You were using Paolo as *bait*," Sam said. "I imagine Paolo tried to contact the person who stood him up for the transfer last night. Am I close so far?"

Brewer said nothing.

Sam nodded. "I *am* close. Maybe his customer arranged a meeting—a time and place. You wanted the big fish, so you staked out the meeting place. Paolo never showed because he was already dead. His partner also didn't show up because he—or she—had already killed Paolo and taken the guns from his shed."

Brewer shrugged, appearing to be reluctantly impressed. "I can't say."

Kit didn't mind showing that she was impressed. "You're right, Sam." And how sexy was that? A nerdy guy in Clark Kent glasses who had a wonderful, gorgeous brain. "And now I'm wondering who Paolo was working with and how they connect to the deaths of Mary Sherman and Laurette Curry."

Who had photos of Akiko on her bedroom wall.

"Which," Lennox said, "is why we're going to let Navarro and the brass duke it out with these guys. If the ATF knows who we're looking for, I'd hope they'd extend professional courtesy and give us a heads-up."

Brewer smirked.

Kit had to take another breath. She was tired. Her temper was frayed. And she still had to tell her sister that Paolo was dead.

"This isn't funny, Special Agent Brewer," she said quietly. "My sister's life is in danger. *My* life is in danger. Paolo is dead and his brother is sitting here grieving. Have a little fucking respect."

Brewer nodded, contrite. "I'm sorry, Detective. You're right. Let's wait for your lieutenant and we'll figure this out."

"Thank you." She looked around at the mess in the kitchen and had an awful thought.

What if Akiko's house was in a similar state because Paolo had used her boat to smuggle guns? Had Paolo's contact tossed Akiko's house, too? What if she'd been home? Would she be dead like Paolo?

Did the Feds suspect Akiko of being involved? Brewer said they had someone "watching" Akiko at the hospital.

Protecting her, my ass.

Kit really was off her game. Those should have been her first concerns.

She wanted to demand answers from Brewer but held her tongue. If they didn't suspect Akiko, she wasn't going to put the idea out there. But the Feds would have been foolish not to.

Goddammit, Paolo. What have you done?

San Diego, California
Tuesday, January 31, 9:45 p.m.

"Oh no." Kit stood in Akiko's living room, surveying the damage. Her sister's tidy house was trashed, just like Paolo's had been.

"Poor Akiko," Sam murmured. "This is a huge cleanup job."

"What were they looking for?" Lennox asked. She'd come with them after Navarro had arrived at Paolo's house. Or, perhaps more correctly, she'd allowed Kit and Sam to come with her. "I mean, I don't expect you to know. I'm just thinking out loud."

Kit sighed. "I know." Lennox had been incredibly helpful, at considerable risk to her own career. "You know you could get dinged for being here with me."

"I don't think so." She moved closer to Kit and lowered her voice. "Navarro and I had a talk. He says I should consider you my mentor for the time being."

Kit blinked at her. "For real?"

Lennox nodded, her black bob swaying around her heart-shaped face. "For real. I don't think you should worry, Kit. Some things are just . . . theater."

"A suspension is not theater," she muttered.

"I agree. It shouldn't be, anyway." Lennox crouched and pushed at a small figurine on the floor with one finger. "Nice carving."

"My father made it for her." Several of Akiko's figurines had been tossed to the floor. It took all Kit had not to sweep them up protectively. But this was evidence, so she left them alone.

"I've heard about his carvings." Lennox stood, looking a little embarrassed. "Actually, I bought one of his carvings at a charity auction a few months ago. I didn't know who the artist was until I'd brought it home. It was going to be a gift for my mother, but once I found out it was a Harlan McKittrick original, I kept it and got my mother something else."

Lennox was much nicer than Kit had anticipated. "What was it that my pop carved?"

Lennox dug in her pocket and pulled out an intricately carved violin. "I played as a kid and my mother still plays. I carry this one for luck."

Kit pulled her own good-luck charm from her pocket. It was a cat with a bird perched on its head, carved by Harlan. *Kit and Wren.* "So do I." Then she felt sick. "Do you think they've broken into my place, too? Taken my other carvings?"

She rarely slept in her boat, which she rented from one of her foster brothers. She'd been staying most nights at McKittrick House for weeks now. But the boat was where she kept her belongings.

She had sixteen small carved wrens on a shelf in her bedroom, gifts from her father. He gave her one every year to remember Wren. Rage mixed with her panic. If someone had damaged her birds . . .

"We'll go there as soon as we're finished here," Lennox promised.

Kit felt too young all of a sudden. Young and scared and vulnerable and she didn't like it.

"You've got good security at the marina, Kit," Sam said calmly. "And that guy who docks next to you is so nosy, I'm sure he'd have noticed someone lurking around. But I've just texted Baz and asked him to drive to the marina and stand guard at your place until we get there."

Baz had stayed behind at Paolo's house, acting as Kit's eyes. Navarro wouldn't allow Kit to stay but tolerated Baz's presence.

"Where is Akiko's security system?" Sam added. "Can we view the footage?"

He was redirecting her anxiety in a way that didn't embarrass her. *He's too good to me.* "It's all online. Akiko should have gotten an alert on her phone that someone had broken in, but she didn't. She would have called me if she had."

She hadn't broken the news of Paolo's death to her sister yet. She was dreading that notification. Akiko and Paolo had been friends since they were children in Ito's San Diego dojo.

"Someone knew how to disable it, then." Lennox went to the kitchen, carefully stepping around broken crockery. "The power is on, but they might have turned it off."

"She has a backup battery," Kit said, following Lennox. "The alarm still should have gone off. Or at least she should have been notified of a power outage."

"You should ask her if she got a notification of a power outage," Sam said. "She might not have paid attention to it since she's been so worried about Ito."

Lennox opened the refrigerator door and touched a carton of orange juice. "It's warm. The power's on now, but it was off. And I'd say it was off for a while. How long has your sister been gone?"

"About twenty-four hours." Kit glanced at Sam. "Right?"

"At least," Sam said. "She was out on a charter yesterday and you got in touch with her about Ito when it had just ended. If she came straight from the marina and hasn't been home since early yesterday morning, that's more than thirty-six hours. But even if she came back here before heading to LA, it's been twenty-seven hours. Long enough that everything in her fridge would be warm."

"Long enough for the battery backup to go dead," Lennox added.

Kit's thoughts were scattered. "That indicates that someone planned this, though. If they didn't set off her alarm—and I'll need to call her to find out if that's true—they purposefully cut off her power and came back when the system was completely dead."

Sam gently gripped the back of her neck, anchoring her. "That makes sense. Especially if they knew she'd gone to LA."

"Can you tell what might be missing here?" Lennox asked. "Knowing what was taken would be helpful."

"I can try. It's hard to tell with such a mess." Which was part of the intruder's strategy. It was hard to determine the intended goal of a robbery until the scene was reorganized.

She walked through each room, her heart sinking at the level of destruction. Walls were damaged, Akiko's bed slashed, the clothing in her closet tossed to the floor.

"There." Kit pointed to the desk in Akiko's home office. "Her laptop is gone, and the contents of her filing cabinet are gone."

"Could she have taken the laptop with her to LA?" Lennox asked.

"Possibly, but I don't remember seeing it. She keeps the current quarter's documents in the filing cabinet. She's really good about staying on top of her filing. Akiko is very organized." Kit opened the closet in the office. More boxes were gone, but not all. "They took the boxes for this month and for the fourth quarter of last year, but no others."

"That would include October," Sam noted.

"What kind of records does she keep?" Lennox asked. "Passenger manifests? Like, maybe the name of someone who was on her boat recently and took photos to hang on Laurette Curry's wall?"

Kit nodded. "The passenger lists are saved to her laptop,

because they're generated by her website. The papers are receipts for business expenses, and the liability forms the passengers have to sign before they can go on the boat."

"So," Sam said slowly, "the name, address, and signature of everyone who was on her boat from October first until this weekend were taken."

"Keeping us from following up on who posted those photos on Curry's wall," Lennox said grimly.

Kit frowned. "That doesn't make sense, though. Whoever killed Curry should have taken those photos down. They had to know that we'd investigate Akiko's passengers since those photos were taken on the boat."

"You're assuming they went to Curry's bedroom," Lennox said. "I know that whoever was in Mary Sherman's house searched it thoroughly, but that doesn't mean they did the same at Curry's house. Maybe they killed her and ran."

"Maybe." But it still bothered Kit because it did not make sense.

They left the office for Akiko's spare bedroom. "I sleep here when I stay over," Kit said, then pointed to the wall opposite the bed, her jaw clenching. It was conspicuously empty. "Her bo staff is missing."

"Her bo staff?" Lennox asked. "Like a long stick?"

"Yeah." Kit took out her phone and found a photo of Akiko with the staff. "It looks like this. She won several martial arts competitions with the staff. It's important to her. I'll send this photo to you."

Lennox took out her own phone, inspected the photo, then sent a text. "I asked Ryland to look for it at Paolo's house."

Kit grimaced, dismayed by both Lennox's implication and

that the other detective was thinking more clearly than she was. *Cut yourself some slack. It's been a crazy few days.* "You think that's what they beat him with?"

"Anything's possible," Lennox said. "But I sure hope not, for your sister's sake."

They checked each remaining room, returning to the kitchen. "I don't know what's missing here. Akiko has a lot of cooking stuff. Sam? Can you see what might be missing?"

Sam pointed at the counter. "One of the slots in her knife block is empty." He opened the door to Akiko's garage and abruptly tensed. "Kit?"

She hurried over to see what was wrong and immediately understood.

Six wooden crates filled the space usually taken up by Akiko's Subaru.

"That can't be good," Kit muttered.

"Probably not," Sam agreed. He stepped by to let Lennox pass.

The detective walked around the crates, examining the exteriors. "They're all empty. The lids have been pried off. Probably using Akiko's missing knife." She leaned in to sniff them. "Gun oil," she said. "These crates may have held Paolo's guns."

CHAPTER FIFTEEN

Carmel Valley, San Diego, California
Tuesday, January 31, 11:05 p.m.

It's a freaking party," Kit murmured as she and Sam walked through the door of McKittrick House.

"Sounds like," Sam said, putting his arm around her shoulders. Six months ago, she would have shrugged him off. Now she realized how much she needed his touch. He grounded her in ways she hadn't known she needed.

"Hey, sweetheart." Betsy met them in the living room, opening her arms to Kit, who walked into them, but not before leaning up to kiss Sam's cheek. He liked it when she did that.

She liked to make him happy.

She rested her head on her mother's shoulder. "Did you talk to Akiko?"

"Not yet," Betsy said, rocking Kit where they stood. "I tried, but your father said she'd fallen asleep. That she'd cried herself to sleep."

Kit's throat thickened, her eyes stinging at the memory of Akiko's sobs. Akiko and Harlan had retreated to a private waiting room at the hospital where Ito remained unconscious, and it was there that Kit had told her Paolo was dead over a damn FaceTime call.

"Dammit, Mom. I hated making that call."

"I know, Kitty-Cat. But I know you told her with all the compassion and love in your heart."

Kit had. But that hadn't made it easier to tell her sister that Paolo had been murdered. Lennox had offered to do it, but Kit had needed to tell Akiko herself. "Notifications are always hard. But with someone you love . . . Mom, she wanted to do the ID. To be sure it was Paolo who was killed. I kept telling her that we were sure, but she didn't want to believe me."

"Denial is a real thing," Sam said from behind her. He stroked a hand over her hair. "You handled it just right. Gave her the facts. But you did it with love, Kit."

Kit sighed, pulling from her mother's embrace. "I had to tell her that Nicchi ID'd him through the tattoos on his arm. That his face had been beaten. That she shouldn't see him like that."

Betsy cupped Kit's face in her hands, her touch tender. "We'll be there for her in the next few days. We'll all hold each other up. It's what we do."

It was. And it sounded like a large group had gathered to lend their support. "Who's here?"

"Sam's parents. All the girls. I'm keeping them home from school until this is over, so they begged to stay up late." Her eyes twinkled. "And Georgia and Eloise. I thought Sam's folks would want to meet them."

"You think of everything, Betsy," Sam said. "Thank you."

"Is Anson here?" Kit asked. She hadn't seen him in months. "His Subaru's outside."

"He's out in the barn, tinkering with the security system." Betsy pointed to the box under Sam's arm. "What's in there?"

"My figurines," Kit said. "We went to the boat to get them." They were the only thing of any real value that she owned. "I didn't want to risk someone breaking in and destroying them."

"Give me the box and I'll put it in your room. Go and get some food. Is Baz coming?"

"I finally got him to go home for some sleep."

"That man needs to take better care of himself," Betsy said. "Sam, your mother's been waiting for you."

"How did she know I was coming here?" he asked.

"She didn't," Betsy said. "But you've ended up here most nights for the past few weeks. Plus, we invited your parents a week ago, as soon as your mom said they were coming."

That Betsy McKittrick and Ann Reeves were becoming friends made Kit a little nervous. If she and Sam didn't work out . . . But that was borrowing trouble, and she'd made a resolution not to do that.

Kit was determined to make it work with him. Whatever that meant.

In the meantime, his mother being friends with hers was a good thing. Betsy deserved friendships with women her own age. She gave everything to the kids who lived here. She needed something of her own.

They were greeted by smiles and hellos from the crowd at

the table. Sam kissed his mother's cheek and hugged his father. Kit was less demonstrative, but she tried to be friendly.

It was hard. She could still hear Akiko's sobs.

Georgia patted the empty chair next to her while Sam sat next to Miss Eloise. The two octogenarians were among Kit's favorite people. She'd met them on a case the previous autumn and they'd become regulars around the McKittricks' table.

"You okay?" Georgia asked quietly. She was a grumpy woman, but that was mostly exterior. Inside she was a marshmallow. She had a quick, biting wit and was one of the most intelligent women Kit had ever met.

One of the things Kit liked about Georgia was that she could be honest with her. She didn't have to put on a brave face. "Not really. You heard the news?"

"That Akiko's friend was murdered? Yes. Your mother told us. I'm so sorry."

"Me too. First Akiko's sensei was beaten and now her friend is dead. She's heartbroken."

"So you are, too. You'd rather be shot at than see her hurting."

Kit smiled at the older woman. "You know me pretty well."

"I *was* you, once upon a time. Not a glamorous detective, mind you. But I was prickly, and people thought I didn't care. I did, of course. I cared a lot. It was just hard to say the words."

"I get you, Miss Georgia. I . . ." She swallowed. "Feelings are hard for me."

"I know. But you're doing really well." Georgia took the filled plate that one of the teenagers had passed down the table and set it in front of Kit. "Eat. We're all finished."

"We've even had dessert," Rita said, "but we can always have more with you." She'd become the de facto leader of the teenagers, having been at McKittrick House the longest. "Miss Eloise made brownies."

Kit choked on the bite of food she'd just taken, and Georgia had to pound her back. "Brownies?" she asked when she could speak. "Miss Eloise made them?"

Eloise fluffed her blue hair. She was an outrageous lady, a peacock among sparrows. "I did indeed. Is there a problem, Detective?"

Kit opened her mouth, then closed it. If they were Miss Eloise's "special" brownies, there would be a lot of problems. Not the least of which would be drug use among minors.

Sam took a brownie and sniffed it. "No hash?"

Eloise frowned. "I would never bring my special brownies here. Not to children. Who do you think I am, Sam Reeves?"

"My favorite baker," Sam said with a relieved smile.

"Oh." Ann pouted. "I wanted to try those."

Eloise patted her hand. "I have some in my purse. I'll fix you up."

"Miss Eloise," Sam groaned.

"She's of age, Sammy," Eloise said tartly. "Stop harshing her vibe."

Kit laughed. "I'm so glad you came tonight, Miss Eloise. I needed to laugh."

Eloise's expression softened. "Everyone at Shady Oaks asked me to send you their best regards."

"Tell them thank you and that I'm mending well."

"How is your sister's grandfather?" Bill asked.

"Not great," Kit said. "He's come around twice but mumbled incoherently and drifted right back out. I hope she gets some time with him."

"To have known him all these years," Ann said sadly, "and just now find out that he's her grandfather. She must feel betrayed."

"She does. He said it was because she was in danger. We're wondering if the trouble with Paolo is connected. It's hard to imagine that it's not."

"He was smuggling guns—is that like organized crime, Kit?"

The question came from Dawn, one of the new girls. The girl who tended to see things other people didn't see.

"Yes, Dawn. Why?"

Sam held up a hand. "Wait. How did you know about the smuggling?" he asked, because they hadn't shared that with anyone.

Dawn hesitated.

Rita sighed. "It was online. Tamsin Effing Kavanaugh."

"Rita," Betsy admonished.

"I calls 'em like I sees 'em, Mom. In this house, that's her name."

"You know it's true, Mom," Tiffany said. "That woman has it in for Kit."

Kit immediately checked her phone. There was the story about Paolo's murder, including the gun smuggling. It even mentioned Akiko and her boat by name.

Kit could feel her rage building and had to take some deep breaths. "I may need to start following her. She's getting scoops almost faster than we are."

Sam made a face. "I don't think you should get that close to her. For her safety."

"Damn straight," Kit muttered, then remembered Dawn's question. "Why did you ask about smuggling, Dawn?"

"Mom said that Akiko's grandfather knew Paolo and his brother. From when they were little kids?"

"Yes. Why?" But connections were starting to fire in Kit's tired brain. *Finally.* "Are you asking if Akiko's sensei is connected to the mob?"

And maybe Paolo worked for him. She hadn't considered it, but it was possible. Especially with how close-lipped Nicchi was being. Maybe he was part of the smuggling operation, too.

Dawn looked at her plate. "Sorry. I shouldn't have said anything." She folded in on herself. "I'm sorry."

The room grew silent, waiting for Kit's reply.

Kit got up and crouched next to Dawn's chair. "Hey. Look at me." She waited until Dawn did so, her heart hurting at both the fear and the tears in the teenager's eyes. Dawn was a tough kid. She didn't cry. She reminded Kit of herself. "You're not in trouble, Dawn. And nobody's going to ask you to leave for asking a question or for speaking your mind."

Dawn's lips trembled. "I shouldn't have said that. Not about Akiko's grandfather."

"I think you should have. I hadn't thought of it until you said something, but it's a darn good question and you are a *smart girl*. Tell me that you believe me. That you're smart and that nobody's gonna ask you to leave."

Dawn blinked, then hastily wiped the tears from her face. "I thought you'd be mad."

"Because you wondered if Akiko's grandfather might be involved in something illegal? Dawn, it's a question I should have asked already."

"Me too," Sam said. "I think Kit and I are both too close."

Kit took Dawn's hand. "You are *safe* here. You are *loved* here. And unless you are a gun smuggler yourself or you hurt someone under this roof, you're stuck here until you're eighteen. Got it?"

Dawn tried to smile. "Yeah."

"And even after you're eighteen," Betsy said. "You must have noticed that we can't get rid of Kit and Akiko. They're always here. And Pop and I love it that way."

Dawn's smile grew stronger. "I have noticed that you're a real loiterer, Kit."

Kit chuckled. "And I mooch meals like nobody's business. You have a home here." She looked up, met the eyes of each of the other five teenagers sitting at the table. "That goes for all of you. If they didn't ditch me, you all are golden. Trust me on that. Right, Mom?"

Betsy stroked a hand over Kit's hair. "Absolutely. This one was a handful, and it was our privilege to keep her. And our privilege to keep all of you until you're eighteen. And once you are eighteen, you still have a place here. Pop and I will make sure you're ready for the world. Nobody gets kicked to the curb. Not in this house."

"Well," Rita said. "Kit did. Tamsin Effing Kavanaugh said so in her article. Kicked to the curb."

"You little shit." But Kit was laughing.

"We need a swear jar," Rita said. "Just for Kit. We'll be rich."

Kit laughed again and her heart felt lighter. "You're such a brat."

"And you love me," Rita sang.

"I do. Brat." Kit gave Dawn's hand a squeeze before letting her go. "Don't be a brat like Rita, okay?"

Dawn's grin was wobbly, but genuine. "I'm probably worse. I have a smart mouth. Gets me into trouble."

"Not with me. You're not in trouble with me. Understand?"

"Yeah," Dawn whispered. "Thanks, Kit."

"You're welcome. And thank *you*. You opened a door in my brain. It's been . . . overwhelming, all of this. I haven't been thinking as clearly as I need to. So thank you for thinking *for* me. Never be afraid to make suggestions, Dawn. I'm serious."

"Sounds like you'll be a great cop someday," Eloise chirped.

Dawn straightened in her chair. "I just might be."

Kit stood up, realizing everyone was staring at her. "What?"

"That was nice," Sam said, his smile sweet.

Ann nodded. "I see what my Sam sees in you."

Kit didn't know what to say. She didn't like being the center of this kind of attention. It made her want to run and hide.

"Just say thank you, Kit," Betsy murmured.

"Thank you," Kit managed to say and retreated to her chair next to Georgia.

At least Georgia wouldn't embarrass her with kind words. The woman was a curmudgeon, and delightfully so.

"Smart kid," Georgia said. "I like her. If she decides to be a lawyer, have her hit me up for contacts. If I'm still around, that is."

"Stop it. You're going to live forever. Eloise says you're too stubborn to die."

"She's right about that. And so was Sam's mother. It's easy

to see what Sam sees in you. I saw it right away. So did Eloise. You're all bluff."

"Not *all* bluff," Kit protested. "I can be a regular bitch when I need to be."

Georgia raised her water glass. "To being bitches when we need to be. And may that reporter get what's coming to her."

"Truth." Kit skimmed the article again. "My God, how is she getting her information?"

"Check your car for a tracker," Georgia suggested.

"I was doing that routinely for a while, but I haven't lately because she's left me alone. I'll have to go back to doing that. And I'll check Sam's SUV, too. I can't believe she listed Akiko's boat in the article. That's gonna hurt Akiko's business."

"I doubt that. But Akiko should consider a defense attorney, just in case the Feds try to scapegoat her for Paolo's crimes."

"I thought of that," Kit said grimly. "The ATF agent said they didn't suspect Akiko, but I don't believe him. I need to find a defense attorney that isn't Sam's ex."

"Damn straight." Bill scowled. "That woman is poison."

Sam's ex had cheated on him. Broken his heart. Kit hated the sight of her.

"I know a number of good defense attorneys who are not Sam's ex," Georgia said dryly. "Just say the word and I'll send you their contact information."

"Thank y—" Kit's cell buzzed, startling her. It was Lennox. "I need to take this." She excused herself into the next room, unsurprised when Sam followed her. "Hey," Kit said when she'd hit accept. "You're on speaker. Sam's here with me."

"Daisuke Takahashi," Lennox said.

"Who?" Kit asked, googling his name.

"Skin under Mary Sherman's fingernails."

Kit sucked in a breath, suddenly a lot less tired as her search results filled her phone's screen. "Akiko's half brother. You've put out a BOLO?"

"I did. His description is consistent with the guy who shot you, Marshall, and Ashton, too."

Kit showed Sam her phone. "Son of a wealthy LA businessman." She tapped on the shooter's Instagram page. "He goes by Danny. Oh, look at this. He's a black belt in karate."

"What do you wanna bet that he studied with Edwin Ito?" Sam asked.

"That's likely a sucker bet at this point," Kit said. "Lennox, do you know if Danny Takahashi has ever been suspected of organized crime?"

"Like gun smuggling? Not that I've heard, but let's check it out. We can check out Ito as well."

We. Kit had been planning to work on the case regardless of Lennox's invitation, but it was nice to have. "You ready for a road trip to LA?"

"Let's leave first thing," Lennox said. "I can pick you up at six a.m."

"We'll be ready," Sam said.

San Diego, California
Wednesday, February 1, 6:15 a.m.

"I packed snacks," Sam said as they set out in the SDPD sedan that Lennox had checked out for the trip. Lennox was behind the wheel, Kit in the front passenger seat. Sam had the whole back seat to himself, but he'd have preferred to have Kit beside him. She and Lennox, however, needed to work on the way to LA.

He'd gotten a few hours' sleep after leaving McKittrick House the night before and made sure his folks were okay with spending the day alone. They were wonderful, as usual, graciously offering to dogsit Siggy. They'd made lunch plans with some of their San Diego golf friends, and then his mother was going back to the McKittricks' to—of all things—take a cooking class from Betsy.

If Betsy could teach his mother to cook . . . There weren't enough gifts in the universe to thank her. His father had always done the cooking, and he simply couldn't anymore.

That his mother was stepping up was sweet. That she and Betsy were becoming friends was good for both women.

"Snacks are good," Lennox said. "I brought a thermos full of coffee."

"And I brought breakfast sandwiches," Kit said. "I didn't make them, so we're all safe."

"I finally get to sample your mother's cooking," Lennox said, holding out her hand. "Gimme."

Kit shook her head, but she was smiling as she passed out what smelled like egg, bacon, and cheese biscuits. "You should have come over last night. It was late, but everyone was still awake, and Mom always makes plenty."

"It was kind of you to offer," Lennox said, "but I had to get my childcare sorted. And prepare my game plan for LA."

Kit's brows lifted. "You have a child?"

Lennox chuckled. "I do. She's seven and the light of my life. You wanna see a picture?"

"Of course." Kit held out her hand for Lennox's phone and made all the appropriate noises as she swiped through the photos. Then she chuckled. "Oh my. She's . . . an artist."

Lennox laughed. "You got to the one where she painted the dog?"

"She didn't make a painting of the dog, Sam," Kit explained. "She painted the actual dog."

Lennox laughed again. "Yeah, that was a day. I went to start a load of laundry and when I came back, she'd gotten out the paints. Luckily it was only watercolors."

"What's the dog's name?" Sam asked, looking at the photos when Kit passed back Lennox's phone.

"She's a shelter Chihuahua who was called Taco Bell. We renamed her Bella."

"My shelter dog is named Siggy, after Freud." He returned the phone to Lennox.

"And my poodle is Snickerdoodle because she's the same color as the cookie," Kit added. "Who watches your daughter when you have to travel?"

"My sister. She's a lifesaver."

Sam wanted to ask more questions. Like, was there another parent? Had there been? Was Lennox divorced? Widowed? Was there trauma he had to tiptoe around?

Once again Lennox laughed. "I can hear you thinking hard, Sam. I'm a single mom, never been married. Never met the right girl. I wanted a child and . . . well, science is a good thing."

Sam nodded, relieved. "I didn't want to misstep."

"It would have been accidentally," Lennox assured him. "I can tell you're a nice guy."

"He really is," Kit said fondly. "He puts up with me."

"Such a hardship," Sam deadpanned. "After our first meeting, the only direction was up."

Kit made a face and explained the circumstances of their meeting to Lennox. That Sam had information on a possible murder, but Kit had taken him for the killer and ended up knocking him to the floor of his apartment and cuffing him.

"And Baz threatened to shoot his dog," she finished. "We're both lucky that Sam's the forgiving type."

"Mostly," Sam said. "I'm still irked at Baz."

"No, you're not," Kit said.

"No, I'm not," he agreed. "I really want to be, though."

"You two are so cute," Lennox said warmly.

Sam glanced at Kit to see her reaction. A few months ago, those would have been fighting words, but today she was smiling.

Sam retrieved Lennox's thermos and poured three cups of coffee into travel mugs. "Coffee for everyone."

"Thank you," Kit said. "I did some research last night, too. Should we share and then decide what else needs to be done?"

"Yes," Lennox said, "but I wanted to update you on a few things. We had to cut Ricky Nicchi loose last night. There wasn't enough physical evidence to hold him for the shooting in front of Ella Sherman's house. Not yet, anyway. He had an alibi that checked out. He was at his office where he was seen by two people. Even though I think those people are lying, we don't have evidence to the contrary right now. We had LAPD search his house for the M40 and they couldn't find it, or any ammo. I put in a request for the lab to try to find a DNA sample in those size thirteen shoes so we can at least place him in Mary Sherman's house at some point."

"Do we know where Ricky is?" Kit asked.

"No. I put a pair of uniforms on him, but he gave them the slip."

Kit scowled. "We need to find him. He's the only one standing who can ID that third man in the photo Leo Sherman took."

"I figured he'd go home to LA," Lennox said, "to see Ito if nothing else."

"I hope so," Kit said. "You said you had a few things to update. What else?"

"I went to see the Sherman twins last night."

Kit's scowl deepened. "I should have done that."

"Navarro wouldn't have told you where they were," Lennox said pragmatically.

Kit winced. "True enough. What did you tell them?"

"That we had a lead on their mother's killer, that their mother was Akiko's aunt, and that Ito was Akiko's grandfather, meaning he's theirs, too. They've attended his San Diego dojo from the time they were ten years old. He was never their direct sensei, but they knew him. They knew that he came in and watched the classes."

"I bet that was a shock," Sam said. "Finding out who Ito was to them."

"Oh yeah. Why would Ito do that? Kit, you know him, right? Why would he keep that kind of a secret?"

Kit sighed. "He said it was because Akiko would be in

danger. And then he slid back into unconsciousness. I don't know him well, so I don't know what kind of man he is. I wasn't the best candidate for martial arts."

"I wasn't, either," Lennox said. "I tried, but I always made some smartass remark that got me in trouble. The sensei told me that maybe I should try kickboxing."

Kit laughed. "That's what Ito said to me!"

Sam smiled as the two women compared experiences. It was like watching a friendship bloom, and he wanted this for Kit. She was slowly coming into her own and he loved seeing it happen.

"Anyway," Kit said when they'd stopped laughing, "Ito was never mean or rude or cruel. He was standoffish, though. Even to Akiko. He was never warm with her. He was simply her teacher. A trusted teacher, but still just a teacher. That's why I was stunned when she said he'd made her his medical power of attorney. Now that makes a lot more sense."

"It could be that that's just his way," Sam said. "But I'm interested in Ito's relationship with Nicchi. Nicchi said Ito was his father when the medics came. Was that a flat-out lie, a symbolic representation, or do they have a legal relationship?"

"Nicchi also had Ito's medical power of attorney," Lennox said. "Kit, can you make a list of questions? Is Nicchi legally related to Ito? And if he is, is Paolo also?"

Kit noted the questions on her phone app. "I'd like to know whether the Sherman sisters know either of the Nicchi brothers."

"They knew Paolo and they remembered Akiko. They didn't remember her right away, but once they got to the safe house they looked through old photos on their phones and realized she'd been their sensei one summer. Raisa remembered thinking that she looked like their mom, but they were fifteen at the time and were not focused on their karate teacher. They're mad that Ito kept them from each other."

"So did Mary," Sam observed.

"Yeah." Lennox sighed. "There was a lot of anger toward their mother, too. More subdued since they're still deep in shock and grief, but they're angry. I told them that Mary had been meeting with Nicchi and Ito in LA. I showed them the photo of the third man, but they didn't recognize him. Although you can only see a sliver of his face. What you mostly see is his glasses."

"What about Danny Takahashi?" Kit asked. "Did Dahlia recognize him as her stalker when you showed her his photo?"

"She said he looked like the stalker, but she never saw the guy's face. They both recognized Danny from their dojo, however. He joined back in August. Dahlia was asked to mentor him since he was new. Knowing that he might have been stalking her after she'd spent time trying to get him settled upset her. They were both even more upset when they realized that he killed their mother, as you'd expect. I never said that he was Mary's killer, but they figured it out and they were angry. Demanded to know why we haven't arrested him. I told them we were looking for him so that we could do exactly that. I did not tell them that Danny was Akiko's half brother or that Nicchi was the second shooter that day in front of their aunt Ella's house. That wasn't information I was authorized to share with the victim's family."

"Are you authorized to share it with Akiko?" Sam asked.

"Navarro says yes," Lennox said. "I figure you already told

her that Nicchi was one of the shooters, but I am authorized to tell her Takahashi's identity. Once I do that, she'll know who her bio dad is, so I'll make sure she's okay with that knowledge before I tell her. Or, better yet, you could tell her, Kit."

"I think that's a better idea," Kit murmured. "Although I don't want to tell her. Her world has already been turned upside down too many times."

"I know," Lennox said sympathetically. "But she's going to find out. Better it comes from you. Plus, we have to make sure that Danny isn't stalking Akiko, too. One of my next steps is to dig into Danny's background. I meant to last night, but I got back from the safe house too late."

"I did that digging last night," Kit said. "I'm glad we didn't overlap. We should make sure we split future research."

"What did you find?" Lennox asked.

"Daisuke Takahashi, aka Danny, is seventeen years old and was born and raised in LA. His mother was Umeko Takahashi. She died when he was eight. Suicide. Danny found her body."

"Oh no." Sam was sad for eight-year-old Danny, but that didn't excuse his crimes. "What else?"

"He's got felony convictions—grand theft auto, carjacking, assault, and possession of a firearm. He hit the woman he carjacked with the gun and broke her cheekbone. He was fifteen at the time. He served eighteen months in juvie and he's been out since July. He dropped out of high school while he was in juvie and hasn't been back."

"He moved to San Diego within a month of his release," Lennox said thoughtfully. "Did he run away from home?"

"According to his father, yes, but I'm not so sure. His father is Kenzo Takahashi, millionaire businessman. Kenzo is fifty-eight years old, born in LA. He took over the family business when he was thirty-eight. The business is privately held and consists of multiple companies, most of which were started by his father, Michitaka Takahashi, during the seventies and eighties."

"What kind of companies?" Sam asked.

"Luxury car exports, construction, real estate—mostly commercial space in the suburbs. Those were the businesses his father started. Kenzo owns one of the smaller casinos in Vegas, which appears to be his primary addition to the family empire. From what I could gather, a lot of the businesses that Kenzo started—other than the casino—have failed, including a vineyard and a brand of frozen foods that both tanked publicly. There was an article in the financial pages that wondered why he hadn't been ousted as the head of the company. The reporter said he was made of Teflon, that his failures didn't seem to stick to him. But despite the failures, he lives very well. He has a house in Bel Air and a condo in Vail. Company jet. He attends galas and charity functions and in every photo, he has two big bruisers behind him. Not the same two guys, but the same look."

"Bodyguards," Sam said. "Because he's rich?"

"For now, we'll think that. I mean, all his businesses fall into the 'classic organized crime' category, but that doesn't mean he's dirty just because his son is."

"Especially if they're estranged," Lennox said. "Why did you say you weren't sure about his son running away, Kit?"

"Well, Kenzo started a charity for troubled kids, stating publicly that his son had had psychological issues that they hadn't been able to address. But some comments on one of the charity's social media posts claimed that Kenzo was a hypocrite who'd disowned his son when he went to juvie. That he'd told Danny that he'd shamed the family and was now disowned."

"Ouch," Lennox said.

"I know. The comment had been left only ten minutes before I saw it. But I went back to double-check the post this morning and it had been removed. Someone didn't like Mr. Takahashi being called a hypocrite."

"Are we going to approach Kenzo?" Sam asked.

Lennox didn't answer. She was glancing at Kit, waiting for her opinion.

He was liking Lennox more all the time.

"I think," Kit said slowly, "not right off the bat. I want to talk to Nicchi first. Or Ito, if he comes around. I don't want to think either of them is involved in something illegal. I'm hoping there's another explanation."

No one said anything, letting Kit gather her thoughts.

"Ito cares for Akiko," she finally said. "He could have kept his identity secret and stayed out of her life, but he didn't. He was always there, watching her. And that could be creepy and nefarious, or it could have been his way of keeping her safe. Danny Takahashi has killed three people that we know of and shot three cops. According to the LAPD detectives who interviewed us at Ito's condo, a person matching Danny's overall description was seen leaving Ito's place shortly before we got there."

"Are you going to involve the LAPD detectives?" Sam asked.

"I don't know," Kit said. "I didn't get a bad vibe off them, but I don't know anything about them."

"I do," Lennox said. "I've got a few friends in LAPD and I asked them. They appear to be good guys. No service record dings, no IA investigations, no complaints against them. They aren't even angry with you for . . ." She cleared her throat. "Being less than honest about why you'd gone to see Ito."

Kit winced. "Did you tell them?"

"Didn't have to. They figured it out on their own. They called me and I told them the details. They knew you'd been suspended. That came up in their Google search."

"Tamsin Fucking Kavanaugh," Kit muttered. "I wish I knew where she's getting her information. Navarro has a leak."

"Add that to your list of questions," Lennox said. "So the plan is to find Nicchi. Then talk to the LAPD detectives."

Kit nodded. "But first, I need to talk to Akiko. I need to tell her about her half brother and her bio father. I want to do that face-to-face."

"Okay," Lennox said gently. "If you don't mind, I should probably be in the room. Just to cover us with Navarro."

"All right." Kit exhaled. "Sam, is there any chocolate in the snacks you brought?"

"A six-pack of full-sized Snickers bars in the bag at your feet."

Kit made a pleased sound. "You're the best. Thank you." She tore into the package of Snickers, then held one out to Lennox. Lennox shook her head.

"I'm not a chocolate lover."

Kit squinted at her. "And here I thought we were getting along so well."

"More for you," Lennox said.

Kit chuckled. "True," she said before taking a big bite.

The little moan she made was . . . well, it was sinful.

Think about other things. Not about how you want to hear her make that sound in your bed. Sam cracked his window an inch to get some fresh air.

Kit swallowed the candy and sighed heavily. "That's better. I'm going to save the rest of these for after I talk to Akiko. I'm going to need them."

And her glum tone was enough to quiet his need, and he rolled the window back up.

"I'm sorry," he said.

"I know," she whispered. "I haven't told her about her house yet, either. It was awful enough telling her about Paolo."

"What do you know about Ito?" he asked, trying to divert her attention.

She flashed him a grateful smile. "Not a lot."

"Then we'll fill in the gaps," Lennox said. "Start with what you know."

CHAPTER SIXTEEN

San Diego, California
Wednesday, February 1, 6:45 a.m.

Kit had spent most of the night reading about Akiko's biological father and her grandfather, the memory of her sister's sobs disturbing her sleep. "Ito's full name is Shigeru Edwin Ito."

"Edwin?" Lennox asked.

"Akiko told me that a lot of Asian Americans have two names—an Asian name from their heritage and a more American name."

"Does Akiko have an American name?" Sam asked.

"No, Akiko just has the one name, but she told me if she were to choose an 'American' name, it would be Raven."

"Why is that?"

"Well, I once told her how much I liked her hair, calling it 'black as a raven's wing.' She said that if she didn't like her own name so much—because her mother had pinned it to her blanket—she'd go by Raven. So I'd still have"—Kit's voice broke—"a bird. Since I'd lost Wren."

"Aw," Lennox said softly. "That's lovely."

Kit nodded, blinking rapidly. She was too emotional today. "It is. But I told her that I preferred her the way she was, that she didn't have to be like Wren for her to be my sister. It was a nice day."

"And you say that you don't know how to do feelings," Sam said. "You do, you know."

"Meh." She waved him off, even though his words warmed her heart. "So I learned a *lot* of stuff overnight. I'll start with Edwin Ito, because everything seems to come back to him. He was born in LA in 1947, joined the Army when he was twenty, went to Vietnam. Was in the Army for six years total. Was honorably discharged, returned to the US, then married one Sakura Yamamoto. I found a copy of his marriage certificate and his divorce decree."

"Lots of vets got divorced after Vietnam," Sam said. "What about his children? What happened to them?"

"Nothing good." She found the notes on her phone. "Bear with me. It took me several hours to uncover all this. I found birth certificates for twins Minako and Ichiro Ito, born in LA in 1973. Ito mentioned them in those few minutes he was lucid early yesterday morning. He called Minako 'Minnie.' However, there's no birth certificate for Himari Ito."

"Aka Mary Sherman," Sam said.

"Yes. I thought her mother might have gone back to her maiden name after the divorce, so I searched for Himari Yamamoto, but I found nothing. Then I checked Mary's marriage license, and her maiden name was listed as Smith."

"She changed her name?" Lennox asked.

"Apparently so. Mary Smith does have a birth certificate that lists both her mother and father as unknown. She was born seven months after Ito and his wife divorced. I figured I had birth certificates for all three of them, but I couldn't find any other mention of Minako and Ichiro anywhere—not under Ito, Yamamoto, or Smith. But my search *did* turn up a Minako and Ichiro Nakamura. And *that's* when things got complicated."

"They're complicated already," Lennox muttered.

"Buckle up," Kit said grimly. "It gets worse. I found an article from 1991 about both Minako and Ichiro *Nakamura*. I figure the likelihood of having more than one set of twins with those names is slim, so I'm assuming they're Ito's children. Or were. The twins were in the news because they'd been murdered."

Sam sucked in a breath. "Oh no."

Lennox clutched the steering wheel. "Fucking hell. I was not expecting that."

"Neither was I, but that all three of Ito's children were murdered has to be connected somehow. I don't buy that they were just unlucky, not with all the name changes. Dawn's theory of Ito being involved in organized crime is looking more plausible."

Lennox exhaled heavily. "Was there a murder investigation for the twins?"

"Yes, but it went cold soon after for lack of evidence. I'll come back to the murders in a minute. I went back and searched for all three of Ito's children but used the name Nakamura. I found birth certificates for all three of them, all with the last name Nakamura, and all listed as being born in Henderson, Nevada. That's just outside of Vegas. The mother is listed as Sakura Nakamura, but no father was identified."

"So the twins and Mary each had *two different* birth certificates?" Lennox asked.

"That's right. The twins as Ito and Nakamura and Mary as Nakamura and Smith." Which, Kit thought, was very sketchy. "There are also differences in their places of birth. The twins as Ito have both parents identified—Edwin and Sakura, with their birthplace as LA. The twins as Nakamura have Sakura as their mother and no father known, birthplace Henderson, Nevada. Himari Nakamura has Sakura listed as her mother and no father known, birthplace also Nevada. *But* Mary Smith has neither parent known and she's listed as being born in San Diego. That's the first mention of San Diego in Mary's background."

"When did Mary go from Nakamura to Smith?" Sam asked.

"I don't know, but the police report says they talked to 'Himari Nakamura.' So Mary didn't change her first name to Mary and her last name to Smith until sometime *after* her siblings were murdered. Maybe *because* they were murdered."

"That makes sense," Lennox said. "Especially since Mary Smith was supposedly born in San Diego and none of these name changes were legally done. Sounds like Mary wanted to hide. Did Ito's wife do a legal name change to Nakamura after the divorce?"

"Not that I could find."

Lennox frowned. "That means she got fake IDs for herself and her children. Hella sketchy."

"I came to the same conclusion."

"Either way," Sam said slowly, sorting through the details in his mind, "both Sakura's name change and her taking her children from LA to Henderson, Nevada, indicates a desire to completely disassociate herself from Edwin Ito. Why? What did he do?"

"That's a good question." Kit had already noted it on her phone app. "I found Sakura Nakamura in the property records. She bought a house in Henderson, Nevada, shortly before Himari's birth. That house was where Minako and Ichiro were later murdered. They were seventeen."

Lennox looked shocked. "How were they murdered?"

"They were both shot in the head and ballistics showed it was with the same gun. It was deemed a robbery gone bad. The autopsy noted that Minako had just given birth, but there was no baby on the premises. The police in Nevada searched for the child, but never found her. Unfortunately, the detective who caught the case died a long time ago, so we can't ask him."

"Okay," Lennox said slowly. "So Mary's brother and sister were murdered when she was . . . how old? Fourteen?"

"Yep. And guess the date?"

"Akiko's birthday or thereabouts," Sam said.

He was smart. Kit really liked that about him.

"Very good. The police report says the twins were murdered in *Nevada* the day *before* Akiko was left at the firehouse in *San Diego*."

"Which is why the Henderson cops never found her," Lennox said. "Akiko was transported over state lines and back then, that would have been much harder to track."

"Exactly," Kit said. "Akiko was a newborn when she was

abandoned. They estimated she was only a few days old. So it seems Minako—or Minnie—gave birth to Akiko and, a few days later, she was murdered, along with her brother."

"Minnie couldn't have dropped her at the firehouse," Sam said. "It had to have been Mary."

"She must have been so frightened," Lennox said. "But what about Mary's mother? She could have left Akiko on those firehouse steps."

"Nope. Sakura Nakamura died the year before, in a car accident."

"How did a fourteen-year-old like Mary get a baby from Nevada to San Diego?" Lennox asked.

"That," Kit said, "is a damn good question. I already noted it."

"Wait," Sam said. "The twins would have been sixteen when their mother died. Mary would have only been thirteen. You said a year later that the twins were murdered in the family home. How were they still there a year after their mother died?"

"The police report says a family friend, Nancy Sayer, came to live with them. Their mother made Nancy the kids' guardian in her will. The property records show that Nancy owned the house next door to Sakura's. She doesn't live there anymore, though. Both houses were sold a few months after the murders. I don't know where the money from the sale of Sakura's house went, but finding that out is on my list. I wasn't able to track Nancy down, but I'm going to keep trying because she might be able to fill in a lot of gaps."

"I'll ask Navarro to find her," Lennox said. "I hope she's still alive."

"I didn't find any death certificate on her." Kit studied her notes. "Now, Mary's daughters said she grew up in foster care, but as of the time that Minnie and Ichiro were murdered, Mary was living with Nancy. I don't know if she continued living with her or not. Mary might have entered the system. If so, she'll have a social service file somewhere, but those are often sealed. But, and here's the interesting part—"

"I thought all the other stuff was pretty damn interesting," Lennox interrupted.

Kit's lips twitched. "About six months later was when Ito opened his second dojo—in San Diego."

"Oh," Lennox breathed. "Mary went to her father for help."

"Or Ito somehow found out that his other children had been murdered," Sam said. "Since they were living under a new name, he wouldn't have been contacted as the next of kin. But clearly Mary and Ito met each other long before the night she talked to Ito outside the restaurant with Leo, just before their wedding. Remember, that's when an 'older Japanese man' saw Mary coming out of the restaurant and he called her Mari, which made her angry. She told Leo afterward that the man was a friend of her mother. In reality, he was her father."

"Do we know that Leo was telling the truth about meeting Ito outside the restaurant that night?" Lennox asked.

"Ito confirmed that," Kit said. "In those few minutes he woke up yesterday. Said he'd put Mary's life in danger that day."

"So Ito opens a dojo in San Diego six months after his granddaughter Akiko is born," Sam said thoughtfully. "And he watches her—or watches *over* her."

"I really want to believe it's the second one," Kit said.

"So do I," Lennox agreed, then glanced at the sedan's

display screen when her phone began to ring. Caller ID said it was Sergeant Ryland from CSU. Accepting the call, Lennox said, "Hey, Ryland. I'm in the car on my way to LA. I've got you on speaker. Whatcha got?"

"I've reviewed the security footage from Laurette Curry's neighborhood."

Laurette Curry, Leo Sherman's mistress, murdered the same way as Leo's wife.

Laurette Curry, whose bedroom wall had been covered with photos of Akiko on her boat.

"Well?" Kit demanded. "Don't leave us hanging."

"The surveillance cameras show two men entering Laurette's house, about an hour apart. The first man has the same body type as Danny Takahashi and his entrance was minutes after the power was cut to Laurette's house."

"Consistent with how Mary was killed," Sam said.

"Yes," Ryland said. "The second man appeared older. Same general size and shape as our 'third man' in the photo with Ito and Mary taken by Leo Sherman when he followed her to LA. The third man was in the house for about ten minutes."

"Long enough to put up those photos of Akiko," Sam said. "That was bothering the hell out of me. Why would Curry's shooter make sure we saw such an obvious clue? If Curry had put up the photos, that would have connected her to the murders. Her killer would have taken the pictures down, not left them up."

"Yes," Lennox said again. "Exactly. That bothered me, too. Someone took a big risk to enter that house and put up photos of Akiko that would lead us to look at her charter boat passengers."

"Which we still need to do," Kit said. "I should have asked her last night, but..." Akiko had been so devastated by Paolo's murder.

"She might not have been able to answer last night," Sam said gently. "She's been through a lot the past few days."

"All of you have," Lennox said. "But he's right, Kit. We'll ask for the names when we see her today. Knowing that a second person went into Laurette Curry's house to make sure we saw that clue changes everything."

Kit frowned. "So this third man broke into Laurette's house and taped photos of Akiko to her bedroom wall because he wanted to... help us?"

"He appeared to be working with Ito, Nicchi, and Mary Sherman to—hopefully—protect Akiko," Sam pointed out. "So, yeah. I think he's trying to help us."

"I'm leaning in that direction, too," Ryland said. "Also, ballistics on the bullets taken from Laurette Curry show a match with the bullet taken from Mary Sherman."

"Danny Takahashi did both murders," Kit said. "But what about Paolo?"

"No ballistics on that bullet yet. I'll let you know when I have the report. For now, though, we know the same gun killed at least two of our victims. That's all I've got for now."

He ended the call and for a moment there was silence in the car as each of them digested this new information.

"I have so many questions," Sam finally said. "The most obvious of which is who or what were the four of them protecting Akiko *from*? Ito knew she existed the same year she was born. Did her biological father know about her? Kenzo Takahashi?"

"Good questions," Kit said. "What else?"

"Why kill Laurette Curry?" he asked. "How does she connect to all this? She was having an affair with Leo Sherman. Does this mean that Leo Sherman is involved in everything? Did he plan the murder of his wife? Did he know about Akiko? I want to think not, because his shock when he saw her seemed pretty genuine, and he's a really bad liar."

"He really is a bad liar," Lennox agreed. "I requested Laurette's bank records last night, but even our initial investigation shows she does have something in common with Paolo. Both of them were swimming in debt."

"I wonder if she was involved in the gun smuggling," Kit said.

"We have to consider the possibility," Lennox said. "Any other questions, Sam?"

"Yeah. Where are the guns? Paolo had them in his shed, moved them onto Akiko's boat, then moved them off the boat. Where did he put them?"

"In Akiko's garage," Kit said. "At least for a little while. Then someone took them."

"Right," Sam said. "But where did they take them? Those crates had to have held at least ten rifles each and there were six of them. Sixty rifles take up some space. Did you look at the neighbors' security footage of Akiko's garage?"

Lennox scowled. "Nobody's camera was facing the right way."

"We'll have to dig deeper on that," Kit said. "Let's request footage from the traffic cams at the nearest intersections. We'd be looking for a small truck or a panel van. I don't think you could fit sixty rifles into a minivan or even an SUV. Connor is good at reviewing camera footage. We can ask him if CSU is too busy."

"You didn't suggest West do it," Lennox said mildly.

"Right," Kit muttered. "Like he's doing anything."

"You are correct about that," Lennox said with a sigh. "We can ask Navarro to have one of his analysts review the footage. Connor is supposed to be recovering."

"Well, I'm supposed to be suspended," Kit said with a scowl.

"True enough," Lennox agreed. "Yet here we are. Sam? What else?"

He pursed his lips, concentrating. "Why didn't Nicchi kill Danny Takahashi outside Ella Sherman's house on Sunday?"

"Yeah, he should have been able to kill him," Lennox said. "So why do you think, Sam?"

"I think Nicchi knew him."

Kit nodded. "You could be right. The options are either that Nicchi lost his nerve and couldn't kill anyone, that he deliberately didn't kill Danny so he could send a message, or that he knew him and couldn't do it. Why do you think it's the third one, Sam?"

"I think Nicchi could kill a stranger without blinking if it was part of a mission. Just my impression of the man," Sam said. "As for a message, what could he have been trying to say?"

"How did Nicchi know to be in front of Ella Sherman's house?" Lennox asked.

"If it were me," Kit said, "I would have come to San Diego immediately upon hearing that Mary Sherman was dead.

Maybe he was worried that whoever killed Mary would come after her daughters."

"Possible," Lennox allowed. "Why didn't Ito come?"

"Very good question," Kit said. "I've wondered that myself. Maybe he couldn't come immediately for some reason and sent Nicchi to protect Raisa and Dahlia. I think he was planning to come himself. When we found him, there was a suitcase next to the front door, like he was ready to leave."

"True," Sam said. "And hopefully Ito will wake up and tell us why he didn't come right away. But sending Nicchi makes sense. And, for whatever reason, he was in front of Ella Sherman's house and he did not kill Danny Takahashi. Also, *Danny* could have shot *him*, but he didn't. He sprayed that van Nicchi was driving with bullets but didn't kill the man who was only a few feet away? Neither of them killed the other. Instead, they both drove away."

"All true," Kit said. "The Sherman twins knew Danny from their dojo, which he joined in August. We need to find out if Ricky taught any classes in San Diego after that. I think you're right, Sam. I think they knew each other, and I don't think that Ricky could bring himself to kill him."

Los Angeles, California
Wednesday, February 1, 9:30 a.m.

"Pop." Kit walked into her father's arms in the ICU waiting room. She, Sam, and Lennox had come straight to the hospital after Harlan had texted that he and Akiko were sitting with Ito.

He'd left Akiko alone in Ito's room so that he could talk to them. The thought of Akiko alone made Kit nervous. She'd check on her sister as soon as she brought her father up to speed.

"Kitty-Cat." Harlan looked tired, and that worried her.

"You okay, Pop?"

"Just ready to go home. I miss your mom and the girls." He gave Sam a quick hug.

"I brought you some more pieces of wood," Sam said. "I don't know if they'll be good for you to carve, but my folks got them for you."

That was a surprise. It warmed Kit's heart in a way she was starting to get used to. Which was scary, if she was being honest with herself.

"That was so nice of them. Thank you, Sam." Harlan lifted an eyebrow at the sight of Lennox, standing near the door. "Who is this?"

"Pop, this is Detective Meghan Lennox, lead detective on Mary Sherman's homicide investigation. Meghan, this is my father, Harlan McKittrick."

"Detective Lennox. It's nice to meet you."

"She's been my window into the investigation," Kit said. "Since I'm . . ."

"Yeah," Harlan said, frowning. "I know."

Suspended. A word Kit never thought she'd be associated with.

"It's so good to meet you, sir," Lennox said. "I've been a fan of your carvings for a long time."

Kit tucked her arm around Harlan's and led him to one of

the waiting room sofas, Sam at her side. "She bought one of your violin carvings for her mother for Christmas, but ended up keeping it for herself."

Lennox let out a surprised laugh. "You weren't supposed to tell him that. Makes me sound like a bad daughter."

Harlan smiled at Lennox. "I imagine you bought something even better for your mother."

"Well, that would be hard to do," Lennox said, "but I tried. How is Akiko?"

Her compassionate tone elevated her even further in Kit's regard. She really hoped that Lennox was as kind and honest as she appeared.

"Devastated. She and Paolo had been friends since they were kids."

"It's hard when you grow up in foster care," Kit said. "Nothing is consistent. Nothing is guaranteed. To have Ito's dojo and all the people in it was an unusual gift. Her friendship with Paolo was something unique in our world."

Sam squeezed her hand and she leaned her head on his shoulder for just a moment, taking the quiet strength he offered. She'd been dreading seeing Akiko. Dreading the sadness she knew she'd see in her sister's eyes, because there was nothing she could do. There was no way to fix this, to make Akiko whole again.

"She'll be okay," Sam murmured. "She's as strong as you are."

And that was true. They were strong in different ways, but they were both children of Harlan and Betsy McKittrick. They'd be okay.

Lennox took the chair closest to Harlan. "Any change on Ito?"

Harlan wobbled his hand. "A little. He woke up two hours ago, but he's on some heavy pain meds. He was awake for a few minutes and went back to sleep. But it's sleep, now, and not unconsciousness, so that's an improvement."

"Did he say anything?" Kit asked.

"Told Akiko he loved her. Asked for Ricky." He sighed. "Asked for Paolo."

"Did Akiko tell him?" Kit asked.

"No. She was afraid of what the news would do to him. He was fuzzy, anyway. Couldn't tell the doctor what year it was or what year he was born."

Poor Akiko. "Then she was right to hold off on telling him. We have other news for her and most of it isn't good."

Harlan exhaled quietly. "Tell me."

"Someone broke into her house, Pop. Made a mess. They were looking for something specific. They did the same thing to Paolo's house and the house belonging to Leo Sherman's mistress."

"Why?" The whispered question came from behind them, the voice achingly familiar.

Kit lurched to her feet to find Akiko in the waiting room doorway. She met her halfway and folded her sister into a hug, tightening her hold when Akiko began to cry.

"Why is this happening?"

Kit's arm was throbbing but she didn't break the hug. "I don't know. But we will figure it out."

"Paolo and Hanshi and . . . my aunt. I never got to know her. And now my *house*?"

Kit's eyes stung. "I know. I'm so sorry."

She held Akiko until her sister's sobs subsided, and then

Kit pulled Akiko onto the sofa so that her sister was between her and Harlan.

"Where's Lennox?" Kit asked, because Sam had moved to the chair that Lennox had been using. The detective was no longer in the room.

"Had to take a call," Sam said. He passed a box of tissues and a bottle of water to Akiko. "You need to replace all that water you just cried out."

Akiko hiccupped a small laugh, her head on Harlan's broad shoulder. "Thank you, Sam."

Kit drew a breath. "Okay, so there's more."

Akiko closed her eyes. "Of course there is."

Kit took her hand. "Paolo was being investigated by the ATF."

Akiko's eyes flew open. "The Bureau of Alcohol, Tobacco, and Firearms?"

"The very same. They said he was using your boat to smuggle guns."

Akiko paled. "What?"

Kit glanced at her father. "You kept her off social media?"

Harlan nodded once. "I forgot to charge her phone."

Forgot on purpose, he meant.

Kit braced herself. "Okay, so some of this has been published online."

"The name of my boat?" Akiko whispered.

"Yes." Kit tried to keep her tone factual. "And your name is listed as the owner, but you're not listed as a suspect in any of the articles I read."

"My business," she whispered. "This is gonna ruin me. Which sounds so selfish of me. People are dead. I'm a terrible person."

"You are not," Harlan said firmly. He kissed her temple. "Worrying about your business is a normal thing. Paolo betrayed your trust, honey. He must have gotten mixed up with the wrong kind of people."

"Exactly," Sam said. "You're good and kind, Akiko, and we'll mount an Akiko-is-good-and-kind PR campaign once this is over. And believe it or not, a lot of people are going to be drawn to the excitement of a boat that smuggled contraband."

"Weirdos," Akiko muttered.

"As long as their money's good," Kit said. "Okay. There's more."

Akiko dropped her chin to her chest. "What?"

"Paolo had the guns on your boat last night, but he ended up not meeting with his client. The ATF wanted the client, so they let him return to dock with the guns. No one is sure where they went after that, but someone wanted it to look like you were involved. The empty gun crates were in your garage."

"I think I'm going to be sick," Akiko whispered.

Sam rose quietly to retrieve a trash can from the corner and Kit offered him a small smile of thanks.

I couldn't get through this without him.

Well, she probably could, but she was glad she didn't have to.

Kit rubbed Akiko's back in wide circles, just like Akiko did for her when she was upset. "They stole your customer files for the final quarter of last year and this year so far."

Akiko looked up, her face a ghastly gray. "Why?"

Kit drew another breath. "There was another murder. The woman Leo Sherman was seeing."

"He was *cheating*?" Akiko's voice rose an octave.

"He was. Apparently had been for a long time. We're still not sure why this woman was killed. Her name was Laurette Curry. Did you know her?"

"No. Never heard of her."

"There were some photos on her bedroom wall. Of you."

Akiko seemed to deflate. "Me? Why?"

"We don't know, but my gut tells me it was to protect you."

Akiko stared at her. "Protect me? What the fuck?"

"Mary Sherman was meeting with three men in LA," Kit told her. "We don't know why. Ricky Nicchi and your grandfather were two of the men. We don't know the identity of the third, but it looks like he might have been the person to post those photos on Laurette Curry's wall. They were taken on your boat, sometime after Christmas. We know because you're wearing the coat that I gave you."

Akiko shrank back into the sofa. "So someone came on my boat to hurt me?"

"Maybe," Sam said. "But the photos clued us to look at your passenger lists."

"Which were stolen," Kit added. "But those are just the liability forms everyone has to sign. You have the passenger lists on your computer, don't you?"

"Yes. Files are stored on the cloud."

"Good. Detective Lennox will need them." She hoped the woman came back from her phone call soon. Lennox had wanted to be present when Kit told Akiko about her half brother's identity.

Akiko frowned faintly. "I thought you didn't like her."

"I don't like her partner. Lennox has been a stand-up cop."

"How has so much changed so quickly?"

"It's been a ride," Kit said.

"Is that it?" Akiko asked. "Everything you needed to tell me? Please say that's it."

Kit hesitated, wishing Lennox would hurry up and return. "There's more."

"Oh God," Akiko whispered. Then she squared her shoulders. "What is it?"

"I have some news," came Navarro's voice.

Heads snapped to the doorway, where the lieutenant stood, looking awkward as hell.

As he should, Kit thought, narrowing her eyes at him.

"Why are you here?" Sam asked, not unkindly.

"Because I have news," Navarro said.

Which wasn't what Sam had meant, and Navarro knew it. Like Kit, Sam wanted to know why Navarro had driven all the way to LA to impart this news. Why not call or text?

"Just tell me," Akiko said wearily.

Navarro pulled an empty chair next to Sam's and sat down. "First, I'm so sorry for your loss. I know you and Paolo were close."

Akiko nodded. "Thank you." But her tone was wooden.

"We identified the man who killed your aunt, Mary Sherman," Navarro said. "His name is Daisuke Takahashi."

Akiko flinched. "Danny? He joined our dojo last summer. He came from the LA dojo, where he was one of Ricky's students. Hanshi said he'd been through a lot."

"So Nicchi did know him," Kit said with satisfaction, nodding at Sam. "You were right."

"Wait," Akiko said, shaking her head. "Just wait. *Danny* is my half brother? Danny Takahashi?"

"Yes," Navarro confirmed. "DNA from the skin cells found under Mary Sherman's fingernails was matched to his criminal record."

"I heard he was in juvie in LA," Akiko said, "but not what he did."

"Carjacking," Kit told her. "And assault on the driver. Plus grand theft auto."

"Oh, Danny." Akiko sighed. "So who's his father?"

And her own father, but that went unsaid.

"Kenzo Takahashi," Navarro said. "He lives here in LA. Wealthy businessman. Have you heard of him, Akiko?"

"No." Akiko pressed her fingertips to her temples. "Paolo and Danny hung out together outside the dojo. Was Danny involved in the gun running?"

"We don't kn—" Kit started, but Navarro said, "Yes."

She looked at Navarro in surprise.

"What's happened?" Sam asked. "How do you know that?"

Navarro looked uncomfortable. "We located the guns that were taken from the shipping crates in your garage. They were in a storage unit rented under Akiko's name."

"No way," Kit snapped, surging to her feet. "You are not pinning this on my sister."

"Of course I'm not," Navarro said irritably. "Please sit down, Detective."

"Not a detective," Kit grumbled as she sat down. "Suspended. Remember?"

"Oh yes, I remember," Navarro said, his tone heavy. Like he was upset at her suspension.

Too damn bad. Kit didn't feel sorry for him.

"Tell us about this storage unit, Lieutenant," Harlan said quietly.

"Yes, *sir*," Kit said. "Please do."

Navarro's shoulders slumped. "Still making 'sir' into a slur."

Kit shrugged and said nothing. Yes, she was being petty and quite possibly immature. She didn't care.

"The storage unit was rented by a man using Akiko's name on a fake ID. I suppose he figured the guy behind the counter wouldn't know that Akiko is a woman's name. At any rate, the signatures do not match yours, nor was your credit card used. The surveillance recordings show a man moving the guns from a ten-foot truck into the storage unit. He had on a long black wig, like he was trying to look like you."

Akiko nodded silently. Numbly.

"I'm sorry," Kit whispered. "I wish this was happening to me instead of to you."

"It shouldn't be happening to either of us," Akiko whispered back. "But you'll fix this. I know you will."

"How did you locate the storage unit?" Sam asked.

"I tracked the truck when it left Akiko's neighborhood," Navarro said. "Those guns had to go somewhere. I used the traffic cams until I found it going into the storage facility."

"We were going to ask you to get one of your analysts to do that," Kit said.

"Or Detective West," Sam said smoothly, watching Navarro's expression.

"I didn't tru—" Navarro stopped himself and shook his head. "Well played, Dr. Reeves."

"You didn't trust West to do it right?" Kit asked.

"Or at all," Navarro said. "Just let me get there, okay? I'll explain what I can."

Kit leaned back, giving him her full attention. "Why did you come here yourself, sir?"

"Because there's another article by Tamsin Kavanaugh. It lists the name of the shooter and his father. Discloses that they are related to Akiko."

Kit closed her eyes against the wave of rage that filled her. "Tamsin Fucking Kavanaugh. How did she know?" Her eyes flew open. "Is West feeding her information?"

"I think so," Navarro said, his tone back to heavy and sad. "I've suspected him for a while but couldn't pin anything on him."

"Have you something to pin on him now?" Harlan asked, his voice harsh and cold.

"Yes, I believe so. The same article states that there was an anonymous tip that led us to the storage unit where we found the guns."

"You fed that information to West on purpose," Kit said. "That's why you did the tracking work yourself."

Navarro nodded. "Yes."

"Does Lennox know?" Kit asked.

Navarro hesitated, then nodded. "Yes. She's the one who had the idea to set West up."

For a moment Kit could only stare. "I'm not sure if I'm annoyed or impressed that she bamboozled us. Either way, we were led."

"Only in that," Navarro said. "She's been telling me for a while that West is shirking his duty and that he often fantasizes about taking you down a few pegs."

"That's why you told her that I should be her mentor?"

"Not entirely. Lennox asked to be partnered with you while Connor is recovering. I told her I'd take it under advisement, then this case erupted."

Kit kept her focus on a fake plant in the corner of the room, because she was too angry to look at Navarro. Sam came to stand behind her, his hands on her shoulders, enabling her to see through her rage. "Is that why you put West on this case?"

"No. He was next in the queue, just like I told you. But it was an opportunity I couldn't ignore. I needed to weed out a dirty cop."

"And you suspended Kit in the process," Harlan said, clearly as angry as Kit was.

"No, I suspended Kit because she defied a direct order."

Kit's gaze flew to his. "An order you knew I would defy."

"It's played out pretty much the way I figured it would."

Sam stroked her hair. "Easy, Kitty-Cat," he murmured. "Don't do anything you'll regret."

"I'm not." She leaned into his touch. "I'm so angry."

"You have every right to be," Sam said, his voice a balm to her frayed nerves. "I thought it was the brass who wanted Kit taken down a peg."

"I never said that," Navarro said. "I only stated that we couldn't show favoritism to Kit by assigning another detective."

"So you set her career back," Harlan said, not a bit mollified. "By engineering this... whatever this is. You knew what she'd do and you kept West on the case anyway. When this is over, what is a suspension going to do to her career, Rey?"

"It'll be negotiated down to a minor infraction," Navarro said, looking exhausted. "It will not interfere with Kit's career.

The higher-ups had already decided that Kit is to be fast-tracked for promotion. That has not changed."

Kit blinked. "What?"

"They want you to take the sergeant's test. They think you'll be a lieutenant before your thirty-fifth birthday."

Kit stared at him. "What?"

Sam lightly gripped her neck. "Sounds like they approve of you, Kit."

"But . . ." Kit frowned. "I'm perfectly happy being a detective. I don't want a promotion." She looked over her shoulder at Sam. "They can't make me do this."

"Of course they can't," Navarro said, sounding relieved. "But they'll try. I'm not supposed to tell you any of this, but . . ." He sighed. "I hated suspending you, Kit. I wish you'd just done what I asked."

"But you know why I couldn't."

"I know. And I did the next best thing by having you mentor Lennox."

Kit shook her head. "I just . . . I don't know what to say."

"Well, act surprised if the captain brings it up," Navarro said dryly.

Akiko raised her hand. "I'm truly thrilled that the department values my sister. But let's go back to guns being found in a storage unit rented in my name. Do I need an attorney?"

"Yeah," Navarro said. "Just to be sure."

Akiko sighed. "I don't know any except for Sam's ex."

"Georgia knows some," Kit said. "We'll call her."

"What next?" Sam asked. "And did Lennox really have to take a call?"

"Yeah," Navarro said. "From me. We're going to meet with the two LAPD detectives working Ito's assault. Sam, I'd like you to come along. Kit, please stay here."

Kit gritted her teeth.

"Please," Navarro said quietly. "I keep hoping that Nicchi will show up here. Last we saw, his car was headed north on the 5. Please be here to talk to him if he shows up to see Ito."

Kit gritted her teeth harder. "Fine." She looked up at Sam again. "You'll update me?"

"Of course I will."

CHAPTER SEVENTEEN

Los Angeles, California
Wednesday, February 1, 11:05 a.m.

The floor of Ito's living room was still stained with his blood.

Sam stared at it for a moment before following Navarro, Lennox, and the two LAPD detectives into Ito's bedroom.

Detectives Burroughs and Desoto had met them at Ito's front door, handing out gloves and shoe covers like party favors. They'd already been searching the apartment for hours.

Sam hoped they'd found some answers. "Do we still think that Danny Takahashi did this?" he asked the group. "Or are we looking at another doer?"

"That's our assumption," Burroughs said. "We never saw the assailant's face, but he matches Danny's size and build."

"We know Danny was in San Diego on Sunday," Navarro said, "when he shot at Kit the second time and then had the shootout with Nicchi in front of Ella Sherman's house. He was in San Diego on Tuesday, because that's when he killed Paolo and Laurette Curry and broke into Akiko's house. But we don't know where he was on Monday. He could have come up here to search Ito's condo and beaten him up and driven back to San Diego in time to do all those other things."

"Knowing that Danny Takahashi came from one of Ito's dojos may explain why Ito isn't dead," Detective Desoto said. "He's the only victim who's lived so far. Well, and Nicchi, assuming it was Danny who shot at him in front of the Sherman woman's house. Danny's shot everyone else in the head."

"But he couldn't shoot Ito," Sam said. He'd thought the same thing.

"He beat him nearly to death, though," Lennox said, clearly skeptical. "And a bullet would have been far less personal. It could be that the beating was to get Ito to tell him where to find whatever it was that he was looking for." She gestured to the mess all around them. The mattress had been gutted, photos knocked off the walls. Knickknacks littered the floor.

It was like that in every room of Ito's condo. The place had been thoroughly searched, just like the other homes—Mary Sherman's, Paolo's, Laurette Curry's, and Akiko's.

That Danny Takahashi might have killed Akiko, if she'd been home, made Sam's stomach churn. He thought about Paolo, how his face had been rendered unrecognizable.

"The severity with which both Ito and Paolo were beaten usually indicates intense emotion," Sam said, "maybe rage or frustration. Or it could have been a psychopath's absence of feeling. We won't know until we find him and talk to him."

"He could have killed Ito, though," Detective Desoto insisted. "Instead he left him alive and able to ID him."

Sam nodded. "True. And he didn't kill Nicchi when he had the chance. Maybe it had something to do with the fact that both Ito and Nicchi were his sensei. Depending on how long he'd trained, there might be an instinctive inability to deal that final death blow."

"Or maybe he thought that Ito was dead," Navarro said. "Like you said, Dr. Reeves, we have to find him and ask him."

Lennox looked around the bedroom. "What have you found here?"

"Photo albums," Burroughs said with a gleam in his eye. "We'd just found them when you knocked."

"They were in that wall safe," Desoto said, pointing to the open safe. "Combo was Akiko McKittrick's birthday."

"Of course it was," Sam murmured. "All those wasted years . . ."

"Yeah," Lennox said quietly.

"Ito's wife divorced him," Detective Burroughs said. "Irreconcilable differences, according to the divorce decree, and Ito signed away his custodial rights."

Desoto held up one finger. "But he paid child support and alimony for years, even though it wasn't court ordered or even mentioned in the decree. Or he tried to, at least."

Lennox looked surprised. "How do you know that?"

"Returned uncashed checks." Desoto picked up a small box from the desk. "Also in the safe. He wrote a very generous check to Sakura Ito every month from the time of their divorce until 1991. But the checks were returned to him. She never took his money."

Frowning, Sam glanced at Lennox, then at Navarro. "He wrote checks to Sakura Ito, but she'd changed her name to

Nakamura. That might be why she never cashed them. But how did he know where to send them?"

"What's this about Nakamura?" Burroughs asked, and Lennox explained what Kit had uncovered.

"And Sakura died in 1990," Lennox finished.

"So he didn't know she'd died," Sam said, the realization making him sad. "Do you know where he sent the checks?"

Desoto held up a clear evidence bag with an envelope in it. "She had a PO box here in LA."

"He didn't know she'd moved to Nevada," Lennox said, then she frowned, too. "How did she keep a PO box if she had all new ID?"

"Maybe she kept her old ID as well," Navarro guessed. "If she was keen on hiding from Ito, she would have wanted him not to look for her. We can check the DMV database to see when her Sakura Ito driver's license expired."

"What the hell did Ito do to make her cover her tracks so thoroughly?" Desoto wondered.

Sam had the same question. "It must have been bad or presented some danger to her or the children. My bet is she feared for her children. That's usually why women leave and that's especially true when they seek new identities." He picked up one of the three photo albums on the desk. "Let's see what was so important that Ito locked it away in a safe." He opened the album and sucked in a breath. "Oh." There was a baby, Japanese, maybe six months old. She was wearing a dress and smiling widely. Carefully he lifted the photo out of the corner mounts and turned it over. *Akiko Jones.* "It's Akiko."

He replaced the photo in its mounts, then turned the page. More photos of a little girl—first a toddler, then a preschooler, then there were school pictures. By the time he got to the school photos, the child more clearly resembled the Akiko he knew. Then there were dojo photos—Akiko in her little gi, her hair in a high ponytail, later as a teenager, her expression focused and almost grim. A final one, a photo of Ito and Akiko together, holding ice cream cones at the beach. Both smiling. She looked to be about eighteen. "Akiko will want these."

"Once they're no longer needed for evidence, we'll return them to her," Desoto promised. "If Ito's . . . you know. Gone."

Which, given his current condition, was a possibility.

"I've got photos of the Sherman twins," Navarro said, holding out the album he held so that everyone could see. "Dahlia and Raisa."

"All the grandchildren he never publicly acknowledged," Lennox said. "But he seemed to have cared for them. Supports the idea that he was trying to protect them by not telling them the truth."

"Protection from?" Burroughs asked.

"We were wondering if Ito was involved in organized crime," Lennox said.

"That makes sense," Desoto said, "because of Danny Takahashi, Paolo, and the gun running. But if Ito was involved, he hid it well. We haven't seen anything resembling a link to organized crime here in his condo. We haven't gotten his financials yet. We're hoping to have them later today. Maybe that'll show us something."

Sam hoped that Ito wasn't involved. For Akiko's sake. But it didn't look good.

He set the album aside and picked up the third. "This album is of Ito as a young man. This one looks like his high school graduation," he said, pulling free a photo that showed three young men in caps and gowns, arms across one another's shoulders. He flipped it over. "Three first names—Eddie, Mitch, and Joe. No last names. Eddie would be Ito. There's also a year—1964." He turned the photo to study it more closely, tilting it when Lennox leaned to look as well. "The sign behind them says MacKenzie High School."

"That's downtown," Burroughs said. "Became a charter school for science and tech about twenty years ago. They'll have old yearbooks, so we should be able to ID the other two. Why are you interested in this photo?"

"Not sure," Sam said, then had a thought. Or more like a memory. He googled Kenzo Takahashi on his phone. Kenzo was only in his fifties, so that wasn't him in the photo. But . . . "Kenzo Takahashi's father was Michitaka Takahashi."

"Mitch," Lennox said with approval. "Nicely done, Doc."

"How did you know that?" Navarro asked.

Sam shrugged. "Kit was talking about Kenzo and his father, the businesses they started. Now, knowing that Kenzo's son studied karate with Ricky Nicchi at Ito's dojo . . . It seems the families are closer than we thought. Has anyone approached Kenzo Takahashi yet?"

"We haven't," Desoto said. "We planned to interview him later today. Why?"

"These three young men look like best friends. If Ito is involved in something illegal—something he might have protected his children and his grandchildren from—and he was friends with Mitch back in the sixties . . . I don't know. It seems like we should get more information before we knock on Kenzo's door."

"Not show our hand too soon?" Burroughs asked.

Sam nodded slowly. "Or not alert Kenzo to the fact that Akiko is his daughter, if he doesn't already know. That might have been what Ito was trying to hide. Otherwise, why wouldn't Kenzo have adopted her out of foster care? But Ito didn't do that. He left her there in foster care, while seeing her every week at the dojo. I don't know much about Akiko's background, but I do know that she was in several homes. At least one bad one before coming to McKittrick House. Maybe Ito didn't adopt her because he didn't want Kenzo to find out about her."

"Mary Sherman left her in the system, too," Lennox said. "Assuming she knew."

Sam thought of Alf Ashton's wife, how she'd surrendered her child for adoption. How she'd hinted that she'd done so because her home life at the time was abusive. How she wouldn't have tried contacting her son unless he was in some sort of danger.

Mary had done just that. Akiko wasn't her child, but she'd been there from the beginning of Akiko's life.

"Akiko's mother and uncle were murdered the day before she was left in a box in front of the firehouse as an infant," he said. "I think Mary left her there. I think Mary and Ito knew all along where Akiko was. And I think Ito planned to take Akiko on as a scholarship student all along. He established the scholarship program the year she was born, so by the time she was five years old, he'd taken in many children already. She wouldn't stand out."

Lennox was nodding. "So whatever Ito was hiding, Mary knew, too."

"I think Ricky Nicchi knows as well," Sam said. He held the photo of the three friends up to the light and examined the details.

The third man in the photo—Joe—had colorful tattoos on his left arm, possibly a sleeve that stopped at his wrist. His raised arm had the sleeve of his graduation gown riding up, exposing about two inches of the tattoo.

They had another, newer photo with a third man. On his phone, Sam opened his copy of the photo Leo Sherman had taken after following his wife to LA. Ito, Nicchi, Mary Sherman, and a third man. "He's wearing a coat in this photo. You can't see his arms. But look at his glasses."

They were the dark frames that so many men wore in the 1960s. The same as "Joe" wore in the 1964 photograph.

"Who?" Burroughs demanded. "Whose arms? Whose glasses?"

"You're right," Lennox said, then explained to the two detectives about Leo Sherman's photo.

"So you may have found the third man," Navarro said. "Well done."

"He might not be the same guy," Sam said. "I mean, who keeps the same style glasses for sixty years?"

Lennox chuckled. "My grandpa does. But even if it's not the same guy, we know that Kenzo's father and Ito were friends. And that these photos were important enough for Ito to lock away in the safe."

Sam replaced the photo and began flipping the remaining pages of the album. "There are more photos of the three of them, sometimes together, sometimes separately, but nothing that indicates who Joe might be."

"We'll work on getting the yearbooks for '64," Desoto said. "If this Joe really is the same guy as the present-day third man, maybe he can tell us what Ito and Mary Sherman were hiding."

Sam flipped to the final photo in the album and froze, staring at the two young men pictured. Joe and Mitch. Ito wasn't in the photo, so maybe he'd taken it. "Oh. Wow."

"Oh wow, what?" Navarro asked, leaning in to look over his shoulder, then sighed. "Oh. Wow."

Sam held the album so that the others could see. "That's a *lot* of ink."

Young Joe and Mitch stood next to a swimming pool. Both wore huge grins.

And tattoos over nearly every square inch of their exposed skin. The tattoos covered their torsos up to the collarbone and went down their arms and legs to ankle and wrist. There was a line of untattooed skin down the center of their torsos.

Sam had seen tattoos like this before.

"Yakuza," he whispered.

"Or the equivalent here in the US," Navarro said grimly.

"There's your tie to organized crime." Burroughs blew out a breath. "Does Ito have tattoos?"

Desoto shook his head. "The hospital never mentioned any."

Sam picked up the album with photos of Akiko and flipped through its pages again. "There are a few here of Akiko and Ito in their gis. She's wearing a T-shirt underneath hers, of course, but he isn't. You can't see any tats on his exposed skin, but they could be hidden under his clothes. We should find out. At a bare minimum, we need to find out who Joe is."

"Especially since Ricky Nicchi is in the wind," Navarro said. "And Ito hasn't been able to tell us anything."

As if summoned, Sam's cell buzzed with an incoming text from Kit.

Ito's in and out. Was awake and talking, but just fell back to sleep. Every time he stays awake a little longer tho. Are you finding anything?

Sam snapped a photo of the graduation picture, then typed his reply. *Found this in Ito's apartment. Ito on the right, Kenzo's father Michitaka "Mitch" in the middle, and "Joe" on the left. Taken in 64. Ask Ito who Joe is. We're on our way.*

Burroughs frowned. "Did you just send someone that photo?"

"I did," Sam said. "Detective McKittrick is with Ito right now and says he's staying awake a little longer each time and is more alert and verbal. I'd rather have her show it to him if he wakes up than wait until we get to the hospital."

Burroughs did not look like he agreed. "I'll take that album back."

Not really caring that he'd annoyed the LAPD, Sam gave the album to the detective. "Let's go."

Los Angeles, California
Wednesday, February 1, 11:30 a.m.

Kit stared at the photo of the three young men taken in 1964. "Eddie, Mitch, and Joe," she said softly, then showed her phone screen to Akiko. "Do you recognize any of these men?"

They sat at Ito's bedside, hoping the old man woke up again. Harlan stood outside the door, ever watchful. One of

Anson's employees stood guard outside the door to the ICU ward and the hospital's security had photos of Danny Takahashi, just in case he tried to enter.

Kit felt that she and Akiko were about as safe as they could be, under the circumstances.

Akiko studied the photo, then glanced at Ito, who lay sleeping. "That's Hanshi on the right. Wow, he was young. Who are the others?"

"The one in the middle is Michitaka Takahashi. Went by 'Mitch.'"

Akiko's eyes met hers. "Father of Kenzo?"

"Yes."

"My two grandfathers then, standing side by side."

Kit nodded. "Yes."

Akiko exhaled quietly. "How could he have kept this secret all my life? How *could* he?"

Kit's chest hurt at the betrayal her sister was feeling. "He said it would have been dangerous for you to know."

"Bullshit." Akiko spat the word with so much venom that Kit blinked.

Her sister never used that tone of voice. Then again, she'd never come face-to-face with evidence that she'd had family and the man she'd trusted had lied to her about it.

Harlan stuck his head through the doorway. "Akiko?"

"I have two grandfathers, Pop," Akiko said, her voice breaking. "I never knew either of them."

Harlan came into Ito's room, disregarding the two-visitor rule. Akiko needed him, so he was there. He glanced at Kit's screen, then sighed.

"I'm sorry, honey. But you know Ito," he said.

"Do I? I think I know what he was willing to show me. What else was he hiding?"

Kit's phone buzzed again with another incoming text from Sam.

Mitch and Joe are HEAVILY tattooed in old pics. Bodysuits. Bright colors. Maybe mob?

Kit's heart sank, because that explained quite a lot without explaining anything at all. Leaving her father to comfort Akiko, she returned to her chair next to Ito's bedside and typed out her reply. *Was Ito tattooed?*

Not that I could see from the pics.

I can't see any either, but he's covered in blankets and bandages right now.

Can you ask a nurse if they've seen any? Sam asked.

On it. Rising, she pocketed her phone. "I'll be right back. Have to ask the nurse a question."

Akiko lifted her head from Harlan's shoulder. "What? What are you going to ask them?"

Kit hesitated, then realized if she didn't come clean, she'd be just one more person keeping secrets from Akiko. "Do you know if Ito has any tattoos?"

"Not that I've ever seen. Why?"

"Because Mitch and Joe have a lot of them. Like, a helluva lot."

Akiko paled. "Like, 'the mob' a lot?"

"Maybe. I'll be right back." Kit went to the desk, where Ito's nurse stood typing into a laptop. "Hi. Can you tell me if Edwin Ito has any tattoos?"

"I can't tell you that. I'm sorry."

"You can tell me," Akiko said, coming to stand beside Kit. "I'm his medical power of attorney, and knowing about any tattoos will help my sister catch whoever put him here."

The nurse closed the lid of the laptop. "Then, yes, he has several tattoos on his back. There's a tiger and a dragon which is kind of curled around the tiger, but the dragon is unfinished. The outline is there, but he never had it filled in. Does that help you?"

Kit nodded. "It might, thank you." She hooked her arm through Akiko's and led her back to the chairs at Ito's bedside. "Let me tell Sam and then we can think about this."

Finished tiger and unfinished dragon. Both on his back, she texted.

Sam's reply was immediate. *Got it thx.*

Kit sat next to Akiko and took her hand. Harlan stood behind Akiko's chair, his big hands on her shoulders.

"That the tats weren't finished might be important," Kit began.

Akiko shook her head. "He was with the mob, wasn't he?"

"Yes," came the whispered reply from the bed.

Akiko's head whipped around to stare at the elderly man. "Why?"

Ito's mouth tightened. "Young. Stupid. Desperate. Take your pick, child."

"Are you still?" Akiko asked, voice breaking.

"No. Not since 1966."

"Why?" she whispered again.

"Couldn't do it. Couldn't kill."

"Couldn't?" Kit asked. "Or wouldn't?"

"Wouldn't," he said. "Not after the first two."

Akiko sucked in a pained breath. "You killed two people?"

"More than that, but the others were in 'Nam."

"You served in the Army for six years," Kit said.

"I did. Killed a lot of people there. But that was different. Or so they said." He was quiet for a few breaths. "I joined the Army to escape."

"Escape what?" Akiko asked.

"Mitch," Kit guessed. "Mitch and whatever dirty businesses he and his family were running."

He huffed a chuckle. "You've been busy, Detective."

"Needed to find out who keeps trying to kill me. And who's succeeded in killing others. Like Mary Sherman."

Ito flinched and the tip of his tongue swept over his lips. "Water?"

Akiko sprang to her feet, lifting his head gently as she held a cup with a straw to his lips. "Slowly." She repositioned his head on the pillow, caressing his cheek before stepping back.

"I'm sorry to be blunt, sir," Kit said levelly, aware that her mention of Mary was quickening his pulse, "but I need you to come clean with me. What's going on here? And who is Joe?"

Ito flinched again, then stilled, his eyes closing as he drew deep, steady breaths. His blood pressure slowly decreased and leveled to something approaching normal.

"Where is Ricky?" he asked.

"He's not here," Kit said curtly. "Stop changing the subject. I need to know who Joe is."

"Where is Paolo?" Ito asked. "Why hasn't he been here?"

Kit opened her mouth to tell him the truth, but Akiko swept in, shooting a glance at the blood pressure monitor. "He's not here, Hanshi. I'm not sure where he is."

"Bullshit," Kit whispered. "I need him to talk to me."

"I need him not to die," Akiko whispered back. "Not yet."

And this was why cops were supposed to recuse themselves from cases involving family, Kit thought. She was honestly tempted to give way to Akiko's wishes. But she couldn't. This was about more than Kit's job. More than Akiko's safety.

More than my safety. People had been murdered, and Ito knew why. Kit was sure of it.

"I'm sorry, Akiko," Kit said quietly. "But we have to get a straight answer."

Akiko turned to Kit, her eyes wounded yet sharp. "You're going to kill him."

"I'm trying to *save* him," Kit shot back. "And you."

Akiko's dark eyes flashed with anger. "I don't care about me. I don't want my grandfather to die. Not today. Save your questions for tomorrow. Please. For me."

Kit's eyes stung at her sister's whispered pleas, but she resisted, raising old barriers around her heart, barriers she hadn't used with Akiko in sixteen years. "Mr. Ito, who is Joe and why were you meeting with him and Nicchi and Mary?"

Another flinch followed by another ragged inhale.

And then another shake of his head.

"You can't tell me that you don't know," Kit said, controlling her anger. But just barely.

"No," Ito said heavily. "I cannot tell you that."

"Who are you protecting?" she demanded. "We can provide police protection for them."

Ito's laugh was utterly mirthless. "No, Detective. You cannot."

Kit tried to hold her temper. "Danny Takahashi nearly killed you. He nearly killed me. And he broke into Akiko's house, searching for something. He killed your daughter, Eddie. Your *daughter*. He killed Mary. Or should I say Himari?"

Ito began to tremble as he opened his eyes and met Akiko's gaze. "Is this true? Danny killed Mary?"

"Kit says so," Akiko said numbly, tears spilling down her cheeks. "And she's rarely wrong."

"Mary scratched him," Kit said. "We got DNA from the skin cells under her fingernails. She fought him, Mr. Ito. She fought hard, but he still killed her."

"*Kit,*" Harlan said. "Don't do this."

Akiko was openly sobbing, and it was breaking Kit's heart.

"I want to stop," Kit said honestly. "I want to walk away and not press this man, Akiko's grandfather, for answers. But I don't have that luxury. Danny Takahashi has killed three people. Wounded three cops. Dammit, Akiko. What if you're next? Is that what you want, Ito? To lose your granddaughter? Or maybe all three of them, because Danny was also stalking Mary's daughter Dahlia. When he kills them, too, will you still say 'I cannot'?"

Kit's voice had risen and, while she wasn't shouting, she was being louder than she needed to be. So she drew a breath. "Who is Joe?"

Ito shook his head. Then he frowned. "He killed my Mary. Who are the other two?"

Akiko dropped her face in her hands, her shoulders shaking with silent sobs. Kit closed her eyes and counted backward from ten. Then she counted backward again. *You're trying to save your sister. You're trying to save them all. Anyone who's on Danny Takahashi's list.*

When she opened her eyes, Ito was staring straight at her.

"Who, Detective?" he demanded. Then he seemed to shrink into the pillow. "Paolo? Is that why he's not here? Did Danny kill my Paolo?"

Kit wasn't going to lie to him. Too much was on the line. "Yes, sir. I'm sorry. Who is Joe?"

Ito stared for another thirty seconds before the tears filling his eyes began to run down his cheeks.

Then, once again, he shook his head. "I cannot," he whispered, his voice ragged and tortured. "My Paolo . . . Did he suffer, Detective?"

Kit thought of Paolo's body, his face beaten until he was unrecognizable. Then she looked at Akiko, whose hands still covered her face.

"No, sir," she lied. "He didn't suffer."

Ito shuddered out a muted wail. "I thought you'd be a better liar, Detective. Paolo was my son. Not by blood, but I've been his legal guardian since he was three years old. I watched him grow up. I bandaged his knees. I dried his tears. Took him to the doctor when he got the flu. I took him to school. I helped him with his homework."

Kit's heart broke a little more. "And when you moved from LA to San Diego to start a new dojo, you brought him with you." It was a guess, but she was pretty certain. The timing matched up with when Paolo met Akiko.

"I did."

"Joe left us clues, you know," she said gently, because she genuinely feared the man would break. "He directed us toward passengers on Akiko's boat. Whatever this is about, sir—whoever this is about—they boarded your granddaughter's boat. They were as close to her as you are to me right now."

Ito closed his eyes once again. He said nothing.

And Kit understood. "You knew, didn't you? You knew they were closing in on Akiko, that they planned to incriminate her in their gun-running scheme. That's why Mary came forward when she did. To warn my sister."

Ito nodded once. And then he turned his face away and wept.

Kit sighed. This was all she was going to get.

"I'm sorry, sir. I truly am. I *hate* having to do this, *hate* having to be the bad guy." Kit's eyes stung again and this time she couldn't hold back her own pain. Her voice broke, but she couldn't care. "I *hate* having Akiko look at me like she is now. Like I'm a fucking monster." Because Akiko was doing exactly that, and Kit wasn't sure she could draw a full breath. Her chest hurt. "But I'll be a fucking monster a million times over to keep her safe. I'm going to find Joe, with or without your help."

She rose and moved to the door of Ito's ICU room on unsteady legs. "Pop? Keep her here, okay?" Angrily, she dashed the tears from her cheeks. "Keep her safe. I have to go."

"Kit, wait." Harlan started after her. "Kitty-Cat."

She shook her head hard and sped up, passing Anson's employee as she left the ICU. She pressed the button for the elevator, then turned to the man guarding the door. His name was Eric, and he was a retired LAPD cop. He could keep them safe. "I have to go. If anyone goes in that you haven't cleared, can you follow them? I don't want Akiko and Pop alone. Ever."

Eric didn't ask her if she was all right, which she appreciated. He only nodded. "You need anything else, you let me know, okay?"

"Thanks." She stared at the elevator display for a few seconds before heading for the stairwell. It was only nine flights, and she had energy to burn.

And answers to find. Because whatever Ito was hiding, it was clearly killing him to do so. Whatever he was hiding was somehow more important than protecting Akiko's life.

Whatever he was hiding had to be big.

CHAPTER EIGHTEEN

Los Angeles, California
Wednesday, February 1, 12:05 p.m.

Sam checked his phone again as Lennox parked the SDPD sedan in the hospital's parking lot. He still hadn't heard from Kit, and he was worried. Something was wrong.

He and Lennox had followed Desoto to the hospital, with Navarro bringing up the rear, all of them using their vehicles' flashers to get them there quickly. Traffic had parted like the Red Sea, but Sam had still been cognizant of every second that ticked by.

They wanted to talk to Ito. They *needed* to talk to Ito.

But at this very moment, Sam was more concerned about talking to Kit. When he'd called the nurses' station to find out if Ito was still awake, he'd learned that Kit had left the ICU in a hurry, visibly upset. And alone. That wasn't like her. She wouldn't leave Akiko unprotected—especially now that they knew Ito's partial tattoo established a real connection to the mob.

"Still nothing?" Lennox asked.

"Nothing," Sam confirmed. "Not from Harlan or Akiko, either." He tapped Kit's name on his favorites list just as the hospital doors slid open.

"There she is," Navarro said, relief in his voice.

Sam's step faltered when he saw her face. She'd been crying. That wasn't like her, either.

"Ito must be dead," Navarro said, but Sam didn't think so.

Kit wasn't close to Edwin Ito. She was, however, close to Akiko, who flew through the sliding door behind Kit, Harlan on her heels.

Sam started to jog toward them.

"Kit!" Akiko shouted. "Stop!"

Kit turned to face her sister and father, her shoulders rigid, her chin high.

Sam upped his jog to a flat-out run. A family crisis, then.

I won't interfere, but I will be there for her.

Always.

"I'm sorry!" Akiko yelled. "Goddammit, Kit, I'm fucking sorry! You're not a monster. I swear you're not."

A monster? Kit?

My Kit?

Never.

"I don't want to hurt you," Kit said when Akiko came to a stop in front of her. Harlan wasn't far behind, his expression filled with sorrow. "I don't want to hurt Ito. But he has to come clean, Akiko. He has to."

"I know." Akiko took Kit's shoulders, giving her the

smallest of shakes. "I told Hanshi that if a hair on your head got harmed because of the secrets he was keeping, I'd never forgive him. You're not a monster."

Sam slowed his steps as he approached, listening.

"You're driven," Akiko went on. "Protective. But so is Hanshi. He thinks he's doing the right thing."

"Did you ask him to tell you who Joe was?" Kit asked, her tone frostier than Sam had heard it in some time.

She was re-erecting those damn walls.

He hated those walls. They'd finally started to come down. She'd finally started to let him in. To let her family in.

To let people love her the way she deserved.

Sam hoped they hadn't set back their progress too far, but if they had, he'd deal. He'd do what it took to pull those walls back down.

"He wouldn't tell me," Akiko said, seeming shaken. "He wouldn't even look at me."

"I'm sorry. I don't want you to damage your relationship with him. He's your grandfather."

"And you're my *sister*," Akiko said fiercely. "And you were right. I was wrong. This has gone way too far."

"He asked who the third victim was," Harlan said in his quiet way, his hands landing on Akiko's shoulders. "He didn't seem surprised when I told him it was a woman named Laurette Curry. He knows exactly what's going on, but he's not talking."

That was disappointing, Sam thought. They needed to find Joe. And if Ito wouldn't even tell Akiko, the secret had to be a big one.

He'd taken another step toward Kit when something

flashed at the edge of his vision. In what felt like slow motion, he turned to see Danny Takahashi emerging from behind a parked delivery truck, a gun in his outstretched hand.

No. Not Kit. Not Akiko. Not Harlan.

Sam didn't take another moment to think. He leapt, propelled by the most all-consuming fear he'd ever felt. He collided with Danny, using his weight to knock the kid to the ground. Before Danny could even react, Sam punched the young man's arm.

Right arm, because that was the one Alf Ashton had hit when he'd shot him. Danny screamed, a high, thin screech of sound. He twisted in Sam's hold, fighting like a cornered animal.

"No!" Danny yelled. "Let me go!"

"Drop the gun, Danny," Lennox commanded. "Or I'll shoot."

From the corner of his eye, Sam could see two sets of women's shoes—Lennox and Kit had come to his aid. Danny still held the gun, but Kit wrenched it free.

Danny threw a punch to Sam's temple, making him see stars, but he held on. Pulling his leg back, Sam kneed Danny's left, where Ricky Nicchi had shot him.

Danny screamed again but stopped thrashing. Sam flipped Danny to his stomach and grabbed his arms, yanking them behind his back as Lennox dropped to her knees beside them.

Lennox cuffed Danny, then yanked him to his feet. "Daisuke Takahashi, you're under arrest for the murders of Mary Sherman, Laurette Curry, and Paolo Feliciano. He's all yours for now, Desoto. We'll transfer him to San Diego after you've booked him for the attempted assault of Akiko here and for Ito's assault."

Sam stood, lungs straining for breath, his adrenaline running high. Kit was at his side, her arm around his waist.

"You okay?" she said, handing Danny's gun to Lennox.

"Yeah. You?"

"Not a scratch." She looked up at him, her lips curving up into a wry smile. "You did it again. Stopped my heart by leaping on someone with a damn gun."

He *had* done that once before.

"No regrets," he said. "Would do it again to keep you safe."

She sighed. "And then you say things like that, and I can't yell at you anymore."

Sam chuckled, relief swamping him. Current threat neutralized. He could rest. Until next time. There would always be a next time with Kit in his life.

He was totally okay with that.

Detective Desoto had gripped Danny by the upper arm while reading him his rights and placing him under arrest for assault with a deadly weapon and the illegal possession of a firearm. Periodically, Danny tried to run, but Desoto shook the boy hard each time.

"You gonna fight me, kid?" he asked when he finished with the Miranda. "Do I need to cuff your ankles, too?"

Danny spat on Desoto's shoes.

"Shit." Desoto yanked Danny up on his toes. "You don't disrespect me like that, you little motherfucker. I don't care who your daddy is or how much money he's got. I'm adding assaulting a cop to the charges."

Danny looked like he'd spit again when Akiko pushed past everyone to stand in front of the seventeen-year-old. She stared at him for a long moment, then brushed a hank of hair from his eyes.

"Hey, Danny. Or should I say 'brother'?"

Danny's mouth twisted. "You're no family of mine."

"You're right. Blood, yes. Family, no. Does your father know about me?"

Danny glared. "Fuck off, bitch."

"Why did you beat up Hanshi Ito?" Akiko asked.

Danny said nothing.

"Why did you try to hurt my sister?" Akiko asked. "For a third time?"

"He wasn't trying to hurt me this time," Kit said. "He was pointing the gun at you, Akiko."

Akiko turned wide eyes in Kit's direction. "He was?"

Sam hadn't realized that. He'd only seen the gun and had assumed Kit had been the target.

Kit nodded. "He was."

"It's money, isn't it?" Harlan asked coldly. "Now that Akiko knows that she's Kenzo Takahashi's daughter, you're no longer content to let her live. You don't want to have to share your inheritance with a newly discovered sibling."

Something flickered in Danny's eyes.

Harlan was right, Sam thought. Mostly. "I don't think Danny would have let her live even if she'd never found out about her biological father. For some reason, keeping Akiko alive served a purpose. I think he was in on the plan to frame her for smuggling guns. That's no longer going to happen, so she's now a liability."

Kit gently moved Akiko out of Danny's spitting range and got in the young man's face. "Who is Joe?"

Danny sneered. "I don't know."

"Liar," Kit said quietly. "We'll find out. Right now, LAPD has you on one count of assault and battery. San Diego PD has you on three counts of murder, three counts of assaulting a cop, and one count of attempted murder of a cop—me, on Sunday. You're young to be spending the rest of your life in prison. Oh well."

"Come on." Desoto yanked Danny toward his vehicle. "Let's go."

Akiko stared after them, then threw her arms around Kit. "You stopped him. He can't hurt anyone else."

Kit winced at the pressure on her arm but held on tight. "But I don't think he was working alone, Akiko. He's only seventeen, too young to mastermind the gun running. We have to find out who's pulling the strings. We need to find Ricky. Or find out who Joe is."

Akiko was the first to pull away. "You're right. Let's go back and talk to Hanshi."

Los Angeles, California
Wednesday, February 1, 1:00 p.m.

Sam wanted to shake the frail old man who currently lay in the hospital bed. Ito had continued to refuse to cooperate with them. He'd continued to remain mute.

They'd asked him again and again to give them the information they sought, and he'd continued to say no. Sam had cajoled, Kit had demanded, and Akiko had begged, tears running down her cheeks.

Ito had categorically refused to speak with them.

Lennox and Navarro had remained quiet, standing by the door throughout their pleas. Harlan McKittrick stood outside in the hallway. The big man appeared to be barely holding it together. His daughters were being targeted, and the one man who could help them was refusing to do so.

It made no sense.

Sam could see that Kit was losing her patience. Frankly, he'd lost his already.

She leaned over the bed, speaking quietly. "Danny Takahashi just tried to *kill* your granddaughter, who you claim to love." Ito grimaced, just as he'd done the first five times she told him. "He did kill Paolo. Why are you protecting him?"

Ito shook his head and remained silent.

"I think the better question is," Sam said, "who could be worth your silence? Who *are* you protecting?"

Eddie Ito turned his face away from Kit and Sam, who stood on one side of his bed, closing his eyes so that he didn't have to look at Akiko, who stood on the other side. "Please stop," he murmured. "Just . . . stop."

Sam stepped back from the hospital bed, shaking out his hands. He'd been clenching his fists so hard that his fingers ached. It was a singularly helpless feeling. Ito knew what was going on. He *knew*. Sam had never been surer of anything in his life.

"This is unbelievable," he muttered.

Never before had he wanted to strike an old man.

"Excuse me." Lennox approached Ito's bed. "Mr. Ito, my name is Detective Lennox, SDPD. I'm the primary investigator on this case. You have evidence that you're refusing to share with your family and their friends. I'm asking you now in an official capacity. Why were you meeting with Mary Sherman, Riccardo Nicchi, and a man named Joe?"

Ito remained silent.

"All right," Lennox said. "You really leave me no choice." She pulled her phone from her pocket. "Will you look at me, sir?"

Clenching his jaw, Ito opened his eyes. Then clenched them shut again when Lennox showed him a photo of Paolo Feliciano's body.

"That's what he's capable of doing," Lennox said. "That's what we're trying to protect Akiko from. I know you can help us."

"Mr. Ito?" The nurse entered his room and frowned at them. She hadn't said a word when Lennox had shown her badge earlier, but she clearly didn't want them all to be there. "What can I do for you?"

Sam realized that Ito held the call button clutched in his hand. *Asshole.*

"Make them leave," Ito rasped.

"Everybody out," the nurse ordered.

"We'll go," Lennox said. "Just know that from here on out, you're a material witness. LAPD has agreed to station a uniformed officer outside your room. Once you've recovered enough to be discharged from the hospital, we'll be putting you in protective custody. You will not be permitted to go home. You will not have your freedom. Do you understand?"

Ito nodded. "I understand."

"You all have to go. *Now.*" The nurse ushered them all out the door, threatening to put them on the no-visit list because they'd caused Ito such distress.

"I'll show him distress," Kit muttered once the six of them had crowded into the elevator. "I'm sorry, Akiko. I honestly thought he'd tell us once he realized that you were in danger, too."

"I thought so, too," Akiko said, visibly depressed. "I thought he loved me."

Harlan's big hands were fisted at his sides. "God forgive me, I wanted to hit him. I wondered why Danny would beat him so thoroughly when he was supposed to have respected him. Now I'm imagining Danny asking him for whatever it was he was searching for and Ito just saying 'no.' It's infuriating."

Sam sighed. "I know. I wanted to hit him, too, and I'm now questioning my own moral compass."

"Don't do that," Lennox said. "Your moral compass is pointed at Kit and Akiko, just as it should be. And neither of you actually hit him, so don't feel guilty for wanting to."

"I wanted to arrest the old bastard for conspiracy," Navarro said, "but I don't know what he's conspiring to do."

"And that should be the focus." Kit linked her good arm through Harlan's. "What were Ito, Mary, Nicchi, and Joe conspiring to do? What was Danny searching for? It's bigger than Danny Takahashi. He's only seventeen years old. He's not planning a smuggling operation on his own. Who is directing his efforts? Is it his father? This Joe person? Ito?" Akiko made a wounded noise and Kit sighed. "I don't want it to be Ito, either."

"But he's not making it easy for me to defend him," Akiko said.

The elevator opened and they left the hospital in silence, because Akiko was right. Ito wasn't making any of this easy at all.

All six of them began looking around when they exited the hospital, no doubt wondering if anyone else was waiting to shoot at them, but all Sam saw was a well-dressed man getting out of the back of a black Mercedes. Two hulking men in black suits also emerged from the car and, together, the three men headed toward them.

And, once they'd gotten closer, Sam saw why.

The well-dressed man was Kenzo Takahashi. He was about five-nine, his hair impeccably styled, his shoes polished to a dazzling shine. His suit was expensive. Must have cost upward of five thousand dollars. He wore dark sunglasses that reflected the light, making Sam want to blink.

But he didn't blink. This was Akiko's father. And Danny Takahashi's as well. That he might defend his son at the expense of his daughter was a distinct possibility, and Akiko had already been through so much.

Beside him Harlan tensed.

Akiko drew a deep breath. "Oh."

Kit's expression became grim. "I suppose we knew this was coming."

Lennox and Navarro said nothing at all. Sam glanced at them from the corner of his eye. Both of them looked . . . prepared.

For what, Sam had no idea.

As a group, they stopped, allowing Kenzo to approach them.

The man looked them up and down, then took off his sunglasses. Sam did blink then. The man's face was gaunt. The sunglasses had hidden the extent of it, but he looked sick. He looked far, far older than his fifty-eight years.

Now that he was closer, it was apparent that his expensive suit hung on his frame. He'd recently lost weight. A lot of weight.

He doesn't just look sick. He is sick. Or has been recently.

Kenzo's gaze lingered on Harlan. Then he focused on Akiko.

"Hello," he said, his voice both softer and deeper than Sam had expected. "My God. You look so much like your mother."

Kit moved closer to Akiko, her body language screaming protectiveness.

Takahashi ignored her, not looking away from his daughter. "I am Kenzo Takahashi."

Akiko nodded once. "I'm Akiko McKittrick."

Once again, Takahashi glanced at Harlan before returning his attention to Akiko. "I didn't know you existed before today. I learned of you in an online newspaper article."

"Tamsin Fucking Kavanaugh," Kit muttered.

Takahashi lifted a brow. "Yes, Tamsin Kavanaugh was the reporter." He took a step closer. "I didn't know I had a daughter. I'm . . . overwhelmed."

He sounded sincere, Sam thought. But there was something about the man—beyond his gaunt appearance—that didn't seem right. He was too smooth. Too confident. Just . . . too much.

"I just found out about you as well," Akiko said. "My aunt

tried to contact me but was murdered an hour before we were to meet. She was the first family to contact me since I was surrendered as an infant."

Takahashi frowned. "Your aunt?"

Ah. There it is. That was what had been bothering Sam. Kenzo Takahashi was lying. He knew about Mary Sherman. How long he'd known was the question.

"Mary Sherman," Akiko supplied, but her irritation was very thinly veiled. She knew he was lying, too. "My mother's younger sister."

Something flickered in Takahashi's eyes. It looked like rage, but it was quickly banked. "I didn't know she existed, either. Not until today."

Kit moved to stand in front of Akiko. "I don't know how long you've known about Mary Sherman and I don't know how long you've known about Akiko, but—"

"I don't lie," Takahashi interrupted. "You're very rude."

Kit didn't blink. "As I was saying, I don't know how long you've known about Mary and Akiko, but your son has known about her for quite some time. He killed Mary Sherman and he tried to kill Akiko only an hour ago."

Takahashi's eyes widened, and Sam thought that his surprise might be genuine. "What?" the man demanded. "What is this?"

Sam stepped to Kit's side. "Danny was arrested and taken into custody by LAPD for assault. When LAPD's done with him, San Diego will prosecute him for three homicides—Akiko's aunt, the man who was Akiko's business partner, and the mistress of Akiko's uncle."

And that they still didn't know why Laurette Curry had been targeted bothered Sam greatly.

"He also shot three cops," Kit said. "Including me. Aimed for my head."

"Then he's a very bad shot," Takahashi said blandly.

Sam saw red, but he bit his tongue to keep his angry words inside. There was a chance that this man knew nothing of Danny's plans. If he didn't, Sam's flying off the handle wouldn't help Akiko have a relationship with her biological father, should she choose to pursue one.

He hoped she wouldn't. He did not like this man.

Sam heard Harlan suck in a quick, startled breath at Takahashi's insolence.

Kit only smiled, equally blandly. "I moved at the last minute. He's killed three other people that we know of. He's a pretty decent shot, Mr. Takahashi."

A muscle ticced in Takahashi's taut jaw. "Please move aside, Detective McKittrick. I came to speak with my daughter. I'd like to have a few moments with her alone."

That Takahashi knew who Kit was wasn't a big surprise. Once he learned of his daughter's existence, it only made sense that he'd research her family.

"Nope," Kit said, her smile unwavering. "Akiko stays with me."

"And me," Lennox added. She was not smiling.

"And me," Harlan said.

Takahashi's gaze flitted to Harlan once again. "And you are, sir?"

Like he doesn't know. If Takahashi had dug deep enough to know about Kit, he knew who Harlan was. Sam's dislike for Takahashi grew.

Akiko took Harlan's hand and stepped around Kit and Sam. "This is Harlan McKittrick. He's my father."

Takahashi's rage was not so quickly banked this time. "I am your father."

Join me, Luke. Sam had to fight not to laugh. It was not the right time for levity and would likely sound hysterical anyway.

Kit had no such compunction. She snickered softly.

Takahashi turned his anger on her. "You are *exceedingly* rude, Detective. Akiko, please come with me. We have matters to discuss. *Family* matters."

Uh-oh, Sam thought. *That was the wrong thing to have said.*

Akiko smiled, but it was frosty. "Look, I don't know you, Mr. Takahashi. What I *do* know is that Kit and Pop are my family. When this is all over, when your son's accomplices are apprehended, I might like to get to know you. But until then, I'm sticking with my family."

Takahashi clenched his jaw. "What accomplices? To whom do you refer?"

"We don't know," Lennox said. "We were hoping you did. There's no way a seventeen-year-old kid acted alone. I'm surprised that LAPD hasn't called you, seeing as how Danny is still a minor and your son."

"If the authorities have called me," Takahashi said, "I haven't been told about it."

"How did you know to come here?" Harlan asked. "How did you know Akiko would be here?"

That was a very good question. Sam had been too thrown by the man's sudden appearance to think about the logistics.

Takahashi regarded Harlan coolly. "I have my sources."

"And what sources would those be?" Navarro asked. His tone was level, but harsh in a way that Sam had only heard a few times.

Beside Sam, Kit stiffened, but he wasn't sure why. Something had happened, though.

"Let's go, Akiko," she said. "Apologies, Mr. Takahashi. We need to be going now. I hope you understand. Akiko was nearly shot an hour ago by your son, and it's simply not safe for her to be out in the open. Do you have a business card? I imagine my sister will be happy to call you when this is all over and she's safe."

Takahashi frowned, and Sam was honestly intimidated. There was a sense of power rolling off him. Sam got the feeling that few people told this man no and that he wasn't at all happy about hearing it now.

Harlan put one hand on Kit's shoulder and the other on Akiko's. "I'm sure you'll agree that Akiko's safety is paramount. Being her biological father and all."

"Of course." The words were gritted out as Takahashi pulled a silver business card case from his pocket and removed a card. He scrawled something on the back, then took Akiko's hand, placed the card in her palm, and closed her fingers over it. "Call me. Please. I can tell you much about your mother."

"I'd like that," Akiko said quietly. "Thank you."

"It's time to go," Kit said. "Lieutenant Navarro, will you please follow us in your car, and Lennox, can you get us out of here?" They hustled Akiko to the SDPD sedan, where Kit put her in the back seat, sliding in beside her. Harlan took his place on Akiko's other side. Lennox got behind the wheel and Sam took shotgun.

"Drive," Kit said tersely, snapping a quick photo out the side window with her phone. "Please."

Lennox obeyed, waiting until they were out of the hospital parking lot before looking at Kit in the rearview mirror. Sam hadn't taken his eyes off her. Her face was tense and a little pale.

"What is it, Kitty-Cat?" Harlan asked.

"Lennox, can you pull into that parking lot?" Kit pointed to the next driveway. "I'd like Navarro to hear this, too, and he's right behind us."

Lennox complied and a minute later, Navarro had stopped beside them and was climbing out of his vehicle.

The lieutenant bent over to lean into the car when Kit opened the back door. "What was that about?"

"There was a man with Takahashi," Kit said. "Got out of the Mercedes and stood there, watching us. It was when Takahashi said he had his sources. He wore a nice suit. Had a gun in a shoulder holster."

"Guns in both shoulder holsters," Lennox added grimly.

Kit leaned forward to see Lennox. "You saw him too?"

"I sure did."

"Who?" Sam asked impatiently. "Who did you see?"

"Yes, Kit," Akiko said quietly. "Who?"

Kit exhaled. "Joe. He works for Takahashi."

"Then why didn't you talk to him?" Akiko demanded.

"Because Ito's keeping secrets," Kit said. "Secrets that involve Joe. And I didn't like Takahashi. He's oily and . . . slithery. Like a crocodile. Until we know what secret Ito is keeping, I don't want to tell Takahashi anything."

"I agree," Navarro said. "I didn't see him, but I agree that Ito hasn't disclosed Joe's information for a reason."

"Is Hanshi safe?" Akiko asked shakily.

"Anson's man is standing outside the ICU," Kit said. "He knows not to let anyone in who isn't cleared."

"But he has no official jurisdiction," Lennox said. "Lieutenant, if you'll stand guard over Ito until LAPD's uniform gets there, I'll drop these guys off at a hotel, then I'll head to LAPD in case Desoto is able to get Danny Takahashi talking. Also, Kit, if you can send me the photo you just took of Joe, I'll have someone in the lab run facial recognition on it. It'll be a better photo than the one Leo Sherman took."

Kit held up her phone. "Just sent it. Also, you don't need to take us to a hotel. We're staying with my brother Anson in Anaheim. He has room. If you stay, text me and I'll send you the address."

That she hadn't included Navarro in the invite was telling. The lieutenant didn't say a word, just returned to his own vehicle, his shoulders slumped.

"Thank you." Lennox put the sedan in gear. "I'll let you know. For now, I'll get you all settled at your brother's house so we can all get to work."

That Kit would continue investigating didn't seem to be a question in Lennox's mind, and Sam appreciated that. So, apparently, did Kit.

"Meghan," she said quietly as Lennox pulled into traffic.

"Yeah?"

"Thank you," Kit said simply.

"You're welcome."

CHAPTER NINETEEN

Anaheim, California
Wednesday, February 1, 3:15 p.m.

I think Joe was wearing a listening device," Kit said.

They'd gathered around Anson's kitchen table after Lennox had dropped them off. Kit's brother had arrived back from San Diego a few hours earlier, leaving Baz to watch over McKittrick House. Kit hadn't seen Anson in a long time, but there was no time for a reunion.

Sam sat at her side, studying the photo of Joe on her phone.

Her father was whittling a piece of wood, his movements shaky and completely unlike the serene way in which he normally carved. He was still tense with anger over the surprise meeting with Kenzo Takahashi. Not because he'd met one of his children's bio parents. Several of Harlan and Betsy's children had sought out their birth parents after being adopted. Her parents were always supportive.

No, Kit figured it was Takahashi's dismissal of his son's attempt on her life that had angered Harlan. He hadn't reacted well when Takahashi had disrespected their family, declaring himself Akiko's father—and, really? Kit had found it impossible not to laugh. Harlan hadn't laughed, though. He'd already been furious.

And he'd asked the most relevant question of all—how had Takahashi known where Akiko would be?

"Why do you think Joe wore a listening device?" Akiko asked. She sat with her hands neatly folded on the table, but her shoulders sagged, and she looked weary.

"Because of when Joe got out of the car," Anson answered. "Right, Kit? You said it was right after Pop asked Kenzo Takahashi how he'd known where Akiko would be."

Kit nodded. "And Takahashi said that he had sources." She frowned at Anson's laptop, which she'd been using to search for more information on Akiko's bio father. "I assume that was Joe. He's working for Kenzo, but also with Ito."

"Playing both sides of the fence," Sam said. "But to what purpose?"

She nodded. "Exactly. We need to know what Joe's role is in the Takahashi corporation. He was armed like a bodyguard, but he's pushing eighty years old. He wouldn't be an actual bodyguard. I need to do more research."

"The girls already have," Anson said wryly. "Rita and Emma have been leading the charge."

Harlan scowled. "How did the girls know about this?"

Anson rolled his eyes. "They read the article identifying Danny Takahashi as Mary Sherman's murderer."

"Tamsin Fucking Kavanaugh," Sam muttered.

Kit snorted. "That is her name forevermore."

Anson chuckled. "That's what Rita says, too."

"So they've been reading up on the Takahashis," Kit said thoughtfully. "What did Dawn say?" Because the girl was insightful.

"She wouldn't say anything for the longest time," Anson said, "but we could tell she wanted to say something. We had to wheedle it out of her."

Harlan put down the block of wood in his hands. "Why wouldn't she speak her mind?"

"Because she feels sorry for Danny Takahashi and didn't want to be disloyal to Akiko."

Kit was surprised. "Why would she feel sorry for Danny? He's killed a lot of people."

"And shot at Kit," Sam added.

"That's why she was sitting silently, biting her lips."

Kit could picture it. Of all the teenagers at McKittrick House, Dawn tried hardest to be tough. *So much like I was.* "Well, tell us what she said."

"Danny's mother died by suicide," Anson said. "It was in one of the articles the girls found on Danny and his father. Danny was eight and he found his mother's body."

"I did read that," Kit said. "My first thought was that he'd had a rough childhood, but that doesn't—"

"Doesn't excuse being a goddamn psycho asshole killer," Akiko interrupted angrily.

"Of course not," Anson said. "But Dawn said she felt for him because his father used Danny's trauma for his own benefit. Google 'Takahashi Los Angeles suicide prevention charity.'"

Kit obediently did so, then exhaled. "I can see her point." She turned the laptop so that the others could view the Takahashi charity's website. "This is a different charity than the one I mentioned this morning. That one used Danny as an example of troubled teens who need help with mental health. This one is suicide prevention. He's posted a photo of Danny at the time of his mother's death. Making people feel sorry for the fact he found his mother hanging from a closet pole. It's all 'Don't let this happen to other kids. Donate and we'll help people not end their lives this way.' Playing off the kid's trauma."

"Think of the children," Anson added with a sarcastic edge. "And open your wallets. Not saying that they don't do good things with that money, but it's a shitty way to raise funds. I kind of doubt Danny was asked if he wanted to be a poster boy for his father's charity."

Kit had to agree. "Either charity. Kenzo uses Danny in both of them."

"He looks catatonic in this picture of him at eight years old," Sam said.

Anson nodded. "Which is what Dawn said. I got the impression she had a personal reason for being so upset, but I didn't ask. And then for Danny to find out that he had a sister out there, one who was fathered while his parents were married." He shrugged. "She knows what he did was wrong, but she can see why he's so angry."

"I hadn't done that math," Sam said. "When did Kenzo and Danny's mother marry?"

Kit checked her notes. "Kenzo married his wife, Umeko, when he was twenty-one. She was eighteen."

"Young," Akiko said thoughtfully.

"They were," Kit agreed. "Danny wasn't born until twenty years later. She was thirty-eight."

Anson came to sit beside her and pulled his laptop closer so that he could type. "Here's the article that Dawn found. It discusses the various charities that were operating in the city at the time. This was nine years ago, by the way. It wasn't written by Takahashi or any of his charity's employees. It says that Umeko Takahashi experienced postpartum depression and had never recovered. That her suicide was tied to that. Who knows whether that's true or not?"

Kit skimmed the article and then glanced at the comments that followed. "Huh. Here's a comment calling Kenzo a hypocrite, saying he didn't love his wife, that he cheated on her 'with abandon,' and that he blamed his son for his wife's mental illness."

"What an asshole," Harlan said, his teeth clenching. "Blaming the child, using the child to get donations? I hope I don't see him again. I'm sorry, Akiko, but I don't think I could stop myself from punching him in the mouth."

"I'll hold your coat," Akiko said grimly. "So far I'm not impressed with my paternal bloodline."

Or her maternal bloodline, but Kit wasn't going to say that aloud. Edwin Ito might be doing what he thought was right for all his grandchildren.

Kit read the comment again, because something was tugging at her memory. "There's something about this commenter that's familiar." On her phone, she pulled up the notes she'd been taking on Kenzo Takahashi the night before. "Here it is. Like I said, Kenzo runs two mental health charities. One is for suicide prevention and uses the photo of the eight-year-old

Danny to tug at heartstrings and open wallets. The other is for 'at risk' kids—kids like Danny who got into trouble and ran away from home. Sam, remember when I mentioned that I saw a comment on the teen charity's website saying that Kenzo was a hypocrite and that Danny had run away because his father had disowned him?"

"Yeah. You said that the comment was taken down within hours."

"I'm glad I took screenshots. The commenter's exact words were: 'Kenzo is a hypocrite. He didn't love his son. He disowned him when he needed him most. But that's no surprise. He's always been a sorry excuse for a man, cheating on his wife *with abandon.*'" She made air quotes around the phrase.

"It's the same commenter?" Anson asked. "'With abandon' isn't a phrase you see every day."

"Maybe." Kit opened the most recent article about Danny and Kenzo Takahashi. "Here's Tamsin Kavanaugh's latest. It's where she names Danny as Mary's killer and names his father as Kenzo. And . . . yep. Another comment. Similar wording. No 'with abandon' this time, but he or she calls Kenzo a hypocrite."

"They really must hate Kenzo a lot," Akiko said. "I'd like to talk to this person."

Kit did, too. "The username is the same in all three comments. *Oneesan.*"

Akiko leaned in to see Kit's phone screen. "'Oneesan' means 'older sister.' I wonder if this woman is Umeko's sister."

Kit wondered the same. "I'll find out who her sister is. She may be able to give us information on Danny. I want to know what went down between him and his father. I want to know if Kenzo was involved in the smuggling operation. But I don't think I'll ever feel sorry for Danny, despite his childhood trauma." She could see Dawn's point, but her aching arm was a constant reminder that Danny really was a goddamn psycho asshole killer. "At any rate, any info we can get will help Lennox when she questions him. She might be able to get him angry enough to give her the information we need."

"I'll make sure Dawn knows she's okay to have these opinions," Akiko said. "I'm not mad. She's right, kind of. But I can't feel sorry for him. He's left too many victims in his wake."

"But *why*?" Kit asked. "I mean, it's most likely that he killed Mary so that she couldn't talk to you, Akiko. But why her and not you? If Pop was right and this is about money, about sharing an inheritance, why not simply kill *you*?"

"I don't think that was the original plan," Sam said. "They wanted to frame Akiko for the gun running. That was either to hurt Ito or Kenzo Takahashi. Or both. Given that Ito has been conspiring with Joe and that Danny has reason to hate his father, I'm more inclined to believe this is about Kenzo."

Kit nodded. "True. And now that we know that Ito, Joe, and Kenzo's father were involved in some kind of organized crime back in the sixties, it's likely that Kenzo has taken over his father's businesses. So what was Danny trying to do? And is Joe a good guy or a bad guy? Was Mary good or bad? And what about Ricky Nicchi and Ito?"

"Hanshi is *not* involved in organized crime," Akiko said quietly but fiercely. "Not anymore. I won't believe it."

Kit wouldn't force her to. Not unless they found incontrovertible evidence.

"So let's say that that Mary, Ito, Nicchi, and Joe are good guys," Sam said. "Let's say they wanted to protect Akiko from whatever it is that Danny is planning. Who's controlling Danny? His father? Joe? Someone else?"

Kit wondered that, too. "Like you said, Joe is playing both sides of the fence. He works for Kenzo, but it was probably Joe who posted those photos in Laurette Curry's bedroom." An important clue that they hadn't followed up on yet. "Akiko, can you check your passenger files? Specifically passengers who went on your boat after Christmas, but go back to October. That was Mary's first trip to LA."

Akiko reached out her hand. "Give me the laptop and I'll check right now."

"Let's check together." Because Kit wasn't sure what they'd see and Akiko was extremely fragile at the moment. "I won't leave you."

"Thank you," Akiko whispered, then logged in to her cloud account. "I'll look at January's passengers first. We make copies of all passengers' driver's licenses for insurance purposes, so I have photos of their faces."

The others gathered near, Sam standing behind Kit, his presence like a warm blanket. Harlan sat next to Akiko and Anson looked over Akiko's shoulder.

Akiko was scrolling through the passengers' driver's licenses when she froze, a photo of Joe filling her screen. The name on the photo was Jim Smith.

Kit sighed. She'd expected something like this, but it was still unsettling. Someone who worked for Kenzo Takahashi had been on her sister's boat. The question was, did Joe work with Danny, too? "It's a good photo, at least. We should send it to Lennox. It'll be better to run through facial recognition than the photo I took in front of the hospital."

Akiko squared her shoulders. "I just forwarded it to you, Kit. I don't have Lennox's contact info."

Kit texted the photo to Lennox. *Joe was a passenger on Akiko's boat on Jan 23.* "Were you on that charter, Akiko?"

"No. This was after I called Mary back and she said she was going out of town, so we had to wait two weeks to meet. I had a bad feeling about meeting Mary and was too nervous to go on the charters without Paolo or you. He had the flu for a week, and we had to cancel several charters, but he was better by the twenty-second. He ran the trip that Joe went on."

Kit sent another text to Lennox. *Akiko was not onboard that day. Paolo took the boat out.*

"So," she said grimly, "*why* was Joe on your boat, Akiko? To meet you? To scope it out? To see if Paolo would be a good smuggling partner?"

Sam lightly squeezed her shoulder. "Wait. If Joe was on the boat on the day when Akiko wasn't, how did he get those pictures of her?"

Kit looked back at him, frowning. "That's a damn good question." She noted it in her phone. "Something more we need to figure out, but right now I'm wondering if that ATF agent—Brewer—knew that Joe had boarded." She angled the laptop toward herself and began scrolling through the remaining January photos. "None of Danny. None of Kenzo." She stopped again, anger roiling in her gut. "Here's Agent Brewer. He boarded on January fourth."

"I remember him," Akiko said. "It didn't seem like he wanted to fish. Spent a lot of time watching everyone else."

"Not a good undercover agent if you noticed him scoping out the other passengers," Sam observed. "Did he go by Brewer?"

Kit huffed. "Joe signed his name as Jim Smith. Brewer signed his as John Smith. So very original."

Harlan scowled. "An ATF agent was scoping out Akiko's boat?"

"Probably looking for contraband," Sam said. "I got the sense he'd been working this case for a while." He put his hands on Kit's shoulders and massaged her tense muscles.

She nearly groaned, it felt so good.

She didn't groan, but she did lean into his touch while she continued scrolling backward from January. None of the faces in December looked familiar. "When did Paolo start doing solo runs?"

"Right after Labor Day," Akiko said.

Kit continued to search the faces of Akiko's passengers, then stopped on Saturday, October 22. "Here's Danny."

Akiko nodded at the photo of Danny Takahashi. "Said his name was Dai Nakamura. Dai is short for Daisuke." She exhaled heavily. "Nakamura was my mother's last name, remember? She was Minako Nakamura after her mother divorced Hanshi. Danny knew. He used her name. Like he was mocking me."

"Were you onboard that day?" Kit said.

Akiko shook her head. "No, we were all at McKittrick House."

"That was Rita's fourteenth birthday party," Harlan said. "Akiko, would Danny have known that you weren't going to captain that day?"

"It was on my website," Akiko said. "We always list who

the captain and first mate will be. It gives passengers confidence. So yes, Danny would have known."

"I wonder if that was when he approached Paolo about the guns," Kit said. "Because he knew you wouldn't be there. But that doesn't make sense. Paolo would have recognized him. They knew each other from the dojo."

"Maybe Paolo was already compromised," Akiko said sadly. "Paolo said he was mentoring the kid, but maybe they were already planning to ship the guns. Did they successfully use my boat to smuggle guns?"

"I didn't think so," Kit said. "Brewer indicated that they hadn't completed a sale. But he also didn't mention that he'd been on your boat."

"I didn't trust him," Sam said.

Kit nodded. "Same. I knew he wasn't telling the whole truth."

"I need to call an attorney," Akiko murmured faintly.

"I texted Georgia earlier," Kit said. "She's going to send me the names of some lawyers that she trusts."

"This is a nightmare," Akiko whispered. "Danny and Joe and that ATF guy? All on my boat? Watching me? Watching Paolo?"

"Sounds like Paolo needed to be watched," Sam said gently.

"Why didn't he ask me for money? I would have given him what I had."

They might not ever know the answer to that question.

Kit examined the photos of Akiko's passengers again. "The main players in Takahashi's circle seem to be Japanese, so let's focus on those passengers."

Sam leaned over her shoulder. "That man. He was on the October charter with Danny and Paolo."

Kit zoomed in on the photo. The man was Japanese, somewhere in his forties or fifties. He wore a huge smile in his photo, like he didn't have a care in the world. His name filled her with dread. "The name he gave was Aki*to* Jones."

"I was Akiko Jones before Mom and Pop adopted me," Akiko said, her voice thin and reedy. "They planned this. From months ago, they were planning to frame me."

"I'd have to agree," Kit said grimly. She opened one of the folders in Akiko's cloud account. "These are the passenger names. Let's see if there's anyone else we recognize." She began to scroll, sighing when she saw Dai Nakamura on five different charters. "Danny was a passenger six times in total, starting in October."

Akiko checked her calendar. "All days that Paolo went out on his own."

Kit frowned. "Who was Paolo's first mate? He didn't go totally alone, did he?"

"No, he hired the son of one of the other captains at the marina. Kid's name is Jorge Montoya. He's eighteen or nineteen."

"Oh, I know him," Kit said. "He's a nice kid. We should talk to him, both for info on Paolo and to warn him. I'll let Lennox know." She dialed Lennox's phone, because she hadn't gotten a reply from her text with Joe's photo attached.

Lennox answered, sounding slightly out of breath. "Hey, Kit. I was just about to call you. Thanks for the photo of Joe."

"You're welcome. I have you on speaker. My father, Akiko, Anson, and Sam are with me. We have another photo for you to run through facial recognition."

"Who?"

"Danny Takahashi and one other man were passengers on Akiko's boat. Neither used their real names. The guy we don't recognize gave his name as Akito Jones."

"Almost the same as Akiko's name before your folks adopted her."

Kit wasn't surprised that Lennox knew that. She was a damn fine cop. "Exactly. You should also talk to a kid named Jorge Montoya. He was Paolo's first mate on all the charters he took out without Akiko."

Lennox got very quiet. "Did you say Jorge Montoya?"

Oh no. "Yes. What's happened?"

"Jorge Montoya was found dead in his parents' house this morning. They'd gone out of town and found his body when they got home. He was shot in the head. Been dead for a few days at least. Ballistics is running the slug the ME took out of him. Navarro just told me thirty minutes ago. He said I should let you know, just in case it was connected."

"They're snipping off loose ends," Kit said.

Alarmingly pale, Akiko lurched to her feet and ran for the bathroom.

"They are," Lennox said. "Nobody knew the connection between the Montoya kid and Paolo until now. I'll let Navarro know."

"Thanks." Kit texted the photo of "Akito Jones" to Lennox. "This guy accompanied Danny Takahashi on Akiko's boat on October 22."

"Only one trip?"

"I think so." Kit searched the spreadsheet containing passenger names and her gut clenched at the result. "Oh shit. Not only one trip. He went on Akiko's boat five years ago." Harlan got up to look over her shoulder, his mouth tight, his jaw tense.

"Not just any trip, Kit. This was Akiko's very first charter. The first time she took her boat out. This guy who calls himself Akito Jones was there at the very beginning."

There was silence in the room, finally broken when Lennox sighed. "I'll get his and Joe's photos to Sergeant Ryland and ask him to run facial recognition. We need real names. Kit and Sam, I'm going to be interviewing Danny Takahashi along with Burroughs and Desoto in an hour. Kit, you can observe. Sam, I'd appreciate an assist in the interview room."

Sam was already looking at Anson. "Can we borrow your car?"

"Of course." Anson pulled his keys from his pocket.

"Lennox, we'll be there ASAP," Kit said and ended the call.

Los Angeles, California
Wednesday, February 1, 5:45 p.m.

"Thanks for coming in," Lennox said as she and Detectives Burroughs and Desoto walked Kit and Sam to the LAPD interview room where Danny Takahashi and his attorney were waiting.

"Has he said anything yet?" Kit asked.

Desoto shook his head. "Only that we're assholes."

"I printed out copies of the driver's license photos you sent me," Lennox said. "Maybe seeing their faces will shake an ID out of him."

"I doubt it," Burroughs said glumly. "His attorney is one of the best in the city."

"Who's paying for his attorney?" Sam asked.

"Daddy," Desoto said. "Kirk LaSalle is one of Kenzo's top lawyers. Normally he takes care of lawsuits, but he has defense experience."

"We might be able to play off that," Lennox said. "I got the impression that Danny didn't like his father overly much."

"Meghan, I know I told you that Danny's mother died by suicide," Sam said. "I don't know what his life was like with his father before that, but afterward, his father used his image to show how sad kids are whose parents kill themselves and, oh, don't you want to donate to my suicide prevention charity? That could be one of the sources of tension between Danny and his father." He showed Lennox and the LA detectives the photo of a grieving eight-year-old Danny. "That had to be humiliating for him, especially as he got older."

Lennox frowned. "That's really disgusting, using a child like that. Good to know. Thank you."

"Oh." Kit had forgotten all about the commenter on the articles about Kenzo Takahashi. "We should find Umeko Takahashi's sister. I think she's been leaving very negative comments on Kenzo Takahashi's website and articles written about him. The one I found on the website was immediately deleted, but Kenzo can't control the articles printed elsewhere."

"Let's find and talk to the sister when we're done with Danny," Lennox said. "Maybe she knows who Joe is. That's one of my goals in this interview. I want to know Joe's last name, who was helping Danny with the gun running, and who this mystery guy is who went on Akiko's first charter—Akito Jones."

"Akiko remembered him," Kit said. "After she gathered her wits." After she stopped throwing up in the bathroom. *Poor Akiko.* "She remembered him remarking that they nearly shared a name. She shrugged it off as small talk. She didn't remember him doing anything but fishing."

At the interview room, Kit and Sam parted ways. Sam followed Lennox and Desoto into Interview, and Kit entered the observation room.

She was surprised to see Navarro already seated. "Sir?"

He pointed to the chair beside him. "Please."

She sat, waiting for him to speak first.

He sighed. "I wish you'd trusted me to get this case solved. I've been working on it along with Lennox."

"I wish you'd trusted me with the truth," Kit replied. "I don't like being 'theater.'"

"Fair enough."

She drew a breath. "Am I really suspended?"

"Yes. But it won't hold. Have you contacted your union rep?"

"Not yet."

"You need to do that. I thought you'd do it the first day."

"I was too focused on finding out who shot Mary Sherman and who she was to Akiko."

"I knew you would be. I should have ordered you to call your union rep. Baz should have, too."

"My rep may have called me. I have a lot of unanswered voicemails." Kit pressed her fingertips against her throbbing temples. "I've really fucked this up, haven't I?"

"No. You'll walk away with a slap on the wrist. The way this is going, you and Lennox will solve this case, and it will just add to your . . . legend."

Her gaze flew to his profile. He was staring at the one-way mirror. He looked tired.

And suddenly Kit felt guilty for not having trusted him. "I have a legend?"

"You know you do. Even Tamsin Fucking Kavanaugh can't make you out to be the bad guy in her articles."

"She said SDPD kicked me to the curb." Which had hurt far more than she'd allowed herself to admit.

"And made SDPD—and me—look like the villains. It'll be okay, Kit. I've been feeding West information that isn't true. Eventually enough of it'll end up in Kavanaugh's column and I'll have him dead to rights. You were a bit of an unintended casualty, unfortunately. It was my luck that West's next case would be Akiko's."

She was quiet for a moment. "Are we okay, sir? You and I?"

"Yeah. Just . . . call your union rep, Kit. I need you back at work."

"Yes, sir."

One side of his mouth lifted. "And it finally doesn't sound like a slur." He nodded at the mirror. "Your doctor is giving Danny Takahashi the evil eye."

Sam was indeed giving the seventeen-year-old the frostiest of glares. "If Sam steps over the line, Lennox will boot him out. She's a good cop, sir."

"I know. When you come back, you'll partner with her. Until Connor returns."

"And then? What will happen to her?"

Navarro turned to look at her, amused. "Have you become attached to Lennox?"

"No, but I respect her. She seems to want to do the right thing."

"When Connor comes back, I may create a three-person team for a while. We'll figure it out when we get there."

"Okay. Thank you, sir."

He nodded once. "They're starting."

Kit sat forward, her attention on Danny Takahashi. He looked smug, the little bastard. His mouth was curved in an obnoxious smirk and he sat in the chair, legs splayed wide.

Just chillin'. No worries.

"Trying to be a little gangsta," Kit murmured.

"Apropos if Daddy is a big gangsta," Navarro murmured back.

On the other side of the glass, Lennox formally introduced herself, Sam, and the LA detectives. Burroughs stood off to the side, leaning against a wall. Desoto sat on Lennox's right, Sam on her left. "So. Anything to say for yourself?"

"I've advised my client to say nothing," the attorney said. He was very polished. A stereotypical corporate shark.

"I figured," Lennox said. "Your client shot three cops and killed four innocent people."

Danny merely blinked.

"Four?" His attorney frowned. "You said he was being charged with three homicides."

"We found another," Lennox said. "Jorge Montoya. He was first mate to Paolo Feliciano. Killed the same way, bullet to the head. Ballistics just confirmed the bullet was fired from the gun that was in your possession this afternoon, Danny. I gotta tell ya, son, it doesn't look good for you."

Danny's teeth clenched. "I ain't your son."

"No," Sam said, "you're Kenzo Takahashi's son and you don't like your father very much. I wouldn't, either, if he'd humiliated me the way he did you. Using your face to raise money for a charity that made a mockery of your mother's death."

"You don't know nothin'," Danny said sullenly.

"I know what you looked like at eight years old," Sam said. "Catatonic. Lights off and nobody home. I can't blame you, of course. Finding your mother the way you did."

Danny's eyes narrowed. "You don't know nothin'," he repeated.

Sam carelessly flicked something from the lapel of his blazer. "I know you couldn't kill Ricky Nicchi or Edwin Ito. Some people might call that weakness."

"Some people would be wrong," Danny said, his anger evident.

Keep pushing him, Sam, Kit thought.

"We met Joe," Sam said conversationally. "Kind of. He's your father's . . . what? Bodyguard? Seems a little old for that, though."

"Lapdog," Danny muttered. "Licks his boots."

Kit expected the attorney to say something, but the man remained silent. Watchful. "The kid's lawyer isn't here for him."

"I know," Navarro said. "He's Daddy's man."

"You know, there's something I can't figure out," Sam said.

Danny feigned shock. "Just one thing?"

Sam smiled. "For now, maybe. Why did you kill Laurette Curry?"

Danny tilted his head, his smirk fading.

"Say nothing, Danny," the lawyer murmured.

About time you did your job, Kit thought.

Danny shrugged.

"Why shoot the cops?" Lennox asked.

Another shrug.

"Why not shoot your father?" Sam asked.

Danny flinched, then glared at Sam.

"I mean," Sam went on, "you don't like him. Maybe you can't kill him. Just like you couldn't kill Ito and Nicchi. Authority figures. They make you . . . weak."

Danny's eyes flared hot with anger.

"Do you have a question, Dr. Reeves?" the attorney asked.

"I have many, many questions. I guess I'm trying to understand Danny's relationship with his father. The grapevine says that he disowned you when you got arrested. You had to go to San Diego to live with . . . who? Nicchi? Paolo?"

No answer.

"And now Akiko is in the picture," Sam said. "She stands to inherit everything since you got removed from the will. That's millions of reasons to kill your sister. You can't deny that's what you were trying to do. But you failed. Badly. You got caught. By me. I'm not even a cop. I'm just a skinny shrink and I took you down."

"You hit me where I was hurt," Danny spat.

"You got sloppy," Sam corrected. "You came at Akiko when she was surrounded by people. Why would you do that?"

Danny didn't answer, but Kit could see that he wanted to say something so badly.

"Keep at him, Sam," she whispered. *And you're not skinny. You're just right.*

"I think your plan to frame Akiko failed and you were angry. You know your father will want her as his daughter. She's the child of his mistress, true, but she's a good person. Doesn't have the baggage you carry. No felony record. Not for your lack of trying, of course."

You go, Sam.

Because Danny was visibly seething. The attorney placed a warning hand on Danny's arm, but the teenager shrugged him away.

"Is that why you came after her today, Danny?" Sam asked. "Because you didn't shoot her on Saturday in front of Mary Sherman's house. You had a perfect opportunity, but you didn't. I'm betting that someone told you not to."

Danny sucked in a breath.

"You're good, Sam," Kit murmured.

Navarro chuckled. "He really is."

"I think Dr. Reeves is right," Lennox said. "Because you knew who Akiko was. You had to have hated her as much on Saturday as you do today, and today you tried to kill her. Someone told you to kill the cop last Saturday, but not your sister. You had other plans for her. Framing her for smuggling guns. Was that supposed to make your father hate her? Because that makes no sense."

"Look at the attorney," Kit whispered. He was watching Lennox and Sam like he was at a tennis match. Back and forth. "He should have ended this interview already, but he wants to know what we know. He's letting them talk. Getting all the details so he can share them with his boss. I don't think Kenzo Takahashi's involved in framing Akiko."

Navarro nodded. "I'm inclined to agree."

Sam leaned forward, his elbows on the table. "Now that you're caught, what do you think will happen? Will the person calling the shots bail you out? I don't think so. I think they'll let you take the fall for all of this. For all the murders, for shooting cops, for assaulting Ito."

Danny started to speak, then stopped himself.

"You know I'm right." Sam smiled gently. "You're expendable, Danny. It hurts my heart to say this, but it's true. You've always been expendable—first to your father and now to whoever is guiding you in all this. You're a pair of hands. That's all. Maybe you should start protecting your own hide. Tell us who's pulling the strings. Who told you to kill Mary Sherman? Was it Joe?"

Danny scoffed.

"Okay, I'll take that as a no." Sam dropped his voice to a conspiratorial whisper. "You're going to take the fall, Danny. Your lawyer works for your father, not you. Do you really think your father wants to protect you? If he did, he never would have thrown you out of the family. You wouldn't have been alone, on the streets, at seventeen."

Danny opened his mouth.

"I'm only here to make sure he doesn't incriminate himself," the attorney said, "until he gets another attorney. He has a trust fund. He'll be hiring someone."

Danny's gaze whipped to the side, and he stared at the lawyer. "I can't access my trust fund until I'm twenty-one."

The attorney lifted a shoulder. "Then you'll be using a public defender. I'm only here for today."

"Oh wow," Kit said. "The lawyer wants Danny to spill *all* the tea."

Danny looked down at the table for a moment. When he looked back up, he was smirking again. "I'll get another attorney. No problem."

Kit recognized that particular smirk. She'd used it often enough as a teenager. "He's faking it because he's scared. Go for it, Sam."

But Sam didn't have a chance to, because the door to the interview room opened and Special Agent Brewer strode in like he owned the place, just as he had when he'd entered Paolo's home the night before.

Stunned, Kit glanced at Navarro. He looked as shocked as she felt.

"What the hell?" Navarro murmured, slowly coming to his feet.

Kit rose as well. "What's he doing here?"

Detective Desoto was already standing. "Can we help you?"

"I'm Special Agent Brewer with the ATF. We'll be taking Mr. Daisuke Takahashi into custody."

Burroughs took a step forward while Desoto and Lennox shared a tense glance. "Why?" Lennox asked. "He's ours. LAPD's and SDPD's. He's been arrested for murder, attempted murder, and assault."

"We found guns in the room he was renting," Brewer said. "They're from the same lot as the guns found in the storage unit rented in Akiko McKittrick's name by Mr. Takahashi here."

Danny lurched to his feet. "No. You're lying."

"Sorry, kid." But Brewer didn't look sorry at all. He looked smug. "We got an anonymous tip that the guns were there and, sure enough, they were. You're under arrest for the trafficking of firearms." He proceeded to read Danny his Miranda rights. "Detective Desoto, please unlock his cuffs. I'll use mine."

Danny stood there for a moment, mouth agape as Desoto hesitated.

Brewer sighed and handed Desoto a piece of paper. "My warrant."

Desoto skimmed it, then gave it to Lennox before unlocking Danny's handcuffs. "It's legit."

"Sorry, guy," Brewer said to Desoto, sounding condescending.

Danny's forehead creased in a scowl. "Who turned me in?"

"It was an anonymous tip," Brewer repeated, recuffing the kid. "We found the guns and the records from your rental of the storage unit."

Danny went still. "You found what?"

Brewer just shook his head. "Come on, Danny. You've got an appointment with a federal judge." He took Danny's arm and gave him a little shove forward. Danny stumbled a step before regaining his balance.

He looked at Lennox and Sam, his expression one of fury. His entire body seemed to crackle with it. "Is that lady detective listening? The one I shot?"

Sam blinked, startled. "Yes. Why?"

Danny looked directly at the one-way mirror. "Joe Fujioka and Bob Fujioka." Then he turned to the attorney. "You can tell my father to express his gratitude to me by hiring me a decent lawyer who's not under his thumb. I just told him how to clean his damn house."

In the interview room, even Brewer seemed shocked, but he regrouped quickly. "Let's go, kid."

"Well, well, well," Kit murmured. "I wonder which one of the two gave him up."

"Who is Bob Fujioka?" Navarro asked.

"I don't know, but we'll find out."

CHAPTER TWENTY

Los Angeles, California
Wednesday, February 1, 6:30 p.m.

"Okay," Kit said once Sam, Lennox, Desoto, and Burroughs had joined them in the observation room. "At least now we know who Joe is." She held up her phone. "Joji Fujioka works for Takahashi Corporation. He was their vice president in charge of security until he stepped down ten years ago. He's still on the payroll as Kenzo's personal assistant and advisor. He's worked for Takahashi, according to their website, for nearly sixty years."

"He was friends with Kenzo's father," Sam said, "so he probably started working for the company from an early age."

"But Ito was friends with them, too, at least when this photo was taken." Desoto set a copy of the graduation photo of the three young men on the table.

Navarro flipped the album pages until he got to the one of

Joe and Mitch by the pool, their tattooed skin exposed. "I think we can assume, from the tattoos, that the three men were part of an organized crime family. And, for the moment, we can assume that Ito somehow got out."

"He escaped by joining the Army," Kit said. "That's what he told Akiko and me, at least. Basically, he couldn't stomach the killing."

Burroughs shook his head. "Very few men *wanted* to join the Army in 1966. He must have been desperate."

"Normally it's not that easy to escape," Navarro said. "He came back to LA after the Army. How did he keep his fingers?"

"That's a good question to ask him," Kit said. "But it seems that Ito trusts Joe, at least enough to meet with him, Nicchi, and Mary." She swiped to another open window on her phone—a photo of the other man Danny had named. "Bob Fujioka is fifty years old. He's Joe's son. He was a passenger on my sister's fishing boat twice. The first time was five years ago when she first started her business. The second time was back in October. Both times he gave his name as Akito Jones."

"What does he do for Takahashi?" Sam asked.

"He became their vice president of security when Joe stepped down. I'm sure being Joe's son helped a lot." Kit rubbed the back of her neck. She was tired and felt a headache coming on. And her arm hurt. She was relieved when Sam put a bottle of ibuprofen in her hand. "Thank you."

"You're welcome."

She took a couple of the pills. "I think it's been Bob pulling Danny's strings."

"Why do you think that?" Navarro asked.

Kit took a moment to gather her spinning thoughts. "Bob was there at the beginning, posing as Akito Jones on Akiko's first charter. That's got to mean something."

"What about Joe?" Desoto asked. "How does he fit in? What do we know about the Takahashi Corporation?"

Burroughs skimmed his notes. "I looked up the Takahashi family after I left Ito's condo—while Desoto was arresting Danny, actually—and found an article written about Kenzo when he took over his family's business after Mitch died in 2003. There was a bit of the family history at the beginning and some Q and A with Kenzo. In 1964, when that graduation photo was taken, Mitch's father Osamu ran the company. The tats on Mitch and his friend Joe point to organized crime, but so far there's been no hard evidence. *But* even if the Takahashis *were* an organized crime family back then, Mitch wasn't the boss when Ito joined the Army to escape. Osamu was. Ito kept his Army discharge papers in his safe. He was discharged honorably before Osamu died, but he didn't come back to LA right away. He took a job in New York City, where he met and married Sakura, Mary's mother. He only came back to LA after Osamu was dead and Mitch had taken over."

"So maybe Mitch was okay with Ito leaving the family business because they were friends, but his father wouldn't have been," Sam said.

Burroughs nodded. "That's what I thought, too. Also, there was a wedding photo in his safe. Joe was his best man."

"Huh." Kit considered that, because it felt important. "That means Joe knew Ito's wife. Maybe even his children. Either way, it seems like Ito and Joe remained friends over the years."

She brought up the photo of Bob Fujioka. "What do we know about Bob? Because Ito trusted Joe, but Bob wasn't in the group of four that started meeting in October."

"Yet Bob knew about Akiko," Navarro said. "From the first day of her charter business, at least."

"Exactly. So who was Ito trying to protect Akiko from? Bob or Kenzo? My gut's telling me that it's not Joe, since Ito won't tell us about him. He's protecting Joe, too."

"Danny said he'd just told his father how to 'clean his damn house,'" Lennox said. "Are both Bob and Joe working against Kenzo?"

Kit nodded. "Good point. But if Joe was the one who went back into Laurette Curry's house and posted those photos where we'd be sure to see them, he led us to Akiko's passenger lists. If we'd had long enough, we could have used facial recognition to get Bob's name from that lead alone. It appears that Joe's trying to help us find Bob, even though Bob is his son."

"Then let's dig into Bob Fujioka," Desoto said. "He seems to be the linchpin in all this."

"If we could find Nicchi, we could stop all this guesswork," Kit grumbled.

"We've got officers out there looking for him," Burroughs said. "They're talking to his coworkers in his protection business and at the dojo."

"I've got people searching for him in San Diego, too," Navarro said. "We've got airports, train and bus stations covered. We'll find him eventually."

"There's more on Takahashi Corporation," Burroughs said. "They're not publicly traded, so the company's worth is difficult to estimate, but they've had a series of business setbacks in the past few months. Starting in October."

Kit's pulse kicked up. "When Bob and Danny went on Akiko's boat."

"Yes. It's been a lot of little things and one big thing. Little things include lawsuits against their hotel chain—guests claiming they've been assaulted, vendors saying they haven't been paid. Clients saying that their conventions have been canceled at the last minute, breaking their contracts. The one big thing is a financial scandal at Kenzo's casino in Vegas. A whistleblower claims that the tables are rigged and that they're laundering money. It might not be true, but the gaming commission is investigating."

"Someone is attacking Kenzo's businesses," Lennox said. "Both now and back when Kenzo took over the reins. Remember, Kit? You told us that, except for the casino, every business that Kenzo started has failed."

"And now the casino has been targeted, too," Kit said.

Lennox nodded. "Exactly. And if the casino's getting investigated, it could lead to law enforcement digging into all their businesses. Any organized crime could be exposed."

"That might be connected to the gun smuggling," Burroughs said. "If Kenzo's already got a spotlight on him for gaming crimes and then both of his children—Danny and Akiko—are indicted for gun running, Kenzo could be investigated for that, too. If he is involved in the gun running, he'd be smart to pull out until the heat dies down. Which means lost revenue."

"*If* he's involved," Sam said. "Can we find out where the

guns found in that storage unit came from? Were they stolen? We know Danny was involved, but who was the boss? Was it Kenzo Takahashi? Or Bob Fujioka?"

"I'll take that," Navarro said. "I'll work with my contacts at the ATF. I'll start with Special Agent Brewer, but I know other people I can ask if I have to. Brewer's a showboating ass, but he's a successful investigator. He had enough evidence to get an arrest warrant, so let's see what he's got up his sleeve."

Up his sleeve. The words triggered a memory and Kit swiped through her phone until she came to the photos taken by Leo Sherman when he'd followed Mary to LA. "Look at this." She held her phone up so that everyone could see. "In one of Leo's photos, Nicchi is sliding an envelope up his sleeve. What was in it? Was that what Danny was looking for when he trashed Ito's condo? When he searched Mary's house?"

"You're right," Lennox murmured. "We had Nicchi's house searched when we arrested him, but we didn't find anything like that envelope."

Sam hesitated, then sighed. "Do we even know if Nicchi is still alive? He could be in a ditch somewhere with a bullet hole in his head, just like the others."

Kit blew out a breath. "It's possible. We need to step up our search for him."

"I've asked one of our analysts to review the camera footage of the hospital's parking areas," Desoto said. "They're searching for his past visits to find out what he was driving. Once we know, we'll put a BOLO out on his car as well."

"Good idea." Kit pulled Joe Fujioka's photo closer and studied the man's face. "We need to talk to him where Kenzo isn't around to hear. Let's do that next."

"I have his address," Desoto said. "Burroughs and I will take that interview."

"If we can find him," Burroughs added dourly.

"If," Kit allowed. "But he wanted us to see him earlier today. He wanted us to know he was with Kenzo. He also wanted us to check out Akiko's passenger list, knowing we'd find his photo along with Bob's and Danny's. I'm hoping he lets you find him now."

Navarro gestured to Kit and Lennox. "What are you going to do?"

"I want to find Umeko Takahashi's sister," Kit said. "She doesn't like Kenzo and, if her sister confided in her, she might have information that no one else knows."

"I found her," Lennox said.

Kit blinked at her. "When?"

"Since we've been talking." Lennox smirked. "I can multitask. Her name is Koharu Carlson. Goes by Haru. She's seventy years old, a widow, and she lives in Santa Monica."

Kit stood up. "Then let's go."

Santa Monica, Los Angeles, California
Wednesday, February 1, 8:30 p.m.

"May I offer you something to drink?" Haru Carlson asked as she led Kit, Sam, and Lennox to a quietly elegant living room.

"No, thank you," Kit said. She sat on a love seat next to Sam while Lennox took a wingback chair that looked like an antique.

Haru was a very beautiful woman who did not look like

she was seventy years old. She appeared to be no older than fifty.

Kit hoped that Danny Takahashi's aunt would give them something helpful. Otherwise, they'd just wasted nearly an hour in traffic. She didn't know how LA cops managed to do their jobs when it took so long to drive less than twenty miles.

"How can I help you?" Haru said, gracefully lowering herself into another wingback chair.

Kit glanced at Lennox, who gave her a go-ahead nod. "We're here because of Danny."

Haru sighed. "Yes, I know. I love that boy, but he's . . . I hope he's not so far gone that I can't bring him back."

"He's killed four people, ma'am," Kit said, trying not to sound unkind.

"I know. And he shot you, Detective. I know what he's done. But I also remember the little boy he used to be. If there is to be redemption, it will now be from behind bars. I know that. It's a difficult thing, watching someone you love take the wrong road."

"You loved your sister," Kit said.

Haru smiled sadly. "I did. Very much."

"I love my sister, too. Her name is Akiko."

"I know. I read all of Miss Kavanaugh's articles. She seems very up to date."

Tamsin Fucking Kavanaugh. Kit wanted to snarl, but she kept her expression impassive. "Then you know that my sister's been drawn into a very bad situation."

"I imagine she was shocked to learn of her parentage."

"Yes, ma'am. Up until this week she didn't have any clue as

to where she'd come from. She does, however, know who she belongs to."

"Your family."

"Yes, ma'am. I will move heaven and earth to protect her."

Haru swallowed. "I understand that desire, Detective."

"I thought you would. You loved your sister, but you don't like Kenzo Takahashi very much. I saw your comments on a number of articles about him."

Haru's mouth pressed into a hard line. "Yes. *Kenzo.*"

"What can you tell us about him?" Kit asked. "Other than that he cheated on your sister 'with abandon.'"

"I used those words on purpose many, many times. I wanted him to know it was me."

"How long have you been leaving comments?" Lennox asked.

"Since my sister died nine years ago. It's become something of an obsession. I've got alerts set on my phone so that every time he's mentioned in an article, I know about it. Up until Danny was arrested, those were mostly self-serving articles about his suicide prevention charity or a business deal he'd completed. He's been able to get my comments taken down on most of those articles. My brother-in-law doesn't like negative publicity. My comments were merely annoying to him, but Danny's arrest was a dealbreaker for Kenzo. After the arrest, Kenzo disowned his son. Danny's been disinherited."

"His lawyer said he has a trust fund," Lennox said. "Where did that come from?"

"From my sister. Our family has our own wealth. We don't need Kenzo's dirty money."

Ah. This was more like it. "Dirty money?" Kit asked.

Haru shrugged. "Not every dollar he makes is dirty, but more are dirty than clean."

"How has he made this dirty money?" Kit pressed.

She hesitated. "I have no evidence that will put Kenzo in prison where he belongs. Otherwise, I would have reported him years ago."

"Just tell us what you know," Sam said. "Let Detectives McKittrick and Lennox worry about putting Kenzo in prison."

"Where should I begin?"

Kit wanted to go directly to asking about Joe, but she wanted to know about Kenzo as well, for Akiko's sake. "Tell us about your sister and Kenzo."

"Umeko was fifteen years younger than me. It was my job to care for her. I did not approve of her marriage to Kenzo Takahashi—at first because she was only eighteen. But I quickly realized that he was not the gentleman he'd purported himself to be. He hit her when she commented that his secretary's clothing was not modest."

"When was this?" Kit asked, not surprised.

"They'd been married only a month. Umeko wasn't quite nineteen. He'd just turned twenty-two."

"Did she try to leave him?" Sam asked.

Haru shook her head. "No. She loved him. I never understood it, but if I'd begged her to leave, I would have lost her. She was a quick learner, my sister. She knew how to work the system to her own advantage. She asked Mitch—Kenzo's father—to give the secretary a transfer along with a raise. Mitch agreed. He always liked Umeko and wanted her to be happy. She'd be the vessel carrying his future grandchild, after all."

There was a bitter edge to her words. "Did you know Mitch Takahashi?"

"Oh yes. Mitch and I dated for a while. He brought Kenzo to a party I was hosting and Umeko was there as well. Kenzo had just turned eighteen and Umeko was fifteen. I didn't like the age difference and forbade her to see him. Which was my folly, I'm afraid. She snuck away to be with him. They met in secret for three years and he proposed—though I believe he loved her inheritance, not her. He wanted them to elope, but I'm lucky that my sister had always dreamed of a princess wedding. That gave me time to convince her to insist on a prenup."

"I'm surprised you were successful," Sam observed mildly.

"So was I. I convinced her that, since the Takahashis were already rich, her money should be held in trust for her children when she had them. Kenzo would still get a lot of her money in a monthly stipend, but he wanted access to it all. He put a lot of pressure on her to ignore me, but she grew enamored with the idea of keeping the family wealth for her kids. Umeko was stubborn—and, like I said, she knew how to work the system. She quickly realized that his desire for her money gave her a means to control him. She liked to play power games." Haru sighed. "All the way up until she died. But she did love Kenzo, and the Takahashis had status in the community. Our family was quietly wealthy. Mitch had already begun building an empire and liked the trappings that went along with it—the fancy parties, the political clout. The power. Umeko really loved the power. So she and Kenzo married after a whirlwind engagement."

"What were the conditions of the prenup?" Kit asked.

"If she died before he did, he'd cease getting stipends and

whatever wasn't held in trust for future children would go to charity. That last part was her idea. I think it was to make sure she remained too valuable to be . . . eliminated."

Sam frowned. "Did she think Kenzo would kill her?"

"She knew that the Takahashis were the local mob. She knew that they killed people who got in their way or who cheated them. I mean, so did I, in a more abstract way. I didn't know for sure what Mitch was back when I dated him, but I knew enough to keep him at arm's length. He was fun to party with, but I never would have married him. Unfortunately, Umeko couldn't control Kenzo as she'd anticipated. She knew his weakness was money. He knew her weakness was him. He knew she wouldn't leave him, even if he cheated, and she never did."

"When did Kenzo's cheating start?" she asked.

"Before they were even married. That's what Umeko told me, anyway. It hurt her deeply, but she kept hoping that he'd 'come around.' That once she had a child, he'd be a better husband."

"She wanted a child from the beginning?" Sam asked. "Because Danny wasn't born until they'd been married for twenty years."

Pain tightened Haru's features. "Yes, she desperately wanted a child from day one. She tried so hard. After two years of trying, she saw specialists. It was the late eighties and in vitro fertilization was all the rage, so she tried that. It was very hard on her body. The hormones . . ." She shook her head. "They really messed with her head. She was so depressed. All the while, Kenzo continued to cheat. They were always around eighteen. Kenzo has a type. And I don't think that they're always consenting. This was the case with your sister's mother."

Kit studied Haru's face. "You knew Minako."

What seemed like genuine regret flickered across the older woman's expression. "Yes, a little bit. She was lovely. Your sister resembles her very strongly. Minnie was seventeen when she came to work for Kenzo. Umeko hated her on sight, virulently hated her. She tried to get her transferred like all the others, but Kenzo refused. He'd laughed at her over the years for getting his secretaries moved to other roles, but he liked Minako. He even loved her, in his own way. But Minnie did not love him. She was so young. Her mother had just died, and she and her brother were trying to survive. Ichiro got a job working in security and Minako started out in the secretarial pool, but Kenzo pulled her out on her first day."

Kit had a bad feeling about where this was going, but before she could ask another question, Lennox spoke up. "They worked for Takahashi Corporation? Why? Why didn't they contact Edwin Ito?"

Haru frowned. "Who is Edwin Ito?"

"A family friend," Lennox replied, evading the real answer.

Haru regarded Lennox for a moment before shaking her head. "I don't know him. Minnie never mentioned him. Neither did Umeko."

That was definitely something they'd be following up on, because the twins should have sought Ito out. They'd been three years old at the time of the divorce, old enough to have at least a vague memory of their father. It made Kit wonder what exactly Sakura had told them about their father. She'd taken drastic steps to create distance between her and Ito, so maybe the kids didn't know where their father was. Or maybe even who he was.

She brought the conversation back to Minnie. "Did Kenzo force himself on Minnie?"

"I believe so. I only met her a few times, when I'd go into the office to see Mitch for lunch—we remained friendly after Kenzo married Umeko. So I didn't actually know her well, but I could see the signs of an abused woman. By this time, I was volunteering with the women's shelter downtown and I knew what to look for. Minnie wore no bruises, but she was . . . defeated. Scared. And pregnant. I could see the signs of that, too. At the time, I didn't think that Umeko knew about the pregnancy, and I didn't tell her my suspicions. I thought it would only make her hatred worse."

Haru went very still. "You must understand that much of this story I heard from my sister shortly before she died. I don't know how much is true and how much was manufactured in my sister's mind. She was not well at the end of her life. Decades of drug abuse and regret tend to catch up to you."

Oh. Kit didn't like this at all. "Did Umeko kill Minako?"

She thought that Haru might flinch or blink or look surprised. That she'd be offended or even angry. But the woman only held her gaze steadily. "Yes. Not with her own hands, of course. She had someone else do it."

Santa Monica, Los Angeles, California
Wednesday, February 1, 9:05 p.m.

"Who did she have kill Minnie?" Lennox asked. "Joe?"

Haru laughed bitterly. "Joe? No. Not because he wasn't a killer. He was. They all were. Still are. But he was the one who'd brought Ichiro and Minako into the company. They were seventeen years old, for heaven's sake. They'd barely graduated from high school. But one day they were just *there*, in the Takahashi offices. They'd moved here from Nevada, just outside of Vegas, and were living with Joe. I don't know how he knew them. I never asked. He never told me."

Joe had brought Minnie and Ichiro to LA? How and why? But it did make some sense.

Kit thought of the wedding photo. Joe had been Ito's best man. He'd known Ito's wife. He'd clearly known Ito's children.

She once again cursed Ito for keeping his silence. "What happened?"

"Umeko was hysterical when it came to Minnie. She wanted her gone because Kenzo hadn't had feelings for any of the others. I caught my sister reading about poisons and I knew she intended to kill Minnie, so I went to Joe. Told him that Minnie was in danger. The next day both Minnie and Ichiro were gone. Disappeared. Kenzo was beside himself."

"He was angry?" Sam asked.

"Yes, but he was more grief-stricken," Haru said thoughtfully. "Minnie was the only woman he'd ever really cared about. He became obsessed with finding her. Accused Umeko of bribing her or forcing her to leave. Umeko became just as obsessed with finding Minnie, so she could 'finish the job.' Those were her words. I don't know that she was in her right mind. I tried to get her help, but she refused. I thought with Minnie out of the picture, she'd calm down, but Kenzo was inconsolable, so Umeko just got angrier. And then one day we got news that both Minnie and her brother were dead. Umeko thought that Kenzo would forget about Minnie and that he'd come back to her and they'd finally have a child. But Kenzo didn't come back. He got an apartment in the city and left Umeko to wander their house, all alone. She started drinking and her mood got darker and darker. I knew she was doing drugs, but there wasn't anything I could do. Mitch tried to get her into rehab, but Umeko wouldn't go. Now, looking back, I think Umeko was being eaten up by guilt."

"Because she'd had Minnie and Ichiro killed," Sam murmured.

"Yes, although I honestly don't think she had anything against Ichiro. Joe was sad, too. His grief was harder to see because he's kind of a robot emotionally. I think Joe just wasn't cut out to be a killer."

Like Ito, Kit thought. But Ito got out. Joe had stayed. Joe still stayed.

"When did you find out what she'd done?" Kit asked.

"It was the day before she took her own life. She was sober for the first time in nearly thirty years—with the exception of the months she was pregnant with Danny. Her pregnancy was the biggest surprise of all. She was finally happy. And, once again, she thought Kenzo would come back to her, but he never did."

"If they weren't together, how was she pregnant?" Lennox asked.

"She'd never given up hope for a child of her own, but she was nearing forty. She asked him to try IVF once more. He said that he'd participate only if she got clean, so she did. And Kenzo wanted an heir for a couple of reasons. First, he'd recently taken over the business after Mitch's death and he wanted a son to carry it on. But the second reason was greed.

Remember the trust for Danny? Umeko set it up so that she'd be the trustee if they were still married or divorced, but if she died, Kenzo would be the trustee until Danny turned twenty-one. Honestly, by that point, if she'd divorced Kenzo, no court would have given her custody of Danny. She was a raging drug addict. By having a child with Umeko, Kenzo was essentially ensuring that most of her money would stay under his control. And, as long as they stayed married, he was still getting his stipend and that was not an insignificant sum."

"Follow the money," Lennox said quietly.

"Yes." Haru drew a breath, as if bracing herself. "After Danny was born, Umeko experienced severe postpartum depression and started drinking again."

"So there was some truth to Kenzo's story on the suicide prevention website," Sam said. "She did have PPD."

"There's always a grain of truth in what Kenzo says. It's what's kept him out of jail all these years. Everything came to a head for Umeko when Danny was eight years old and asked her not to be drunk for one night. He had a school concert coming up and he wanted her to come. To be a normal mother. He didn't want her to embarrass him. She loved him so much. So she quit. Cold turkey. It was not pretty. But she made it to the concert and she was stone-cold sober. That made her think about all the things she'd done, though. And why she'd been drinking so much to start with. We had dinner together one night soon after the concert. I hadn't seen her sober in eight years, not since Danny was born. I was so happy to have my sister back, you know?" She sighed heavily. "But then Umeko started talking. Told me that she'd arranged Minako's murder. She knew about Minnie's pregnancy, and it had made her even angrier, so she told her lover to do the deed. To kill Minnie and the baby. She was afraid that Kenzo would divorce her if he had a child with someone else. I think he would have. I also think that if he had divorced her, my sister might still be alive today."

"Who was her lover?" Kit asked, but she was starting to think she knew.

"Bob Fujioka, Joe's son. They'd started sleeping together shortly before Minnie's death."

Kit had been right about it being Bob, but she was stunned at the length of the affair. "Wait. Minnie was killed thirty-two years ago, because that's how old Akiko is. Umeko died by suicide nine years ago, when Danny was eight. Your sister and Bob had an affair for twenty-three years?"

"That's what she said." She sighed again. "Bob started in the mail room part time when he was sixteen but two years later got a job in security. That was Joe's department, and he hired whomever he chose. Mitch left all the decisions up to Joe. He trusted him implicitly. They'd been friends since they were kids. Bob was Joe's son, and Joe indulged him. Bob asked to become Umeko's bodyguard, so that's what happened. He was her bodyguard for nearly ten years."

"Oh," Kit said.

"Yes, oh. I thought maybe he saw it as a way to get ahead. He was always ambitious. But it turns out that Bob really hates Kenzo. With good reason. See, Kenzo is a sociopath. You wouldn't know it just talking to him, but he is a stone-cold killer. He likes it. He doesn't do the dirty work himself anymore, but back when he was younger, he liked it. And one day—now, mind you, all this came from Umeko at the end, but I don't think she was lying—she told me that Bob's father worked for Mitch and had done something wrong. Stolen money from one of the businesses. Probably one of the illegal gambling dens they ran in those days. Whatever it was, it was bad, because Bob's father was targeted for . . . elimination."

Sam frowned. "I thought Joe was Bob's father."

"That came later, after Bob was orphaned. Joe adopted him. You see, Kenzo killed Bob's parents. Both of them. Bob was twelve. Kenzo was only twenty, not yet married to Umeko, and he was wild. Mitch was trying to teach him some responsibility, so he sent him with Joe to punish Bob's father. Joe and Kenzo were only supposed to kill the father, but Kenzo went crazy, even though Joe tried to stop him. Bob told Umeko that he was hiding in a closet and saw the whole thing. He heard Joe yell at Kenzo not to kill his mother. After that, Joe adopted Bob."

Kit was surprised. "Joe adopted Bob even though the kid knew what they'd done?"

"I don't think Joe knew that Bob had witnessed the murders of his parents."

"Why would Bob confess this to her?" Lennox asked. "Wasn't he concerned that your sister would tell Kenzo?"

Haru looked suddenly weary. "At that point, Umeko had been a drunk for so long that no one would have believed anything she said, even once she was sober. I don't know that *I* even believed her. She'd finally come to the place where she was ready to leave Kenzo. She was sober and seeing that he'd never loved her. But she thought that since she and Bob had been sleeping together off and on for years, he'd want her to move in with him when she left Kenzo. He laughed at her. Told her that the only reason he'd been with her was to have access to the house, because Kenzo kept his less legal business records in the house and not in the office. He'd been searching Kenzo's office and spying on Kenzo's businesses for twenty years and killing all of Kenzo's new initiatives from the inside."

Now that makes sense, Kit thought. "I read that the only new business Kenzo successfully started was the casino. That his father began all the other businesses."

"That always frustrated Kenzo. I think he knew that someone was sabotaging him, but he could never figure out who. Guess who he had spearheading the investigations?"

"Bob," Sam said. "Talk about the fox in the henhouse."

"Did Bob love your sister, though?" Lennox asked, sounding sad.

"No." Haru sounded equally sad. "He said he only slept with her because she belonged to Kenzo. He never loved her. She was merely a pawn, a weapon to use against Kenzo. And then he threatened that if she told anyone he'd turn her in for arranging the murder of Minako and Ichiro. She'd go to prison and never see Danny again."

Kit frowned. "He'd be turning himself in, too."

Haru shook her head. "He's smart. He left no tracks, no way to prove it was him. He had Umeko on tape ordering him to kill the twins, but he never says anything incriminating during the conversation. Just a few grunts and *uh-huh*s. And, like I said, who was going to believe a drug addict? She didn't dare turn him in."

"So your sister ordered Bob to kill Minnie?" Kit asked, just to be sure.

"Yes. That's my understanding. She saw Minnie as a threat.

Back then, I hoped that Umeko didn't know that Minnie was pregnant, but she did. She told Bob to kill Minnie and the baby. I'm not condoning it in any way, Detective. My sister did a monstrous thing. She made a terrible choice in the heat of the moment, and I think that drove her to drink and do drugs for the rest of her life. She regretted her actions, but it was way too late for her to make it right. Sober, she couldn't live with herself. I should have stayed with her the night she told me. But I was . . . horrified. I'm sure she saw it on my face. I had to leave." Haru's voice broke. "I left her there. And the next day Danny found her body."

Kit had so many questions. She wasn't sure what to ask first.

Sam stepped in. "Why didn't you say something? Why didn't you tell someone what Bob had done?"

Haru's eyes were wet and filled with agony. "Don't you think I wanted to? I had no proof beyond a dead addict's ramblings. She told me that secret and I had to live with it. You can't know what that feels like."

Sam exhaled. "Yes, ma'am. I do. If a client tells me that he killed someone twenty years ago, I can't tell a soul. I'd lose my license."

But when faced with that choice one year ago, Kit thought, Sam had chosen to do the right thing. He'd suspected that one of his clients had killed a teenager and he'd told someone.

He called me. They'd never met, yet Sam had trusted her with a dangerous truth. She respected the hell out of him for that.

He was the best of men.

Haru's nod to Sam was respectful. "I suppose that's true.

I'm not going to ask you what secrets you hold in your heart, Dr. Reeves. I'm sure they're legion."

"That's what I agreed to when I chose this profession," Sam said, his tone as gentle and compassionate as always. "You're not a psychologist, Mrs. Carlson. Holding a secret like that must have been difficult. But I think you misunderstand my question. Were you afraid that Bob would retaliate if you told someone? Or that Kenzo might, in some way, retaliate?"

"I was afraid of Bob, certainly. But, in the aftermath of Umeko's death, I was focused on Danny. He was so little and broken and there wasn't anything I could do except hold him."

"Did you take him to therapy?" Lennox asked.

"I wanted to, but Kenzo refused. Told me that if I pushed it, I'd lose all access to my nephew. I couldn't have that. Danny needed me. And I needed him, too. I considered turning Kenzo in, hoping that CPS might take custody of Danny. Then I could raise him. But Kenzo has expensive attorneys, and I didn't know specifics. I might have said, 'Kenzo Takahashi is the head of the local mob.' But I had no proof. So I stayed in Danny's life and did the best I could. Clearly, it wasn't enough. Not that Kenzo ever cared. He got what he wanted—Umeko's money. Once she died, he became the trustee of Danny's trust fund and he got the rest of her money, too."

"I thought it would go to a charity if she died," Lennox said.

Haru's smile was sharp. "It did. The charity he started in my sister's name. She didn't specify a charity by name, so Kenzo started one."

Kit understood now. "The anti-suicide charity he used Danny to promote."

Haru nodded. "Kenzo is smart. He saw the loophole and

he took advantage of it. He now controls all of what belonged to my sister. And now, with Danny going to prison, he'll be able to 'oversee' the boy's trust fund even after he's twenty-one."

What a bastard. "How loyal is Joe to Kenzo?" Kit asked. "Because we've gotten the impression that Joe is trying to help us."

This seemed to surprise the older woman. "Really? Well, like I said, Joe was the one who brought Minnie and Ichiro into the company. They needed jobs after their mother died. And I went to Joe when I suspected that Minnie was pregnant and worried that Umeko would try to poison her. Joe whisked them away, which must have been very dangerous for him. Kenzo was still wild and liked to kill. If he'd found out that Joe was responsible for taking Minnie away from him, he would have killed Joe himself and I don't think Mitch would have been able to stop him."

Once again, Kit wondered who Joe was to the twins. He'd taken dangerous chances for them. She also wondered where Ito factored into all of this. She wondered if he'd known that his children had come to LA. She wondered if he'd spent time with them. She wondered why it had been Joe that the twins had turned to after their mother's death.

"Bob didn't kill Akiko when she was a newborn baby," Lennox murmured. "Did he tell your sister that he had?"

"I assume he did, or Umeko would have made it her mission to track the child down." She shrugged. "Maybe there's a line even Bob won't cross."

"Or maybe Mary was hiding with the baby," Kit said.

"Also possible, since your sister exists. I can't help you with that part of the story."

"Why kill Ichiro, too?" Sam asked. "I can see Bob killing

Minnie even if Umeko *hadn't* ordered him to do so. Killing Minnie would hurt Kenzo, especially if Kenzo had real feelings for her. But why the brother? Unless Ichiro tried to protect her and got caught in the crossfire."

"Or," Kit said, "Bob was jealous of Ichiro. Bob was Joe's son and all of a sudden, Joe brings strangers into his home. Gets them jobs. Takes care of them, like they're family."

"Or both," Lennox said. "We'll just have to find Bob and ask him. Do you know where he might be hiding, Mrs. Carlson?"

Haru shook her head. "I avoided him after Umeko's death. I was afraid I'd lose control and hurt him. Or say something that would get me killed. Or, worse, Danny."

Danny, who could not have coordinated a gun-smuggling operation on his own. Who'd given up Bob when he'd been taken away by the ATF.

"Were Bob and Danny close?" she asked.

Haru shook her head. "Danny never mentioned that. Why?"

"Just trying to connect the dots," Kit said. "Is there anything else you think we should know?"

"No. If I think of anything, I'll call you."

Kit rose, as did Sam and Lennox. "Thank you for talking to us."

"I hope you find Bob quickly." Haru walked them to the front door, where a large burly man stood on the porch. "Can you see the detectives to their vehicle?" she asked him.

The man appeared to be Haru's security, and Kit was relieved. After this case broke open, Haru was going to need all the protection she could get.

"Yes, ma'am." Without saying another word, they were hustled to Lennox's department sedan. Anson's car was parked at a nearby shopping center. They'd followed Lennox that far, then they'd driven to Haru Carlson's house together so that Kit wouldn't have to flash her badge to gain entrance. Since she was still suspended, after all.

We need to scan the car for trackers or listening devices, Kit thought.

As if reading her mind, Lennox took a handheld scanner from her bag.

I really like her.

When they were back on the road and headed for Anson's car, Lennox asked, "What do you think? Did Haru tell us the truth?"

"I think so," Sam said from the front seat. "Kit?"

But Kit's attention was on her phone and the three voicemails and fifteen text messages she'd received while they were talking to Haru Carlson.

All of them from Anson. All of them within the last fifteen minutes. All of them begging Kit to call him. Each more frantic than the last.

Hands trembling, she dialed her brother, holding her breath as he answered.

"No," he rasped, once the call had connected. "Get that away from me. I have to take this."

"Anson?" she asked, her voice high and reedy. Something was wrong.

"Meghan," Sam said, "pull over, please." He twisted to stare at Kit, his expression grave. Lennox pulled the car into the parking lot of a grocery store.

Kit met Sam's worried gaze, knowing her own was panic-stricken. *"Anson?"*

Anson coughed, the sound painful to hear. "Kit?" he whispered. "She's gone. Taken."

Kit forced herself to stay calm, because there was only one *she* he could mean. "Akiko is gone?"

"Fuck," Lennox said through clenched teeth as she brought the car to a stop. "When? How?"

Her heart racing, Kit put her phone on speaker. "What's happened, Anson?"

"Fuckers used drones. Flame-throwing drones." He started coughing violently. *"Stop."*

"Sir, you need to let us treat you," a voice said in the background.

"Not *yet*," Anson snapped, continuing to cough. "I need to *tell* her."

Breathe. Breathe. Don't panic.

It was no use. She was panicking. "Anson? Are you all right?"

"Yeah. Pop's hurt."

No, no, no. Her mouth opened but no words came out.

Sam was out of the front seat and sitting beside her in the back before she could blink. He took her hands and held on tight. "Anson, it's Sam. Where's Harlan?"

"Ambulance took him already. Two drones flew over my house. I have jammers." Another coughing fit. "Drones got past them. Set my house on fire. We got out, but he got through my gate." More coughing. "Was waiting with a rifle. It was the guy on Akiko's boat. Her very first charter. He shot Pop." Anson's voice broke into a sob. "Kit, he shot Pop."

"Bob," Kit whispered. *He took her. He hurt Pop.*

No, no, no. Please, no.

"Which hospital?" Sam asked.

In the front seat, Lennox was already on her phone, calling . . . somebody.

Kit couldn't think. She was shaking, her teeth chattering.

Akiko.

Pop.

Another voice came on the line. "I'm the paramedic treating Mr. McKittrick. He and his father are being taken to UCI."

UC Irvine. It was not the closest hospital.

But it did have a Level I trauma center.

She opened her mouth again to speak, but still no words came out.

"Sir," Sam said, "I'm with Mr. McKittrick's sister. Will he and their father be going into surgery?"

"I'm not the doctor—"

"I know that," Sam cut in. "And I apologize for interrupting, but I need to know if I should take her to the police station to work on finding her sister or to the hospital. If they're going into surgery, there won't be anything she can do for the next several hours."

"I think surgery is a definite possibility for her father."

"Thank you. Can your partner radio the responding officers to contact Detectives Burroughs and Desoto?" Sam cupped Kit's face as he continued talking to the paramedic. "And please tell Anson we'll be there as soon as we can, but we're going to find Akiko."

"I'll tell him."

The line went dead.

Kit couldn't breathe. Her lungs wouldn't work. Her panic escalated and black spots began dancing in her field of vision.

And then Sam was pulling her into his arms. "We'll find her. And your father is the strongest man I know. We'll get through this, Kit. You and me. Now, sweetheart, I need you to breathe. In and out."

She laid her head on Sam's shoulder and sucked in a breath. And then another and another until the black spots faded away. She couldn't think. She needed to think. "We're wasting time. I need to find Akiko."

Another door opened and Lennox was crouching next to them. "Where do you want to start, Kit? I vote for Kenzo Takahashi. If Joe's with him, we will find out what the fuck is going on here."

Kit nodded. "Yeah. Let's do that."

And if either Kenzo or Joe gave her any shit . . .

I'm already suspended. I'll beat it out of him if I have to.

CHAPTER TWENTY-ONE

Los Angeles, California
Wednesday, February 1, 9:55 p.m.

Sam listened with one ear to Lennox briefing Navarro and the LAPD detectives as she drove toward Kenzo's house, but most of his focus was on the woman sitting beside him. Kit was pale, trembling, but her chin was up, her mouth set in a determined line.

Akiko. He was terrified for her. She'd been at the center of this from the beginning. That Bob had come for her was not a shock, except that it was.

Akiko. She'd become like the sister he'd never had. But he couldn't allow his fear to consume him. Kit needed him. So he shoved his fear into the corner of his mind. He'd deal with it later.

For now, he would focus on getting her back to LA.

"You with me?" he asked Kit.

"I have to call Mom. I need to tell her about Akiko and Anson and . . ." Her voice broke. "And Pop."

That Harlan had been shot was . . . Sam couldn't even go there. If something happened to Harlan, Kit would shatter into a million pieces.

So don't *go there. Make sure Kit doesn't, either.*

"Let me call my mom first. I'll have my folks go sit with your mother and the girls. Between them and Baz, I think they can keep everyone at McKittrick House. I don't want Betsy driving when she's upset, and she's going to be upset."

"They have to stay put." Kit's voice was high and panicked. "It's not safe here. Bob might go after them, too."

That was true. That Bob would try to eliminate Kit again when she tried to stop him was pretty much a given. Danny had already tried to kill her twice. But there was no way Kit was staying put, not when her sister's life was on the line, so he wouldn't even try. He pushed that fear to the corner of his mind as well.

His Kit was smart. She could take care of herself.

I'll still be by her side if she needs me.

He dialed his mother and, putting the phone directly to his ear, asked if she and his father would go to McKittrick House and requested they not ask him why. To their credit, they immediately agreed.

"Love you, Mom," he said quietly.

"I love you, too. It's bad, isn't it?" Ann asked, and he was glad he hadn't put the phone on speaker. Kit was watching him, her heart visibly breaking.

"It is. But we'll work through it." He briefly met Kit's eyes when he said the words, and she swallowed hard. "Gotta go.

Call me when you get there." He ended the call and put his phone away. "I wasn't lying, Kit. We *will* work this out."

She swallowed again. "I keep thinking about Akiko with that man. He killed her mother, Sam."

He tried to have you killed, too. But Kit wasn't thinking about herself right now. *That's my job.*

"I know," he murmured. "I'm sorry, baby."

"I have to find her."

"And we will. Akiko McKittrick is a powerhouse. She's a black belt, right?"

"Right."

"She can kick Bob's ass."

"Not if he has a gun."

That was true, but he didn't want her dwelling on that point. "Well, he wants her for something, and it has to do with Kenzo. I don't think he'll hurt her until he has Kenzo where he wants him. I think that all of this, this entire scheme, is to cause Kenzo maximum harm."

She nodded once decisively. "I think you're right."

"I know I am. You know what else I think?"

"What?" Her tone was becoming firmer with every word she spoke.

His Kit was not going to be defeated by this. They'd find Akiko, and Kit would kick some ass of her own.

"I think there's a good chance that Bob has been doing things to hurt Kenzo for years. He destroyed Kenzo's businesses and slept with his wife. And who knows? Maybe Umeko's death wasn't a suicide. Maybe Bob killed her and made it look like one, just to hurt Kenzo—his reputation, anyway."

"I thought of that. Of course, Kenzo just turned it into a money grab. I bet that charity has some significant overhead and Kenzo's lining his pockets."

"Because Kenzo's evil, too." They had no shortage of bad guys here. "And now Bob's got Kenzo's son in his pocket. Who knows how long he's been worming his way into Danny's mind? Into his life? First, he took Kenzo's wife and then took his son. We'll have to find out when Bob's influence began, but I wouldn't be surprised if he was working on Danny long before that carjacking arrest."

"I hadn't thought of that."

"You would have, but you're distracted."

"And you're kind." She drew a breath. "Can I tell you something?"

"Always."

"You told Haru that if you shared secrets like the one she's been keeping about Minnie's murder, you could lose your license."

"Yes."

"But you did that a year ago. You risked your license, your *livelihood*, to share a secret with me, to tell me that you thought one of your clients had committed murder. You risked everything because it was the *right* thing. You do the right thing, Sam. It's one of the things I l-like best about you."

Sam's heart was about to club through his chest. That little stutter on *like* could have been *love*. And even if it was just a stutter . . . "You see me."

"And you see me. Haru Carlson might have had a good reason, in her own mind, to keep her sister's secret. But, in my mind, she was afraid. A lot of people would have been. Most people would have taken that secret to their grave, so at least she told us now. But you took the risk."

"And it paid off. You got the bad guy, and I got you."

"I'm glad you did. I'm glad you're here."

"Oh my God," Lennox said from the front seat, and Sam startled. He'd all but forgotten about her. "Could you two be any sweeter? Baz would simply vomit if he were here."

Kit barked a surprised laugh. "Then I'm glad he's not. But I am glad you're here, Meghan."

"Aw," Lennox said. "Same. Now that our little love fest has concluded, I have Kenzo's address, Sam. And Joe Fujioka's. And Bob Fujioka's. Do we still want to start with Kenzo?"

Sam was glad she was here, too. She'd made Kit laugh. "Yes. Let's start with Kenzo."

Kit exhaled, letting her head fall forward. She was centering herself. Calming her mind. The energy coming off her began to quiet. When she lifted her head, she was composed. His Kit was back. "Why now?" she asked.

"Why now, which?" Lennox asked.

"Why is Bob executing this grand plan now? And, other than hurting Kenzo, what exactly *is* his endgame? I doubt he'd go to all this trouble just to make Kenzo sad. He's been playing a very long game. He knew about Akiko and her boat five years ago. He started sleeping with Umeko over thirty years ago. He's spent the last twenty years tearing down nearly every business Kenzo tried to start, and he's been causing a lot of recent trouble to the businesses Kenzo has managed to keep. So why now?"

"Why do *you* think it's now?" Sam countered, because he bet she'd already thought this through.

"I think Bob's endgame is to overthrow Kenzo and take everything, but maybe he didn't have the support he needed, so he consoled himself with ruining Kenzo's businesses," Kit said. "I think he's been trying to overthrow Kenzo all this time by making him look incompetent, but it hasn't worked. I think he's upped the ante now because Kenzo is sick. Did you notice how thin he was when he talked to us outside the hospital this afternoon?"

God, was that only this afternoon? It felt like a week ago.

"I did, actually. I wonder if he's got cancer or something."

"Something," Kit agreed. "He's had some kind of medical trauma."

"Perfect time for Bob to stage a coup," Lennox said. "And the recent troubles aren't enough to ruin Kenzo's business. Burroughs said that Kenzo's businesses had been having mostly little setbacks."

"All but the casino," Kit said. "This new investigation could shut the casino down. And that's Kenzo's only legacy. Do you think Bob wants the company for himself, so he's not permanently damaging the businesses he wants to keep?"

"That's a distinct possibility," Lennox said. "Just so you're aware, LAPD has unmarked cars at all three addresses. They're also looking for Ricky Nicchi's gray two-year-old Lexus SUV. One of Desoto's analysts found him driving it on the hospital's parking lot cam. The officer on guard outside Ito's hospital room knows to grab him if he shows his face and hold him until we get there."

Kit managed a weak smile. "Thank you."

"Doin' my job. And you'd do the same."

"I would. So what would a coup of an organized crime business look like? What would Bob need to do to truly take over?"

"I'd think he'd need to get a lot of people on his side first," Lennox said. "He's VP of security, but everyone knows that Kenzo is in charge. A Takahashi's been at the helm for seventy years. We'll have to find someone on the inside to help us understand the company's inner workings. But I'm betting he's been sowing dissent for a long time, making Kenzo look incompetent. Making himself look more powerful. More in charge. Getting Danny to so publicly unravel is a way to do that. Kenzo can't even control his own son. How can he be expected to control an empire?"

Kit nodded, her expression thoughtful. "I wondered at first why Bob would risk telling Brewer and the ATF where to find the guns—because only he knew where they were. He had to know that Danny would try to drag him under the bus, but Bob's pretty much made it so that no one is going to listen to a word Danny says."

"Well, Danny did that to himself," Sam said. "He's not blameless in this."

"Oh, I know. My throbbing arm reminds me of that all day long. But who's going to listen to him, for real? He's killed four people, shot three cops. Got caught with guns. The guns are still puzzling me, though. What was Bob's angle? Why try to implicate Akiko?"

"Ah," Lennox said. "There might be an answer coming on that one. While you were verbally smooching back there about how wonderful Sam is, I was talking with Navarro through my earpiece. I brought him up to speed—he's going to sit in the surgical waiting room for news of your father, by the way. Your family won't be alone."

"Oh," Kit breathed, clearly touched at the gesture. "That's kind of him."

"He wants to help you," Lennox said. "He feels like shit about the suspension. You might be able to get some concessions out of him. Like a monthly Snickers bar allowance or something."

"I'll keep that in mind. So what about the guns? Was Brewer helpful?"

"He was. He and Navarro had a chat. The boss is supposed to call us with an update right about now. He also has information about what happened at Anson's house. That's why I interrupted your conversation."

Lennox didn't have to continue sharing information with Kit. Sam knew this meant a lot to her. He hoped a friendship between the two women would extend beyond this case. Kit needed friends.

"He didn't give you a hint?" Sam asked.

"Nope, but— Oh. Here he is." She answered the call and put Navarro through to the sedan's speaker. "I'm in the car with Sam and Kit," she said.

"Kit," Navarro said. "I'm in the waiting room at UC Irvine. Your father is in surgery right now. The paramedic I talked to said that his vital signs were strong. He was shot in the chest, and the paramedic thinks his lung may have collapsed, but they were giving him oxygen and brought his blood pressure back up. The bullet missed his heart. I haven't talked to the surgeons, but your dad is a strong man. The paramedics said he kept saying to make sure you knew what happened, to tell you to go after Akiko."

Kit shuddered. "Thank you. I didn't know how bad he was hurt. We're on our way to Kenzo Takahashi right now."

"I know. Lennox has been keeping me up to speed."

Kit managed a small smile for Lennox. "She's a good cop. A good person."

Lennox looked away and said, "What about Kit's brother? Anson? How is he?"

Sam couldn't help but notice that Lennox was as bad at taking compliments as Kit was. She tended to deflect back to the case, just like Kit did.

"Being treated for smoke inhalation, but he didn't get shot. He said that his smoke alarms started to go off, so he got Harlan and Akiko out of the house—just as he heard an ambulance approaching. The ambulance used its yelp siren to get through his gates."

"Yelp siren?" Sam asked.

"It's a special tone that emergency vehicles use," Lennox explained. "Activates the gate opener."

"Anson said he didn't think twice about the siren. The smoke was visible, and he thought a neighbor had called 911."

"Bob was driving the ambulance?"

"One of his lackeys," Navarro said. "Anson had run back into the house to get his cat. As he was coming back out, he saw Bob grabbing Akiko. Your father tried to stop him and Bob shot him, dragged Akiko into the back of the ambulance and it drove away. He . . ." Navarro hesitated.

"Tell me," Kit said grimly.

"Bob had to hit her pretty hard, Anson said. She was

fighting Bob like a wildcat, but he knew some martial arts as well and was countering her attacks. She went limp, but Anson thought she was more stunned than knocked out. Just so you know for when you find her."

"Did Burroughs and Desoto find Joe?" Kit asked.

"No, he wasn't home. They're on their way to Kenzo's house to provide support."

"Thank you," Kit said again.

"We've got your back, Kit. I promise." Navarro cleared his throat. "I also have information on the guns. Special Agent Brewer said that he'd been working with an anonymous source who tipped him off about the gun running and the use of Akiko's boat. The source said that the op was being controlled by Kenzo and implicated both Akiko and Paolo. Brewer was told that if the ATF watched the boat, they'd get enough evidence on Kenzo to take down his operation. The ATF has suspected Kenzo of smuggling guns and drugs into Japan for some time, specifically using his luxury car business. The car trunks are packed with illegal firearms and drugs, then the cars are loaded onto shipping vessels and unloaded once they reach port in Japan. Money changes hands at the docks for safe passage. It's very lucrative for Takahashi."

"Where does Akiko fit in?" Kit asked.

"Not sure and neither was Brewer. But if Bob has it in for Kenzo, it may have simply been emotional torment. Here's the daughter you didn't know you had, but whoops, now she's going to prison and so are you. He wouldn't be able to contact her and he'd know she went to prison even though she was innocent. That's the best we can figure. When you find the bastard, you can ask him."

Kit nodded. "We will find him."

"I know you will. A task force is forming to search for your sister. LAPD, the ATF, and the FBI are involved. You're not alone."

Kit closed her eyes. "Thank you."

"Keep me informed." He ended the call.

"Meghan?" Kit opened her eyes. "Can you drive faster?"

Bel Air, Los Angeles, California
Wednesday, February 1, 10:35 p.m.

Kit studied the view through the iron bars of Kenzo Takahashi's front gate. Only one corner of the immense house was visible, as the driveway seemed to twist and turn and wind through a thick copse of trees. Strategically placed spotlights came on as they approached the gate intercom.

"Yes?" a deep voice asked. It sounded like Takahashi himself.

"Dr. Reeves, Detective McKittrick, and Detective Lennox of the San Diego Police Department, here to see Mr. Takahashi on an urgent matter," Lennox said.

The massive iron gates didn't make a sound as they opened. After what seemed like hours, Lennox stopped the sedan. Only two more minutes had passed.

Takahashi's house was more than immense. It was three stories of stone. A veritable fortress. "It's a castle," Lennox said.

Sam was also staring up at it. "I'm expecting a dragon to fly over at any moment."

"Let me go first," Lennox said. "Kit, you stay behind me.

Sam, please bring up the rear. I want Kit protected. We don't know what we're walking into here."

Kit wanted to disagree, but Lennox was right. "Where are Burroughs and Desoto?"

"They followed us in," Sam said.

Kit looked behind them, and sure enough, there was a black SUV. That she hadn't noticed them told her exactly how out of it she was. Lennox was right to go first. Kit would be a danger to herself and everyone else in this frame of mind. "Are they coming in with us?"

It felt surreal, not being in charge. But she was too numb for it to bother her as much as she'd always feared it would.

All she could think of was Akiko. *And Pop.*

The conversation with her mother had been heart-wrenching. Betsy was so scared, as were the girls. Harlan being shot, Akiko being taken. Anson losing his house. Any one of those things would have been devastating, but all three?

Kit was hanging on by a thread, but Akiko needed her. Her father was in surgery and getting the finest care at a Level I trauma center. Anson was being treated.

Still, she could hear her mother's voice breaking. She was so grateful to Baz and to Sam's parents. They'd provided the support that Kit wished she could. But getting Akiko back would be the best use of her time and skill right now.

"No," Lennox said. "Burroughs texted that he and Desoto are going to wait outside. They're backup, in case we need them, but they agree that we don't want to gang up on Takahashi. He knows they're there. It's statement enough. Let's go."

So Kit found herself sandwiched between Lennox and Sam

as they stood at the front door. Then it opened, revealing Kenzo Takahashi.

He wore a silk robe and honest-to-God silk pajamas. Kit had never actually seen anyone wear silk pajamas before.

"What is it?" he asked wearily. "It is very late."

Even in the dim light Kit could see that he looked ill. He was much paler tonight than he'd been earlier. It occurred to her he might have been wearing makeup when they'd met him outside the hospital.

Now he looked old and frail.

"We need your help," Kit said from behind Lennox. "Akiko has been taken."

He gasped. "What do you mean, taken?"

Kit stepped to one side so that she was no longer behind Lennox. Lennox was taller and blocking her view. She wanted to see Kenzo's face when she told him the truth.

"I mean your VP of security, Bob Fujioka, set my brother's house on fire and when my family evacuated, Bob shot my father and kidnapped Akiko." Kit stared hard at the man, watching the confusion flicker across his face. Watched the confusion become denial.

"You are mistaken."

"I am not." Kit showed him the photo of Bob on her phone. "This is him, yes?"

"Yes. Where was that taken?"

"It's from a fake ID he used when he boarded my sister's boat. She owns a fishing charter. This was her first trip out of San Diego, five years ago. Bob was a passenger."

Kenzo shook his head. "This makes no sense."

"It does," Sam said. "Did you know that Joe Fujioka adopted Bob after his parents were killed?"

"Yes. I remember when Bob came to live with Joe. I thought he was a nephew or something."

"No, not a nephew." Kit looked Kenzo right in the eye. "Do you remember a visit you paid with Joe to a married couple? You were twenty years old. You were only supposed to kill the husband, but you killed the wife, too. Guess who was watching from the closet? A kid named Bob."

Kenzo froze, anger slowly taking over his expression. "You overstep, Detective. No such thing ever happened."

"You lie, Mr. Takahashi." She'd seen the fear in his eyes before the rage took over. "And it matters. Because Bob Fujioka has been slowly chipping away at your empire, at your *life*, ever since. He slept with your wife for more than two decades. He killed Minako Nakamura because your wife told him to."

Kenzo's mouth fell open. "Minnie?" he whispered.

Kit didn't let up. "He's been working with Danny to frame Akiko for smuggling guns. He's been sabotaging your businesses. He *hates* you, sir."

Kenzo gripped the edge of the front door, swaying slightly, his face cycling through a myriad of emotions—shock, recognition, acceptance, betrayal, sorrow—before becoming blank and cold. "You are mistaken. Get out of my house. Off my property. Or I'll call security to escort you out and they will not be gentle."

"Call security," Kit challenged. "Call Bob. When you reach him, ask him where the *hell* my sister is. If he hurts her, there will be no place on this earth that either of you can hide from me."

But Bob had already hurt Akiko. He'd hit her in the head so hard that she'd been stunned. *Don't think about that. Don't think of Akiko scared and hurting.*

"Get. Out." Kenzo seemed to transform, his body no longer weary and frail. He exuded power and rage. In that moment Kit understood how the man could command his own mob. He hit a button next to the door and a siren began to wail. "Get out *now*."

"Where is Joe?" Kit demanded, surging into Kenzo's space and taking a quick look around the foyer. "Is he here? Maybe he knows where we can find his son."

"Get out."

She'd reached for those silk pajamas when Sam gripped her elbow, tugging until she stepped away from Kenzo. "Come on. Let's go."

She was vibrating with rage as Sam settled her in the back seat of the department sedan. And then . . . it hit her. Akiko was missing. She was gone.

And I enraged one of the only men who might have been able to find her. She sucked in a huge gulp of air that burned her lungs, held the breath until her head began to spin. Tears pricked at her eyelids, and she couldn't make them stop.

She dropped her face into her hands and began to cry.

"Get us out of here, Meghan," Sam directed.

Lennox complied, and Sam's hand squeezed Kit's thigh. "We will find her, Kit."

She's gone. She's gone.
Just like Wren.
I didn't keep her safe.
Just like Wren.

Lennox sped down Kenzo's long, winding driveway, out into the street. She drove for a block, passing more gated driveways. The vehicle slowed to a stop and Sam pulled Kit out of the car and into his arms, one hand on her back, the other in her hair. "I've got you."

"I lost her." She could barely breathe, the sobs racking her body. "I didn't keep her safe. Just like Wren."

"Akiko is not Wren," Sam said fiercely. "Wren was a vulnerable, helpless fifteen-year-old. But Akiko is strong. She is not helpless. And neither are you. You are not fifteen years old, nor are you helpless. And you're not alone. I'm here. People who care about you are out there trying to find her. There is a whole task force searching for Akiko. You are not alone."

Her forehead resting on his chest, she fisted his shirt, holding on for dear life. He was solidity. He was safety. He was a rock. *My rock. He's mine.*

"I lost my temper. I shouldn't have lost my temper."

Lennox got out of the car to stand beside them. "I think you should have. It shook him up. And now, when Bob calls him with his demands, Takahashi will know exactly who he's dealing with. You got to him, Kit. He claimed he didn't believe you, but he did. I think a lot of pieces fell into place for him. So it's okay. When he finally meets with Bob, he will not go unprepared."

"He won't protect Akiko. He'll just want revenge."

"I don't think so," Lennox said. "I think he'll fume and seethe about what Bob has taken from him over the years. He'll be determined not to let Bob keep Akiko—or kill her. She's the one thing Bob hasn't yet ruined and Kenzo will want to save her, if for no other reason than to thwart Bob."

Kit nodded slowly, Lennox's words making sense. "What do we do now?"

"We find that fucker Ricky Nicchi," Sam growled.

"Or Joe," Lennox said. "Come on, Kit. Get back in the car. We have work to do."

Sam gently put her back in the car and fastened her seat belt, caring for her like she was spun glass. But she felt like shattered glass.

"My head hurts."

"I guess it does." He kissed her temple softly, pulled the bottle of painkillers from his pocket, and gave her a bottle of water. "Take two and don't argue."

"Wasn't gonna," she grumbled. She swallowed the pills, chased them with water, then drained half the bottle. Damn tears. She was dehydrated. "Where are we going?"

"I'm taking you to that shopping center so you can get Anson's car," Lennox said gently. "You need to go to the hospital to sit with your father."

Kit frowned, instantly suspicious. Lennox sounded different. She wanted to demand what the other detective would be doing, but she thought she knew. Five minutes later, she was proved right when they stopped by Anson's car.

A black SUV pulled up on the other side of them and Lennox rolled her window down. The passenger-side window of the other car lowered, and Burroughs gave Lennox a quick nod. "We need to hurry."

Lennox winced. "I'm going with Burroughs and Desoto. Kit, you've done all you can do. Let me take this the rest of the way. I'll find your sister. I promise."

Kit drew a deep breath, reining in her temper. "*Where* are you going, Detective?"

"A vehicle just pulled into Joe's garage. We're going to interview him. You need to take a break. Yelling at Kenzo may have worked, but you can't yell at Joe Fujioka. I think he knows everything, and we need him to talk. Take Anson's car to the hospital and take care of your family."

Kit nodded once, her jaw clenched. Like she wasn't taking care of her family right now? *Fuck this shit.* "Have fun."

She got out of the sedan and held the door for Sam, who was shaking his head, his expression weary.

"Kit," Lennox started, then sighed. "I'll let Navarro know you're on your way."

Kit smiled sweetly. "Okay."

Lennox motioned to Sam. "She needs some rest, Sam. Please."

"She's not a child, Meghan. I'm not going to tell her to take a nap. Good luck."

Kit's heart squeezed and then . . . grew. Grew into something huge. She was continually surprised by this man. *And I shouldn't be. He's proven so many times that he knows who I am.*

And he wants me anyway.

Lennox pursed her lips, but she nodded. "Don't do anything stupid, okay?"

Kit leaned around Sam to push her face through the open window. "I said, *okay*. Go and do your *job*, Detective."

Reluctantly, Lennox closed the window and followed the LAPD vehicle.

Kit got into Anson's car, waiting for Sam to slide behind the wheel. She kissed his cheek. "Thank you."

"You're welcome." Smiling a little, Sam waited until Lennox's taillights had disappeared around a curve. "Where are we going?"

"Back to Kenzo's neighborhood. We're going to sit there and wait for Takahashi to leave. Bob will be contacting him soon."

"I agree."

One side of Kit's mouth lifted. "I don't hate her, Sam. I might not trust her, but I don't hate her."

"I might," Sam admitted. "A little."

She brushed her fingertips over his cheek. "You always know the perfect thing to say. Now I need to make a call." She punched in a number on her phone and put it on speaker.

"Kit," Anson said in a gravelly voice, "are you all right?"

"I'm fine. Sam's here with me. Where are you?"

"Just finishing in the ER and I'm heading up to the surgical waiting room to wait for news about Pop. Are you coming?"

"As soon as I have Akiko."

He made a sound that hurt her heart. "Kit. I'm sorry. I should have . . ."

"Anson, stop." She softened her tone. "You didn't do anything wrong. Your house has amazing security. But Bob is Takahashi's VP of security, so he's good, too. Maybe we should have anticipated something like this, but we didn't. Listen, Lennox is about to tell Navarro that I'm on my way to the hospital."

"But you're not," Anson said. "Did she dump you?"

"She tried," Kit said. "She's going to talk to Joe. We're going to be waiting outside Kenzo's house because I know Bob will be contacting him soon. So when I don't show up for Pop in the next forty-five minutes, don't go thinking that I'm dead."

"I wouldn't anyway. I'd be there to back you up if I could."

"I know. Take care of Pop. Tell him I love him, okay?"

"He knows, Kit. He knows."

She swallowed hard. "Tell him anyway."

"You know I will. Sam? Make sure she stays alive."

"I always do," Sam said.

Kit gave him a look that she hoped expressed everything in her heart. "He really does. I'll text you with updates."

"Wait. Did you call Mom?"

Kit's face fell. "I did. Sam's parents were with her and so was Baz, so she's not alone. She'll hold up, for the girls if for nothing else."

"That's good. Go now. Bring Akiko home."

Kit nodded, feeling grim. "I will."

She was *not* losing another sister.

CHAPTER TWENTY-TWO

Bel Air, Los Angeles, California
Thursday, February 2, 12:30 a.m.

Kit stared at the gate in front of Kenzo's house, mentally willing it to open. Worry for Akiko burned inside her. "I thought Bob would have called him by now."

"I did, too." Sam sounded calm, but Kit knew that he was as tense as she was.

It had been more than three hours since Bob had taken Akiko. He could be hurting her.

No. She couldn't think like that.

Sam was right. Akiko was not Wren. Akiko could defend herself.

And I am not alone.

"Thank you for staying with me."

"Always," he said softly.

"And for being willing to aid me in my potentially felonious stalking."

He smiled. "I hear that Georgia knows some good lawyers that are not my ex."

Kit's laugh surprised her, and she was grateful to him for that, too. No one else could make her laugh in such a situation. *I want to keep him. I want him to keep me.*

The buzzing of her phone had her heartbeat stuttering. It was Navarro.

Pop.

She hit accept, putting Navarro on speaker. "How's Pop?"

"I thought you were with him. Lennox said so."

Kit narrowed her eyes. "I thought *you* were with him. Lennox said so."

He hesitated. "I was, but I had to leave. I came back to San Diego. I located Nancy Sayer."

It took Kit a second to place the name. Sam was faster on the uptake.

"The woman who became Mary's guardian after her mother died?" Sam asked.

"Yes," Navarro said. "I'm with her now. She wants to talk to you. Can I switch you to FaceTime?"

Kit shared an expectant glance with Sam. "Yes, of course," she said.

A moment later, Navarro's face filled the screen. He readjusted his angle, bringing an older woman into the frame. "Kit, this is Nancy Sayer. Miss Sayer, this is Detective McKittrick."

"I know who you are, Detective," the woman said, her voice raspy and unsteady. Lying in a hospital bed, she wore an oxygen cannula, and her skin was stretched tight across her face. "I've known your name for sixteen years. But I know about you from Tamsin Kavanaugh's articles over the last few years."

Kit couldn't find it in herself to even scowl at the mention of the reporter. "You knew about me sixteen years ago? You knew that Akiko was placed with my family?"

"I did. I helped watch over her for her whole childhood."

So many people had watched over Akiko. "You knew Mary?"

"I did. I helped her change her name to Smith after the twins were murdered. She was terrified and so was I. But she was so very strong. I can't believe she's gone."

"I'm so sorry for your loss," Kit said. "I wish we could have known her."

"Can you tell us about her?" Sam asked, and Nancy smiled crookedly.

"You're Dr. Reeves. I've read about you, too." She wheezed a rattling breath. "I knew Sakura from college in New York. I moved around after graduation. Following a man." She made a face. "He landed in Vegas, so I did, too. Didn't work out with him, but I loved the sunshine, so I stayed. I became a social worker. Sakura met Eddie Ito while we were college seniors. She married him right out of school, and they went to LA. When I finally broke up with my ex, I called her. The twins were three and she was pregnant again, even though she didn't know it at the time."

The older woman drew another rasping breath, then went on. "She wasn't happy. She thought she was going to get a life of excitement in California. Hollywood and movie stars. But she was stuck in a tiny apartment all day with twins. Eddie worked all the time. He was an accountant by day, but he was also starting his own karate dojo."

Kit was surprised to hear that Ito had been an accountant, too. That hadn't come up on any of his background checks. It must have been a long time ago. "Did you ever see Sakura in LA, Miss Sayer?"

"Once. We met for lunch at a restaurant. She didn't want me coming to see her apartment. She was ashamed of it. Ashamed of Eddie. Of how poor they were. In New York, she'd been comfortable. Her parents had spoiled her. But they hadn't liked Eddie and when she married him, they cut her off. She was miserable. I hated to see it. I asked about the twins that day, and she said that she'd left them with Eddie's best friend—Joe. He'd been the best man in their wedding, so I'd met him. He . . . well, I didn't like him. He'd looked at Sakura the way a man shouldn't look at the woman marrying his best friend."

"Oh," Kit breathed, realization dawning. "Joe loved Sakura."

"He really did." Nancy sighed. "Anyway, she was desperately unhappy and wishing she'd never left New York. Wishing she'd never married Eddie. But I noticed she wore a very pretty necklace that was not cheap. Joe had given it to her. He gave her other things, too. Jewelry. Dresses. Eddie didn't like it, but Sakura didn't care what he thought." She shook her head. "I told her that she shouldn't be taking presents from anyone but Eddie, but she said she wanted something pretty. She was mad at Eddie because Joe had found him a job as an accountant in his company, but Eddie refused, even though it would have been a huge pay raise. The lunch was mostly her complaining about Eddie, and I was glad when it was over. Then three weeks later I got a phone call. Sakura was hysterical. She was going on about gangs and tattoos and mafia. I had no idea what she was talking about, but I finally got her calmed down."

"Did she see Eddie's tattoo?" Kit asked.

"Oh, she always knew about Eddie's tattoo. He told her that he got it in 'Nam."

"He didn't," Kit said.

"No, he didn't. She'd thought Eddie's was just a pretty tattoo, but then she saw Joe's tattoos and that's when she called me in a panic. I didn't know back then that the Japanese even had a mafia, but Sakura did. She said her parents had warned her away from men with tattoos. When she saw Joe's tattoos, she knew who he was. *What* he was. And she knew that Eddie had lied to her, because Joe had the same tiger and dragon on his back that Eddie had. Joe's was all filled in, of course. She'd confronted Eddie, asked if he was in the mob. He admitted that he had been, but he'd escaped. She was scared and angry because Eddie was still friends with Joe, and Joe was mafia. She didn't feel safe. Eddie had lied to her, and she wanted a divorce. I told her to come and stay with me in Henderson, Nevada, while she figured things out. But nothing was simple. She showed up with the twins and a baby bump—and a new last name. She'd changed it to Nakamura. She had ID and everything, for herself and the twins. She said that Joe got them for her."

"Were you scared?" Kit asked. "Of the mob?"

"Of course I was," Nancy snapped. "I wasn't stupid, Detective. But she said she wouldn't stay with me long and she didn't. She bought herself a house there in Henderson. With cash."

"Joe again," Kit said, a few more pieces falling into place.

"That's how he knew where to find the twins after she died. He bought her the house. Did Joe visit her there?"

"First Sunday morning of every month, like clockwork. Never stayed long and he never went inside. I don't think she ever saw him or even knew he made the trip. He stayed in his car, just waiting on the curb up the street. When Sakura would come out with the kids to go to church, he'd watch them and then he'd leave."

"You watched him waiting on Sakura's street?" Kit asked, then remembered that the two women had lived next door to each other. "Did Joe buy you a house, too?"

"He did. I was afraid to take it, but I was more afraid not to take it. He told me to watch over Sakura and the children. And maybe send him photos sometimes. Of the children," she added meaningfully.

"Of the children?" Kit repeated, and suddenly she understood. *Oh. Ohhh.* "Was Joe the father of the twins?"

"He was. I was so angry at Sakura. She'd cheated on Eddie and then divorced him for lying to her. She was a hypocrite. And she agreed with me. But, back in LA, Joe had brought her presents. Brought toys for the kids. He had money to burn. And Sakura wanted money. Until she learned it was mafia money."

"Miss Sayer," Sam said, "how did she not know that Joe was the mob when she had children by him? Surely, she'd seen his skin."

"She said he always kept his shirt on. Claimed he had scars that he didn't want her to see. He didn't mean for her to see him with his shirt off. She walked in on him when he was changing, and she immediately knew. Joe didn't want her to leave LA, but she said if he really loved her, he'd let her go. Ironically enough, she said the same thing to Eddie. Both men loved her. Both men let her go."

"She wanted to escape but she let Joe get her new ID and buy her a house?" Kit frowned. "Apologies, ma'am, but that doesn't make sense."

"It would have if you'd known Sakura. She acted tough, but she was really just a scared girl. She was terrified of the mob, but she was more terrified of being homeless and not being able to feed her children. So she accepted Joe's help. He gave her a fresh start and promised not to bother her anymore. He kept his word, mostly. Except for the monthly drive to watch them go to church. To my knowledge, Eddie Ito never knew where she was. Sakura told the twins their father had died."

"Probably why Minako and Ichiro didn't seek him out when they went to LA," Sam said. "Was Joe Mary's father, too?"

"Sakura was pretty sure that Eddie was Mary's father, but at that point she just wanted to get away. She didn't want anyone in Joe's 'family' to know that she or the twins existed. She was genuinely terrified they'd take the kids."

"But Eddie tried to take care of her," Kit said. "He sent her money every month."

"I know. Joe made a monthly drive to San Diego to see the kids. I made a monthly drive to LA to empty Sakura's PO box. She needed to keep her Sakura Ito persona alive so that Eddie wouldn't go looking for her under another name. These days, with the internet, he could have found them easily. I mean, how many twins are named Minako and Ichiro?"

"That's how I found them," Kit said. "Not a common name combination. Did you send the money back or did Sakura?"

"I did, at her request. She finally found a job that paid enough for her to feed the kids. She sold the expensive jewelry that Joe had given her. Losing the diamonds was penance, she said, for cheating on Eddie. That money helped her buy necessities for the kids. Eventually, she got a two-year degree and became a respiratory therapist. Then things were easier for them. Until she died."

"Do you think she would have left Eddie for Joe had he not been in the mob?" Kit asked.

"I do. She loved Joe, but she wanted no part of that lifestyle. She asked Eddie if he'd killed, and he was honest with her. He said he had. She asked Joe and he said that he hadn't. But she knew he was lying. She never mentioned Joe to the kids, to my knowledge."

"But when she died, Joe came to get the twins?"

"Yeah, he did. I said *no*. But the kids recognized Joe's face. Sakura kept a wedding photo hidden in her important papers, and Minnie had found it when she was going through her mother's things after the funeral. When Joe showed up for his monthly drive and no one came out to go to church, he knocked on my door. The kids were with me. And they recognized him from the picture. When Joe offered them jobs in LA, I said *no*. That Sakura wouldn't have wanted that. But Ichiro wanted to be the man of the family, wanted to support his sisters, and the money that Joe offered was ten times what he could make as a seventeen-year-old with a high school diploma. Joe told me privately that if I stopped fighting him about the twins, he'd let me keep Mary. He was quiet but threatening. I was scared. So I agreed. And then, about four months later, he brought them back. Told me that Minnie was pregnant and the baby's father's wife was insane and wanted Minnie dead. This was Sakura's worst nightmare, that her kids would get caught up in mob violence. Joe told me to hide them. I told him I would, but that he needed to leave and never come back. I tried to hide the twins and Mary in my house, but Minnie wanted to have her baby in the house she grew up in. Said she felt closer to her mother there. She didn't leave once during her entire pregnancy. Ichiro found a job in an all-night diner in Henderson. He was at work the night the killer came."

She slumped back into the pillows, breathing hard, Navarro still at her side. They let the woman catch her breath. "What happened that night, Miss Sayer?" Kit asked.

"I was in my own place next door and Minnie, Mary, and Akiko were in Sakura's house."

"Wait," Kit said. "The house hadn't been sold? A year later?"

"No. Sakura left it to the kids and the twins wanted to keep it. That's one reason they agreed to go to LA with Joe. They needed the money to pay taxes on the house."

"Thank you." Kit wasan't sure that she wanted to hear the rest of the story, but she made herself ask. "I interrupted you. I'm sorry. What happened that night?"

"Mary said she was feeding the baby when she and Minnie heard a noise. Minnie made her hide in the closet with Akiko. She said that if anything happened to her, no one could ever know she'd had a child. Mary said she heard Minnie calling Ichiro at work, begging him to come home. Then she heard a strange man asking Minnie where the baby was. At first Minnie didn't answer, just begged the man not to kill her, but he kept demanding to know about the baby. So she told him that she'd left the baby on the firehouse steps. And then Mary said she heard nothing. No sound. Until Ichiro came home and screamed Minnie's name. And then he went silent, too. After a little longer, Mary came out of the closet and saw her brother and sister dead on the floor. Bullet holes in their foreheads. She was fourteen and freaked out."

Kit sighed. "Who could blame her? Did she take the baby to the firehouse?"

"We did it together, but we knew we couldn't leave her in Henderson. The cops would know that Minako had just given birth and would be looking for a newborn Japanese baby."

"So you went to San Diego," Kit murmured.

"We did. I had friends there who we could stay with. We drove straight from Henderson to the firehouse in San Diego. I put Akiko in a box and wrapped her in a blanket. It was Mary's idea to pin the paper with her name to the blanket."

"Was there a photo of Minnie in the box?" Sam asked.

Nancy blinked. "Why would we do that? We were trying to hide Akiko's identity."

"Then that was just a story someone told Akiko to make her feel better," Kit said. "Who left her on the firehouse steps?"

"I did. Then Mary and I waited across the street until a firefighter found the box. Akiko entered the system."

Akiko would at least know how brave her mother and Mary had been. Both had given their lives to protect her. "Mary kept track of Akiko."

"She did, with my help. I knew the firefighter would call Child Services and then I'd be able to keep track of her from there. It was the only reason I agreed to the plan. I was a social worker in Nevada, you see. I was able to get a job with Child Services in San Diego, so I knew where Akiko was at all times.

I came clean with Mary that same night as the firehouse. Told her that her father hadn't died. That his name was Edwin Ito. I didn't tell her that the twins were Joe's, though. I didn't think that was anything she needed to know. I just said that Joe was a family friend. A week later, Mary disappeared. She left me a note saying she was taking the bus to LA to find her father. That she needed to keep Akiko safe from the mob and she needed help. She came back with Eddie Ito."

"Eddie opened a dojo in San Diego shortly thereafter," Kit said, and Nancy nodded.

"He kept tabs on Akiko until she was old enough to get a scholarship to his dojo. He was there for her. Not in the way he wanted to be, but he made sure she was healthy and safe. I wasn't her caseworker, but I knew the woman who was and together we—she, Eddie, and I—made sure that her foster homes were good ones. But then Akiko got placed in a bad one. The foster father was a predator. One night, Akiko had to defend herself from his advances. Broke the guy's ribs. I'd heard about your parents, Detective. I'd heard that Harlan and Betsy McKittrick were good people. I asked her caseworker to approach your folks, and they took her in. You know the rest of the story."

"I know the rest of Akiko's story, yes. Thank you for making sure she stayed safe. That's going to mean a lot to her. But what about Mary? She told her daughters that she grew up in the foster system. Did she live with you?"

"No. I couldn't keep her. Whoever killed her brother and sister might come looking for her, and that she'd been living with me was public knowledge. Himari Nakamura needed to disappear." Her eyes snapped with fire. "I was so *angry* with

Joe. I'd *told* him that Sakura wouldn't want the twins working with the mob, but he was insistent. He didn't tell the twins what kind of business he ran before he took them, and threatened me so I wouldn't tell them, either. He was responsible for their deaths. So was I. I should have told them about the mob, even if Joe would have killed me. I have to live with the fact that I didn't. But afterward, I knew Joe could get Mary a new ID, because he'd done it once already for Sakura. At first, Joe wanted to adopt Akiko. But I said *no*. Hadn't he caused enough trouble by getting Minako and Ichiro murdered? I caved the first time, when he came to get the twins after Sakura died, but I kept seeing Minnie's and Ichiro's bodies on the floor."

She had to stop talking as she was gasping for breath. Navarro gave her some water and they waited until she could speak again.

"So I did not cave again. I wouldn't tell him where Akiko was and threatened to tell the cops if Joe didn't stop demanding the baby. He finally agreed to help Mary. He got her a new identity and she 'showed up' at a shelter as a runaway. I got her placed in a home I'd personally vetted. I was the executor of Sakura's will, so I sold her house and mine. The proceeds from Sakura's house went into a trust for Mary's college. She went to college here in San Diego because she wouldn't leave Akiko. She was nineteen when Akiko started at Eddie's dojo. Mary would wait outside the dojo for a glimpse of her, but Eddie was our main contact. He saw her every week and made sure she was okay. It was a bad situation all around, but Eddie, Mary, and I tried to make the best of it."

The old woman sighed wearily. "That's all of it. I have photos of Sakura, Minnie, and Ichiro. Mary didn't want her husband to find them and ask questions, so I kept everything. It's in a storage locker. Tell your sister to come see me."

"I will." *When I find her.* "Thank you."

"Akiko needs to know how many people loved her. How many people risked everything to keep her away from her father. He would have made her work for the mob. Please tell her."

"I promise," Kit said, then looked away from her phone screen when Sam stiffened beside her. "We need to go, ma'am. Please rest now. Thank you, Lieutenant," she said to Navarro, who'd turned the phone back to his face. "I'll call you, sir, and bring you up to speed when I have information."

"Kit," he said. "Wait."

"I can't, sir." Because Kenzo Takahashi's gates were opening. "Bob appears to have finally contacted Kenzo for whatever it is he's planning. We're going to follow him. I'll call Lennox for backup."

She ended the call as he demanded answers.

She winced. She was going to get in trouble for that. But she'd worry about that later.

It was time to get her sister back.

Bel Air, Los Angeles, California
Thursday, February 2, 1:00 a.m.

"He's going to know we're following him," Sam said as he put Anson's car into drive.

"I know."

Kenzo Takahashi had left his massive fortress, driving a Bentley.

No driver. No security. He was also driving at a steady pace and making no sharp turns. Kenzo didn't seem to want to shake them. At least not yet.

"I didn't expect to learn that Joe is Akiko's grandfather," Sam said.

"Same. I'm wondering if Ito knows. If he doesn't, finding out the truth about Joe and Sakura might make him finally spill the tea on Joe." She bit at her lip. "I hate this for Akiko. At least when Ito was her grandfather, she knew he cared about her. But finding out that it's really Joe? It just keeps getting worse. But I'll worry about that when she's safe."

"She will be." *I hope. Please let her be safe.* He'd tried to stay positive for Kit's benefit, but every hour Akiko remained missing was . . . well, it wasn't good.

From the corner of his eye, Sam saw Kit's phone light up with a new text.

"Oh thank God," she breathed. "Anson says Pop's in recovery and his vital signs are stable. He's gonna be okay. And so is Akiko." She pulled her gun from its holster and checked the chamber. "But Bob is going down. Where's your gun?"

"In my back holster." He'd applied for a concealed carry permit after being hired by the police department but hadn't started carrying his gun consistently until recently, when he'd really needed a weapon and hadn't had it with him. Luckily Navarro had loaned him a gun when he'd needed one. It had enabled Sam to keep Kit safe. Since then, Sam was never without his firearm. Because he'd continue to protect his Kit.

"When was the last time you fired it?" she asked.

"Last week at the target range."

He'd been practicing for the past few months. Sam hoped

he wouldn't need to shoot anyone tonight. His one experience with shooting a human being had left him shaken. That feeling would stay with him always, but he was pragmatic enough to know he'd do it again. He'd do almost anything to keep Kit McKittrick safe.

The Bentley put on its turn signal as it slowed for a right turn, cementing what Sam had suspected. "He's letting us follow him."

"I thought he might," Kit said. "He wants to save Akiko. He knows we want the same. And, if push comes to shove, we can be his cannon fodder."

He was startled into a breathless laugh. "I can always count on you to see the situation clearly." He turned right, sticking closer to Kenzo's sedan. The Bentley was slowing and pulling over. He followed suit, coming to a stop behind Kenzo's parked car. "What's this?"

"Let's find out." Kit got out, her gun held loosely at her side.

Gripping his own gun firmly, Sam followed Kit to the Bentley. Together, they waited as Kenzo slowly emerged.

He now wore a suit and tie, his silk pajamas retired for the evening. He looked gaunt and utterly exhausted.

For a long moment Kenzo and Kit regarded each other silently, opponents sizing the other up for weaknesses. For strengths. For commonalities.

Akiko.

"Detective," Kenzo finally said. "Dr. Reeves."

"Mr. Takahashi," Kit said. "Did you hear from your VP of security?"

Kenzo dipped his head in a nod. "I did. He asked me to meet him at one of our warehouses. The code to the lock on the rear door is six-one-three-four-star. I intend to go through the front door as I was instructed."

"You want me to come in through the back?" Kit asked. "Come to the rescue?"

"Whatever it takes."

"Bob wants to hurt you," Kit told him.

"I know. I am grateful for your insight into my VP of security. I admit to none of his accusations, of course."

She lifted a brow. "Of course."

"The warehouse is mostly one big, cavernous space, but there is a back hallway that runs the width of the building. You'll be able to use that hallway to access the storage area."

"Do you think Bob has reinforcements?" Sam asked.

"From what I've ascertained from the local authorities, Bob used a stolen ambulance to gain access to your brother's residence. He had at least one person helping him, the man driving the ambulance. I don't know who that is, but his people are very well trained. If they shoot you, they will not miss. Now, I need to hurry. I've been given a deadline. I must meet him in a few minutes. He says he wants to 'show me something.'" Kenzo used air quotes. "I'm quite certain that he knows you stopped by my house. He has access to my external security cameras."

"Did he mention Akiko at all?" Kit asked.

"No. At this point, I don't know if he knows he is a suspect."

"I'm going to assume that he knows," Kit said. "Are you going in alone?"

"I am. I wasn't told to come alone, but if my VP of security is corrupted, my bodyguards may be as well. I don't know who, within my household or my company, I can trust."

"But you trust me."

"We share a goal, Detective."

"Yes, we do. Is there any other security that we'll need to bypass in order to get inside?"

"The keypad code is nine-two-one-five, if the alarm has been set. That should be all. The warehouse itself is filled with crates, most of which are filled with products we ship."

"Guns?" Kit asked.

"No, Detective. They're supplies for our hotels. Towels and toilet paper. My point was that there are many places to hide among the crates. Be careful."

"Thank you." She gestured to his car. "After you, sir."

She waited until she and Sam were back in the sedan before speaking again. "I don't believe there's toilet paper in that warehouse."

"Neither do I. We never did find out where Danny got those guns."

"I thought the same thing," she said. "Kenzo has to know by now that Special Agent Brewer arrested his son."

"And that Danny named both Joe and Bob as being involved," Sam added. "Maybe not as co-conspirators, but at least as people of interest."

"That expensive attorney definitely told Kenzo he named Joe and Bob. Especially since Danny made a point of saying that he was helping his father clean his own house."

Sam waited until Kenzo turned back onto the road and then followed him. "It's possible that Kenzo didn't believe Danny until Bob called him tonight. Danny has been out of control lately. Or at least out of Kenzo's control."

"He's been under Bob's. There is a very small part of me

that almost feels sorry for Danny Takahashi. He's been either manipulated or groomed ever since he was born. His mother was a drunken viper who ordered Minnie Nakamura's death. His father used him to raise money for a phony charity and discarded him when he went to juvie. And Bob has been using him for God knows how long to get revenge on Kenzo."

"You sound like Dawn." Sam thought about the outspoken teenager whose own upbringing had forced her to become wise beyond her years. "She was sorry for him, too."

"Yeah, yeah. I'll tell her later. It'll make her feel not so guilty. But I did say 'almost.' I can pity his upbringing and still not feel sorry for the young man he is today. People make choices, and Danny's made some bad ones."

"He couldn't kill Ito or Ricky."

"I know. So . . . brownie points there? Although, I think that was more a dojo mentality than any kind of moral compass. Do you think he's redeemable?"

"I don't know. I want to believe so, but he'll have to find redemption behind bars. What do you think we're going to discover in that warehouse, other than boxes that are not filled with toilet paper?"

"I have no idea. I'm wondering if this is a trap to hand Kenzo over to Brewer. We've been so sure that Bob intends to hurt Akiko as a way to hurt Kenzo, but that might not be Bob's plan at all."

It would be beyond terrible if they got there and found Brewer and his people but no Akiko.

"I've thought about that. Bob's worked for Takahashi Corporation since he was sixteen years old. He's been silently attacking Kenzo all this time. But he could have turned him in at any point. He could have *killed* him at any point. As Kenzo's VP of security, he had full access and the ability to cover it up. But he hasn't."

She turned in her seat to study him. "What do you think Bob's endgame is?"

"I still think he's going to ruin Kenzo, but not go all scorched earth. If he turns Kenzo over to Brewer, it could topple the entire Takahashi empire, and I don't think that's what Bob wants. He wanted Akiko arrested, but I don't think he ever planned to turn Kenzo in to Brewer. He wants the throne. And once he's sitting on it, he can gloat over having crushed Kenzo Takahashi like a bug."

"Which killing his daughter might do."

"In *front* of him," Sam emphasized. "I think Bob wants Kenzo to see it. Just like Bob saw his parents killed while hiding in the closet. We still have time to get her out."

"Either way, we could be walking into a trap."

"But we're going in anyway."

"You can stay back, Sam."

He reached for her hand and gave it a gentle squeeze. "You know I'm not going to."

Her exhale sounded relieved. "Then let's do this."

"Are you going to contact Lennox and tell her where we're heading?"

"I just texted her. Told her the direction we're going and to stand by for a location." A few minutes later she made a surprised sound. "She says to wait for them before going in, that they're five minutes out."

"How?" Sam frowned. "Are they tracking us?"

"I don't know." Her fingers flew over her phone screen.

"Are . . . you . . . tracking us?" A moment later she laughed, a flat sound. "She says, 'Oof. Um, no.'"

"You hurt her feelings."

"Not gonna apologize. I think it was a fair question. Then how do you know where we are?" She spoke aloud as she typed. "Oh. Well, that's unexpected. She says Ricky Nicchi told them where to go. That Joe wasn't at his own house, but Ricky was. She says she'll explain when she meets us."

"Are we going to wait?"

Kit was quiet for a long moment. "I think that from the second that Kenzo walks in the front door, Akiko's time will start running out. I think we should go in, get eyes on Akiko, then wait to see what Bob has planned. If he makes a move toward her, I'm aiming for his head. But I will give Lennox the combination to the rear door lock so she can bring in the cavalry." She typed for a few seconds. "It's done."

And it was just in time, because Kenzo Takahashi turned in to a warehouse complex and pulled into a parking place right next to the front door.

"Stop here," Kit said. "Don't take us into the parking lot. I don't want to give Bob any more warning than we have to."

Sam did as she'd requested, parking Anson's car on the street just before the warehouse's driveway, and then he shut off the engine. "Let's go."

CHAPTER TWENTY-THREE

Tarzana, Los Angeles, California
Thursday, February 2, 1:05 a.m.

*S*ix-one-three-four. Kit glanced up at Sam before she hit the asterisk key to finish the code and unlock the warehouse's rear door. Sam nodded once, expression grim.

Thank you, she mouthed, and he smiled, his eyes filled with that emotion she was too terrified to name.

Star. She pressed the final button, and the lock whirred, then clicked. Carefully, she opened the door just wide enough for the two of them to slip through.

Eyes on Akiko. That was the plan until reinforcements arrived. There was no way she was allowing her sister to be hurt in the crossfire.

I'm coming. Hold on a little longer.

She moved warily down the unlit hall. It took a moment for

her eyes to get used to the darkness, but once they had, she moved with more confidence.

She could feel Sam's heat at her back. He was close. Almost touching.

He'd had her back so many times already. She trusted him with her life.

More importantly, at this moment, she trusted him with Akiko's life.

They came to a door on the other side of the hallway wall and, holding her gun in a firm grip, she slipped through first. Looking both ways, she nodded at him to follow.

This was the storage area of the warehouse. It was at least four stories high, the area separated by rows and rows of metal racks that rose at least thirty feet in height. Each shelf of every rack was filled with boxes shrink-wrapped onto pallets. The overhead lights were dim, creating shadows everywhere Kit looked.

Kenzo was right. There were too many places to hide.

Keeping to the shadows, she checked the aisles between the racks, row after row, but there was no one around. Where was Kenzo?

Where was Bob?

Where is Akiko?

This feels like a trap.

But she kept going until she'd searched two thirds of the warehouse. She crept across one of the aisles until she came to the end of the row. She paused, drew a silent breath, then edged forward until she could see around the corner.

Her heart stopped.

Akiko.

Her sister sat tied to a straight-backed chair, her long hair trailing behind her, her head tilted at an awkward angle. Her hands were bound in front of her. The ropes that tied her to the chair appeared to be the only thing keeping her upright.

She looked dead.

No, no, no.

Sam's hand gripped her shoulder, offering his support. "She's breathing," he whispered.

Reassured, Kit tamped down her panic and saw that he was right. Akiko's chest moved in and out with rhythmic breaths. She was alone in the center of an open area. An empty chair sat about five feet in front of her.

Kit guessed that was for Kenzo. She looked over her shoulder at Sam. "Bob's gone to get Kenzo from the front," she whispered. "Let's get her out of here before he comes back."

He nodded and they left the shadows at a run. Kit pulled her Swiss Army knife from her pocket as she dropped to her knees next to her sister.

Akiko's head jerked up, her eyes wide. "Kit."

Kit fumbled the knife in her surprise as a sudden rush of sheer joy filled her. "Are you hurt?"

"A headache. He hit me, then drugged me, but I woke up a while ago. I was pretending to still be out. Where did you come from?"

Kit sawed at the ropes at Akiko's ankles, conscious of the seconds ticking away. Sam had his pocketknife in his hand as well and was working the ropes that bound Akiko to the chair.

"Bob went to get Kenzo from the front entrance," Sam said. "We came in through the back. Can you run?"

"Yeah," Akiko said grimly. "Or I'll die trying."

Kit glared up at her. "Not funny."

"Not kidding," Akiko shot back. "This is the guy from my first charter. Who is he and why is he doing this?"

Kit had forgotten that Akiko didn't yet know Bob's identity. "His name is Bob Fujioka, and he hates Kenzo because Kenzo killed his parents back in the day."

She'd save the news about Joe being Akiko's grandfather for once they were out of here.

"Shh," Sam whispered. "They're coming back."

She could hear two male voices, and they were growing louder.

"I appreciate you coming out," a man said. "I thought this was something you should see."

That had to be Bob.

"What seems to be the problem?" Kenzo asked.

"Shit," Kit whispered.

"Go," Akiko said fiercely. "Hide."

Kit shook her head hard. "I'm not leaving without you." She broke through the rope at Akiko's ankles just as Sam finished cutting the rope around the chair.

Wrists still bound, Akiko stood up and began weaving on her feet. "Dammit." She tried to take a step but stumbled. "Goddammit."

Whatever they'd given her hadn't worn off yet.

Sam didn't blink. He just hoisted Akiko over his shoulder in a fireman's carry. "Let's go."

He took off at a run, Kit on his heels. They got to the door they'd come through, but it was locked.

Kit yanked on it in desperation, then stopped, making herself breathe.

She looked up at Sam. "We have to hide until Lennox gets here," she whispered.

They turned to run—and hit a brick wall of a man. He was nearly as big as Ricky Nicchi. Kit had seen him before. He was one of Kenzo's bodyguards. He'd been at the hospital the day before when Kenzo had first met Akiko. It appeared Kenzo had been right about not being able to trust his people.

The bodyguard had a gun in his hand, and it was pointed at Sam's chest. "Put your gun down, Detective." But he didn't wait for her to do so, instead grabbing her wrist and wrenching the weapon from her hand.

But the bodyguard didn't go for Sam's gun. Sam no longer held it. Where had he put it?

Then she remembered the holster he wore at his back. He hadn't wanted to wear it on his hip. His private practice patients might see it and become alarmed.

Sam hadn't moved a muscle. He just held on to Akiko, who was starting to gag. Her sister had a notoriously weak stomach and did not do well with anesthesia.

The bodyguard made a face. "What's wrong with her?"

"You drugged her," Kit said. "She's probably gonna puke."

The man looked like he might do the same. Roughly, he pointed Kit's own gun at them. "Let's go back."

Kit wanted to say no. She wanted Sam to run, to take Akiko and just run.

Instead, she walked back to where Akiko had been held, Sam at her side, Akiko still draped over his shoulder.

The man who'd taken Akiko's first charter five years ago waited for them by the two chairs. Bob Fujioka held a gun on Kenzo Takahashi, who sat in the other chair. Kenzo tugged at his cuffs and crossed his legs at the knee. He had the appearance of a man who was only mildly irritated.

Kenzo gave the bodyguard escorting Kit, Sam, and Akiko a shake of his head. "I never thought you'd betray me like this, Torrence."

Torrence shrugged. "He paid me more. Sorry."

Bob nodded toward the empty chair. "Put her down." He waited until Sam had lowered Akiko's feet to the floor, where she began weaving again. Her face alarmingly pale, she gripped the back of the chair to which she'd been tied, determined to remain standing, but Torrence shoved her into the chair.

"You took something that's mine," Bob said to Kit. "And you've trespassed. Really shameful, considering you're a cop."

"I'm suspended," Kit said blandly. "I don't have to follow the rules right now."

Bob laughed. "You'll follow my rules. Sit, Detective. You've crashed my party, so you might as well join us. Have a seat."

"No chairs. I'll stand, thank you."

Torrence shoved her to her knees, then did the same to Sam.

Kit winced, because the jolt hurt her knees and caused pain to shoot up her arm. But she wasn't going to panic.

Because Lennox was coming.

Bob smiled down at them. "You're thinking you just have to hold on for a few minutes, right? No. Your friends aren't coming to help you. They were delayed."

"By?" Kit asked, starting to panic. A little.

Or maybe a lot.

"Another one of my men. Don't worry. I told him to make it quick. Your friends felt no pain."

Kit's heart rose to fill her throat and she thought she'd be sick. Lennox, Burroughs, and Desoto were dead?

Later. She'd think about them later.

"How did you know they were coming?" she asked.

"My father bugged Kenzo, I bugged my father."

Kenzo was looking up at Torrence. "Sullivan betrayed me, too?"

"Yep." Torrence shrugged. "Sorry."

He was clearly not sorry enough, Kit thought. "Who's Sullivan?"

"My other bodyguard," Kenzo said. "How many of my security force did you buy out?" he asked Bob.

"All of them. Took me several years. Had to fire a lot of people before I got a crew who was solely loyal to me. You should have paid them better."

Kenzo still appeared unruffled. "You wanted me here, Bob. Tell me why."

Bob looked annoyed. "You already know why. The detective spoiled my surprise when she showed up at your house tonight."

He seemed like a toddler denied a toy.

"God, you're all assholes," Akiko muttered, her glare glacial. "You. Bob. You came on my boat. Twice. Why?"

"The first time was because I could. The second time was to inspect your boat to see if my cargo would fit."

"Your illegal guns," Akiko said. "Why me?"

"You were a means to an end," Bob said simply. "Nothing more. Your arrest would have caused your father pain."

"He didn't know I existed until yesterday."

"He would have found out about you when you got arrested. Do you know that he still keeps a framed picture of your mother next to his bed? Do you know how much you resemble your mother? He would have moved heaven and earth to keep you out of prison. To keep you by his side. I would have cleared you—for a price."

Kenzo looked angry but still unsurprised. Kit wondered how much of this he'd already figured out. She wondered if Kenzo would have paid that price. She doubted it.

"You wanted his business," Kit said.

Bob nodded once. "He'd have to hand it over to me with a full endorsement. He would have crawled away knowing that I owned everything that meant something to him."

"And if Kenzo had said no?" Kit asked, at this point buying time. Even if Bob's thug had killed Lennox and the others, Lennox would have informed Navarro of where they were going. She did things by the book.

Mostly.

Navarro would be sending help. Either way, she needed to keep Bob talking until that help arrived.

"Then he'd go to his grave knowing he was the one who sent his daughter to prison. Either way, he'd be in pain."

"But he's dying," Sam said. "Why not just wait until he was dead to take over?"

"Because that wouldn't have hurt him," Bob said. "Unfortunately, he won't hurt nearly long enough."

"Bob has been making moves against Kenzo for more than

thirty years," Kit murmured to her sister. "He killed your mother."

Akiko drew a breath. "So Bob murdered her after Kenzo raped her?"

Kenzo frowned. "I never raped her. I loved her. And she loved me."

"She was *seventeen*," Akiko said.

"Bob seduced Kenzo's wife, too," Kit said, still buying time. "And he turned Danny against his father."

Where's our backup, Navarro? It's time to bring in the cavalry.

"And," Sam added, "he's also been sabotaging Kenzo's businesses. Some of the sabotage has stretched over the past twenty years. Any new business Kenzo started after his father's death. Recently, though, he's attacked the hotels and the casino, which were the most profitable ventures. Which seems counterproductive, since his goal appears to be a business takeover."

"No," a new voice said. "The recent attacks were me."

Kit turned to see Joe Fujioka walking into their circle. He held a gun in his hand, as did the bodyguard who had accompanied him.

Joe's gun was steady. "Bob, let the girl go."

Tarzana, Los Angeles, California
Thursday, February 2, 1:25 a.m.

Kenzo was staring up at Joe, shocked bewilderment on his face.

Sam knew how he felt. *Joe* was behind the recent attacks on Kenzo's business? Was this what Joe, Nicchi, Ito, and Mary

Sherman had been working on? *This* was how they were protecting Akiko? That didn't make any sense.

"What is this?" Kenzo asked softly.

"My father has been damaging your businesses," Bob said. "All those anonymous calls to the gaming commission? My father. The audits that showed missing money that looked like I stole funds? All the canceled conventions and complaints about your hotels? That was my father, too. He's trying to take you down."

Kenzo pursed his lips. "Is this true?"

"No," Joe said. "I've been trying to take you both down. I wanted you to suspect each other. I wanted you to take each other out."

Bob stared. "You wanted him to kill me? Your own son?"

Joe shrugged elegantly. "I would have said no before October. But then you sought to use Akiko McKittrick as part of your vendetta against Kenzo. I was going to stop you, by whatever means possible. Once Kenzo knew Akiko existed, he had to go, too."

"Explain," Kenzo ordered.

"It's simple," Joe said. "Bob wants to cause you maximum damage—personal and professional—before you draw your last breath."

Kit glanced at Sam. *Be ready,* she mouthed.

Sam nodded once. Joe and Kenzo were talking to each other like Bob didn't exist, and that was making Bob very unhappy.

The man was a classic narcissist.

"Why have you betrayed me, then?" Kenzo asked, still sounding dignified.

Joe exhaled wearily. "Because Bob found out about Akiko. He would have used her to hurt you. And I didn't want you to know about her. Ever."

"Why?" Kenzo demanded. "Why keep her from me?"

"Because you would have brought her into the business and made her your heir," Joe said. "I wanted to keep her safe from you, because you use people. You *hurt* people. And when they displease you, you kill them. You've done it your whole life. But Bob found out about her. He wanted to use her to hurt you just like he used Danny to hurt you."

Bob was grinding his teeth now. Sam didn't think this was going as the man had planned. Unfortunately, he hadn't lowered his gun. Now there were four guns in play—Bob's, Torrence's, Joe's, and Joe's thug's.

Sam hoped they didn't start shooting at each other. *We'll be dead.*

Sam still had his weapon. It was tucked in his waistband holster, behind his back. If necessary, Sam would defend them, but at least one of those four men was sure to turn his gun on them if Sam fired.

"But why *you*?" Kenzo pressed. "Why are *you* involved? Why are *you* protecting *my* daughter? I understand why Bob's doing this. He blames me for the death of his parents."

"Because you fucking killed them!" Bob snarled.

"My name is Inigo Montoya," Akiko muttered. "Prepare to die."

Sam almost laughed, the line from *The Princess Bride* was so perfect.

Bob glared at Akiko. "Cover Kenzo," he said to Torrence and turned his gun on Akiko.

Beside Sam, Kit sucked in a disbelieving breath. "You are such a hypocrite," she said to Bob. "You killed Akiko's mother, and you have the nerve to stand there being angry that Kenzo killed your parents? And now you're holding a gun on my sister? What the hell is *wrong* with you?"

Bob moved his gun so that he aimed at Kit's head. "I'm going to start with you, Detective. Because I'm tired of hearing you talk."

Sam moved his hand slowly, going for the gun at his back. He wouldn't allow Bob to kill Kit, but help came unexpectedly.

"Bob, drop the gun or I will kill you where you stand," Joe said quietly.

Sam's gaze whipped to Joe, who was watching his son, his expression cool but determined.

Bob gave his father a look of contempt, but his gun remained pointed at Kit's head. "You wanted Kenzo to kill me? Your own son? Because of *her*?" He gestured at Akiko. "You've teamed up with Eddie Ito? To protect her? Just tell me why."

"Allowing Kenzo to kill you," Joe said, "was the plan. But five minutes ago, I learned that you knew who killed your parents. I had no idea how long you've nursed this desire for revenge. I had no idea it was you who killed Minnie Nakamura. You are but my adopted son. She was my blood daughter, and you killed her. So now there's a new plan." With no further discussion, he shot his son in the chest.

Wide-eyed, Bob stumbled backward but didn't fall. There was no blood on his shirt. He wore a vest.

Joe's next shot found its mark, and this time Bob did fall, a hole in his forehead. His hand opened as he fell, the gun skittering across the shiny gray floor, coming to rest in the middle of the circle.

Akiko's gasp wasn't audible over the gunshot, but Sam didn't need to hear it. Her wide-eyed shock was clear to see. He couldn't blame her. Joe's declaration that Minnie had been his daughter—and, therefore, Akiko his granddaughter—along with the fact that Joe had killed his son in cold blood? Akiko had a right to be shocked.

Sam figured the shock would hit him later. He was too busy trying to get them out alive.

Kit was shaking her head, muttering, "Dammit."

Torrence made a sudden grab for Akiko, but Joe's third shot brought the bodyguard down. The man fell to his knees, then to his stomach. His body twitched for a horrific moment, then went still.

Akiko's scream was muted, her bound hands pressed to her mouth.

Kenzo's eyes had widened at Joe's revelation about Minnie being his "blood daughter," but his expression was now back to stoically blank. Slowly he rose and gave Joe a nod. "Thank you." He looked to the man behind Joe. "Thomas. I'm happy I can still trust you." His words were muffled through the ringing in Sam's ears, but he could understand Kenzo well enough to be horrified by what came next. "Take care of the detective and her psychologist, please. Not here. Take them away and dispose of their bodies."

No, Sam thought, and went for his gun, but froze when Joe fired a fourth time.

Kenzo Takahashi looked shocked. And then he sank to the floor.

Dead, like the others, a hole in his head.

Akiko slowly turned her stare from Kenzo's body to Joe. "*You're* my grandfather?"

"I am."

"Not Hanshi?"

Joe shook his head. "No. Your mother and I . . . well, I loved her, but she didn't want to be part of this life. I understood that."

Akiko made a choked noise. "And all this . . . this was to *protect* me?" Her voice had risen, becoming nearly shrill.

"Yes. Your father would have corrupted you. We were trying to avoid that."

"We," Akiko said dully. "You and Hanshi and Ricky and my aunt."

"Yes. Bob had to be stopped because he wanted to expose you to Kenzo. Kenzo would have dragged you into his world. Neither could be allowed to succeed."

"I just can't." Akiko shook her head, seeming dazed. "So . . . we can go now?"

"You can. But not them. I really am sorry." Then Joe turned his gun on Sam.

Sam's lungs stopped working, the breath frozen in his chest.

Akiko leapt to her feet, coming between them even as her body swayed. Her hands, clenched into fists, were still bound in front of her. "No. You'll have to kill me first."

"You can't mean that," Joe said. "I spent the last thirty-two years keeping you safe."

Akiko widened her stance, gaining some balance. "You'll have to kill me first," she said again. "You know I'll tell. You won't let me live."

Joe frowned. "Of course I'll let you live. I'll keep you secure until you decide where your loyalties lie, but I won't kill you. You're my granddaughter."

Akiko lifted her chin. "Kit is my family and Sam is my friend. I won't let you hurt them."

"You really don't have a choice, my dear." He motioned to the man standing behind him. "Remove the doctor and the detective from this place. Kill them."

"Fuck this," Kit muttered, then dove for the gun Bob had dropped, rolling onto her back to aim high. She cried out in pain a heartbeat before she fired.

Joe dropped to his knees as blood gurgled out through the hole in his throat.

The man standing behind him still held a gun. *Thomas.* Kenzo had called him Thomas. He'd shot Kit, who lay on the floor writhing in pain.

Sam's wits returned to him in a rush, and he grabbed his gun from his back holster and shot Thomas twice, first in his upper arm, then again at his wrist. He'd practiced the move at the target range over and over again.

Debilitate. Don't kill.

Thomas looked at his arm in stunned surprise. His hand had fallen open, the gun dropping to the concrete floor, but he was already bending over to pick it up with his other hand. He'd barely missed a beat.

Sam threw himself on top of Kit, aiming at Thomas's head. He'd never wanted to kill anyone ever again, but he wouldn't let Kit die.

Akiko was suddenly behind the man, faster than Sam could blink. The thud vibrated through the floor when Thomas fell, going down hard. She'd swept his legs out from under him in a move she'd taught Kit. Akiko kicked the gun out of his hand, landing on Thomas's back, her knees in his kidneys, her bound hands gripping his hair. "Sam! Help me!"

Sam crawled across the floor. He held his gun to Thomas's head, his own head spinning.

Kit dragged herself over to them and pulled her handcuffs off her belt. She wasn't gentle as she cuffed Thomas's bloody wrist first, then the other. She pointed her gun at Thomas's head. "If you twitch, I will blow your head off."

Sam holstered his gun, then retrieved his knife from his pocket and cut through the ropes binding Akiko's wrists. She shook her hands out and said, "I'll keep him here. You take care of Kit."

Kit rolled to her back, panting. "I need something to bind my leg so we can get out of here before any other mobsters show up." She lifted her head to stare at the bodies littering the floor. "Dammit. This is a mess."

So was Kit. The leg of her trousers was dark with blood. "I'm going to start carrying bandages in my damn pockets," Sam muttered. He found a first aid kit mounted to the warehouse wall and used it to bind Kit's wound, which wasn't as bad as he'd feared.

Then he called 911 on his cell phone, tersely giving the operator the details while Akiko stared at Kenzo's body, her expression blank.

She might be in shock. Or simply relieved that this was over.

"I've got help on the way," the operator said.

Sam lay beside Kit, not caring that the floor was hard. Or that it was bloody. He cupped Kit's face in his hand, and she leaned into him.

"Thank you," she said quietly.

"You're welcome."

CHAPTER TWENTY-FOUR

Costa Mesa, California
Thursday, February 2, 3:25 p.m.

"Pop." Kit's smile lit up the room and Sam's heart lightened as he pushed her wheelchair close to Harlan's bed.

Sam had finally gotten her to the same hospital where Harlan was recovering around three that morning. They'd had to stay in the warehouse, sitting with four dead bodies and one live prisoner, until the cops came.

The delay had arisen from an "officer down" call fifteen minutes away. Sullivan, Bob's other guard, had been sent to kill Lennox, Burroughs, and Desoto, but he hadn't counted on Ricky Nicchi being in the vehicle in front of them.

Sullivan had forced the LAPD SUV off the road, sending it down an embankment. He'd stepped out of his car and, after he'd gotten off a few shots at the cops in the SUV, he was run over by Ricky Nicchi in his own vehicle.

Lennox, Burroughs, and Desoto had been transported to the same hospital as Edwin Ito, in downtown LA about an hour away. Lennox and Burroughs had head injuries from the crash but would survive. The prognosis for Desoto, who had been shot, was grim.

Sullivan was dead, his neck broken.

Nicchi had been treated for a broken arm and then released. As far as Sam knew, Nicchi was sitting at Ito's bedside. They hadn't heard from the big man all day.

Sam and Kit still had so many questions. After Kit visited with her father, they were headed to see Ito in the hospital in LA to get answers to those questions. Nicchi and Ito would talk to them. Sam wouldn't leave until they did.

But this moment was for Kit to spend with Harlan, who was sitting up in the hospital bed, being spoiled rotten by his family. As it should be.

They'd moved Harlan from the ICU into a regular room, so he'd had a constant stream of visitors—Kit, Akiko, Anson, the teenagers, and a host of former fosters who'd driven hours to see their dad. Betsy, of course, hadn't left her husband's side.

Harlan was clearly enjoying the attention. Sam thought that Harlan needed his kids as much as they needed him. He'd started to back away when Harlan shot him a wry look.

"Sam. Come here."

"Sir," Sam said, resting his hands on the bedrail. "You're looking better than you were last night." When he and Kit had stopped by after leaving the ER.

Kit had needed more stitches, but there was no long-term damage.

They had much to be grateful for. Last night could have ended so much worse.

Harlan lifted his hand and Sam took it. The big man just stared up at him for a long moment before clearing his throat. "Thank you. You brought my girls back to me."

"Kit helped," Sam said.

Harlan smiled for a moment before his expression hardened. "I want you to talk to Ito. I want to know why he kept secrets that nearly got my daughters killed."

"Oh, trust me," Sam said quietly. "I'm going to find out."

"Thank you, son. Pass on my thanks to your parents and tell them I'm sorry we've been lousy hosts."

"I think there were extenuating circumstances. But I'll tell them. Rest if you can." He squeezed Harlan's hand. "I'm glad you're all right."

Sam leaned down to press a kiss to Kit's cheek. "Take as long as you want. Text me when you're ready to head out. I'll come back and roll you to the car."

Her cheeks had a pretty blush from his quick kiss. She slipped her hand around his neck and drew him down, giving his lips a kiss in return. "I won't be long."

Ignoring the pleased expressions on her parents' faces, Sam backed out of the room, watching her until he was in the hallway.

Back in the waiting room, Sam found his mother. "I know you made arrangements for Siggy, but where is he?" He hadn't seen his dog in days.

"We took Siggy, Snickerdoodle, and Petunia to Connor's," Ann said. "Connor says he's bored and the dogs will keep him occupied. His mother says she'll make sure the dogs are taken care of."

"Since when do you know Connor's mother?"

"Since she and I took Betsy out to lunch yesterday before everything hit the fan. We got mani-pedis and everything."

Rita sat down beside Sam and his mother. "They had fun," she said morosely. "Left us at home all alone."

Ann's lips twitched. "Baz was there."

"He wouldn't let us do his nails." Rita pouted. "He said he was on guard duty and needed to be able to shoot any intruders."

"He did offer to teach us to shoot, though," Dawn said. "I'm starting lessons next week."

"For when she becomes a cop," Emma said loyally.

Dawn looked embarrassed. "Maybe."

"Or maybe a psychologist," Sam said. "You have a lot of empathy. Hey, you know who else was feeling sorry for Danny Takahashi last night?"

Dawn frowned. "Who?"

"Kit."

Dawn shook her head. "No way."

"Way. She saw the same thing you did. That Danny was just a kid who'd been manipulated his whole life. It doesn't excuse any of the things he's done, but we can feel sorrow for the child he was while still wanting him held accountable for his crimes."

Dawn's smile was shy. "That's what I thought, too. You really think I could be a shrink like you?"

"I do indeed."

"But that takes college. I can't afford college."

"I think you'll be surprised what you can afford," Ann said. "For one, foster kids can attend some colleges in California for free. And if you want a different school than is included on that list, your parents have set up a college fund for you guys."

Sam was touched. "Can Harlan and Betsy afford that?" he asked his mother.

"They've got some help. A sponsor. Or two or three."

Sam's lips curved. "You and Dad. And Connor and his family."

"I never said that," Ann said lightly, but it was clear that Sam was right.

He kissed his mother's cheek. "Love you, Mom."

"I love you, too, Sam. We're proud of you, your father and I."

He held on to her hand, content to simply sit by her side. He'd been lucky to have her and his father in his life since birth. Kit, Akiko, and the other McKittrick fosters had not been so fortunate. He was so glad they had people now.

He was glad he could be one of those people.

"A college fund?" Dawn said, wonder in her tone. "For us?"

"For you," Ann said, putting her arm around the girl. "We believe in you. All of you."

"I told you that everything would be all right, Dawn," Rita said. "That you have a home *and* a family."

Sam saw Akiko watching them, her expression melancholy. He told his mother he'd be back and went to sit with Akiko.

"You okay?" he asked.

"Not really. I mean, I'm alive. Kit's okay. Pop's gonna be fine. But . . . dammit, Sam. This is hard. I always wondered about my family. My bio family, I mean. And now that I know, I wish I'd never found out. I have a sensei who might still think he's my grandfather. I don't know if anyone's told him yet that his wife cheated with Joe. He watched over me my whole life without telling me the truth as he knew it, and I don't know how to handle that. I have two legit grandfathers, both mobsters, both dead. A mobster father, who's also dead. And a half brother, who'll spend most of his life in prison."

"Don't forget the business empire," Sam murmured. "With Danny going to prison, you're the only Takahashi left."

"I am not a Takahashi. I am a McKittrick."

He smiled at her. "So you are."

"I don't want any of it. Not the company, not the blood money. And maybe not even the pseudo-grandfather." Tears filled her eyes. "Hanshi was my person for so long. The only constant in my life until Mom, Pop, and Kit. But he *lied* to me. All these years, he's honestly believed he was my grandfather, and he never told me. He can say it was to keep me safe, but I'd rather he'd told me the truth."

Sam considered his words carefully. "Ito left the Takahashi organization. Joined the Army to get away—and at a time when very few people wanted to join. What he escaped was what he was trying to protect you from. Let's let him explain first. And Kit and I will go with you to talk to him. You won't be alone."

Los Angeles, California
Thursday, February 2, 6:45 p.m.

Ito looked better, Kit thought as Sam wheeled him into his hospital room. Like her father, Ito had been moved from the ICU into a regular room, which allowed for more people to gather.

Ito was sitting up in bed, Ricky Nicchi in a chair at his side.

Nicchi's arm was in a sling, and he had some cuts and bruises on his face.

Navarro gave Kit a nod as she entered. He'd returned from interviewing Nancy Sayer in time to meet Kit in the ER as she was being treated. He'd stood at her side as she gave her statement to the LAPD. He'd been quietly supportive, listening as she'd recounted the night's events and adding his own details—the murders of Minako and Ichiro thirty-two years ago and Joe Fujioka's role in the events of the past and present.

His initiative in finding Nancy and getting those answers had gone a long way to smoothing his and Kit's relationship, both personal and professional. Some of what he'd learned was relevant to the case. Some was relevant only to Akiko, and Kit appreciated it.

He hadn't mentioned Kit's suspension, not even once. Now that she'd had a few hours' sleep, she was going to find out exactly what she needed to do to get her suspension either dropped or resolved.

She still needed to call her union rep—but she'd been a little busy the past week.

Kit took a moment to study Ito's face. Both he and Nicchi looked so very sad. They'd suffered a lot of loss this week. Paolo and Mary and Joe. She didn't think that Ito knew about Joe being Akiko's bio grandfather, so Kit would tread lightly, but Ito deserved the truth. There had been enough lies in Akiko's biological family for a lifetime.

Lennox was already in the room, also in a wheelchair. She looked tired, her face drawn with pain. She had a bandage on her head and a splint on her leg, which was elevated. She gave Kit a nod when Sam parked her wheelchair next to Lennox's.

"Meghan," Kit said quietly. "You okay?"

"I will be. Hurts like a bitch, though. How's your pop?"

"Better."

"And your sister? I thought she'd come with you."

"She did. She's talking to Ito's new nurses."

Lennox eyed the old man in the bed. "I hope he talks to us now."

"He'd better," Kit said.

"I'm right here, Detectives," Ito said, his voice much stronger than it had been. "I can hear you."

"Good," Lennox said, a bitter edge to her voice. "If you'd been honest with us, none of us would have gotten hurt."

Ito's mouth tightened. "For that, I am sorry."

Kit didn't accept his apology, because it wasn't all right. But he cared for Akiko, so she'd afford him the minimum of respect. "We're sorry for your loss, Mr. Ito," she said instead. "We know that you were friends with Joe Fujioka for many years."

There was no reaction to Joe's name other than sadness. No anger or bitterness. So he probably didn't know yet.

"Thank you, Detective." Then Ito's gaze focused on the doorway because Akiko had just come in. "Akiko."

She inclined her head in a small bow. "Hanshi."

Ito winced at the formality. "Will you come sit near me?"

Akiko did as he asked, murmuring a thank-you to Navarro when he pushed one of the visitor chairs next to Ito's bed. She lowered herself into the chair and looked at Nicchi. "Are you all right?"

"I'll live," Nicchi said. "I'm glad Kit and Sam got you out. We were on our way to help you when we were attacked by one of Bob's men."

"I know. I'm happy you were able to stop him."

Everyone had spoken so primly, so stiffly. They weren't going to get anywhere like this.

Kit cleared her throat. "We have a few details to share, but we have a lot more questions. I assume you two have answers. Can we begin? Because I'd like to get back to my father."

"Ask your questions, Detective." Ito held out a hand for Akiko, but she kept her hands tightly clasped in her lap. The old man seemed to sag into himself. "I will say that we thought we were doing the right thing. If we'd been successful, it would have been. Akiko would have been protected and never brought into her father's orbit. Now, the point is moot."

Kit briefly considered telling Ito the truth now but dismissed the thought. The truth could upset him to the point that he might be unable—or unwilling—to give them the information they needed. Ito owed them that information. So she waited.

She assumed that Navarro had brought Lennox up to speed. It seemed that the others were letting Kit take the lead. *Fair enough.*

"That's what Joe said last night." *Before I killed him.* Kit wasn't sorry. If she hadn't acted, she and Sam would be dead, and Joe would have made Akiko his prisoner until she decided not to tell anyone what he'd done. So . . . forever. "But he wasn't very specific in exactly what you'd done. Please tell us."

"We knew that Bob had discovered Akiko's existence," Ito began.

"Wait," Akiko interrupted. "How? We don't know how he found out about me." She glanced at Kit. "Do we?"

Kit shook her head. "That's one of my questions. Mr. Ito?"

"I'm not entirely sure," Ito admitted. "I was hoping you knew. It had something to do with her boat, because Joe saw photos of Akiko and her boat on Bob's desk. That's how he knew she'd been exposed. Then Joe came to me."

That Bob had photos made sense. He'd been on her boat twice, the first time on her first day of business, so he'd known for at least five years. Hopefully they'd be able to figure out how he'd known, if only for Akiko's peace of mind.

"So Joe came to you," Kit said. "Why? Were you still close?"

"No. We'd stopped speaking after my twins were murdered. Joe had brought them here to LA, given them jobs, and never told me they were here. When I learned that they were dead—from Mary, who was only fourteen—and that Akiko had been surrendered to the foster system . . . Well, I was furious. I let him know just how angry I was. He asked what he could do to make amends, and I told him to make sure that Kenzo never discovered that Minnie had a child. That if Kenzo did, he'd seize custody, and Akiko would be raised to be a criminal. Like Joe. He agreed to listen for any mention of Akiko. He didn't expect that it would come from his own son."

Kit understood why Joe had been so solicitous. He hadn't wanted to admit to his affair with Ito's wife. "So Joe came to you and said, 'Bob's got a photo of Akiko.' Then what happened?"

"Joe said that when he asked Bob who the photo was of, Bob said the woman owned a boat he planned to use to move contraband. I knew my Akiko wouldn't do that, that Bob would have to frame her. She would only be safe if we could get Bob and Kenzo to take each other out before Akiko was involved. Initially, we didn't know why Bob had chosen Akiko, just that we had to keep Bob from framing her. It wasn't until we got into the Takahashi ledgers that we realized that Bob had been stealing from Kenzo for years."

"Did Mary find the stealing?" Kit asked.

"It was Mary and Hanshi together," Ricky replied.

"Mr. Ito was an accountant back in the day," Kit observed.

"He still is," Akiko said. "His license has lapsed, but he handles the accounts for both dojos, and he helped me set up my business accounts. How much did Bob steal?"

"Not a lot," Ricky said. "Which was puzzling. It wasn't enough to buy an island in the Caribbean or anything. But it was enough to bring down several of Kenzo's businesses in the past. He'd manipulated the accounts to make it look like there was a lot less income into the businesses Kenzo started up. The businesses his father started were left alone. That was our first red flag that Bob was trying to undermine Kenzo's position. I studied Bob's hiring and firing of security personnel and that also raised a red flag. He'd steadily fired bodyguards and other personnel that had excellent records. He personally hired their replacements. He built himself an army of loyal soldiers."

"We met one of them last night," Kit said. "His name was Torrence. Joe killed him."

"We met one of them, too," Lennox said dryly. "His name was Sullivan. Nicchi took him out before he could kill us."

Nicchi didn't deny it. "At any rate, we began to see that Bob was trying to take over the business. We figured if Bob knew about Akiko, he somehow knew who she was to Kenzo. Joe insisted he'd been careful, that Bob couldn't have found out from him, but I was doubtful."

Joe hadn't been all that careful, Kit thought. Nancy Sayer

had seen him watching Sakura's house once a month for fourteen years. And if Nancy had observed him, maybe Bob had, too. After all, Bob had known where to find Minako and Ichiro the night he'd killed them.

Nicchi was watching Kit shrewdly. "I had a lot of questions for Joe, but he was good at evading them. I wanted to know how he recognized Akiko from a photo on Bob's desk." Nicchi met Kit's eyes. "You know, don't you?"

Kit didn't reply. Nicchi had kept secrets for days. He could have helped their investigation, but he hadn't. She'd hold on to her secrets for a few more minutes.

"Joe said he was responsible for the attacks on Kenzo's businesses," Sam said when the silence became awkward.

Nicchi sucked in his cheeks and settled in his chair, his expression angry. But he didn't push. For now.

Ito shook his head. "That was mostly Mary and me. Joe had access to Kenzo and to the company's servers, so we'd give him files and he'd upload them. As accountants, Mary and I were able to develop fake books to make it appear that Bob was embezzling a lot more than he was. We wanted Kenzo to notice."

"Mary had just finished last week when she was in LA the last time," Nicchi said. "She focused on the casino, because that was Kenzo's pride and joy—and his only legacy because Bob had ruined his other startups. The casino was already being investigated by the gaming commission because we anonymously called in accounting discrepancies."

"Which you had engineered," Kit said.

Nicchi nodded. "Joe was supposed to have uploaded the fake books this past Monday, but then Mary was murdered and everything fell apart."

"I created fake memos signed by Bob," Ito said, "and I canceled several convention reservations. That cost the hotels money and hurt their reputations when the clients complained. One or two instances could have been smoothed over, but we dropped a lot of bombs quickly and across all Kenzo's businesses. Kenzo finally noticed and tasked Joe with finding the culprit."

"But Joe was the culprit," Kit said.

Lennox frowned. "Why didn't Joe just tell Kenzo that Bob was trying to overthrow him?"

Nicchi scowled. "That was my idea at the beginning, but Joe said that Kenzo would have killed Bob, maintained control, and still found out about Akiko, since Bob had been taking photos of her and her boat. Which is probably true, but I never trusted Joe. He was playing both sides of the fence." He focused on Kit. "Why did Joe even care about Akiko?" He glanced at Kit's sister. "No offense."

Akiko shrugged and said nothing.

Kit sighed. "Okay. Well, like I said, we do have a few things to share. Some of them might not be easy to hear. But I'm going to go back to Bob for a moment. He didn't just want Kenzo's business. He hated Kenzo and had since he was twelve years old. Kenzo killed his parents. Joe didn't know he knew when he took him in."

Ito's eyes had widened, and he and Nicchi shared a glance. "That explains a lot," Nicchi said. "What else did Bob do?"

"He killed Minako and Ichiro."

Ito gasped. "What? Bob?" The machine monitoring his pulse began to beep, so he pursed his lips, taking deep breaths through his nose until his heartbeat had slowed. "I wish I'd killed him."

"He also turned Danny against Kenzo," Sam added. "They were working together."

"I figured that out for myself." Nicchi once again focused on Kit. "Why did Joe care?"

Kit glanced at Navarro, who nodded. She turned her attention to Akiko, just in case her sister wanted to be the one to break the news, but Akiko shook her head.

"You say it," Akiko said quietly. "Please."

So Kit braced herself, just as she did every time she did a death notification to the next of kin. Because sharing this felt like a kind of death. "Sakura cheated, Mr. Ito. The twins weren't yours. They were Joe's. Joe was Akiko's maternal grandfather. Not you."

At first Ito went completely still and it felt like everyone in the room was holding their collective breath. And then he closed his eyes, his throat working as he tried to swallow. "I wondered. Ichiro had a widow's peak and no one in my family did. But Joe did. He gave Sakura lavish gifts and spent time with her when I was working. She denied that there was anything inappropriate between them. But I wondered. How do you know?"

Kit told them about Nancy Sayer and their phone call, adding in the details they'd learned from Haru Carlson. Throughout the tale, Ito held himself still, his eyes remaining closed. When she was finished, he inclined his head.

"Thank you, Detective. You are correct, this was not easy to hear. But I appreciate the information."

He'd taken it better than she'd expected. "I wish I could have kept it secret, but you deserved to know."

Nicchi blew out a breath. "A lot of things make more sense now. If Joe was making monthly visits that this Sayer woman noticed, he wasn't being all that discreet. I bet Bob followed him. He'd have known that the twins were somehow important. He might not have known their paternity, but he knew they meant something to Joe. And then, when they turned up in LA, working for Takahashi, Bob would have been so angry. That explains why he killed them both and not only Minako, as he'd been tasked to do by Kenzo's wife. And he waited to kill her until after the baby was born. He knew Kenzo had a daughter out there. Maybe he decided then to use Akiko against Kenzo when the time was right."

"I thought the same thing," Kit said. "I think he hated Joe, too. I mean, Joe was there the night his parents were killed, and he brought his 'real' kids into his house and gave them the same job opportunities he'd given to Bob. Last night Joe told Bob that he was his adoptive child, but that Minako was his by blood. That was right before he shot and killed Bob. I wonder if taking down Kenzo was also taking Joe down, too. Danny called Joe his father's lapdog. I wonder if he heard that from Bob."

"All that could be true," Sam said. "But we still don't know how Bob knew to board Akiko's boat on her very first fishing charter."

Ito's eyes flew open as he gasped again. "He did?"

"He did," Kit confirmed. "Bob went on two of Akiko's charters. He said he went the first time because he could. The second time was because he wanted to see if his gun shipment would fit in her hold. Things escalated before we could find out how he knew about her boat, though."

Ito sighed. "I might know. Bob was trying to overthrow Kenzo's business, but how much did he know about Kenzo's personal affairs?"

"Quite a lot, I imagine," Kit said. "Bob was sleeping with Kenzo's wife Umeko for twenty years, off and on, according to Umeko's sister. When she offered to leave Kenzo and move in with Bob, he said he'd slept with her to get access to Kenzo's personal life. He knew that Kenzo kept a photo of Minnie on his nightstand to this day. So I think he knew a lot about Kenzo's personal life."

"Kenzo knew I was Minnie's father—at least on paper," Ito added with a touch of bitterness. "He came to my dojo months after Minako had disappeared from LA. I later found out from Mary that Joe had taken the twins to LA, then returned them to Nevada after Minako got pregnant. Kenzo sounded insane that day. I'd never met him before. I knew he'd been born, that Mitch had a son, but I never saw him. I hadn't seen Mitch since I left for Vietnam—Mitch was Kenzo's father and my friend, the other man in that high school graduation photo you found, Detective. Mitch said I'd be safer that way, that he could better protect me from his father if I wasn't in his life. Because I'd run away from the family. His father considered me a traitor, but I was a low man, and he forgot about me. Mitch didn't, but we still never spoke again."

"Which is why Joe was in your wedding party, but Mitch wasn't?" Akiko asked. "You looked like you were three best friends in that graduation picture."

Kit had almost forgotten how much that graduation photo had upset her sister. Her two grandfathers, she'd said. And, even after Joe's revelation, that was still accurate. She'd thought that Ito and Mitch were her grandfathers but in reality, they were Joe and Mitch.

"Yes," Ito said, turning to Akiko. "We were once great

friends, but I'd never met Kenzo, and I was surprised he knew me. Kenzo said he'd had one of his security people search for Minako when she disappeared. His man had found the twins' original birth certificate, listing me as the father. Kenzo had known *of* me. Knew who I was to his father. I was in a lot of Mitch's photos from our childhood. I was alarmed. I wanted to know who in the Takahashi organization had this information—that I was Minako and Ichiro's father. He said he'd kept it close, that he'd asked Joe's son to do the search."

"Oh." Kit sat up straighter. "So Bob believed you were the twins' father all this time until Joe told him differently last night. But I'm still not following how he knew about Akiko's boat or even who she grew up to be."

Ito was still looking at Akiko. "I wasn't truthful with you about several things, child. You remember when I found someone to loan you the money for your boat?"

Akiko's expression became carefully blank. "You said it was an elderly woman and her daughter who wanted to invest in a woman-owned business."

"That wasn't true. The money came from me."

"Hanshi," Akiko breathed. "Why didn't you tell me?"

"Because you would have said no," Ito said. "I took out a second mortgage on my condo building."

Kit noticed that Nicchi's expression had become surly. She wondered if he'd known that Ito believed himself to be Akiko's grandfather. She also wondered how much Nicchi had resented Ito's relationship with Akiko.

Still, he'd aided Ito, Mary, and Joe in their plot to bring Kenzo and Bob down. His love for Ito was stronger than his resentment of Akiko.

Akiko sucked in a breath. "You're right. I wouldn't have let you do that."

"It's done," Ito said simply. "I hated that I couldn't adopt you. I hated that you had to live in foster homes your whole childhood, but if I'd brought home an infant, Kenzo would have known. He would have figured out who you were, that he was your father. And he would have taken you. So I had to let you grow up in foster care. I . . . owed you better. The boat was my attempt to make it up to you."

Akiko's eyes grew shiny. "Hanshi," she whispered.

Ito held out his hand, and this time she took it. "I don't care that Joe was your grandfather by blood. You've been my granddaughter since the moment you were born. And . . ." He cleared his throat. "I love you."

Akiko blinked, sending tears down her cheeks. "I love you, too."

Ito turned to Nicchi. "Don't resent her," he said quietly. "You've been my son since the moment I laid eyes on you. You and Paolo. You were the children I could publicly claim. I've given you everything else."

Nicchi dropped his gaze, but Kit could see that his cheeks had darkened, probably from embarrassment at the gentle admonition. "I know. I'm sorry, Hanshi."

"You're my son," Ito said again. "Don't believe otherwise."

"I won't." Nicchi lifted his head. "So you think that Bob knew you'd taken out a loan? That he was watching your finances?"

"It makes sense. From what we learned over the past months, he'd been trying to take Kenzo down for a very long time. He wasn't successful. Seems like he'd want to know everything that affected Kenzo, and that included me." He turned his gaze to Kit. "We thought that Bob had chosen to frame Akiko now because Kenzo's time was drawing to a close. He had pancreatic cancer and he wasn't going to live much longer."

"He needed Kenzo to feel the pain while he was still breathing," Kit said.

Ito nodded. "That would be my guess as well, Detective."

"I just have one more question," Kit said. "Why did you two refuse to tell us any of this when we begged you?"

"Because you would have ruined everything," Nicchi said. "You kept asking questions that would have exposed what we were doing to bring Kenzo and Bob down. There was still a chance of success until Hanshi ended up in the hospital. Joe said that he'd . . . take care of it. But that if we told anyone, the plan would fail and Kenzo would walk away scot-free. Then he'd be able to claim Akiko as his daughter. Joe didn't want that to happen. Neither did Hanshi."

"Well, Joe did take care of them," Kit said. "He killed both Bob and Kenzo without blinking an eye."

"I'm glad they're dead," Ito said fiercely. "Joe included."

The room went quiet at Ito's words. Kit wasn't sorry they were dead, either.

Los Angeles, California
Thursday, February 2, 7:15 p.m.

Sam was glad that Kenzo, Bob, and Joe were all dead, too. He still wished he hadn't seen the killing up close and personal, though. Those images would stick with him for a long time.

"I have questions," Lennox said into the silence. "Bob had Danny kill Mary. How did Bob know what Mary was doing?"

Navarro stepped away from the wall he was leaning against. "I can answer that one. Bob bugged Mary's house. When he told Danny to kill Mary, he made sure to tell him where the bugs were so that he could pick them up."

Everyone turned to Navarro. "How do you know that, sir?" Lennox asked.

"Because Special Agent Brewer called me after interviewing Danny, who's cutting a deal with the ATF. Danny's been very forthcoming. He and Bob communicated using the Signal app and Bob had the messages set to disappear after ten seconds. But that stressed Danny out because he was afraid he'd forget a detail, so he began to make screenshots of Bob's messages. On Saturday morning Bob messaged Danny that Mary was home and it was time to 'do it.' He didn't say to kill her, just 'do it,' and afterward to get rid of all the 'insects' and search for the items they'd discussed. Which Danny said was any kind of data storage—thumb drives, etcetera. Guess who planted the bugs?"

Both Kit and Lennox inhaled sharply.

"Laurette Curry?" they asked at the same time.

"*That's* how she fits in," Lennox added. "That's been driving me crazy. I knew she'd been paid by someone and knew it had something to do with Bob and Danny, but I didn't know what or why."

But neither Ito nor Nicchi looked surprised.

"You knew about Laurette Curry?" Sam asked.

Ito nodded. "Mary came home from a garden club meeting

unexpectedly early one Saturday in early January. Found Leo snoring in their bed and a naked woman in her bedroom, searching through her drawers. She snapped a few photos of the woman's face before she was seen and left the house. We were able to identify her as Laurette Curry. She works at Leo Sherman's hospital. That told us that Bob was on to us."

"Leo and Laurette had been sleeping together for nearly a year, according to the other nurses in Laurette's unit," Navarro said. "Long before you organized yourselves in October. We don't think Leo was involved. It seems like Bob just took advantage of Laurette being in Leo's house."

"How did Joe know that Laurette was dead?" Kit asked. "He was at her house not even an hour after Danny left. He posted those photos for us to find. How did Joe know to enter her house at that moment?"

Nicchi hesitated, then lifted one shoulder in a half shrug. "Joe called me yesterday. Told me that he'd dealt with Laurette, so I didn't have to worry about her. He wanted to find out who hired her. He was almost certain it was Bob, but she might have just been trying to steal from Mary. He waited for her outside the hospital after her shift, posed as Hanshi, said his daughter was dead and that Laurette would make a prime suspect. She wasn't a hardened criminal. She broke immediately. Told him that she'd been hired to search for portable hard drives. She didn't know by whom. They communicated via Signal, too. Joe demanded she show him the messages. She showed him her phone, but of course the messages had been set to disappear. Joe grabbed the phone and started to walk away, but he was really sending a message to her single saved contact saying

'More money or else.' When she started to scream for him to give her back her phone, he did. Then he went to her neighborhood and waited for Danny to show up and kill her, after which he went inside and tacked up those photos."

Sam stared at Nicchi, horrified. "He set her up to be killed?"

Nicchi nodded but didn't look nearly as horrified as Sam felt. "She betrayed Mary by cheating with her husband. She was willing to betray her again by selling whatever she found in Mary's house to a stranger. Look, Bob would have had her killed anyway. She was a loose end. Joe simply made it happen sooner. You should be grateful. He posted those photos so you'd know to look at Bob."

Sam didn't know what disturbed him more—Joe's actions or Nicchi's calm acceptance of them.

Wow. Just . . . wow. Then he thought about the photos. "How did Joe get the photos of Akiko that he taped to Laurette's wall? He didn't go on Akiko's boat when she was captaining."

Nicchi sighed. "Joe asked me for the photos. I didn't know what he wanted them for. I got them off my brother's phone. Paolo took those photos."

"Thank you for asking that, Sam," Lennox said. "It was on my list, too."

"But," Ito said, "we still don't know how Bob knew that Mary was involved?"

"You weren't that careful," Lennox said. "Leo Sherman managed to take several photos of the four of you talking outside Ricky's office."

Ito sighed. "One time. There was just one time we all left together. We stood outside talking for no more than two minutes."

"Long enough," Navarro said. "Besides, Danny said that Bob suspected that Joe was up to something."

"Did . . ." Nicchi cleared his throat. "Did Bob force Danny to do the murders? Or did Danny want to?"

Oh. Of course Nicchi would want to know if killing Paolo was Danny's idea.

"Danny says he didn't kill Paolo," Navarro said. "He said he couldn't. Nor did he hurt you, Mr. Ito, and the messages from Bob to Danny back this up. Bob was furious that Danny didn't follow his instructions."

"Of course Danny couldn't," Akiko said. "I was shocked when you told me that he'd beaten Hanshi and that he'd . . . that he'd hurt Paolo so badly before killing him. It would have been breaking basic dojo etiquette. We are trained not to hurt a fellow student. The thought of truly harming our teacher is incomprehensible."

Lennox and Kit looked at each other. "Danny is about the same size as Bob," Kit said. "We should have thought of that."

"What about Laurette?" Lennox asked. "Did Danny admit to her murder?"

"Yes," Navarro said. "He admitted to killing Mary, Laurette, and Jorge Montoya. He said that Bob told him that Mary was trying to steal the company away from him to give to Akiko, that it was Danny's birthright. So Mary had to be stopped. Still, Danny was hesitant. That's why he was following Dahlia on campus. He wanted to know if Mary was really trying to steal from him, but he could never find the courage to ask Dahlia. Bob showed him a photo of Joe and Mary together, told him that Mary was working with Joe and that they were close to success. So Danny killed her, thinking it would be just one murder. But after he'd done the one murder, Bob threatened to turn him in if he didn't do the others. That's when Danny realized he was being used, that Bob didn't care about him like he'd always claimed."

"Which is why he gave Bob up when Brewer came to arrest him," Kit said.

"Exactly. Danny definitely killed three people, but he wants Bob to be punished, too. He doesn't know yet that Bob is dead. Brewer's hoping to squeeze the kid dry before he finds out."

"Why did Bob beat Paolo?" Nicchi asked. "I mean, I suppose I can understand the motivation for killing him. He knew about the guns, which could have come back on Bob in a big way, especially if he'd managed a corporate takeover. But why . . ." His voice broke. "Why beat him like that?"

"Paolo needed money." Navarro's tone had become gentle. "Danny said he was doing drugs."

Akiko gasped. "No. I would have known."

"The toxicology reports showed heavy usage of both heroin and ecstasy," Navarro said. "I'm sorry, but Paolo had addiction issues."

"Yeah," Nicchi said heavily. "I know."

"You knew?" Akiko asked, her eyes widening. "Why didn't you help him?"

"Don't you think I tried?" Nicchi snapped. "He didn't want my help. He didn't want anyone's help. Except Bob's, apparently."

Navarro's expression was sympathetic. "Bob asked Danny if anyone in Akiko's circle had a vulnerability. Danny is an addict, and he recognized it in Paolo."

"So that's why Paolo agreed to work for Bob," Nicchi said, "but why did he beat him?"

"Paolo was supposed to be carrying contraband on Akiko's boat, but only when Akiko was onboard," Navarro explained. "Time and time again, Paolo would schedule his drop-offs when Akiko was off or sick. Bob was getting more and more impatient with Paolo because he was impeding Bob's plan to frame Akiko. But Paolo just couldn't do it. If Paolo had done what he'd been told to do when Bob first told him, Bob's plan would have already been accomplished. That's why Bob beat him. Bob was also responsible for beating you, Mr. Ito."

"I figured," Ito said. "But Danny was involved. I heard a noise on Monday afternoon. I got up to investigate and was hit upside the head with a club. I'm old but I'm still able to defend myself. I was able to quickly restrain my attacker, but there was a second man. He hit my head again, then injected me with a sedative of some kind. When I woke up, I was tied with rope."

"Same with me," Akiko said. "Bob hit me with something, then I felt the needle. It was fast acting."

"Fentanyl," Ito said. "That's what the doctor told me I'd been given. But Danny was there, even if he didn't throw a punch. Bob knew how to deflect my strikes long enough for the sedative to kick in. They were looking for the files that we'd faked. There were a number of documents that we'd created but hadn't yet utilized that would have been damaging to the company when Bob took over. But I didn't have any of those documents in my condo. Joe had a master copy on a portable hard drive."

"The work was done on a laptop in my office," Nicchi

added. "I'll give it to you. My network and office are secure. It was the safest place for us to work." He rose with a grimace. "I need to go. The ME released Paolo's body this morning. I need to arrange for his burial."

"Ricky, wait." Kit tried to stand, but Sam gently pushed her back into the chair.

Nicchi turned. "Yes?"

"Why did you leave your shoes in Mary's house? If her husband thought she was cheating, why would you leave something Leo could use against her?"

Nicchi shook his head. "I didn't know she had my shoes until you mentioned it that first time in my office. She must have taken them with her when she left LA that last time. Seeing Laurette naked in her bedroom really hurt Mary. Maybe she wanted Leo to believe she'd found someone else. Now, I really have to go."

The room was quiet after Nicchi made his exit. Navarro finally broke the silence.

"Detective McKittrick, can I see you out in the hall?"

"Yes, sir."

Sam pushed the wheelchair out into the hall, then started to back away to give her and Navarro privacy, but she grabbed his arm. "Stay. Please."

"Of course."

She drew a breath and looked up at Navarro. "Am I still suspended?"

"No. I dropped the suspension yesterday after we talked in the LAPD observation room. When you went into that warehouse last night to save your sister, you were an active detective. Off-duty because you're on med leave, but not suspended."

"Thank you, sir."

"Trust me next time, okay?"

She studied her hands for a moment before looking back up. "Don't play suspension games with me next time. You used me to get at Detective West. Lennox knew, but you didn't tell me."

Sam had nearly forgotten about Detective West.

Navarro nodded. "That's fair. I apologize."

"Thank you. And thank you for investigating this personally, sir."

He looked like he wanted to say something more but only nodded again. "When will you head back to San Diego?"

"I don't know. It depends on when Pop is ready to go home."

Sam wanted her to leave today so that she could get some much-needed rest, but he knew better than to push. Her family had some healing to do, physically and emotionally. He'd just be whatever she needed when she needed it.

EPILOGUE

Linda Vista, San Diego, California
Wednesday, February 8, 11:30 a.m.

"The ramp is new," Kit said as Sam pushed her wheelchair onto Alf Ashton's front porch.

"I think they had it installed for you," Sam said, dropping a kiss atop her head.

She twisted to stare up at him. "For me?"

"Alf can use crutches. You can't, not with a wounded arm as well."

"But . . . oh my God, Sam. That was so nice of them."

She said it like she couldn't believe anyone would treat her so well.

"People like you," Sam said, amused.

She huffed. "Now I'm glad I brought cupcakes for dessert."

They were having lunch with Alf Ashton and Kevin Marshall

and their wives. Alf said it was to celebrate Kit's reinstatement and Sam knew that was partially true. Apparently, however, Alf and Kevin had been bored out of their minds for the ten days they'd been on leave and their wives wanted to give them something to do.

The two detectives also had a surprise for Kit. A couple of surprises, actually.

Stacey Ashton met them at the door as she had once before. "Welcome!"

Kit held up the box of cupcakes. "My mother made them."

Stacey took the box. "Now I finally get to sample the famous Betsy McKittrick baked goods. Follow me."

Sam pushed the chair into the living room and grinned when Kit gasped. Connor Robinson was sitting on Alf's couch, looking excited to see Kit, too. Connor struggled to his feet, leaning heavily on a cane, then walked to Kit's chair and hugged her hard.

"You got shot again," he muttered. "You promised me you wouldn't do that."

"Sorry." She let him go and studied his face. "It wasn't part of the plan. You look good, Connor."

"So do you. And now I've got to sit down again. I promised CeCe that I wouldn't overdo it."

Sam pushed her closer to the others, who were waiting their turn.

"You just had to one-up us, didn't you?" Marshall said dryly. "I got a bullet in the arm, Alf got one in the leg, and you had to go and get both."

Alf harrumphed. "Show-off."

"I missed you guys, too," Kit said.

"How's your father?" Leslie Marshall asked.

"Better. He's at home, supposedly resting, but the house is filled with all the fosters coming to visit. Pop's having a ball. Mom keeps looking at him with a haunted expression, though."

"I can relate to that," Stacey said.

"Same," Leslie said.

"Same," Sam echoed, sitting in an empty chair next to Kit. He hadn't yet had a night without at least one nightmare about that hour in the warehouse.

"How's Akiko?" Connor asked.

Kit sighed. "She's okay. She's grieving still. Paolo and the aunt she never got to meet."

"Not her bio dad, though," Connor said.

"No." Kit shuddered. "Kenzo was a terrible person. They were all terrible people—Kenzo, Joe, and Bob. I hate that Ito lied to her all her life, but I have to be grateful that he kept her out of that den of vipers. I think Akiko is, too, but her relationship with Ito will never be the same. Ito will recover physically, but Akiko will have trouble trusting him again. On the bright side, she's got two cousins she didn't know about before. The three of them have already had lunch three times."

DNA testing had confirmed that Mary was Ito's biological daughter, so once the threat was over, the Sherman twins had made the trip to LA to greet Ito not as their sensei, but as their grandfather.

"Are your parents still in town, Sam?" Connor asked.

"They are. They were staying at McKittrick House to make sure the girls got to school while Betsy was in LA. Harlan's back home now, so Mom and Dad are back in their condo. We're going to their place for dinner tonight."

"We're ordering takeout," Kit said with a laugh. "Sam's mom is a worse cook than me."

Sam had to smile. After she'd gotten over her nerves, Kit and his parents had gotten along beautifully. It was a huge relief to have everything going so well.

An even bigger relief was that he could watch over Kit from the comfort of his own condo. She couldn't make it up the stairs at McKittrick House and neither could Harlan, who had taken the sofa.

For the past two nights, Sam had fallen asleep with Kit in his arms. So when he had those nightmares and woke up with a start, his heart pounding, he could tighten his hold on his detective and go back to sleep, knowing that she was safe.

Their arrangement wasn't permanent, of course. She'd soon be able to take the stairs at McKittrick House again. But for now, he was grateful.

"Well, we have a surprise for you," Ashton announced. "Office gossip."

"More than gossip," Marshall said. "Documented as true."

Kit straightened in the chair. "Tell me."

"West got fired!" the two men sang together.

Kit fist-pumped the air. "Yes!" She reached over and high-fived Connor. "Did they walk him out and everything?"

"He's lucky that they're not pressing charges," Connor said. "He was *selling* information to Tamsin Fucking Kavanaugh. Navarro's going to tell you this afternoon when you meet with him, so you have to pretend to be surprised."

Kit practiced her surprised face.

Connor winced. "That was . . . not good, Kit. In fact, that was terrible. Just tell Navarro that Baz told you."

Kit laughed. "You want me to throw poor Baz under the bus?"

"Yes," Sam said.

Kit laughed again and Sam's heart swelled in his chest. He wanted to hear her laugh every day forever.

"We invited Baz to come today," Stacey said, "but he said his wife was coming home from her cruise. He's picking her up at the port in LA."

"I have a feeling he's going to have some explaining to do," Kit said ruefully, "but he was never in much danger."

"He was with you when you got shot at the second time," Sam pointed out.

"But not the first or the third," Kit said.

Sam shook his head. "Too soon. Way too soon."

She smiled at him. "Sorry. Did you ask Lennox if she wanted to join us?"

Sam was surprised. "Really? I thought you didn't trust her after she wouldn't let you go with her and the LAPD guys that night."

"Well, I was mad in the moment, but it worked out in the end. Except for them nearly getting killed, of course. Burroughs and Lennox escaped the wreck with a few broken bones, but they'll be okay. Desoto is going to make it, but he'll probably have to retire early."

There was quiet around the room for a long moment.

"But it did work out in the end," Connor said soberly. "If you'd gone with them, you wouldn't have found Akiko in time."

"I know. I think about that a lot. But we did find her, Sam and I. And she's healthy. Sad for now, but she's on the right side of the grass, so I'm just going to be grateful. Anyway, Lennox is a good cop. We should invite her next time."

The other detectives nodded, and Sam could see that they understood that when Kit said there would be a "next time" for socializing it was a big deal. He liked these guys. They were good for Kit.

"Well, lunch is ready," Stacey said. "Let's eat and toast Kit and Sam solving this case."

Alf reached for his wife's hand. "And for bringing down a mafia operation. We can't forget about that."

Because they had brought down a mafia operation. Or at least they'd started the ball rolling. Brewer had gotten a warrant for all the Takahashi warehouses and had hit the jackpot. The warehouse where Kit, Sam, and Akiko had nearly lost their lives had been filled with hotel supplies—paper towels and toilet paper. But mixed among those boxes were guns. Crates and crates of guns. Ammo, too. The key players in the corporation were dead, but there was a whole slew of people who were alive and in big trouble with the ATF. Second-in-command all the way down to the runners.

Sam waited until the others had moved to the dining room before leaning in to kiss Kit's smiling mouth. It was mostly sweet but a little rough, and Kit hummed into it as she gripped the back of his neck and pulled him closer.

Mine. You're mine.

But he'd hold the words a little longer. He pulled back, then brushed his lips over hers once more. "That was nice, asking them to include Lennox."

"Thank you," she whispered.

"For what?" he whispered back.

"Not giving up on me."

"Not gonna happen." Tenderly, he brushed her hair off her face. She was wearing it down today. He loved seeing her relaxed.

He loved seeing her intense, too.

He just loved seeing her.

He just . . . loved her.

"Let's eat," he blurted out before he could say the words that wanted to escape. "We need to have lunch."

She met his eyes, hers warm and honest. "And dinner. And breakfast, too."

For how long, he wanted to ask, but he didn't. It was enough that she was making plans for them. Even if it was just food. Making plans of any kind was a big step for Kit.

"Kit!" Connor called. "Hurry up. We're waiting for you."

She looked away, the moment broken, and Sam wanted to hit Connor on the head with his own cane. But he didn't, pushing Kit into the dining room instead.

For now, lunch. The rest would come.

Linda Vista, San Diego, California
Wednesday, February 8, 12:30 p.m.

Kit took Sam's hand under the Ashtons' dining room table. She was happy. They'd had good food with good friends and Detective West had been shown the door.

Akiko was alive and so was Harlan.

Anson was recovered except for a cough and was in the process of rebuilding his house. The fire damage wasn't that severe, thanks to the sprinklers he'd installed. Most of the damage was from the smoke.

Her family was okay.

Sam was okay.

Sam was better than okay, actually. Sam was wonderful, and everything with him was going so well. He'd held her tenderly for the last few nights. A little too tenderly. She kind of hoped he'd try something, but she knew he was waiting for her to give the go-ahead.

She'd been thinking about doing so. A lot. Waking up in Sam's arms had been the best start to her days. She didn't want to think about the time in the future when she wouldn't need to stay with him. She didn't want to leave and that was . . . scary. But that was a problem for next week or the week after.

For now, in this moment, she was happy.

Lunch was finished, her mother's cupcakes had been devoured, and a comfortable silence had fallen around the table.

And then Marshall cleared his throat. Kit's gaze flew to his and she was instantly tense. Marshall looked like he wanted to say something. No, like he *needed* to say something, but it was making him uncomfortable.

Ashton had also become grim, and the two partners stared at each other, having some kind of a silent conversation.

Kit glanced at Sam first, then Connor. Both looked as clueless as she felt. "Kevin? Alf?"

Marshall seemed to brace himself. "We have one more piece of news. We still have remote access to the computers at the office. So, while you were up in LA working Akiko's case, we were watching security footage."

"What kind of footage?" Kit asked, but she thought she

knew. Her stomach did a slow greasy slide, and she had to breathe through a sense of panic.

"Footage from the bus station locker room," Marshall said.

He was talking about her sister's murder case that had gone cold for seventeen years. A name in the notebook of a killer who'd blackmailed other killers was the closest they'd come to a lead in all that time. The name of someone who'd thrown his unnamed fifteen-year-old victim in a dumpster.

Just like Wren had been.

Except the name of the killer was John Smith, which hadn't been helpful at all.

Kit tried to breathe, but no air was filling her lungs. "What did you find?"

Ashton took up their story. "The blackmailer's list provides the name of the blackmailee and the date, place, and time where they were to drop off their payments. The places included the bus station, the train station, sometimes lockers at the gym."

"I know all this," Kit gritted out. "Please, guys. What did you find?"

"We were able to match the name on the dead man's list to a time for a money drop-off at the bus station," Ashton said. "We found him on the security tape and traced him back to the vehicle he arrived in. But there's a problem."

Sam squeezed her hand hard. "Breathe, Kit. I'm right here."

She inhaled raggedly, clutching Sam's hand like a lifeline. "What is the problem?"

"The person who dropped off the blackmail payment was a child, barely tall enough to reach the locker. They left the bus station and got into the back seat of a black minivan.

The license plate had been reported stolen. But we have a clear picture of the child's face. If we can find the child, we may be able to find the adult driving the van."

"Which could lead us to the man who threw a fifteen-year-old girl into a dumpster," Kit whispered. She looked up at Sam, her eyes burning. "Do you think . . . ?"

Sam wrapped his arm around her shoulders and kissed her temple. "We won't know until we investigate. But we *will* investigate. You have my word."

"Ours, too," Ashton said. "We're with you, Kit."

"We've got your back," Marshall said.

"All of us," Connor added grimly.

Her heart was pounding so hard that her head spun. Finally. After seventeen years, she was going to catch the bastard who'd killed her sister. She'd get justice for Wren.

She met the gaze of each of her colleagues, ending with Sam. His green eyes were steadfast, determined. Filled with that emotion she was still too afraid to name.

"When do we start?" she asked.

"Today," Sam said. "We start today."

ACKNOWLEDGMENTS

My friends Kay, Terri, Christine, Sheila, Dan, and Sonie for lifting me up and letting me talk my way out of my plot holes. I'm so lucky to have you all in my life.

Sarah Hafer for your expertise in Japanese culture and language. And also for your eagle eye! You catch my mistakes before anyone else can see them.

Martin Hafer for making sure I don't get scurvy.

Sonie Lasker for your expertise in martial arts. I'm so honored to have studied with you all those years ago.

Beth Miller for the proofreading when I've stared too long at the words to see any mistakes.

Margaret Taylor for answering my questions on police procedure. I hope Kit does you proud.

As always, all mistakes are my own.